TREE
of
SOULS

Lavender Crow

HEDDON PUBLISHING

www.heddonpublishing.com
www.facebook.com/heddonpublishing
@PublishHeddon

About the Author

Lavender Crow was born in Hamburg, Germany and spent most of her childhood travelling to far-flung destinations such as Tripoli, Aden and Kenya, her father having served with the British Army. Lavender also lived in Christmas Steps, Bristol, where, with her interest in the supernatural, the story began.

For Arlene, Poppy, Oscar and Buster

Chapter 1

Christmas Steps
Bristol, 1985

Christmas Steps is one of the oldest and most charming places in Bristol. A mix of residential and commercial properties, sitting proudly either side of a stone staircase constructed by a wealthy merchant in 1669 and rumoured to be haunted by a Cavalier Officer called Lonsford, killed at the top of the steps during the siege of Bristol in the English Civil War.

Over the years, many unexplained incidents set tongues wagging in the small community of Christmas Steps, giving credence to its reputation of being haunted.

Set mid-way up the stone staircase was No. 26; a terraced property with shop frontage and residential accommodation above, set over three floors and boasting a small, secluded back garden; a rarity in central Bristol. In 1985, the property was occupied by Donald Adams, a sad alcoholic, along with his two children, Jane and Tommy.

The sister and brother had lost their mother, Marjorie, to a brain aneurysm when she was just thirty-four. After Marjorie's death, Donald turned to the bottle and reverted from life, his only shining light being his son. This blatant favouritism caused rivalry and resentment between the two siblings. They constantly battled for their father's affections but, despite this petty squabbling, Jane and Tommy tolerated each other.

Life in No. 26 continued without too much trauma until Eve, Tommy's girlfriend, moved into the household, shattering the fragile harmony. Jane had no say in the matter; it was ultimately her father's decision and he agreed to let the couple have the run of the house for a month whilst they looked for a flat of their own. That month turned into a year.

Tommy and Eve dropped the pretence of searching for a flat, instead settling into No. 26 and reaping the benefits of cheap rent. Meanwhile, the relationship between brother and sister evolved into something more intense and volatile.

As a result of escalating problems at home, Tommy took to disappearing for long periods. Eve began to question his whereabouts and Tommy started to feel like his every move was being monitored. Eventually, he retaliated the only way he knew.

The violence started slowly, with a push or a shove, then a slap, graduating to a punch; another following in swift succession. It didn't take much to send Tommy into a rage, normally set off by something quite trivial and then quickly escalating. His anger was exacerbated if another man showed the slightest interest in Eve; his red-haired girlfriend seemed to attract the attention of most men she encountered.

The week everything came to a head began with problems at work and Tommy vented his frustrations on everybody in the household. By Wednesday evening, he was in a foul mood but agreed to go out to a bar with Eve and some of his friends. As he grumbled to Stephen about the shit week he was having, he noticed Eve laughing with another friend, Ben. Tommy was incensed, convinced there was something going on between his friend and his girlfriend. His temper pushed him over the edge.

He pulled Ben aside and growled in his ear. "I know your game, I've seen the way you look at my girlfriend. I'm warning you, keep your hands off." Tommy started jabbing a finger into Ben's chest to hammer home his feelings.

"Look mate, you've got hold of the wrong end of the stick." Ben pushed Tommy away, trying to placate his friend, whose fists were now clenched, ready to take a swipe.

"I am not your fucking *mate*! You leave my girlfriend alone or I will—" Tommy didn't get chance to finish the sentence as he was pulled away by Stephen, who'd seen the row brewing and decided to intervene.

Stephen managed to calm Tommy down but his outburst angered Eve and, shortly after the altercation, they left the pub. During the short walk home, Tommy was quiet and sullen. Eve became apprehensive of what was in store for her. In his present state of mind, there was no doubt there would be repercussions.

The house had a strange air of foreboding as they entered. Eve shivered as she followed Tommy, climbing slowly up the stairs to the first floor. Determined not to give him any ammunition, she kept quiet, but once the bedroom door was closed behind them, Tommy's drink-fuelled mood erupted and he turned on her.

"What was that about in the pub? Are you trying to make me look like a fool in front of my friends?"

"What the hell are you talking about?" Eve never gave in to a fight, despite knowing the likely consequences.

"You know exactly what I'm talking about. You were all over Ben, like a common slut."

"Don't you call me a common slut. You've got a bloody nerve, the way you've been acting lately. For God's sake, Tommy, grow up. I was only being friendly. I've no interest in Ben whatsoever."

"That's not what it looked like to me."

His face was in hers now but she wasn't going to back down.

In Tommy's mind, all he could see was how Ben and Eve looked at each other; the way they laughed at private jokes, making him feel as though they were conspiring against him, maybe already having an affair behind his back. As the thought entered his mind, Tommy snapped. Lunging at Eve, he grabbed a handful of her long red hair then threw her on the bed and jumped on top of her. She was powerless to stop him as he began pummelling her viciously with his fists until she blacked out, her screams turned to silence.

When she came to, one eye was so badly swollen she could hardly open it. She tried to move but a shooting pain in her side immobilised her. A glance around the bedroom told her the curtains dressing the small casement window were open.

It was dark outside and the bedside light was still on. Gradually, she became aware of a strange noise coming from the corner of the room. Amid the shadows she could see Tommy in the rocking chair she'd brought with her when she moved in, his head in his hands, mumbling incoherently to himself. As her eyes lingered on his rocking shape, he lifted his head and stared in her direction. It was too late to feign unconsciousness; he had already seen she'd regained her senses. Eve froze as she watched him stand up slowly and walk the short distance across the room, to the side of the bed where she lay. Her whole body trembled, anticipating another violent attack, but instead of another beating, Tommy fell to his knees beside her, sobbing like a baby, apologising and swearing it wouldn't happen again.

She turned away from him, letting him babble on about how things would change and how he would make it up to her. She knew they were idle promises he would never keep. Eve had suffered enough of Tommy's unpredictable mood swings and escalating violence. In the midst of last night's beating, she had seen something dark behind Tommy's eyes, which terrified her. It was this last image she remembered before she had lost consciousness.

As she listened to his pleading and sobbing, Eve felt the strange madness which had overwhelmed Tommy receding, leaving in its wake a pathetic excuse for a man. She lay on the bed, staring at the far wall, not daring to turn to face him, or say anything. Her mind was made up.

She would leave him.

Faced only with Eve's back, Tommy gave up trying to excuse his violent behaviour and stumbled to his feet, padding to the other side of the bed and climbing in. It gave Eve time to close her eyes, in the vain hope he would take the hint and leave her alone. The mattress sank under his weight and his alcohol-breath lingered on her face as he reached over. For one horrendous moment she thought he was going to hit her again. Instead, Tommy kissed her gently on the forehead. Then, after what seemed like an eternity, where, through closed eyes, she felt him assessing her face for signs of wakefulness, he turned and fell into a deep sleep.

Tommy had the ability to sleep no matter what was happening within and around him; a habit at that present moment in time Eve blessed. Once she heard snoring, she began to think back to where everything had gone wrong. When she first moved into Christmas Steps, everything was exciting and, whilst it was evident Jane was not enamoured with the situation, on the whole the two women got on well. Donald had welcomed Eve, insisting that she and Tommy stay as long as they liked in order to save for a decent deposit.

At first, they had made a concerted effort to look for a home of their own but rents in the part of Bristol they favoured were far above their budget. It had been almost a year now and Jane's patience and acceptance were starting to wane. She made her feelings known to Tommy on more than one occasion but he chose to ignore his sister's grumblings. It seemed to Eve that this was the moment when his behaviour had begun to change, beginning to spend more time away from the house and gradually distancing himself from his girlfriend.

Besides his good looks, it was Tommy's easy-going personality that had initially attracted her. Now, he was a person she barely recognised. Instead of the man she loved with a heated passion, she found herself living with someone she didn't like and, more alarmingly, a person she'd come to fear. Jane had also remarked on the change in his personality, when they were talking in the kitchen before Tommy got home from work one night. At the time, Eve had shrugged off the comments, putting his behaviour down to pressures at work, but the more she thought about the strange things he'd been doing, the more she found herself agreeing with Jane. She knew she had to do something before it was too late and a plan began to form in her mind but, even as it took shape, doubt crept in as to whether she would have the courage to follow it through. Beside her, Tommy was snoring loudly, oblivious to the turmoil his girlfriend was facing.

Eventually, Eve fell into a troubled sleep, her fears about their relationship seeping into her dreamtime so that she tossed and turned all night but Tommy did not wake.

The following morning, bruised and battered, Eve slipped quietly out of bed before Tommy woke. As she shuffled painfully across the short distance to the bathroom, she was grateful that at least the rest of the household were still asleep, Donald and Jane blissfully ignorant of the events which had taken place during the night.

Jane, however, who had been in her top-floor bedroom reading a book, had heard the commotion coming from the floor below, but as rows were a common-place occurrence had ignored her brother's ranting. She had been told in no uncertain terms, on more than one occasion, to keep her nose out of their affairs. Jane remembered only too clearly the last time she had tried to intervene, coming close to being the recipient of an angry fist. She now gave the feuding couple a wide berth.

In the early hours of the morning, as Tommy's ranting had reached screaming pitch, she had rummaged in her bedside cabinet for a set of earplugs, stuffing them into her ears. With the noise reduced to a muted silence, Jane picked up her book once more, eventually falling asleep, entirely unaware of the events unfolding on the floor below.

Jane's morning ritual was to shower first but as Eve was occupying the bathroom she descended the stairwell to the kitchen, where she prepared a lunch box for work then sat to have breakfast. As she finished the remnants of cereal in her bowl, there were no signs the bathroom had been vacated. Looking at the kitchen clock, Jane started to get impatient. Time was marching on and if she didn't get in the bathroom soon she was going to be late for work.

Inside the bathroom, Eve had just stepped out of the shower and was inspecting the cuts and bruises Tommy had inflicted on her body. Wiping down the steamy mirror on the medicine cabinet, she stared at the reflection of her battered face, realising no amount of make-up was going to cover the tell-tale signs of violence, and dreading what work colleagues were going to think when they saw the shining black eye. As she assessed the damage, trying to pull down her hair to hide the bruising, the pain in her head returned with a vengeance, then another loud noise began to pierce her brain, making her jump back from the mirror. It took a moment to realise someone was outside, banging on the bathroom door.

"Will you hurry up, Eve, I'm going to be late for work!" Getting no response, Jane hammered again, prompting Eve to open the door. Eve pulled her dressing gown tightly round her neck, to hide the ugly bruises. She was in no mood for confrontation and in her haste to get past Jane, who was blocking her way, she accidentally pushed her into the doorframe. Jane's temper flared; she was too wound up from the wait for the bathroom to take in the damage Tommy had inflicted on Eve's face.

"How fucking rude! I've spent the best part of an hour waiting to get in this sodding bathroom and then you push me aside, as though I have no rights in my own home."

The commotion propelled Tommy out of bed and within minutes all three were going hammer and tongs at each other. The screeching argument spilled from the first-floor landing down the stairs and into the kitchen, where Donald was at the table in his dressing gown, drawing deeply on a cigarette and reading the *Racing Roundup*.

"Will you bloody kids give it a rest, I'm trying to read!" Slamming down the paper, Donald ground out his cigarette in the overflowing ashtray. As he got up from the table, he was subjected to another onslaught of incoherent screaming, the two siblings blaming each other for starting the row.

"Will you stop this fucking screaming? It's going right through me!" As Donald raised his voice, silence prevailed. He stormed through the lounge and up the front stairwell to his bedroom, leaving the feuding threesome in no doubt he had no intention of getting involved in their petty domestics.

With Donald out of earshot, the argument turned ugly once more. Tit-for-tat insults were slung at each other until Jane, in an effort to get in the last word, said something that about their mother that left her brother reeling; telling him that, shortly before she died, Marjorie had been planning to leave Donald.

"Take that back. It isn't true, she wouldn't do that!"

"Yes, it's true. I heard them talking about it." Jane's tone was harsh, wanting to hit Tommy where it hurt the most.

The minute the words were out of her mouth, however, she realised she'd taken the argument to another level. Seeing the look in her brother's eyes, she beat a hasty retreat back up to the bathroom. She attempted to shut the door but Tommy was right behind her, his foot wedged inside the frame.

Jane heaved against the door with all her strength, trapping his foot and making him howl out in pain.

"Oooooouccchhhh, you fucking cow, you're fucking crushing my foot. Open the bloody door." Frightened by what she'd inadvertently done in an effort to escape, Jane eased her hold on the door. Preoccupied with his throbbing foot, Tommy didn't register the door slamming and the sound of the lock engaging.

Exhausted and terrified of her brother's temper, Jane collapsed on the bathroom floor and listened in silence as her brother ranted and raved on the landing outside. Eventually, with the intervention of their father, who reappeared from his bedroom to give Tommy a dressing-down, Tommy stomped back to his bedroom. Fifteen minutes later, the front door slammed and Donald was knocking the bathroom door, informing his daughter it was safe to come out as both Tommy and Eve had left the house.

Opening the door, Jane fell sobbing into her father's arms. "Dad, this cannot go on any longer, I'm frightened of what he will do next."

"Hush now child, don't fret, I will have a word with him." Donald, unaccustomed to shows of affection since the death of his wife, held his daughter at arm's length, reassuring her. "Now, go and get yourself sorted and ready for work, or you'll be late. I will talk to Tommy tonight."

It was unusual for Donald to get involved in his children's arguments. He had long since lost interest in his children, especially Tommy, who'd gone down in his estimation with the carry-on with his girlfriend, but lately he was beginning to realise how out of control the situation was becoming, under his own roof. Watching his deflated daughter slump back upstairs to her bedroom, he was determined to have it out with Tommy, reflecting that his daughter may have been right and perhaps it had been a mistake to allow Eve to move into the household.

The last thing Jane wanted was to go to work but she had to get out of the house in case Tommy returned to continue their argument. All day, the precarious situation at home weighed heavily on her mind. The thought of another confrontation with her brother sickened her but there was no option other than to face the situation head-on and have it out with him. Despite her father's promise and good intentions, Jane knew Donald would gloss over things. After a word of warning, Tommy would carry on as though nothing had happened and, like clockwork, Donald would make his way to the pub.

As she left the office, walking the short distance through Queen Square into the centre of Bristol, Jane was oblivious to early evening commuter traffic. Her mind was in turmoil, going over the blazing argument and the hurtful words they'd slung at each other; recalling what she had told him about their mother, cementing the fact that living under the same roof with Tommy and Eve was an impossibility. As she passed a rank of shops, Jane stopped at Jazzy's Unisex Hairdressers to look at some of the latest styles. She caught a glimpse of her unkempt reflection. Normally fastidious about her appearance, she barely recognised the shabby person looking back at her. It was a wake-up call, letting her know how far things had slipped and forcing her to make a decision to rectify the situation.

She briefly toyed with the idea of spending the evening with friends but, realising it would only prolong the agony, and maybe make a volatile situation worse, she continued her journey past the rank of shops and on towards Christmas Steps.

At No. 26, Jane reluctantly unlocked the front door, mentally bracing herself for the inevitable onslaught. Shoulders squared, head held high, she marched in, and through to the lounge, ready for confrontation. Finding no one at home, her rigid stance relaxed slightly, but on entering the kitchen the shambles greeting her ignited her rage.

"Bloody hell, it looks more like a navvies' canteen than a kitchen," she cursed to herself, casting her eye over the overflowing ashtray, newspapers and magazines strewn across the kitchen table. Taking off her jacket and hanging it on the back of a chair with her handbag, she turned and started to tackle the sink full of dirty dishes.

Moments later, Tommy entered the house and, hearing Jane in the kitchen, prepared himself for a fight. The sound of booted feet on the flagstone floor alerted Jane to Tommy's presence. She turned to face him, the morning's hurtful words echoing in her head, prompting a long list of grievances to pour unabated from her mouth and giving Tommy no opportunity to speak.

"You and that girlfriend of yours have outstayed your welcome. The arrangement was for a month and you have been here for almost a year. I am fed up with being treated as your housekeeper, continually clearing away your shit. Enough is enough, Tommy, you have to find somewhere else to live." Barely stopping for breath, her words came out in a heated rush.

"You fucking cow! Who do you think you are? You have no right to tell me to leave. It's my home as well as yours." Tommy's face was inches from hers as he spat the words back at her. Incensed beyond all reasoning, he wasn't going to be spoken to like that by anyone, least of all his bastard sister.

Before Jane could move away, Tommy lunged towards her, his strong hands encasing her slender neck in a vice-like hold, from which there was no escape. As his hands tightened round her throat, squeezing the lifeblood from her body, something inside him exploded, sucking out all traces of humanity. A seething rage possessed him, distorting his face into a demonic mask.

With her brother's hands around her throat, Jane was forced to look at his deranged face. The sight terrified her. The man with her life in his hands no longer resembled Tommy. He seemed controlled by an unknown force, and beyond reasoning. Grunts and howls spewing from his mouth were akin to those of a feral animal in a feeding frenzy. Jane fought for her life, tugging at his hands in desperation to ease the pressure on her suffocating windpipe.

She started to claw at his face. Tommy howled in pain as her long fingernails sunk into soft tissue, just under his right eye. A struggle for dominance ensued. Jane was no match for the beast who flung her like a rag doll against the Belfast sink then began to bang her head against the polished stone surface until she stopped struggling and slipped into unconsciousness.

No longer in possession of his own mind, Tommy threw his sister's unresponsive body on the flagstone floor, tore off her dress and panties, then brutally raped her.

As soon as it was over, the force controlling Tommy vacated his body, leaving him confused and horrified in equal measure as he found himself on top of his sister, trousers round his ankles.

"What the fuuuuucking hell have I done?" Tommy screamed at the top of his voice as lurid flashbacks of the rape bombarded his brain, chilling him to the core.

Tommy staggered up against the kitchen units to steady himself, pulling his trousers back up. Apart from the horrendous flashbacks, Tommy could not think clearly about what had happened. It was as though something had climbed inside him; used his body, taken his soul, and was now taunting him cruelly, replaying the horrendous act into his conscious mind, asserting its dominance on him.

As he clutched the kitchen units for support, Tommy could still feel its presence, moving around his internal organs, making his body tremble in fear as he wondered what it was going to make him do next. Then, as though his questions had been answered, the temperature inside his body reverted from ice-cold back to a sickly warmth as the obstruction dissipated and his blood supply started pumping normally again. As the residue of evil left his body, Tommy found himself suspended in that moment in time, a strong smell of sulphur lingering in his nostrils as he looked down at Jane's lifeless body.

Tommy remained fixed to the spot, staring down on his macabre handiwork, shockwaves bombarding his mind as his sister's screams echoed through his head. His first impulse was to run away from the terrible act he'd committed. Glancing at the kitchen clock, a moment of blind panic knocked him sideways as he realised Eve was due home any moment. Faced with an impossible situation, he lashed out, slamming his fists against the kitchen wall. The resulting pain brought his mind into sharp focus. He remembered his girlfriend was going to visit her mother after work. He hated the interfering old bag with a passion. She took every opportunity to poison her daughter's mind against him but in view of the beating he'd given Eve the previous evening, he had bitten down his usual objections to the visit.

With his girlfriend out for the evening, Tommy knew his father would not pose a problem; Donald would be ensconced in the Three Sugar Loaves pub until closing time.

With a small window of opportunity, Tommy had to act quickly if he was to save his own skin. Walking to the lobby area in the front of the house, where they kept their bikes, shoes and umbrellas, he pulled aside the thick net curtains dressing a large glass window and peered outside. Something behind one of the bikes caught his eye but as his mind was in deep turmoil he didn't consciously acknowledge the object, which looked like a holdall.

As it was still early evening, the footfall on the narrow, cobbled street was light. Tommy watched a middle-aged couple saunter past the window. Once they had disappeared down the bottom of Christmas Steps, he retrieved a set of keys to his van from the ornate wooden key box located on the side wall, opening the front door and leaving it on the latch. Nobody was around to see him as he ran up to the top of Christmas Steps and down Colston Avenue, where his van was parked displaying a resident's permit. He started the engine and drove the short distance around the centre of Bristol, negotiating several sets of traffic lights. Luck was on his side as the lights were all green, giving him unhindered passage to his destination. When Tommy arrived at the loading bay at the bottom of Christmas Steps, it was empty, allowing him easy access. Turning off the engine, he sat for a while, trying to get his jumbled thoughts together. From where he was parked, he had a bird's-eye view of the cobbled street. With no one in sight, he climbed out of the van and opened the back door, leaving it slightly ajar, then ran the short distance back up the cobbled street to No. 26.

Tommy clambered up the narrow stairwell to the first floor. In his haste to get up the second set of steps to Jane's bedroom, he tripped and knocked his knee. Cursing, he picked himself up and limped up the remaining stairs. In Jane's room he spotted a rucksack hanging on a set of chrome hooks behind the door and began to fill it with clothes and toiletries then he reached for a dressing gown, removing its cord belt. Satisfied he had what he needed to make it look as though Jane had packed in a hurry, Tommy shouldered the rucksack and ran back downstairs into the kitchen. All the while, he was concocting a cover story for his missing sister, convincing himself that after the blazing row they had that morning Jane would have a plausible reason to leave the house and it would be logical to assume she'd gone to stay with friends for a while, whilst the dust settled.

Back in the kitchen, Tommy averted his eyes from his sister's face as he lifted her limp body onto the rattan mat that had pride of place in the middle of the kitchen floor. Rolling her inside, he held the rug together against the kitchen units and fastened it with the dressing gown cord. After checking it was securely tied, he dragged the hefty load through the lounge and dumped it in the lobby. Back in the kitchen, he picked Jane's jacket and satchel bag from the back of the chair. Stuffing the lightweight jacket into the satchel, Tommy slung it over his shoulder then put his arms through the rucksack straps, resting its bulk against the crook of his back and hurrying back into the lobby to retrieve Jane's body. Lifting the curtain again, he peered up and down the street before opening the door. The coast was clear. He slung the rolled-up rug over his shoulders, his sister's body still encased within, then gently closed the door behind him and made his way as quickly as he could to the bottom of Christmas Steps and his waiting van.

Just as Tommy was about to throw the load into the back of the van, Donald staggered out of the Three Sugar Loaves. Seeing his father, Tommy froze momentarily before panic-fuelled adrenaline kicked in. Opening the back door, he manoeuvred the mat off his shoulders and into the van, with the ease of bodybuilder lifting a set of dumbbells. His actions were so quick that Donald stumbled past him, oblivious; such was the level of his intoxication, his interest solely focused on the next watering hole and getting another pint of ale down his throat.

Once his father had staggered out of sight, Tommy threw Jane's rucksack and satchel onto the front seat, locked the van, then went back up to the house to clean the bloody mess in the kitchen.

Unbeknown to Tommy as he stumbled back up the cobbled street to No. 26, Eve had just walked down from the top of Christmas Steps and let herself into the house. She was in the lounge and about to go into the kitchen when she heard the front door opening. Not wanting to be found, as it would scupper her plans to leave, she desperately looked for somewhere to hide. Slipping into a gap behind one of the sofas and the wall, she waited silently, praying for an opportunity to get out of the house unseen.

From her hiding place, Eve heard someone enter the lounge. She could tell from heavy footsteps on the bare floorboards that it was Tommy who stopped beside the sofa. Thinking he was going to sit down and turn on the television, she cursed her foolish choice. A few moments passed, as though he were thinking about something, then Tommy walked straight past her hiding place and through the open glass-panelled doors which led into the kitchen. Dizzy with relief, Eve peered from behind the sofa and flinched when she saw him moving around in the next room.

Running the taps, Tommy started to wash down the work surface and sink, then he stripped off his clothes and threw them into the washing machine. Curiosity made Eve inch back out from her hiding place to get a better look at what he was doing. His peculiar behaviour puzzled her. She had never known Tommy to clean up the kitchen, let alone wash his own clothes.

Suddenly, dressed only in boxers, he turned around. Her hand went to her mouth to smother a gasp as he looked straight at her. Terrified, Eve darted back into her hiding place, cowering; sure he would pull the sofa back from the wall to expose her and initiate another thrashing. Her heart was beating so fast it felt like it was coming out of her chest as the sound of his bare feet padded towards her. Eve's terror went into overdrive, her whole body shaking in anticipation of the first punch, but instead of pulling the sofa back from the wall, Tommy walked straight past her. The lounge door closed behind him and she heard him walk upstairs. Not quite believing he hadn't seen her, Eve seized the moment and crept out from her hiding place. She rifled in her handbag and left on the coffee table a letter she'd written earlier. Quietly, she left the house.

Eve ran as quickly as she could to a waiting taxi at the top of Christmas Steps. Seeing her struggling with two heavy bags, the driver got out and helped her put them in the boot. The young girl was agitated and, in her haste to get inside the cab, stumbled on one of her high heels and fell against the door. By the time the man had put the bags in the boot and got into the vehicle, she had picked herself up and thrown herself inside. Eve broke down in tears.

The taxi driver looked in his mirror. "Are you alright, love?"

"Yes, just a tiff with my boyfriend, I'll get over it." Eve didn't want to get into the ins and outs of her tumultuous relationship with a complete stranger. Little did she realise that another woman, just a short distance away, was not going to have the chance to get over anything.

During their two-year relationship, Tommy had changed from happy-go-lucky into a belligerent, arrogant individual she hardly recognised. At first, the change was gradual then, once the other side of his personality emerged, the love she felt for him started to diminish. She found herself wondering whether he was the same person; knowing if she pandered to her growing suspicions as to the monster he'd become, it would have turned her mind inside out.

A voice broke her introspection. "Where to, love?" The taxi driver stretched across to adjust his meter.

"Chester Crescent, Winterbourne," she replied, dabbing the tears running down her cheeks with a tissue from her pocket.

Eve had been looking for a way out. She had found a small bedsit she liked, in a Victorian house on Chester Crescent. It was in an area of Bristol Tommy rarely visited so there was little danger of bumping into him. As long as she conducted her life in and around Winterbourne, at least until he got used to the idea she wasn't going back to him, she was safe.

Eve had thought long and hard about her decision. It meant leaving her job and friends behind, and, more importantly, her mother. She had gathered her courage in both hands, telling Tommy it would be a good idea for her to stay with her mum for a couple of days, to give him and his sister time to resolve their argument. In between cursing Jane from her head to her toe, Tommy had reluctantly agreed with his girlfriend's reasoning.

Guilt had consumed Eve as she spun the concocted story, knowing she had no intention of staying with her mother, who would undoubtedly have to deal with the fallout when Tommy turned up on her doorstep. Eve resolved to call her once out of harm's way, deciding the safest thing was to tell no one and to disappear until things blew over. She hoped Tommy would eventually give up searching for her. The thought of spending another moment with him turned her stomach.

She had signed the rental agreement, paid the deposit and a month's rent in advance, and arranged to meet the landlord at the property, where she would start a new life without Tommy.

As Eve was driven away from Christmas Steps she looked through the back window of the taxi one last time and breathed a sigh of relief. It seemed a miracle Tommy hadn't discovered her hiding behind the sofa. When she thought now of the way he'd stared at her, it was like he was looking straight through her; as if she wasn't even there. She could only surmise that as he stared straight into her face, his mind was elsewhere.

She had a sense of unease when she thought of No. 26 Christmas Steps and she shuddered at all she had witnessed there. It was as though the place was cursed.

It was just after 10pm when Tommy returned, after disposing of his sister's body. The house was empty and he was relieved to find his father still out, presumably in the pub. Walking into the kitchen, he cast a critical eye over the freshly cleaned work surface and sink, looking for signs of blood. Satisfied there was nothing to suggest to the naked eye that a crime had been committed, he took a black bag from a kitchen drawer then clambered upstairs. Inside his bedroom, Tommy stripped off his clothes and put them in the bag, intending to throw them in a skip far away from his home.

After showering to remove any traces of his sister, he went straight to bed. Sleep, however, didn't come easy and when he eventually drifted off he dreamt of Jane sitting at the bottom of his bed; her dead, accusing eyes making him scream out in terror and wake with a start. So real was the image burnt into his brain that he was convinced he'd actually seen her, although this was a complete impossibility as her body was trussed up like a turkey and wedged into a garbage bin somewhere in Somerset. Turning over quickly, he flicked on the bedside light and saw nothing out of the ordinary in the room. He realised the grisly vision was something conjured up by his imagination. Looking at the clock on the bedside table, he saw it was 3.15am and the space in the bed Eve normally occupied was empty.

"Where the fuck is she?" Still groggy, Tommy mumbled to himself as he slung on a dressing gown and went down to the kitchen to make some tea. Guilt-ridden and fearful of seeing his dead sister's face again, he knew any more sleep would be impossible.

By 3.35am, his mind was in meltdown. He had forgotten that Eve was staying with her mother. Sitting on the sofa with the TV turned on low as background noise, he fretted over whether he'd left anything incriminating behind, mentally dissecting the disposal of his sister's body. Everything that could identify Jane had been removed from her satchel and transferred into the rucksack with her jacket. On the drive back into Bristol, after dumping the satchel with her body, Tommy discovered a wooded area beside a river. Driving deep inside the wood, he parked close to the river bank. He left the van's lights on as he hunted for stones and rocks, which he put into the rucksack. Then he threw the bag as far as he could into the water, dimly making out its shape as it sank below the surface and vanished into the river's murky depths. Tommy was already beginning to regret his hasty decision to dump the body in the garbage bin, wishing he'd come to the river first. It was then that he remembered the rattan mat.

Panic flared as he visualised the empty space where it had been in the kitchen. A replacement had to be found as soon as possible. Eve would spot its removal straight away and an inquisition would begin. His father was less likely to notice. Donald didn't know the time of day, let alone whether there was a mat missing from the kitchen.

Desperate thoughts crowded Tommy's mind, forcing him to face his demons. Why had he done this terrible thing to his sister? What was happening to him? He could remember coming into the house, confronting Jane in the kitchen, and a powerful rage consuming him until he was no longer in control of his own actions.

A window opened in the dark recesses of his mind, where regurgitated thoughts stirred up something undeniably evil. As it permeated through him he began to fight against unseen restraints, his body contorting into unimaginable positions in a vain attempt to ward off the malevolent intruder.

Clutching his head, Tommy screamed out. "Nooooooooo, no, noooooooo! Get away, get away from me, whatever or whoever you are, get awaaaaaay!" Tommy fell to the floor on his knees, sobbing like a baby, thrashing at his head as though he was trying to ward off a swarm of angry bees.

The entity left as quickly as it had consumed him, the seed already planted, its mission complete. Suddenly, there were no angry bees, and no deviant thoughts, in Tommy's mind. He lay on the floor, cradling his head for some time, shielding himself from the unseen intruder and waiting for another attack to begin.

Eventually, sensing the danger had passed, Tommy dragged himself up from the floor and onto the sofa. In a deep state of shock, he momentarily questioned his sanity. What had just happened to him was bordering the realms of fantasy. Was it deep-rooted guilt making him conjure up these imaginary things, or was this insanity really happening? Either way, Tommy knew he had to get a grip of himself as he was in danger of losing all sense of reality.

In an attempt to stem foolish thoughts of unearthly visitations, he went into the kitchen to make some tea. He was shocked to discover it was 5am. An hour had passed which he couldn't account for. As the kettle boiled, his thoughts reverted to Eve, wondering where she was and, more importantly, who she was with, and what was she up to.

His jealous streak conjured up images of her and Ben laughing together, igniting his temper. Not paying attention to what he was doing, Tommy narrowly missed scalding his hand as he poured boiling water into his mug. Cursing, he wiped the spilt water with a tea towel and took the tea into the lounge. Putting the mug on the coffee table, he reached for the remote and started to flick through the TV channels. It was then that he spotted an envelope with his name on it. Tommy recognised Eve's handwriting and turned the envelope over, ripping open the gummed seal.

The simple act of opening the letter bought him back to reality, jolting his memory. He remembered Eve suggesting she stay with her mother. Momentarily, he felt relieved, knowing where she was and who she was with, but as he pulled the single white sheet of paper from the envelope and read its contents, his whole world fell apart. On top of everything else, Eve had left him.

"Fuck, fuck, fuck, fuuuuuucccck!" Screaming at the top of his voice, he ripped the letter into shreds and flung it on the floor. "Fucking bitch, I'll teach her a lesson she'll never fucking forget when I get my hands on her." He punched and kicked over the coffee table in a fit of rage.

Storming back upstairs, Tommy threw some clothes on and started packing. With thoughts of law enforcement breathing down his neck in the wake of Jane's disappearance, he had nothing to keep him in Bristol now. There was one place he was going to visit before he left, then he would disappear forever. He would also leave behind his father; a stinking drunk whose life was permanently lost to alcohol and who would carry on his ways regardless of his son's absence.

On the top floor of the house, in the bedroom next to Jane's, Donald stirred in his sleep, oblivious to what was happening in his home. No amount of noise would wake him. When he surfaced hours later he would shower, shave, shovel a bit of breakfast down his throat, and catch up with the footie or the racing news in the paper, then wait for the pub to open.

Day in, day out; year in, year out, the routine never changed. No matter how much his kids badgered him about his drinking – especially Jane – he took no notice. Donald told them on numerous occasions it was his life to do with as he wished and they had no right to interfere whilst they lived under his roof.

"If you don't like it – leave."

Chapter 2

Somerset, 1985

In a leafy suburb of the town of Street in Somerset, the early morning mist shimmered in pockets; promising signs of another sunny day. Freddie, a rotund refuge collector, head full of thoughts of a date with a curvaceous redhead he'd met at the Flag & Bull a couple of nights ago, was oblivious to what was to unfold in the next few minutes, throwing his daily routine into an uproar.

The moment he wheeled the green garbage bin onto the truck's mechanical lifting equipment alongside the other bins, it had struck him as unusually heavy. As he watched the mechanical lift upend its rubbish into the truck, his suspicions proved correct. The load dropped out in a great lump, stemming the flow of rubbish into the bottom of the truck. Cursing to himself, he immediately shut off the whirring machinery and leaned over into the bowels of the truck, looking for the obstruction. It didn't take long to spot the source; a rattan mat with a leg hanging from it, which Freddie initially assumed was part of a mannequin. As his gloved hands tugged at the mat it fell open, revealing the bloody face of a woman. Freddie instantly dropped the mat and jumped away, stumbling over a curb in the process. Regaining his balance, he ran around to the front of the truck to alert the driver.

"Charlie, for Christ's sake stop the truck!" he screamed.

"What the fuck is wrong with you?" Charlie turned off the

engine, hauling himself out of the truck. Thinking Freddie was off on one of his fits of fantasy, he strolled round the back after his colleague, to investigate.

"Jesus Christ, Mary and Joseph," the bald-headed Irishman exclaimed, flicking his body with the sign of the cross the moment his eyes followed Freddie's pointing finger to the woman hidden amongst the rubbish.

The commotion alerted the rest of the team, who stopped what they were doing and congregated around the truck to find out what was going on. Davey, the team leader, who'd stopped to take a crafty ciggy break at the side of one of the houses, dropped his cigarette and rushed over to his team, instructing them to stand aside.

"What the fuck is that?" The sight of the bloody body shocked Davey, who stumbled away, retching up last night's Tandoori chicken onto the pavement. The gathering of men fell silent, each panic-stricken, not knowing what to do. As Davey was in no fit state to take charge of the situation, Charlie jumped in and started issuing orders to the team.

"Andy, there's a phone box down the road. Phone the coppers and get them here double-quick." Like a seasoned sprinter, Andy shot off down the street.

"Steve, move those sodding bins away from the truck and the rest of you stand over there." There was no backchat from the men as they adhered to Charlie's instructions.

Meanwhile, Charlie, for the sake of common decency and not thinking about contamination of evidence, covered the woman's face with the rattan mat. Saying a silent prayer over her before moving away, he realised Freddie's quick actions had saved the body from being crushed.

Local police responded to the 999 call within ten minutes. On arrival at the scene, DS Gerald Spencer, accompanied by DS Robert Rye, flashed his badge at one of the early responders; a fresh-faced constable looking a little green around the gills. Issuing orders to his men to take statements from the shocked garbage collectors, DS Spencer called the medical examiner and ordered the area to be cordoned off with blue-and-white police tape.

Donning latex gloves, Spencer and Rye approached the garbage truck. Peering inside, they immediately saw the rattan mat, and, spotting the exposed leg, Spencer steeled himself as he gently lifted the top part of the mat. As the woman's face was revealed, the extent of her injuries temporarily shocked him, giving way to a fleeting sympathy for the young copper who'd been one of the first to see the body.

"Jesus fucking Christ." Standing next to him, DS Rye recoiled at the sight. "What sort of a fucking animal has done this?" he ranted, watching as Spencer respectfully covered the battered face, assessing there was nothing they could do for the woman now but await the arrival of the medical examiner.

Twenty minutes later the ME, Patrick Callaghan, a morose and sallow-looking man in his late fifties, arrived. A forensic tent was erected beside the garbage truck, to give privacy to their activities; away from prying eyes of onlookers, some of whom had shamelessly jostled for position nearest the truck to get a glimpse of the body, a body bag, or some other morsel to verbally dissect over a pint in the local pub later on.

Photographs were taken of the body in situ before it was carefully lifted out and set down on the plastic sheeting covering a section of pavement inside the tent. Another set of photographs were taken of the body prior to unwrapping the mat in its entirety. The revelation was shocking; the woman's face was so mutilated, it barely passed as human.

Crouching down to inspect the battered body, the ME was therefore taken aback when he discovered a faint pulse. Double-checking his discovery, Callaghan moved his face close to hers, detecting signs of shallow breathing, confirming that the woman was still alive. The investigation catapulted to another level; what had started off as a suspected murder became a fight for life.

Within minutes, the woman's battered body was transferred to a gurney, then into a waiting ambulance, which was dispatched at neck-breaking speed on blue flashing lights to Frenchay Hospital in Bristol. A call had been placed ahead, with theatre staff on standby for her arrival. The young woman underwent live-saving neurosurgery to remove blood clots, reducing the swelling in her brain. After the operation, DS Spencer was informed by the lead neurosurgeon, Nicolas Patel, that although the woman had survived the surgery, the prognosis was bleak. It was Patel's opinion that it would be a miracle if the woman regained consciousness and, if she did, there was no telling how much brain damage she'd sustained in the savage attack.

A press conference was called, police pleading with the public to come forward with any information to help identify the woman. No photographs were released to the media to aid their search as the woman's injuries were so severe that, even with the passage of time, her face would never regain its original features. The scant description which was issued informed waiting reporters that the victim was estimated to be in her late twenties, brunette, and of slight build. Nothing was found on the body to identify who she was or where she came from. Another frustration for the police was the fact that most of her teeth had been smashed or knocked out in the frenzied attack, making identification through dental records impossible.

Despite coverage in newspapers and on local news channels, no one came forward to report a missing woman fitting the sketchy description. Days turned into a week and then Hugo Fitzallen, a partner at Fitzallen & Goode, a company of solicitors, called with concerns about one of his secretaries, Suzette Morris, who had failed to turn up for work. It had been over a week and no one had heard from Suzette. Fearing the worst in the wake of the brutal attack, Fitzallen contacted the police. Hoping this was the break they were looking for, Spencer and Rye arrived at Fitzallen & Goode's offices located in Pembroke Road, Clifton – one of the most upmarket areas of Bristol – to question Mr Fitzallen and his staff. It later transpired the employee in question arrived at work unscathed and unmolested the following Monday, having taken an impromptu holiday with her boyfriend. Hugo Fitzallen, infuriated by his employee's irresponsible behaviour and the fact he was made to look like a complete fool in the eyes of the law, promptly sacked Suzette.

On hearing about Suzette's safe return, DS Spencer was deflated, as hopes of identifying the woman in the hospital bed were diminishing. It was an unusual situation for a young woman to disappear without someone reporting it and, with no clues to her identity, the investigation stalled.

Two months passed whilst the unidentified woman remained unresponsive in a coma and, despite continued appeals for information, nothing was forthcoming from the public. IV lines and drains from bags suspended on drip stands running into her arms and abdomen made her look more alien than human. Her injuries were extensive, consisting of a fractured skull, broken jawbone, smashed nose, and lacerations across the whole of her body, but the catalogue of brutality paled into insignificance in the wake of a recent discovery. After the woman had been stabilised, a rape kit had been conducted. Semen had been found inside her, together with vaginal tearing and bruising, confirming rape had taken place.

Worse was to come when it was discovered that over the course of time, a rogue seed had germinated, resulting in pregnancy.

The medical team caring for the woman faced moral and ethical dilemmas, not knowing whether she would regain consciousness. If she did, would she be capable of understanding what happened to her?

It was doubtful she would live long enough to carry the baby full-term. Test results concluded she was nine weeks pregnant, confirming the baby growing inside her was the product of rape. DS Gerald Spencer went into overdrive when he heard the news and, despite warnings from the powers-that-be banging on about budgets, he initiated another search, enlisting the help of local recruitment agencies, figuring at some stage she might have approached one of them looking for work. He knew he was clutching at straws but was prepared to give it a try in the desperate hope the search may jolt someone's memory and provide a lead.

Meanwhile, in another part of Bridewell Police Station, an aggrieved Mr Christianna, having decided his problems were escalating, had barrelled through the revolving doors into the foyer. The tenants of No. 26 Christmas Steps owed him unpaid rent, totalling the princely sum of three thousand pounds. As other elements in his business empire were suffering, the money was desperately needed. William Batey, the duty sergeant on the front desk, suffered the brunt of the man's grievances as Christianna whinged on in explicit detail about the numerous occasions he'd knocked the tenants' door then called into a local pub he knew Donald Adams frequented. Christianna's mood darkened as he explained that the pub landlord informed him Adams hadn't been seen for ten days, adding that it was out of character for the man as he spent most of his time in his bar. Fearing his tenant had done a moonlight flit, the disgruntled Christianna demanded the police intervene in the matter. Sergeant Batey, who started to take a dislike to the arrogant man, assured him they would look into it and contact him when there was any further news. Not used to being dismissed by anyone, least of all a public servant,

Christianna held his ground, insisting on speaking to someone in higher authority.

"Sir, this will be passed on to the relevant team, just give us time to make our enquiries." Batey's words were tinged with impatience. Realising he wasn't going to get the results he wanted, Christianna's impatience boiled over and he turned on his heel.

Watching the disgruntled landlord stomp across the foyer and slam back through the revolving doors, Batey thought the man's behaviour reminiscent of a spoilt child who couldn't get his way. However, rude behaviour aside, the sergeant's inner radar told him all was not well with the elusive tenant; a known alcoholic whose landlord had just cause to be worried. Batey's lengthy experience with drunks taught him routine dictated they never strayed too far from their patch, making them an easy target to locate, and as Christmas Steps was only a stone's throw away from the police station, two constables were dispatched to investigate.

PCs Brian Davies and Ken Smithers spoke to Paul Bower - the landlord at the Three Sugar Loaves, the proprietor of a small newsagents just around the corner where Donald Adams picked up his daily papers, and a young woman who owned a bridal shop opposite. All were concerned by Donald's unexplained absence. According to the bridal shop owner, Donald's son, his daughter, and the son's girlfriend had not been seen for some time.

Davies and Smithers knocked the door at No. 26 Christmas Steps. Receiving no response, Smithers looked through the letter box and spotted a wedge of untouched mail. The young PCs realised there was something not quite right about the man's disappearance. Local information pointed to one course of action; to gain access inside the property and find out what was going on.

PC Smithers fired his burly shoulder at the flimsy door, which, after several thrusts, gave way under his weight. The house looked as though it had been ransacked; rubbish and uneaten food littered work surfaces in the kitchen. Empty beer cans and bottles, some of which were broken, were strewn on the floor in the lounge, giving the constables reason to believe there had been a disturbance of some kind.

"Police, Mr Adams. Are you at home?" PC Davies called as they cautiously made their way through the house, batons drawn, ready to encounter any trouble.

Having satisfied themselves that the ground floor was clear, they started to search the rest of the house. All was deathly quiet as Davies and Smithers climbed in single-file up a narrow stairwell to the first floor, where they came across a bedroom, then a bathroom full of vomit and shit. As they edged their way up the second stairwell to the top floor of the property, the putrid smell increased, hinting at what lay ahead. On reaching the top floor landing, Davies entered the first bedroom with Smithers hot on his heels. An overpowering stench made him gag and bring his hand up to cover his nose, in a futile effort to ward off the evil smell, but the sight on the floor was far worse. Ken Smithers, however, was oblivious to the obnoxious stench, having lost his sense of smell six years earlier after a blow to the head whilst attempting to pull apart two rival football supporters intent on beating the crap out of each other. It was only when Davies moved aside, allowing him to see the full extent of the bedroom, that he realised why his colleague was struggling to control his retching.

Lying on the floor, fully clothed, by the side of the bed was Donald Adams, his body in an advanced state of decomposition. Struggling to gain composure, Davies clambered downstairs, seeking fresh air and meaning to report their discovery to the station whilst Smithers remained upstairs.

Careful not to disturb anything, Smithers opened a small window, allowing a flow of fresh air in. He surveyed the room and looked over the decomposing body but there were no visible signs to suggest any criminal intent and, despite the strange deadlock grimace on the man's face, he assumed Adams had died from natural causes.

Smithers inspected the second empty bedroom, which, judging by the bottles on the dressing table, seemed to have a female occupant. Leaving the room, Smithers was about to make his way downstairs when he felt something brush up against him. Turning to see what it was, he faced an empty landing. A quick scan of the second bedroom also confirmed no one other than himself and a dead body were on the second floor of the house. As he stood alone on the landing, knowing Davies was downstairs, he couldn't shake the feeling he was being watched.

Walking a couple of paces along the hallway, Smithers was heading for the staircase when a powerful force lifted him from his feet and pinned him to the wall. As the unseen force held him there, he felt like something was feeding on him, his lifeblood being sucked from him, stripping away his earthly existence. Smithers struggled violently against the unknown entity, kicking and screaming for his life, but nothing dislodged the force.

Davies, who had just ended his call to the station, heard the commotion upstairs. Knowing the property was clear, and there was no threat to either himself or Smithers, he was alarmed by the sudden screaming. Unbuttoning his baton, he quickly ascended the stairwell in search of his colleague. As Davies approached the second floor, he could hear Smithers' screams intermingled with a low, guttural voice. Someone or something other than himself and Smithers was in the property. With no time to wait for back-up, he followed the source of the screaming, which increased in volume with every step he took. Raising his baton, he charged up the remaining steps onto the landing outside the two bedrooms, where he saw Smithers suspended in mid-air, pinned up against the far wall.

"Jesus Christ, what's happening here?" The sound of Davies' booming voice broke the entity's spell and Smithers fell to the floor in a crumpled heap.

Davies dropped his baton and rushed over to Smithers, who was too traumatised to speak. Helping his colleague to his feet, as Davies' hand touched him he was flung across the hallway then tumbled down the stairwell to the floor below. Adrenaline kicked in when he came to a halt at the bottom of the stairs. Getting to his feet, Davies charged back up the stairwell, ready to take on the invisible attacker. This time, there was no retaliation when he helped Smithers back downstairs and out of house, where he sat him on the pavement. In an effort to establish what had happened, Davies tried to question Smithers but the traumatised PC was in a world of his own, mumbling incomprehensively to himself. The normally level-headed Davies was totally unnerved by Smithers' mental state and what he'd seen, not to mention the physical assault he been subjected to. Looking back at the narrow terraced house, he was suddenly very afraid.

A dark shadow appeared at the window, which had been left ajar. Davies felt compelled – challenged, even – to return to the house. He was mesmerised by the shadow, which metamorphosed into a black mass. He was on the point of surrendering to its spell when a scream brought him back to reality. Smithers, who was sitting on the pavement by his feet, had also seen the mass and, recognising it as his tormentor, let out an anguished howl of revulsion, wrenching Davies from its dark world. Momentarily stunned by the shadow's hypnotic influence, Davies realised how close he'd come to being under its spell. As he tried to calm his distraught colleague, the entity disappeared, leaving him in no doubt that whatever had possessed Smithers and attempted to gain control of his mind was still in the house. As he wrenched his eyes away from the window, a clutch of officers arrived at the bottom of Christmas Steps, signalling the arrival of back-up.

As the rapid response team rounded the corner, they saw one officer on the ground and another beside him, looking totally disorientated. By this time, the commotion in Christmas Steps started to attract attention from local shopkeepers and residents, who ventured out of their properties to see what was happening. Gerald Spencer, the team leader and a seasoned veteran when it came to dealing with death scenes, quickly assessed the situation. Issuing orders to members of his team, the house was swiftly sealed off from the public and a PC stationed on guard outside the property. Davies and Smithers were dispatched to the Bristol Royal Infirmary on upper Park Row, for medical attention.

After Forensics had conducted their investigations, Adams' body was removed from No. 26 and the house was shut up. No further incidents occurred whilst the remainder of the team were in the house and in view of Smithers' precarious mental condition – he was in such a state as to be unable to corroborate Davies' report – doubts were cast on its accuracy.

Word spread amongst the lads at the station concerning the strange events at Christmas Steps. Many took to ribbing Davies about the ghostly, out-of-this-world apparition, nicknaming it ET. None of his colleagues seemed to grasp the fact that the thing they'd encountered at the property, which had rendered Smithers, a normally able-bodied officer, a gibbering idiot was far from the friendly alien from outer space depicted in a children's movie.

Donald Adams' post-mortem revealed several anomalies. The man's clothes were removed, his body displaying a mass of welts and bruising, indicating foul play had taken place. Jack Watkin, the duty coroner, was baffled by Adams' injuries, which were consistent with fingers being pushing through his skin, as though his flesh were putty.

An idea started to form in his mind as the body was sliced open, giving credence to speculation Donald Adams had been attacked internally by something pushing his internal organs out of his body. The discovery, coupled with the putrid stench emanating from the open cavity, made Watkin and his assistant Colin Ward stagger back from the body in pure revulsion. Embarrassed by his bizarre reaction to the corpse, Watkin, who possessed a wicked sense of humour that came to the rescue in difficult situations, made light of the incident, taking the opportunity to leave the autopsy room. Colin Ward joined him in the ante-room, where the stench that followed them was neutralised by an air filtration system. As both men took deep breaths of clean, uncontaminated air, Watkin stared through the viewing panel at the mutilated body. Ward, who had his back to the window, didn't see the translucent mass emerge from the corpse's body.

"Bloody hell, Colin, take a look at that."

Watkin's assistant turned quickly and looked through the viewing panel in time to witness the mass vanishing into thin air. "Jesus, what was that?"

Both men stood awhile, pondering what they'd just seen.

Jack Watkin put the incident down to a build-up of gases in the deceased's body, explaining that once the incision had been made, those gases were released, forming a cloud of vapour which lingered momentarily before dispersing. As he aired his theory to his assistant, Watkin knew the mass was no vapour cloud. The moment the scalpel cut through Adams' dead flesh and he peered inside the cavity he'd created, Watkin sensed something else happening within the body. The mass had taken on a life of its own as it ascended, lingering over the dead corpse as if in final judgment, before vanishing.

Ten minutes later, when both men re-entered the autopsy room, all evidence of its presence was gone. In its place, the lingering smell of death prevailed. Thankfully, Colin Ward had also witnessed the strange phenomenon but Watkin knew he was going to have a battle to write a factual autopsy report incorporating what they'd seen, without it sounding like an extract from a supernatural thriller.

***

At Bridewell Police Station, Davies' colleagues were gradually starting to take his account of events seriously, in the wake of the post mortem report, which made for startling reading. Prior to the information in the report coming to light, it had been assumed that Adams, with levels of alcohol off the Richter scale, had injured himself in a drunken stupor, accounting for upturned furniture and broken glass found on the lounge floor. Watkin, however, disproved this theory by evidence of the unknown finger-gouging and discovery of skin under the deceased's fingernails, matching deep claw marks in his neck and pointing to the likelihood he was trying to fight off something. Forensics also established that a fight had started downstairs in the lounge and continued upstairs, where Donald made his last stand against the unidentified force in his bedroom. Plaster had been dislodged on a top section of the bedroom wall, where a bloody hand print had been found, matching the deceased's.

There was no logical reason for the position of the hand print and it was surmised Adams had been thrown against the wall with such force that he had flung his hand out in a vain attempt to cushion the impact. The fact remained, however, that whoever or whatever had propelled the body of a nineteen-stone man was something so powerful that it had obliterated his internal organs and in all likelihood Adams was dead before his body hit the ground. Other injuries on the deceased's body were consistent with external violence, where Adams had tried to defend himself. Internal trauma triggered a massive heart attack, culminating in sudden death. Nothing, however, could explain what Watkin witnessed in the autopsy room after making the first incision into the body. Level-headed and not normally given to fanciful thoughts, he shivered as he recalled the mass lingering over the body and wondered whether it had continued into the afterlife after Adams.

Further questioning of the landlord at the Three Sugar Loaves pub revealed that Adams told him his daughter had left home after an argument with her brother. Adams had also found torn pieces of paper littering the lounge floor. When he pieced them together, he discovered they made up a letter addressed to Tommy, from his girlfriend, telling him she was leaving him. Shortly afterwards, his son had packed up and vanished too, leaving the old man on his own; all suggesting it was not a family member who attacked him. With no trace of the son, who appeared to have vanished off the face of the earth, the search for Adams' daughter and Tommy's girlfriend proved problematic.

Meanwhile, with Smithers on long-term sick leave, PC Brian Davies was following a fresh line of enquiry for the daughter, who he discovered had worked as a temp for Avondale Recruitment; an agency located in the centre of Bristol. Tanya, the recruitment consultant who had dealt with Jane's job application, confirmed that Jane had left the temp job without notice. The consultant, clearly annoyed with her applicant and thinking about her lost commission, told Davies Jane worked three days into the month's assignment then left. No one in the agency had heard from her since, despite numerous calls and voice messages left on her home phone. Assuming Jane Adams had moved onto a better-paid position, or found a permanent job, Tanya had archived her details.

Upon requesting sight of the archived file, Davies found a photocopy of a recent passport photograph amongst the paperwork. As he studied the grainy black-and-white photocopy the hairs on Davies' neck stood on end, his thoughts immediately going to the woman who'd been found in Somerset. Armed with copies of Avondale's paperwork, Davies went back to the station and reported his findings to DS Gerald Spencer, who was spearheading the case. The discovery at Avondale prompted further searches through medical records, revealing Jane Adams had a scar on her lower back, resulting from the removal of a cancerous mole. Spencer visited Frenchay Hospital and, after speaking to Doctor Josephine Lacey, the consultant overseeing the woman's healthcare, discovered the unidentified woman also had a scar in the same location, confirming the victim of the vicious attack was Jane Adams.

Spencer was elated by the recent development, which allowed the investigation to move forward. At the morning briefing, he broke the news of the woman's identity, to loud cheers from his team, who had worked tirelessly on the search.

"Okay, okay, listen up, now we've got a name we need to find the bastard that did this to Jane."

Spencer gestured for silence as he proceeded to write on the whiteboard in pride of place at the front of the small briefing room.

- Jane Adams – Last known movements – temp job through Avondale Recruitment just off Broad Street – stone's throw from Christmas Steps.
- Donald Adams – father - deceased suspected foul play – daughter and son argued resulting in Jane leaving home.
- Tommy Adams – brother - whereabouts unknown – disappeared shortly after splitting with his girlfriend.
- Girlfriend – who is she and where is she?

Family at No. 26 Christmas Steps
Donald Adams (Father)
Jane Adams (Daughter)

Tommy Adams (Son)
Girlfriend of Tommy (Name Unknown)

Jane Adams
Left temp job with Avondale Recruitment
Left No. 26 after row with brother
Rucksack and clothes missing

Tommy Adams
Row with sister
Break-up letter from girlfriend
Left home taking clothes and money from Whisky Jar
Girlfriend - Name and whereabouts unknown

Donald Adams
Landlord at Three Sugar Loaves reported him missing for approx. 10 days
Christianna complaining about rent arrears – fearing his tenant doing a moonlight flit
Body found in upstairs bedroom
Signs of a disturbance in the lounge and a struggle in the bedroom

Looking at his writing on the whiteboard, it was obvious to Spencer and the rest of the team that their main suspect was the brother, Tommy Adams. Despite the fact Tommy had disappeared long before Donald's death, it wasn't discounted that he could have returned to the house and fought with his father. Tommy was also their major suspect in the attack on Jane. The landlord of the Three Sugar Loaves corroborated the argument had taken place between the two siblings; information he'd gleaned from their father as he was rambling into his beer one night. Energised by the discovery of the victim's identity, the team's main focus was Tommy Adams and the whereabouts of his girlfriend.

For such a small community, Spencer was surprised to find that door-to-door enquiries revealed nothing of interest on Christmas Steps. It wasn't until officers went into the newsagents in Christmas Street that information about their suspect started to come to light. Dorothy Baker, the proprietor and a willing gossip, who served Tommy and his girlfriend with cigarettes on numerous occasions, supplied a Christian name for the girl. Eve. On questioning Dorothy further, officers got a full description of the redheaded beauty, including the fact the proprietor of the shop mainly dealt with cash purchases as she didn't possess a card machine. However, as luck would have it, Dorothy occasionally accepted cheques from regular customers and recalled Eve paying by cheque for cigarettes and magazines on one occasion just before pay day. Leaving the officers in the shop, Dorothy went into her storeroom, where she kept her accounts in a battered steel cabinet. Rifling through the drawers, she found the book she was looking for and searched through the items paid in until she came to the cheque entry. Taking a post-it note and pen from a nearby desk, she wrote down the cheque number with Eve's Christian name against it and gave it to the waiting officers. The new information provided a glimmer of hope. Tracing the cheque through the banking system could yield a surname, making the search for Eve easier.

After hours of wading through banking protocol, the Branch Manager of HSBC in Corn Street agreed to initiate the search. Geoffrey Digby returned Spencer's call on his direct dial number and supplied him with the name he was waiting for.

Eve Shalinski.

Chapter 3

Jenna (Childhood Memories)
Bristol, 1990s

Jenna muttered under her breath as she watched the documentary about the Russian scientist crowing on about his new discovery. The invention – photographic equipment –purportedly captured the soul leaving the body at the moment of death. This was nothing new, she thought sourly. She herself had witnessed many strange phenomena since the age of five. Sadly, her parents, being good Catholics, didn't understand what she saw, or chose not to understand, and dismissed her claims as being the result of a child with an over-active imagination.

As she continued watching, her first experience of the afterlife came flooding back. At that stage in her life, when Nana Coleman visited her, she'd been a young, impressionable girl. Memories transported Jenna back to her childhood bedroom, where she saw herself sitting on her bed, playing with her favourite doll, Sarinda. It was early evening and her brother Timmy, who was three years older and allowed to stay up later, was outside in the back garden, playing football with his friend Owen. Her mother and father, Martha and James, were downstairs in the lounge, watching a film. Everything in the household that evening had been very normal but upstairs in Jenna's bedroom something was going to happen that would change the course of her life.

It began with a pungent smell of lilacs and lavender, which

invaded Jenna's senses. It seemed familiar as it wafted around the bedroom, distracting her. Abandoning the delicate task of dressing her doll, Jenna's eyes searched the room for the source of the aroma. What she saw next made no sense. One minute, she was looking at the shadows cast from her bedside lamp then the next, her room was saturated by a blinding light. Emerging from the light was a glowing orb, which came to rest at the bottom of her bed. Jenna felt no fear; its appearance was reminiscent of the shards of light she often glimpsed flitting on her bedroom ceiling and walls. Inevitably, when she turned to look for them they vanished, leaving her wondering whether they had been a figment of her imagination.

As Jenna continued to stare mesmerised at the orb, she ran through the possible explanations for its presence. It was nothing like the vanishing shards of light and it wasn't one of Timmy's silly little games; she could hear him in the back garden, bouncing his football against the side of the house. As she started to formulate a third possibility, the brilliant orb began to materialise into a humanlike form. When the metamorphosis was complete, Jenna instantly recognised the shimmering form as her grandmother. The overwhelming excitement at seeing Nana Coleman again, after her leaving so abruptly, was too much for Jenna, who wanted to share her presence with the rest of her family. Jumping off the bed and scampering out of her bedroom, she ran to fetch her mother and father.

"Mummy, Daddy, come quickly, Nana Coleman is here!" Jenna shouted excitedly at the top of her voice as she bounded downstairs into the lounge.

As she gabbled excitedly to her parents about the brilliant light; how it turned into Nana; likening her to an angel surrounded in a halo of light, instinct told the five-year-old this was another occasion her parents chose not to believe her. The strange look passing between her mother and father made Jenna think she'd done something seriously wrong. It wasn't until later that she would come to realise neither parent had the capacity to comprehend what had taken place in the tiny bedroom with its pink walls and stuffed toys.

The revelation she had seen her dead grandmother came as a complete shock to Martha and James. They were used to their daughter's strange ways and imaginary friends but this was something they'd never encountered before. Martha dealt with the strange situation in the only way she knew: complete denial. Taking her daughter's hand, she led her back upstairs. As they walked, Jenna sensed her mother's great sadness but on entering her bedroom and witnessing the shimmering orb in front of her, Jenna's own sadness transformed into extreme joy.

"See, Mummy, I told you so, there she is," Jenna pointed towards her bed. "Look, she is here." Jenna broke away from her mother and ran to the glowing form, stepping unafraid into its all-embracing brilliance. Martha saw nothing apart from her daughter standing by the side of her bed and hugging herself. The gesture was strange but it gave her no cause for alarm, until she tried to put Jenna back into bed. From the moment Martha put her arms round her daughter, she felt like she was being sucked down a long, narrow tunnel, at the bottom of which was a brilliant light. Momentarily stunned, Martha was unable to resist the mesmerising power pulsating through her body but then the voice of reason rang in her ears.

This can't be happening. No, it's not happening, I will not let it happen. Martha's determination was so great she was able to break free from the mesmerising light.

Once the spell had been broken, she was free to observe Jenna, who appeared to be in some kind of trance. A fleeting glance at a milky, translucent substance covering the whole of her daughter's corneas instilled fear into Martha's heart. Then suddenly it was gone, leaving no trace and making her wonder whether this was something else she had conjured up in her own imagination. All thoughts of her own safety were abandoned and in desperation to get her daughter back from the unknown force which seemed to be controlling her, Martha snatched Jenna away from the bed. As she grabbed her daughter, a low-frequency whooshing noise rang in Martha's ears, making her fear she was going to be sucked in by the light again. Undeterred, Martha started shaking Jenna so hard that it not only took the breath out of her but brought her daughter back to reality, spluttering and gasping for air.

"Oh Mummy, it was soooooooooo beautiful, didn't you see her?" Jenna's breathy voice cooed as she came back to reality.

The strange experience shook Martha to the core. Her young daughter appeared unharmed, which made her momentarily question her own sanity. As her mind feverishly searched for possible answers for Jenna's condition, the only plausible explanation that presented itself was that her daughter had suffered some sort of fit. The explanation, however, didn't account for the sensation Martha had personally experienced when she touched her daughter. Another theory was forming in her mind and, being a religious woman, she was beginning to believe that whatever had taken place in that tiny bedroom wasn't of this earth.

"Mummy, Mummy, you must have seen Nana." Jenna's pleading voice tore her back from the shocking, speculative thoughts.

Martha held her daughter at arm's length once again, inspecting her body and face for any residue of the fit. Satisfied Jenna was physically unscathed by the experience, she cuddled her, protesting, to her breast and sat back down on the bed. Rocking the child in her arms, Martha attempted to calm Jenna, explaining that Nana Coleman couldn't be in her room as she had gone to live in a better place, called Heaven, a year ago, where she was happy and well again.

Jenna remembered only too clearly the day it happened as they had all been living with Nana whilst waiting to move into a new home. Nana told her that she was going upstairs to have a lie down as she had a headache. An hour later, when her grandmother failed to come back down, Jenna went to find her. Nana Coleman was fully dressed, lying on her bed with her eyes closed. At first Jenna thought her Nana, who had a wicked sense of humour, was playing a game with her. No amount of cajoling woke her, though, and the girl ran back downstairs to tell her mummy. Martha, ordering her daughter to stay in the front room, bolted up to her mother's bedroom. Shortly, the thud of footsteps stopped and a loud wailing noise could be heard coming from upstairs.

"James, James, phone for an ambulance, there's something wrong with Mother," Martha screamed from the top of the stairs then ran back into the bedroom, propelling her husband to the phone in the hallway to call the emergency services.

After that, everyone in the household was in a state of panic, waiting for help to arrive. Jenna heard the ambulance pull up outside their home and watched as two paramedics came hurtling up the pathway. On opening the door, her father directed them upstairs and followed them, where he found his wife kneeling on the floor and crying, her head resting on her mother's breast. The paramedics prised the distraught woman away but, even before examining the old woman, who was lying stock-still on the bed, it was clear there was nothing they could do. Jenna, waiting downstairs, sensed a strange stirring in the air and knew something very bad had happened.

Five-year-old Jenna watched her mother's mouth opening and closing whilst she cuddled her. She was not listening to the words of denial she knew not to be true; she could see Nana Coleman very clearly, hovering close by. It has been over a year since she'd gone but it felt just like yesterday to Jenna. Sadness overwhelmed her when it dawned on her that Mummy could not see Nana but at the same time she was elated her beloved grandmother was back from Heaven to visit her. Eventually, Martha, believing she'd reasoned with her daughter, tucked Jenna back into bed and turned off the bedside lamp. Going back downstairs and knowing her husband wouldn't entertain something he couldn't understand, Martha decided it was best to put the strange incident down to Jenna's wild imagination.

Meanwhile, back in Jenna's bedroom, Nana remained with her for some time. There was no need for words between them and the experience of seeing a dead person became a pivotal point in Jenna's life. From that moment, a veil lifted. Jenna was stripped of all innocence and plunged into a world no one could ever seem to understand.

After enlightenment to the spirit world, Jenna's abilities developed quickly and with them came something far beyond her comprehension. At first, it felt like a game, as Nana introduced her to an extraordinary world filled with beauty the like of which she'd never seen before, making her hanker for more with each visitation.

Then, on the eve of Jenna's sixth birthday, something happened to destroy the beautiful visions, bringing with it a sickening reality. It began with a nightmare, then the nightmares turned into visions, depicting a girl about the same age as her entombed under a timber floor. At first, in her bewildered state, she thought the girl in the shallow grave was her. Each time the vision came, it filled her with a dreadful fear.

As time passed, the death vision became less frequent and although she never understood why the dead girl chose to come to her, it forced Jenna to accept that evil, as well as extreme joy, was part of her new, astonishing world.

As she grew up, Jenna got used to concealing her extraordinary gift. At the age of fifteen, she was involved in a school project where the class were given several topics to choose from, one of which was family history. With the aid of school computers and knowledge from her parents, Jenna chose to research her family tree. The search on the maternal side bought up a relative called Albert, who had fought in the battle of Jutland, and an aunt who'd been privileged to experience a maiden voyage in one of the first iron ships ever built. So much fascinating information came to light that it was difficult for Jenna to decide which one of the long-deceased relatives to select for her project. Although her mother's side of the family seemed so intriguing, coming from a military background, for some reason she was drawn to her father's side. Going back to the 1750s, she discovered a branch of the Thornleigh family; farmers living in Cornwall. In particular, a man called Joseph caught her attention. Joseph had married a woman called Catherine, and they went on to have seven children, five of whom were boys who all followed in their father's footsteps and became farmers. For some unknown reason, Jenna was fascinated by the family of farmers and they became the focus of her search. The oldest of the sons, Matthew, married and settled in a small hamlet called Lawhitton, where on the death of his parents he inherited a farm; a sizeable place called Hydlebury, with land stretching down to the River Tamar. Matthew and his wife Beatrice had been blessed with two children; a boy, Luke, born in 1792, and later a girl called Mary. What was startling about Mary Thornleigh was that she was born in the same month and on the same day as Jenna, although the year had been 1795. There was a three-year gap between the births of Mary and Luke, just as there was between Jenna and her brother Timmy. One coincidence was strange but two made her think there might be something in the theory of parallel lives. She was aware of the theory of split incarnation, where two identities could derive from one soul, and Jenna toyed with the idea, making

Mary Thornleigh the point of her fixation.

Over the years, armed with the acquired knowledge from her 'gift', she learned it was possible for up to seven separate existences to be derived from the same soul. In encounters with Nana Coleman, she came to understand it was like a beam of light splitting into two or more beams, each owning a separate existence and separate life. These lives spanned centuries without knowledge of each other but occasionally something happened during their lifetime to invoke previous memories, which could be very harrowing if the previous soul had met with an untimely end. Briefly, she wondered whether the nightmares she suffered as a girl were connected to Mary.

During her research, Jenna learned about the hard times bestowed on farming communities during the 18th century. Series of poor harvests culminating in a disastrous potato crop, a staple food for most rural communities, resulted in many families losing everything. It was during these times that a census showed many households growing in number. Families and friends moved in together, sharing rents and making do with what meagre pickings the land could offer. Matthew Thornleigh's household expanded, with the addition of his brother Henry and his family, who had fallen on lean times. The farmhouse, although large, barely accommodated two families, resulting in Henry's two boys; John, aged twelve, and Thomas who was fourteen, sleeping in one of the out-houses. Despite overwhelming difficulties the families worked side-by-side, toiling on the farm, bringing their depleted produce and livestock to sell at the surrounding markets. Old farming accounts recorded the pitiful prices and substandard produce sold at the farmers' markets, making Jenna wonder how any of them survived at all.

She became obsessed with family history, often spending hours researching the more menial aspects of her ancestors' lives whilst her fellow students chose more exciting topics and characters to base their projects on.

Jenna's search took an unexpected turn when she stumbled on a series of murders towards the end of the 1790s, committed in and around the small hamlet of Lawhitton. A piece of information caught Jenna's interest; it concerned a missing girl by the name of Mary Thornleigh.

Around the time of Mary's disappearance a seven-year-old called Catherine Kernow had been brutally murdered, her body found on the outskirts of the neighbouring village of Rezare. Seven months after Catherine was found, a second child was murdered; a young boy called John Peese. Local newspapers reported the community being in uproar over the murders. Mothers closeted their children to their breasts, fearful the beast in their midst would strike again. News travelled quickly and it wasn't long before the whole country knew about the demise of the two children.

Fingers started pointing as speculation grew as to who could have committed such atrocities. Two local officials responsible for the Lawhitton area and familiar with the farming community also dealt with Mary Thornleigh's disappearance. Concluding that, although she was a wilful child and could have run away from home, it was likely she had also fallen foul to the unknown killer. Jenna discovered that the criminal justice system in those days relied on the existence of the 'Bloody Code'; a list of crimes that were punishable by death. Lesser offences such as poaching, burglary and common damage didn't escape punishment but above all, murderers and perpetrators of crimes against children were destined for the hangman's noose. People were baying for blood and before long a list of suspects was rounded up for questioning.

Jenna unearthed every scrap of information available but record-keeping in the late 1790s was vague, leaving a lot of gaps to fill. Every possible moment was spent searching through library records for old newspapers that may have carried the story about the child murders. Going through microfilm frame by frame in the public library, Jenna came across an old copy of the *Royal Cornish Gazette* and was stunned to discover Thomas Thornleigh was on the list of suspects rounded up for the murders. Later editions of the newspaper reported he had been questioned and consequently found guilty of the cruel, premeditated murders of John Peese and Catherine Kernow. Jenna's eyes lingered on the story, in particular the line that read, *The young fellow son of Henry Thornleigh turned pale and coneffcdhe he had bean guilty of murder*. The shock discovery completely overrode the type-setter's spelling mistakes.

After sentencing, Thomas Thornleigh was taken to Bodmin Gaol, where he was slung in a stone cell, with a wooden plank for a bed, and fed a meagre diet of bread and gruel. Old prison records indicated that during the week leading to his execution, two women – one of whom was Thomas' mother – came before the governor, asking to see him. The governor denied the mother's request. The other woman, who suffered from tuberculosis – known as the 'King's Evil' – requested Thornleigh touch the infected parts of her body, as it was widely thought at that time the 'hands on' brought about a healing from one who was imminently to meet his maker, and in return the prisoner was expected to agree as a sign of repentance. This request was granted and the woman was escorted to Thornleigh's cell, where she was left alone with the young boy, who had one last self-satisfying experience before he died. The guards, thinking they were hearing screams of rapture coming from the sick woman – a sign of being cured from the dreaded curse that had befallen her – failed to investigate. When the cell was eventually opened, the woman's lifeless body was discovered. Thomas was sitting nearby, staring at the corpse, his face a picture of smug satisfaction and a far cry from repentance. The guard who unlocked the cell door went berserk when he saw the woman's dead body. Launching himself at the prisoner, he started kicking and punching him, until he was dragged off by two other guards. The governor was alerted and, as the woman died with no known relatives, her body was quickly dispatched to a mortician for disposal. The guards involved in the incident were sworn to secrecy and threatened with the loss of their jobs should they breathe a word to anyone about the woman's death. The incident was lost in prison gossip, which only came to light after the governor's demise, strangled by an escaping prisoner who was hell-bent on getting revenge for his incarceration.

When the day arrived for Thomas Thornleigh's sentence to be carried out, people flocked far and wide from across the countryside to Bodmin Gaol, to witness the execution. Crowds mocked the condemned prisoner as he was dragged onto the gallows to be hanged. At the stroke of nine in the morning, a silence fell as Thomas was asked if he had any last words of repentance. From his position on the gallows, Thomas stood rigid, head held high, defiant to the end, taking one last look at the baying crowds and scrutinising faces closest to him, making them shiver with fear as his gaze fell upon them. No words were uttered from his mouth but his message was clear: death would not destroy him. The executioner placed a black hood over his head then released a bolt from the trapdoor, dropping Thomas' body eight feet to oblivion, to the sounds of the cheering crowd.

After Thomas was cut down from the scaffold, the executioner divided the rope that hanged him into neat, short lengths and sold them for a shilling each to an eager crowd, who clambered and bartered for the piece of rope nearest the noose. To get possession of this piece of rope was a prize as it was deemed to have a stronger power to cure all types of rheumatism, arthritis, fits and distemper, and guaranteed to keep its owner free from harm in the years to come. The final insult to Thomas was his landing on a dissection table in the doctor's surgery, where his body was cut into bits and stored in bottles of formaldehyde, in the pursuit of medical research.

Jenna had shuddered at the shocking revelation of Thomas' demise, and the fact a murderer formed an intricate part of her family history. Mary Thornleigh's disappearance, however, remained a mystery and although Thomas confessed to murdering Catherine Kernow and John Peese, he went to his grave with no mention of his cousin. Without the presence of a body, Mary, it appeared, had simply disappeared, and life in the farming community went on regardless.

Investigations into her family history troubled Jenna and left many unanswered questions, invoking a night vision in the guise of a young man she instinctively knew was Thomas Thornleigh, lying on his belly in a cornfield and spying on a young girl.

The target of his obsession was wearing a knee-length cotton printed dress, her face hidden by a mass of blonde corkscrew curls as she played on her own, completely oblivious to the danger lurking just yards away. The vision felt so real, making Jenna scream out in her sleep in a vain attempt to warn the girl. As her screams faded, a darkness set in, through which more visions appeared, enabling Jenna to view a snapshot of the lives of the Thornleigh family. A strong sense of kinship and belonging also presented secret intimacies.

Cramped conditions in the farmhouse had made Thomas' parents, Henry and Elizabeth, take to lovemaking in the woods. In one of the visions, Jenna saw Thomas swimming in his favourite part of the River Tamar, then the scene switched to him walking home through the woods, where he stumbled across his parents. Heavy breathing and grunting made him turn from his path to Hydlebury, to investigate the strange sounds.

Approaching quietly through a thicket of trees, he came across a clearing, where he witnessed his father, bare-arsed, pushing his mother up against a tree. Disturbed by the sight, Thomas darted back behind the thicket of trees for cover, careful not to disturb them. From his hiding place, he was able to view clearly the strange activity his parents were involved in, the like of which he'd never seen before. As he watched his father insert his huge penis in and out between his mother's shapely thighs, it was also the first time Thomas had seen a woman's lower regions. The sight excited him so much that he found a hardness growing in his groin. Undoing his trousers, Thomas took the hardness in his hands and emulated his father's thrusts into his mother until he came to a glorious release.

He remained in his hiding spot for some time after his parents left, revelling in his new-found experience and reliving it time and time again, until he was spent and exhausted. After that, it became a regular occurrence for Thomas to spy on his parents, who quickly worked out a pattern to their clandestine rendezvous. Each time he witnessed their lovemaking, Thomas was rewarded with another sexual experience, culminating in seeing them completely naked, his mother on all fours, being mounted by his father from behind. It was a turning point for Thomas, whose sexual frustrations had grown to a point where he started looking for other ways to satisfy his needs.

Jenna's vision switched back to Thomas as he watched Mary playing in the dirt by the side of the field. As the boy stroked his enlarged penis, his vile thoughts bombarded her mind. He fantasised about killing the spoilt little brat, who he hated with such passion it took his breath away. With his parents' lovemaking fresh in his mind, Thomas was driven to the brink of madness, his sole goal to re-enact what his father had done to his mother. Moving slowly through the cornfield, he edged nearer his quarry, stopping several times to manoeuvre through the tall corn stalks. Fortunately for him, as Mary had a habit of humming and talking to herself, his progress went unheard. When he was within reach, Thomas pounced on his cousin, who was caught totally off-guard. The five-year-old was no match for the boy, who'd grown into a strong young man, pumped with sexual urges beyond his control.

The first attempt to rape Mary was met with a spirited resistance, which only served to fuel his rampant desires as she put up a valiant fight, struggling, kicking and clawing at him. Yanking both arms to her side, he pushed her to the ground and straddled her, then, putting his hands round her tiny throat, Thomas strangled the lifeblood from her body. He pulled Mary's cotton dress up to cover her face and repeatedly raped her lifeless body until he was fully satisfied. Once Thomas finished abusing her, he carried Mary back to the barn, knowing his brother was in the nearby village of Lansan with their father on errands so he had free rein and wouldn't be disturbed for some time.

Once inside the barn, he located the trapdoor, under which was a cellar where they stored discarded farm implements. A perfect place to hide a body. Opening the trapdoor, he heaved Mary through and let her lifeless body drop, landing with a dull thud on the wooden floor below. Momentarily, he stood looking down with elated pride at his sadistic achievement, then he climbed down a crudely forged wooden staircase after his prize. Thomas pulled the body over to a spot where he started to remove several floorboards. Jumping down into the void beneath the barn he started to dig a hole in the dirt deep enough to accommodate Mary's body. The soil was hard and compact, taking some time to break, but once he'd got through the first layer the rest came away with relative ease. Before long, he'd dug a hole big enough to bury his young cousin. Climbing back out of the hole, Thomas raped Mary a final time then flung her like a heap of unwanted rubbish into the black hole. Jumping down after her, he covered her body, tamping down the top soil. His last task was to reposition the wooden floorboards and hammer them back into place, leaving no trace of his despicable crime.

Jenna woke with a strangled sob, bathed in sweat. The horrific visions confirmed what her search failed to reveal: centuries before her time, Mary Thornleigh had been killed by her cousin, Thomas. It was a cruel and abominable demise for the young girl, whose parents went to their graves not knowing what had happened to their daughter. The visions not only enlightened Jenna to an ugly hidden truth but also left her with a strange sense of foreboding and a prelude of what was to come.

In the wake of the disturbing visions, Jenna abandoned the original idea of writing about the farming family as the story was too horrendous to reveal. Instead, her school project was based on Albert Matthews, who was killed in the Battle of Jutland, and the undisputed heroism he displayed under tortuous conditions. Jenna knew a hero would pass muster with her school friends, whereas revealing a murderer in her family history would invoke all kind of strange thoughts and prejudices.

It had taken a long time to bury the secret Jenna had accidentally unearthed all those years ago. Little did she know then that the past was about to come back to meet her.

Chapter 4

Daniel (The Therapist)
Bristol

Daniel's violent rages, coupled with vivid, bloodthirsty dreams, were spiralling out of control. He feared it could be something neurological and was on the point of seeking medical advice when a chance meeting with a friend of his ex-girlfriend, at a dinner party, gave him another avenue to explore. Listening to Jackie's fantastical stores about regression, Daniel was curious and wanted to know more.

The next day, after the dinner party, Daniel researched the internet and came across Anton Fallier; a regression therapist, who reportedly had acclaimed success in this field. Intrigued by what he read, and paranoid about privacy, Daniel rang and booked an appointment under the false name of Simon Day.

It was two weeks later that Daniel eventually met with Anton. Despite having seen pictures of the therapist on the internet and researching him fully, he was surprised to find the man was not the person he imagined him to be. In his mind, he'd built up an impression of a detached professional; not the friendly, open man who greeted him in the reception area of his Clifton Wood surgery. Fallier took him into a large, airy room just off the reception area and overlooking an immaculately lawned garden. Here, Daniel was invited to relax on a sumptuous white leather couch. The therapist instantly put him at ease as he explained it was his aim to bring to the forefront any past memories his patients were not consciously aware of. By releasing these memories, many found they were able to understand the problems they were experiencing in their current lives. To Daniel, this seemed all very plausible and logical and he readily agreed with the theory that, without clearing the past, the future would always be hindered in some way. As instructed, Daniel closed his eyes and focused on the therapist's voice, which had a gentle, calming quality, and instantly found himself relaxing; open to Fallier's directions without question.

The first exercise Fallier gave him was to visualise a door and then to go through that door. Daniel had no difficulty conjuring up an image almost immediately. The therapist instructed him to pass through the door, into whatever lay beyond, encouraging him to describe what he saw in the process. The image Daniel's mind created was of an old barn and sturdy wooden trapdoor set into the floor. He saw himself kneeling down to lift the trapdoor. Once it was opened, he walked down a dark wooden staircase to a lower level.

At the bottom of the staircase, Daniel paused to assimilate the foreign surroundings. Urged on by the therapist to explore his imaginary world, he found there was no fear; only confusion and curiosity. The only light in the underground room emanated from a battered iron wall sconce containing a burning tallow candle, reflecting off the crudely constructed timber walls that surrounded him. Metal shelves housing all manner of tools, many of which were rusted and covered in thick cobwebs, sat above wooden cabinets running the full length of one of the walls. As his eyes grew accustomed to what lay in front of him, Daniel realised he was in an underground cellar or workshop. Turning, he took in a 360-degree view of the space to find that this was no ordinary cellar. In front of him was a wooden bench equipped with leather restraints, on top of which was something that didn't quite register in his thought process. Taking another look at the object on the bench, he could make out it was a female body, caked in blood. As his eyes took in the rigid white carcass, with its tell-tale signs of brutality, Daniel realised she was dead. His whole body shook whilst his eyes remained wide open, transfixed by the naked female. As he struggled against conflicting emotions, Daniel's inner fear mechanism was replaced by a sense of detached fascination, compelling him to linger and savour the brutality spread before him.

Anton Fallier, who had been monitoring his patient's erratic breathing and body movements, instinctively knew Daniel was experiencing a critical episode during the regression and immediately prepared to guide him back to the present. But before completing the exercise to bring him back, his patient launched into a shaking spasm so violent it forced Fallier to restrain him on the couch, for his own safety. Whilst holding down his struggling patient, Fallier noticed the man's facial expressions changing. At first this didn't unduly alarm him, as it was a common occurrence for displays of distorted facial muscles when patients revisited painful memories. However, as Fallier battled to bring his patient back, for the briefest of moments the therapist witnessed a complete metamorphosis, which revealed another person's face. Fallier gasped in horror at the grotesque mask, his own fear mechanism flinging him away from the couch like he'd been struck by a bolt of lightning.

The regression progressed to another level that couldn't be stopped. Like changing television channels, Daniel was hurled into another time span, where he found himself encased in something wooden and solid. Gone was the grisly vision of the woman's corpse in the cellar; it was replaced by a total blackness. A sinking sensation made him feel as though he was being lowered into the ground. He could hear a voice above him, sobbing, then the blackness vanished, revealing a young woman being comforted by an older man, who Daniel instantly knew from their strong resemblance was her father. Then, as clumps of earth hit the wooden contraption encasing him, an awful realisation hit him that he was in a coffin, watching on the periphery of helplessness whilst gravediggers began to bury the funeral box, with him inside it.

His whole body shook violently as he fought desperately to be released from the restraints of the wooden prison. His screams thundered from his mouth yet no one above the grave pit heard him. As he lay entombed beneath tonnes of soil, deep in the bowels of the earth, bitterly contemplating his own demise and what had bought him to this catastrophic end, a surge of energy engulfed him. The force was so powerful it separated his soul from his body and for the briefest of moments allowed him access from his final resting place into the world of the living. An image of himself emerged above ground in the empty graveyard. Daniel read the inscription on the tombstone above his body.

Sean Baxter
Beloved husband of Sophia
Will always be remembered
12th August 1954
Aged 28

A black rage overwhelmed him at the injustice of being caught between worlds, reliving another man's death. Who the hell was Sean Baxter? Nothing stirred in in his memory banks. Daniel had no idea why he'd been in another man's grave, nor could he recollect the young beautiful blonde known as Sophia, who wept with her father at the graveside of the deceased man.

As Daniel struggled to get a grip on reality, salvation came in the form of the therapist's urgent voice, guiding him back from the dark, foreboding world to the present. The voice sucked him from the visionary nightmare back into his own living body, where traces from past lives festered and lingered in the vaults of his memories.

A darkness followed him back through the time portal where, suspended in a world outside of his own, Daniel experienced the gruesome art of butchery and murder. The fleeting image of the beautiful blonde crying over Sean Baxter's graveside provoked a host of hostile thoughts, invoking present-day memories of ex-girlfriends, many of whom he had subjected to savage beatings in pursuit of his sadistic sexual urges. After the beatings, the frightened young women were too terrified to go to the police, fearful that Daniel, who made sure he knew every aspect of their lives and in some cases even had keys to their homes, would carry out his threats to pay them a visit.

The regression brought to the surface hidden memories of a violent past, making Daniel realise without a shadow of a doubt that he was capable of carrying out those threats. The bloody, dismembered body lying on the wooden bench in the cellar cemented the fact that the murderous fantasies filling him with a lustful excitement were not only a by-product of his past life but the very essence of his existence. These last thoughts stayed with him as Daniel opened his eyes and saw Fallier cowering against the desk on the other side of the room, watching his patient with growing fear.

Daniel instinctively knew something monumental had occurred, bringing a re-birth of his former self who had one sole purpose on this earth: to kill.

The moment his patient opened his strange hazel-flecked eyes, Fallier knew the metamorphosed face with radically different features and skin colour belonged in the man's past. The appearance of another presence emerging as an earthbound spirit shocked the therapist, whose fear had propelled him away from the leather couch to the other side of his surgery. On shaking legs, Fallier grabbed hold of his desk to steady himself and watched with trepidation as the man on the couch sat up and looked at him. Expecting some sort of emotional fall-out from the man emerging from the regression, the therapist was unnerved to discover his patient seemed unaffected by the experience. As Fallier studied him from across the room, their eyes locked for the briefest of moments and he witnessed something resembling pure evil, beyond his comprehension. Daniel's gaze shifted as he nonchalantly swung his legs off the couch, stretching his tall frame as though he'd just woken from a refreshing sleep. Completely oblivious to the therapist's distressed state, and concluding the session was at an end, he made his way out of the surgery.

Anton Fallier, who was too shaken to speak, followed him. As it was late, his receptionist had finished for the day and, being a small practice, he and this man were the only people left in the building. Normal procedure would have been for the therapist to book another appointment to discuss a way forward, addressing any issues arising during regression, but as the patient had already paid in advance for the session and he was afraid of the man, he wanted rid of him quickly. As they walked in silence along the long corridor, Fallier scurried ahead and, reaching for the latch, he opened the door to let the patient called Simon Day out of the building.

Once the therapist had closed the solid oak door and heard the man walk back down the stone stairs leading onto the street, he went back into his surgery and sat at the desk opposite the leather couch, trying to make sense of the face he'd seen. Never in twenty years of practising regression had he come across anything quite like it. Whatever or whoever it was, he knew something evil from a past life had attached itself to the man, surrounding him like a black cloak. Despite his fear, Fallier knew there was no alternative but to make contact with Simon Day again and somehow send back the malevolent spirit before it was too late and the entity bonded with its earthly host.

Booting up his laptop, he searched for the patient's contact details and found a company name and address with a mobile number. Ringing the number, he was connected to an automated voice on the other end announcing the number was unobtainable. Trying to stop his hands from shaking, Fallier tried again. 'Number unobtainable' was again the response. On the third attempt, Fallier took his time, studying each digit to ensure it matched the contact number Simon Day had given. Satisfied there was no error on his part, he listened with dismay as the same announcement came. The number the patient had given was bogus. Fallier did a search online for the man's office address, only to find it was non-existent; as, of course, was the company.

With no means of making contact, Fallier could only hope the patient contacted him to book another appointment.

He made a mental note to speak to Amy, his receptionist, when she arrived in the morning, and to give her instructions to reschedule all appointments should Simon Day call, making sure to get him back into the surgery at the earliest possible opportunity. Fallier realised that whatever the purpose of the man's visit, he'd unwittingly played a part in bringing something evil back to this earth and, whether he liked it or not, the responsibility lay at his door. For the time, being the therapist could only hope that the man would call back. The alternative was unthinkable.

A week after visiting Anton Fallier, it was clear that a monster had awoken in Daniel. Flashbacks to previous lives became a regular occurrence. Piece by piece, he started to get a flavour of what type of person he had been before, and revelled in it. Now that he knew nothing neurological was wrong with him, the revelation he'd lived before in other guises spanning the centuries, committing heinous crimes, made him feel powerful and whole again. He now remembered Sophia; the young woman he'd seen crying over the grave during the regression session. Sean Baxter's life had been easy to recall, as it had been his last. The year was 1954 and the woman called Sophia Baxter was Sean's wife of two years; a snivelling bitch whose needy ways suffocated him. Fate, however, had been on Sophia's side, as it had been him in the grave instead of her. She had been destined to be the next victim, had Baxter's life not been cut short.

Flashbacks to this previous life revealed he'd been a sergeant major in the British Army, based at Catterick Camp, where he had free reign to abuse his authority, drilling the recruits within an inch of their lives, knowing they would be too frightened to report any form of bullying, for fear of reprisal. The camp, surrounded by barbed wire and protected by guard dogs, fuelled the feeling of terror amongst young boys, many of whom were fresh from home for the first time. The weak were soon weeded out, becoming prime bait for the bullying sergeant major, whose favourite form of punishment for insubordinate behaviour was cleaning the toilets with a toothbrush. The humiliation was compounded by onlookers, who were encouraged to scorn and mock their fellow recruits. The higher commanding officers were no better than Baxter, choosing to turn a blind eye to these barbaric practices as it was commonly considered as 'character-building'. Sergeant Major Sean Baxter was known to the recruits as SB, aka Sick Bastard, for his perverse, intimidating tactics.

From of a motley selection of fresh-faced recruits, Daniel remembered with fondness how the next boy was singled out for the Baxter 'special attention'. Little did sixteen-year-old Adam Fetter, known amongst his fellow recruits as Baby Face for his cherubic appearance, know how he was going to suffer at the hands of SB. The moment Baxter clapped eyes on Fetter, he started grooming him for his personal needs until the young lad was completely under his spell and had become so brainwashed that he'd carry out any instruction with no qualms. As Baxter's bullying escalated, so did his perverted sexual urges. It soon became the norm for Baxter to bait Fetter up against other recruits, where he would watch his protégée engage in sexual acts with other young men, forced against their will to take part in all manner of depravities. None of his victims uttered a word to the hierarchy, having seen first-hand the torture a 'squealer' would endure.

Nobody dared challenge Baxter at the camp but life at home was another matter. One evening, after a particularly violent argument with Sophia, he reported back to the barracks for duty early, after storming out of the house. Seething from the argument, Baxter called on Fetter and together they hatched a plan to kill Sophia. Baxter would supply Fetter with a key to his army quarters, a stone's throw away from the barracks. Fetter would murder Sophia whilst Baxter was on duty, providing him with an alibi. To cover his tracks, in front of other recruits Baxter would issue orders to Fetter to complete a specific task where he would be left unsupervised, allowing him to slip out from the barracks unnoticed.

Fetter, fully versed with Sophia's movements, would access the property from the rear. The house was the last one in the row, looking out onto an empty field. Once inside, he would kill Sophia then set up the house to make it look like a botched burglary.

It took weeks of careful planning before the plan was perfected but before he could give Fetter the key to his quarters, Baxter suffered a massive heart attack and dropped dead whilst on the square, drilling a new set of recruits.

In the wake of Baxter's death, the spell on Fetter was broken and he later left the army, discharged on medical grounds after a horrific beating from several of his victims. It left him mentally impaired and physically unable to perform his duties. Despite extensive investigation by the military police, nobody was charged for the ferocious attack. Victims of Baxter's brand of depravity closed ranks, choosing to remain silent and certainly not wanting to drag their painful ordeals into the public domain. With no-one willing to give evidence in Fetter's assault, there was no way for the military police to bring the perpetrators to justice. The case was closed and the cover-up conveniently forgotten.

Revisiting these memories, Daniel felt short-changed; his past life ended so abruptly and he briefly wondered what became of his pathetic little wife. Although Sophia always infuriated Sean, she possessed an extraordinary beauty, enhanced by a curvaceous figure and big blue eyes. Doing some calculations in his head, Daniel estimated Sophia, who had been twenty-six in 1954, would now be eighty-eight. Realising the bitch was either dead or senile, he laughed to himself. It was a lifespan he had no intention of revisiting, or had any need to exploit.

Flashbacks were now a common occurrence. It was the earlier memories that rocked Daniel's world. In them, he visited the cellar; the same place he'd been to under regression with the therapist, where the mutilated body of a woman was strapped to a wooden bench. This time, however, as he waded through past memories unimpeded by the therapist's presence, there was no mutilated body. An overwhelming sense of evil engulfed him, telling him that the cellar had been the site of multiple killings. Invoking images of the trapdoor Daniel recalled being above ground, lifting the trapdoor then walking down the wooden stairwell. He tried to envisage what lay above but nothing came to him. Then, without warning, a vortex of past memories swept before his eyes. Like a horror film, the cellar was transformed into a bloody underground torture chamber, where women in all guises were subjected to excruciating torture. As he witnessed everything in hideous technicolour, another memory erupted from his deep past, in the form of a young girl in her early teens, who was strapped to the wooden bench. Daniel watched on the periphery of another dimension as the girl begged for her life. Mesmerised by his other persona, he watched himself strip thin pieces of skin from the girl's leg, until it resembled a slab of meat; a bloody mess dripping onto the wooden floor. The girl bravely clung to life as he continued the macabre disfigurement of her body, working his way up to her face. When the steel ribbing knife sliced her cheek, she screamed one last time, then her heart stopped and he experienced her last gasp before she died. After the girl's death, he continued skinning her body, placing selected pieces of skin to one side on a steel platter located on a wooden cabinet by the side of the bench.

Daniel watched the butchery, revelling at his handiwork, until the last piece of skin was removed, leaving the body unrecognisable as human. The girl, who had once been extremely beautiful and self-possessed, now resembled a bloody pulp. The knowledge he'd been responsible for destroying such a beautiful human being empowered Daniel, fuelling a desperate need for other conquests to be revealed. As if on cue, all forms of torture invaded his warped mind, but before he could indulge his lustful fantasies the visitation in the cellar ended and he was back in the present, unremorseful for the pain and suffering he'd inflicted on another human being. After experiencing the thrill of killing in another lifetime, Daniel was hell-bent on unravelling his family lineage. He realised, if it still existed, this would be key to finding the location of the underground torture chamber.

Daniel's background was sketchy, at best. His adoptive parents withheld his mother's name, only supplying when pressed that she'd died during childbirth and that he'd been adopted soon after he was born, on 12th August 1985. Life for Daniel with Stanley and Heather Overton, who were well-off, and childless up until his adoption, had seen him privileged, brought up with the best that money could buy. Stanley had built up a successful construction business in the commercial and private housing sectors and was often away for long spells at a time, surveying new sites, which gave young Daniel plenty of quality time with Heather.

He remembered only too clearly the day he unearthed the information relating to his adoption. He was eight years old, playing hide and seek with his mother, when he'd gone into his parents' bedroom and hidden in the depths of their huge walk-in wardrobe. In the process of trying to squeeze his tiny body underneath the built-in shoe rack, he discovered a box, which was preventing him from getting into the small space. Pulling it out, he looked at it and was about to pull off its lid when he heard his mother come into the bedroom.

Hearing her footsteps edging their way over to the wardrobe, he hurriedly put the box back under the rack of shoes. He was desperately searching for another hiding spot in amongst the hanging clothes when the door opened, his mother caught him, and the game was over. Heather collapsed in squeals of laughter as she caught her son red-handed trying to slide underneath the hem of long ball gown, oblivious to the fact his feet beneath it would have been a dead giveaway, had he not been caught in the act.

Daniel accepted that he had lost the game this time and laughed along with his mother as they went down the stairs to the kitchen, where Heather brought out a new batch of her scrumptious, homemade cookies. They had sat at the kitchen table, eating the cookies and drinking cups of hot chocolate; a sweet indulgence which never failed to win Daniel over when things weren't going his way. As he bit into a second cookie, the hidden box which had piqued his interest was on his mind. It was then that he decided to return to the wardrobe in his parents' bedroom, when the coast was clear.

The opportunity arose sooner than he had dared to hope for. That afternoon, his mother opened the front door to a friend who had dropped by for coffee and as Stanley was working away it was the ideal time for Daniel to explore the wardrobe uninterrupted. As the women settled themselves in the kitchen, Daniel snuck into his parents' bedroom, where he tiptoed over to the walk-in wardrobe and opened the door. The shoe rack was adorned with a dizzying selection of shoes, mostly belonging to his mother. Daniel got down on all fours and crawled on his belly into the space beneath it. Stretching his arm out, he felt the sharp edges of the box and eased it out of its hiding place. Daniel knew what he was doing was wrong but, fuelled by excitement and mischief, he didn't care about his parents' rules. His only goal was to find out what was in the box. He knew it had to be very important to be hidden so well.

Lifting the lid, Daniel discovered a lot of old paperwork, amongst which were three certificates. A marriage certificate, a death certificate and a birth certificate. Daniel, who was well advanced for his years, knew the importance of these documents, especially when he saw his name on the birth certificate. He'd grown up knowing he was adopted and was happy to accept his mother had been very sick and died when he was a baby, and that he had a new mummy and daddy, called Stanley and Heather Overton.

He picked up the birth certificate and studied it. In the column underneath the father's name was the word 'unknown'. Looking along to the mother's name, it was denoted as 'Jane Adams'. Beside the mother's name was the father's occupation, under which was also written 'unknown'. The next column was for the signature description and residence of informant. As his eyes lingered on this column, Daniel was confused and shocked as in it was written his adoptive mother's name: Heather Overton. Putting it aside, Daniel reached for the death certificate, which was for a woman called Marjorie Adams, who had died at the age of thirty-four of a subdural haematoma. He was pondering what a subdural hematoma was when he noticed that the woman's maiden name had been Thornleigh. Trying to make sense of everything, he looked at the last document, which was a marriage certificate. Daniel found this document easy to understand as it related to his adoptive parents. As Daniel studied it, he spotted his adoptive mother's maiden name, which registered with something he'd seen on the death certificate. Looking at it again he saw that Marjorie Adams' maiden name was Thornleigh, the same maiden name as on his mother's marriage certificate. Things started to fall into place. Daniel also linked Marjorie to Jane Adams, as Marjorie's married name was Adams. As he sat on the floor amongst the contents of the box, holding the birth certificate tightly between his hands, he came to the conclusion that his adoptive mother, despite telling him otherwise, had actually known his birth mother, as she'd not only registered his birth but was related to her. His adoptive mother was the sister of Marjorie Adams, who in turn was the mother of Jane Adams, his dead biological mother. This made Heather Overton née Thornleigh his great aunt.

Daniel's head pounded with the information he was trying to process and the implications it brought as he stashed the box back under the shoe rack. Sneaking out of the walk-in wardrobe he closed the door and left his parents' bedroom. As he padded along the corridor to his bedroom he could hear his mother saying goodbye to her friend at the front door then coming upstairs to find him. Running to his bed, he threw himself on top and pretended to be asleep. He didn't want to speak to her.

With his eyes squeezed shut, Daniel heard his mother come into his bedroom and linger by the side of the bed then he felt a kiss on his forehead before she left the room, satisfied her son was fast asleep. Going over the story his adoptive parents had told him about his biological mother, he knew now it was all a lie. The only truth was that they had adopted him shortly after she died.

Two questions bombarded his mind: who was his father, and if Marjorie Adams nee Thornleigh was his mother's sister why hadn't she told him about her? The only sister he knew his adoptive mother to have was the woman he called Aunt Peggy, who lived in Somerset, whom he didn't much care for and had only met on a couple of occasions, under duress.

After his mother left his room, Daniel crept out of bed and rummaged through his toy cupboard. Finding one of his used colouring books, he wrote down the links he had discovered between the certificates in the hidden box.

Jane Adams was my mother.
Marjorie Adams/Thornleigh was Jane Adams' mother.
Heather Overton was Marjorie Adams/Thornleigh's sister.
Who was my real father?

All he had to do was bide his time until the opportunity arose to use this information to find out why his parents had hidden the truth from him. Daniel was confused and angry. Why had they lied to him? The more he thought about the cover-up, the more he became obsessed with finding the truth.

In the wake of the discovery, Daniel's feelings towards his adoptive parents changed overnight. From an affable young boy, he became resentful and argumentative, always questioning their authority. As time progressed, Daniel's feelings festered. The brunt of his resentment focused on his mother, who was often left alone with him whilst her husband was away working. One Saturday morning, when things between them came to a head, Heather phoned Stanley at work, breaking one of their cardinal rules.

Stanley was showing a group of investors round a site he was developing when he received a message via the on-site radio, telling him there was an urgent call from his wife. In no mood for distractions, in view of the amount of money at stake, he was annoyed at the interruption. Knowing it must be something important, however, he ushered his investors to a safe area outside the building and left them with the site foreman, reviewing the progress that had been made on the exterior since their last visit, then made his way off the windswept site to the Portacabin to take the call. Julie, the weekend temp, transferred it to his workstation at the far end of the room.

As luck would have it, Julie and Stanley were the only ones in the Portacabin, as most of the engineers on the weekend shift were out on site, checking and detailing snagging works. Stanley snatched the phone out of its cradle on his desk. As soon as his wife's tearful voice filled his ears, his annoyance was replaced with concern.

Heather completely broke down during their conversation; pent-up emotions she had held back for so long came tumbling out. It all came as a shock to Stanley as Heather confessed that during his absences Daniel had been playing her up to the point his behaviour had become uncontrollable. As he thought about his wife's tearful confession, Stanley wondered how long this had been going on as Daniel, albeit sometimes a bit awkward, never displayed any signs of disruptive behaviour in front of him. He managed to calm Heather down, with a promise to get home as soon as possible. Thinking ahead, he was already delegating tasks. Twenty minutes later, after joining his foreman and investors, he finished the exterior tour of the partially-constructed lobby area of the high-end hotel. Another meeting was set up for phase two of the construction, which was scheduled for completion in three months.

The investors left the site impressed and happy with progress, blissfully unaware of Overton's troubled home life. After thanking the foreman for his help with the investors, Stanley caught up with Robert Finlay, his business partner. Reorganising his shift pattern, Stanley left Robert at the helm and drove the 180-mile journey home.

He found his wife upstairs, outside their son's bedroom, in a state of total meltdown. As he crouched down to hug her, the hem of her cullet pants rose up, exposing the lower part of her legs. He noticed her bruised and badly swollen right calf.

From inside the locked room, Daniel heard his father helping his mother to her feet then they moved away from the door. Once Stanley had manoeuvred Heather into their bedroom and calmed her down, he questioned his wife about her leg and discovered that in the heat of an argument with his friend Eddie, Daniel had slammed a cricket bat against Heather's leg and run off. Since then, their son had barricaded himself in his bedroom, screaming obscenities from behind a closed door and refusing to come out.

Seeing the colour rise in Stanley's face, a sure sign of an escalating temper, Heather quickly explained that it had been an accident and that Daniel was playing cricket with their next-door-neighbour's son when it happened. Stanley listened whilst Heather told him how the boys started squabbling and, hearing raised voices coming from the back garden, she had gone to investigate, finding the two boys squaring up to each other and hurling insults. In an effort to defuse the situation, Heather got in between the two boys but Daniel was beyond reasoning, insistent that Eddie had started the argument. Eddie, determined to have the last word, was cursing her son and calling him a weirdo. In retaliation, Daniel lashed out with his bat, intending to shut him up, but Eddie ducked out of the way and instead of Daniel hitting his friend, the bat caught his mother's leg. A sickening thud reverberated through the air. She had howled in pain and fell heavily to the ground, clutching her right calf. Eddie stopped cursing, watching in horror as Daniel threw the bat against the makeshift wickets and ran off into the house, leaving Eddie to face the aftermath of the childish tantrum.

Not knowing what to do, Eddie burst into tears, trying to apologise to Mrs Overton, who was on the floor nursing her throbbing leg.

"Go home, Eddie, I will be all right," Heather told the young boy through gritted teeth as waves of pain shot through her leg. Eddie didn't need telling twice. Leaving Heather on the ground, he slipped off with his cricket bat trailing the ground. Heather was in no doubt that he would give his parents a blow-by-blow account of her son's shocking behaviour. She felt a sickening jolt in her heart, knowing they would undoubtedly receive a visit from Mr & Mrs Shortridge in the near future, to discuss the unfortunate incident.

Heather had struggled to her feet and limped painfully into the house. There was no sign of her son in the kitchen or the living room and, hobbling up the stairs, Heather made for Daniel's bedroom. The door was closed and locked. She started trying to cajole her son out. Daniel screamed back at his mother, telling her to go away, but despite Heather telling him he wasn't in trouble and that she knew he didn't mean to hurt her, Daniel refused to come out. An hour later, Heather gave up trying to reason with her son and hobbled back downstairs. At her wits' end, she scooped up the phone. Knowing Stanley didn't like being called at work, mainly due to hazardous working conditions on the sites he developed, Heather reluctantly dialled her husband.

After speaking with Stanley, Heather painfully climbed the stairs back to Daniel's bedroom, hoping against hope that in the time she was gone her son had calmed down enough to be reasoned with. The door was still locked but this time a deadly silence greeted her as she tried talking to him. Heather resigned herself to the fact it was a position of stalemate and she was getting nowhere. From her slumped position on the floor, she tried to make sense of the situation and how a silly spat between two boys could escalate into something far beyond her comprehension. She was in the same spot when Stanley found her after his drive home.

As he listened to the sequence of events leading up to the accident, Stanley wondered what had got into his son. Clearly, his wife's attempts to get him out of the bedroom had not worked and his patience with his son was running thin. Insisting that Heather rest on the bed, Stanley told her that he would sort out the situation. Leaving their bedroom, he walked the short distance to his son's bedroom to confront him, battling to keep his temper in check. He knocked the bedroom door, trying to coax his son to come out.

The minute Daniel heard his father's voice addressing him directly his rage erupted and all the resentment he harboured from the secret he discovered spilled out.

"Fuck off, you bastard, I've told that bitch I want to be left alone," Daniel screamed.

Stanley was shocked by his son's bad language. "Come on, son, open this door and we can talk about this. I know it was an accident."

"No, you both lied to me, you told me you didn't know who my mother was but you knew all along."

Stanley realised his son had somehow found out what they'd kept hidden all those years in an attempt to give Daniel the semblance of a normal life.

Eventually, after hours of coaxing and careful negotiation, Daniel opened the bedroom door into the loving arms of his parents, who attempted to rebuild the bridges destroyed in the wake of the discovery of the box in their wardrobe.

Taking Daniel downstairs into the lounge, his parents sat him on one of the sofas, where Heather told him about her older sister called Marjorie. Daniel learned that Heather was twenty-one when Marjorie died of a brain aneurysm, leaving two children, Jane and Tommy, and a husband called Donald Adams, who Heather had never got on with. Heather explained that after Marjorie's death Donald, who wanted nothing to do with their side of the family, took his children away. Years later, being next of kin, Heather was contacted by the police, who informed her Donald Adams had died, Jane was seriously ill in a coma, and Tommy was missing. It also transpired that Jane, who was pregnant, died shortly after but her baby survived. After Jane's death, Heather and Stanley adopted Jane's baby boy and called him Daniel.

The boy realised then realised his suspicions were correct, that his adoptive mother was in fact his great-aunt, prompting more questions. When he asked Heather how Jane died, he was told she was involved in a car accident and had been in a coma for months before eventually succumbing to her injuries. Now that the family lineage had been exposed, Daniel couldn't help staring at Heather, who possessed the same strange hazel-flecked eyes as him. It was clear now why she was so much older than most of his friends' mothers and why, despite being adopted, he had so many characteristics similar to Heather's. Something still nagged at him, though. Why had the secret been hidden from him? Deep down, his gut told him something wasn't right. There was something else his adoptive parents were keeping from him and he knew in time he was going to find out what it was.

Thinking back to the discovery of his identity prompted another flashback in Daniel, irradiating his childhood memories. He was propelled him into another age, where he saw a fifteen-year-old boy, born into a farming family. This time the year was 1910. It was a time of great social change and tumult – a time when farming was becoming increasingly mechanised at home and abroad and the world was moving gradually towards war. Farmers diversified into fishing, mining and market gardening, and had to master the industrial advances of the Edwardian age. Women's dresses were simpler and more flowing in design; hairstyles either curled or bobbed, on top of which sat cloche hats.

Hemlines began to creep up past the ankles and to the fifteen-year-old boy the wearers of such garments appeared more like ladies of the night.

Women started to have a voice, many inspired by Emmeline Pankhurst and the other Suffragettes, some of whom employed violent methods like breaking windows and blowing up mailboxes to make themselves heard. The authorities responded with mass arrests and police brutality, delving into torture, and force-feeding when they women went on hunger strike. In the persona of the boy, Daniel felt himself sharing sheer contempt for these women, standing firmly with the male hierarchy who ignorantly deemed the women interfering troublemakers. In this previous life, Daniel's self-appointed role as exterminator of these troublemakers spurred him to extraordinary lengths to fulfil what he saw as his mission.

Once again, Daniel was transported back to the cellar. Nothing much had changed in the intervening years; it was still the same dank, run-down structure he remembered from his first vision. During months of preparation, the boy plotted revenge on these women for daring to spew out such blasphemy against the male fraternity. In the cellar, below the floorboards, Daniel saw the existing grave and remembered the killing of the young girl in his previous life. The boy in this timeline seemed to acknowledge the existence of the older grave and had dug other shallow graves, ready to accommodate multiple bodies.

As Daniel struggled to comprehend the images his brain was receiving, the vision flashed to an ale house, where two old men were huddled by a roaring fire, supping from pewter tankards and discussing a rumoured mid-day meeting of suffragettes in Launceston. Daniel, in the boy's body, was standing at the bar, listening with great interest to details of the meeting which, according to the two old men, was taking place amongst a slew of others throughout the country, Suffragettes protesting in an effort to make their voices heard and their cause known. The boy immediately saw this meeting as an opportunity too good to miss, to carry out his vile plans. Although abducting a woman in broad daylight would be tricky, it would not be impossible.

The flashback moved forward in time, to a small market square in Launceston, where Daniel saw a large gathering of women. The crowds spilled out into the small side streets, down to a church called Mary Magdalene where, on each street corner, members of the Suffragettes were stationed, chanting their vile insanities. Standing on the periphery of the chaos, Daniel experienced feelings of sheer loathing as the women argued their case. Boiling hatred consumed him as he listened to their condemnation of the male race and the injustices suffered at the hands of men, which he felt was a completely unjustified affront to all men. The idea the Suffragettes were feeding to other feeble-minded women in the crowd, to petition to be able to vote, was too far-fetched to contemplate. It was at this point that Daniel and the boy became united, each experiencing a fury that grew to such a level it could not be controlled.

As the crowds jostled to get nearer the front for a view of the main speaker, the boy was scanning the crowds. Through the boy's eyes Daniel saw a young woman who'd just joined the rabble. In her mid-twenties, she appeared nervous and at complete odds to her counterparts, who were in full throttle. Standing at the back, she was completely entranced by the speaker's words and unaware of the fifteen-year-old boy with the strapping build of a man older than his years as he sidled up to her with one eye on the crowd and a mind set on the deserted graveyard running to the side of the Mary Magdalene Church. Whilst all eyes were riveted on the main speaker, the boy saw his chance and grabbed the woman from behind. In a flash, he pulled her round the corner, into the graveyard. The woman had little time to react or scream as his hand was firmly clamped round her mouth, the other gripping her from behind in a crushing bear hug. As he carried her the woman lashed out with her foot, her sturdy-heeled boot landing a sharp kick on his leg. Howling in pain, the boy momentarily loosened his grip and the woman wriggled free. Within seconds, she was screaming and running out towards the back entrance of the church, the boy in hot pursuit. Her shouts for help, however, were drowned by the noise of the crowds applauding the speaker, who had just finished a rousing speech.

Just as the young woman was about to flee through the back entrance, her boot became entangled in the hem of her skirt and she stumbled. As she fell to the ground, she put her hands forward to break the fall but her efforts were in vain as her attacker flung himself on top of her, slamming her head against the stone path. The impact knocked the woman unconscious and she lay still. Reaching for her shoulder, the boy turned the woman over and Daniel saw her face, the bleeding gash to her head jarring a vague memory loose in his subconscious.

After that, everything happened so fast there was no time for the recollection to surface. Realising the woman was temporarily immobilised, the boy slung her over his shoulder and ran through the churchyard, out to the other side and up a side lane, where he'd hidden the horse and cart he had commandeered from his parents, in the guise of carrying out some errands in Launceston. Slinging the unconscious woman in the back, he tied her arms firmly with rope and covered her with a blanket. Satisfied his victim couldn't escape a second time, the boy jumped in the cart and cracked a crop against the horse's rear, spurring the animal away from the thronging crowds, into the sanctuary of the surrounding fields and countryside.

The vision shifted back to the cellar, now with the unconscious woman stripped of all clothing and restrained on the wooden bench. Daniel experienced the boy unbuttoning his trousers and repeatedly raping the woman, until all his sexual urges were satisfied.

During this horrendous ordeal, the woman remained unconscious, allowing the boy time to observe the body without interruption. Before him lay an under-nourished female, her hands rough with chipped fingernails, which made him wonder briefly whether she was a maid employed at one of the surrounding manor houses. As his hands explored her full breasts, squeezing her brown nipples cruelly between his fingertips, he admired her young face. Apart from the gash on her forehead, it was unblemished compared to the boy's own acne-ridden skin. Her mousey hair lay lank and long, just below her shoulders, making her appearance waif-like and not worthy of his wrath. Momentarily, guilt bit at the boy, but it was quickly dismissed when he recalled the gathering of women baying for blood over the injustices suffered at the hands of men, for which the young woman would pay the ultimate sacrifice. Selecting a bone-handled blade amongst the tools which lay on the battered cabinet, he started work on her body. The first time he cut into her flesh, the girl didn't flinch, but as he slowly worked on her leg the incisions became deeper and she began to stir from unconsciousness.

The first thing she saw was a boy not much younger than herself in bloody clothes, looming over her with a knife. Glancing down at her body, she saw she was naked, her right leg a mass of blood, chunks of missing skin, and the source of the excruciating pain she was suffering. She screamed and then shock set in, making her wet herself. Through the boy's eyes, Daniel watched with detached fascination as a trail of urine ran between her legs and pooled on the floor while she continued screaming and struggling against the leather restraints anchoring her to the bench.

"Why are you doing this to me? Please let me go. Please, pleeeease, I won't tell anybody about it, just let me go before it's too late."

It was already too late. The boy shoved a dirty rag in her mouth to silence her and continued his vile ministrations unhindered, until the blood loss and fear ultimately triggered a heart attack. Taking the rag from her mouth, Daniel watched as the girl's body shuddered her last breath, leaving as a gasp. Undeterred by her demise, the boy continued skinning her body until she was no longer recognisable as human. Satisfied his prey had been obliterated from the face of the earth, the bloody carcass and torn clothing were unceremoniously thrown into a shallow grave under the floorboards and covered with soil. The boy replaced the floorboards then set about clearing the bench, taking care to store some of the larger pieces of skin in a glass jar containing the formaldehyde he'd stolen from the druggist in Launceston.

Daniel had witnessed this theft in an earlier flashback; the boy entering the shop and sneaking through to a side room, where all manner of herbal potions, ointments and jars were stored. When the druggist was occupied with a customer, the boy seized the opportunity to duck behind the counter. Within seconds, he had secreted several apothecary jars into his sack and was able to get back into the shop without being caught. Once the druggist had finished with his customer, his attentions turned to the boy, who bought a bottle of medicine that was on his mother's regular supply list. Placing the medicine into his jacket pocket, he carefully gripped the sack containing the stolen jars then left the shop, the druggist unaware that a thief had stolen some of his prized possessions.

After the boy stored the body parts in one of the glass jars containing the formaldehyde, Daniel saw him scrawl words on a cardboard label, describing the victim's physical appearance, and attach it round the top of the jar, which was placed on one of the shelves above the wooden cabinet. Daniel knew instantly that this was the first of many murders he would be a party to. The macabre flashback still lingering in his head, and the realisation that he'd reincarnated back to the earthly plain once more – albeit some one hundred years apart – to the same farming family as a young boy blew his mind.

Chapter 5

The Sighting
Bristol

In two previous lives, it occurred to Daniel, he had failed to survive to middle age and now, aged thirty-four, having surpassed those milestones, he felt invincible. The flashbacks left him unsure when or how the boy in the 1800s had died. Mulling over the emotional triggers that evoked the evil in him, he realised there was not just one stand-alone trigger; there were many. It could be the way someone talked or looked, or their attitude.

One recent trigger building an obsession in him was women he viewed as the 'Towie Type' – named after a popular reality show which, in his mind, was a load of self-indulgent shit pandering to a group of people parading their lives and loves in the pursuit of one-upmanship. The show's petty squabbles, 'must have' attitude for designer labels, cheating partners and desires to be seen in the 'in' places made compulsive viewing for many viewers. As a result of the show's success the young, impressionable and clueless started emulating its stars. Daniel found there was no shortage of humanity who were so self-obsessed and it became a sport to observe them in their favourite watering holes. The falseness enraged him as he watched air-kissing whilst listening to loud conversations between friends intent on bragging about their latest acquisitions.

Most of these women were so engrossed with their appearances that when it came down to the wire it was as though nobody but them existed in their world. It sickened him to watch how they never missed an opportunity to pout into the nearest mirror, or stare lovingly at the reflection bouncing back at them from their partner's mirrored sunglasses, checking out their surgically enhanced features. Daniel blended into the background, careful not to be noticed, and favouring a look and style of clothing that passed without attracting attention in the trendy upmarket bars.

One night, after trawling several wine bars, Daniel came across Hotel Papiar; an upmarket boutique hotel with a bar and restaurant. Tucked away in a side street off Bristol's city centre, it felt like a gentleman's club, with its leather armchairs, oil paintings and wood panels.

Shortly after crossing its threshold, he spotted a woman whose beauty stood head and shoulders above a group of average-looking wannabes at the far side of the bar.

Moving closer and picking up a comprehensive wine list, Daniel studied its contents, briefly glancing over and trying to mask his interest in the woman. With shoulder-length blonde hair, cornflower-blue eyes and pink cupid lips, she resembled a young Debbie Harry, an '80s icon he was obsessed with, and just his type. Ordering a glass of French Chardonnay, he took the drink over to a leather armchair by an open fireplace and continued his surveillance of the woman. The natural way she flirted with both men and women made her an irresistible magnet amongst the company she kept. It was evident she had caught the eye of several admirers, one of whom was heading in her direction.

Seeing the competition advance, Daniel decided to break his cardinal rule of observing from afar until the time was right to strike. He gulped down his wine and rose quickly from the armchair, heading through the crowded bar towards the woman and reaching her before the competition.

Realising he'd been headed off at the pass by someone else, the man strutted off in a childish sulk, launching himself at another pouting female. All attention shifted to the man, who pushed through the crowds to present himself into the heart of the group. At first, nobody challenged his presence as he confidently ingratiated himself amongst them; each assumed that one of their number must already know him.

Unbeknown to Daniel, however, his black aura was visible to one person. The very woman he had been watching. Jenna. Red flags of warning raised immediately in his presence, even though her friends seemed to be enchanted by the handsome stranger.

Throughout the conversation, Daniel edged closer to Jenna and his charming persona gradually broke down the barriers of suspicion. Despite the strange aura warning her otherwise, Jenna was persuaded to accompany him when he offered to buy a round of drinks for the group. As they pushed their way through the crowds to the bar, where people were standing three-deep waiting to be served, Daniel turned to face Jenna. With mousey, shoulder-length hair and a chiselled face supporting a tightly trimmed goatee beard, his appearance was appealing, but everything was brought back sharply into focus the moment she stared into his strange hazel-flecked eyes. The people around them seemed to disappear as Jenna felt him try to encroach her inner self. It was as though he was attempting to claim her soul. A battle of wills raged as Jenna fought to break his hypnotic spell. With a mammoth effort, she managed to move her physical body but his solid, muscular arm blocked her way. The movement broke the spell, however, bringing the crowds surrounding them back into focus. Panicking, Jenna scanned the room for her friends but they were too far away to see what was happening. As she looked back at the man, searching for an escape route, it was evident from the smug smirk on his face that he was revelling in her fear.

Daniel was completely turned on and, unable to control his desires, grabbed Jenna and manoeuvred her through the crowds to the side of the bar, where he pinned her up against the reclaimed mahogany, pushing his hardness against her. Jenna struggled to push him aside, her attempts thwarted by tightly packed revellers, all intent on getting served by two overworked bar tenders; her angry voice lost amidst people shouting drink orders.

As she frantically considered her options for freedom, Jenna was aware of another commotion coming from the crowds as someone bulldozed through the throngs, much to the annoyance of several men who took umbrage at being pushed aside. As the crowds parted, she recognised a familiar face.

Peter's muscular build afforded him unhindered access as he pushed the rest of the way to get to Jenna. Sensing trouble, people in close proximity started to move away, creating a space away from Daniel, who was too busy with lustful designs on Jenna to notice the change in atmosphere. A sharp blow between his shoulder blades stopped him in his tracks.

"The lady is not interested, mate. Leave her alone." Peter flung Daniel aside like a rag doll, freeing Jenna.

Outraged that his sport had been interrupted, Daniel rounded on the blond bodybuilder but was stopped short as his arm was yanked behind his back, causing him to yelp in pain. No one attempted to stop the altercation between the two men, for fear of reprisal.

"What the fuck do you think you're doing?" Daniel demanded through gritted teeth as he was frogmarched through parting crowds towards the door and shoved unceremoniously onto the pavement. Once he was released, the urge to retaliate was so great that Daniel almost jumped on the bodybuilder's back as he turned to go inside. However, realising he was no match for the muscle-bound hulk, Daniel quelled the urge, deciding to deal with him later when, with an element of surprise on his side, he would have the upper hand. Smarting from the altercation, he stormed off, muttering obscenities under his breath and threatening that they would pay for what they'd done to him.

From a short distance away, in a side street opposite the Hotel Papiar, Daniel had a bird's-eye view of the comings and goings of the wine bar. He waited, shifting occasionally to other locations, to avoid attracting attention. Just before midnight, his patience was rewarded when he spotted the young Debbie Harry lookalike arm-in-arm with the blond bodybuilder, heading towards Christmas Steps. Dodging oncoming traffic, Daniel ran across the road, reaching the bottom of the steps just in time to see them stop outside one of the terraced properties.

Loitering around the corner, he made a show of stopping to light a cigarette as a group of rowdy party-goers passed him, using Christmas Steps as a thoroughfare on their way to a club venue on Park Row. The drunken rabble passed Peter and Jenna and disappeared at the top of the steps, screams of laugher echoing into the night; in their wake, a hushed silence.

Daniel strained for sounds of conversation between the two people he had followed but was unable to make sense of anything they were saying. As he inched closer, he heard the sound of footsteps retreating down the stone steps towards him. Panicking, Daniel rushed back around the corner and found an alcove leading to a shop doorway where he could hide. Moments later, the bodybuilder passed him, completely unaware of the shadow watching as he made his way to the taxi rank in the city centre.

When he was certain the bodybuilder was out of sight, Daniel made his way back to Christmas Steps to locate the property he'd seen the pair talking outside. The terrace of shops and cafes was deserted as he made his way up the flight of stone steps, the bulk of night-time revellers having moved on to other venues to continue partying. Mid-way up, he stopped outside a recruitment business called Stepz 2 Recruitment. He was puzzled as to why the woman had gone into an office building so late at night then he remembered that some of the properties also had residential use. Looking up at the three-storey terrace, he spotted a light in an upstairs window, confirming residential use above the office. Seeing movement, he darted back into the shadows and watched the Debbie Harry lookalike draw back the curtains in one of the windows. The sight of the woman made Daniel want to cheer out loud. Knowing where she lived and presumably what she did for a living would make his plans easier but as he walked back down the street he felt a shiver, as though someone had walked on his grave, and a feeling of familiarity about the building he couldn't quite place.

It was primarily violence that excited Daniel; the more extreme, the bigger the high. Over the years, he had perfected ingenious ways of inflicting pain, revelling in the god-like power it brought. Sex was just a by-product; a throwaway part of the process. Victims attempting to appeal to his better emotions begged to stop the torture but it was futile. Empathy and compassion were qualities he did not possess. There were no feelings of guilt or remorse; just tremendous elation and a great smugness that, through centuries of reincarnation, being reborn and living other lives in different bodies with the same dark soul, he'd evaded justice for his horrendous crimes against humanity.

Lately, however, everything in his dark world had begun to evolve into something beyond his comprehension. He realised he'd been out of control the moment he spotted the woman in that pretentious wine bar. There was something about her that made him want to throw caution to the wind, making him unveil his dark side prematurely and thwarting his plans to slip GHB into her wine then transport her to the van he had parked in a loading bay at the bottom of Christmas Steps. Adding to his mounting fury was the intervention of the blond bodybuilder, who was ultimately going to pay dearly for the humiliation he had caused.

Daniel's normal preference was for women. Picking them off was easy; all he had to do was wait for the right opportunity, when they were alone, but he was prepared to make an exception for the bodybuilder. Dealing with a strong, fit man would be difficult but, as with the Debbie Harry lookalike, he had plans. Ultimately, Daniel was going to make the bastard beg for his life before he killed him. No one made a fool out of him and got away with it.

The first thing Daniel did after returning home in the early hours of the morning was make himself a strong black coffee. Going into a spacious study at the back of the house, he turned on a light and sat at a large oak desk. Setting his coffee on a silver coaster by the state-of the-art Mac, he booted up the machine and began an internet search to learn more about his intended victim. His first search was Companies House, where he checked out Stepz 2 Recruitment. After paying a small fee, he was privy to company details, discovering the business had three directors: Alannah Corby, Abbey French and Jennifer Thornleigh. He wondered whether the Jenna he had met at the Hotel Papiar was Jennifer. Daniel initiated a search on the property, obtaining access to title deeds, and found the proprietors were Alannah Corby and Jennifer Thornleigh, who had purchased the building eighteen months previously. Now he had two names and the full address it would be easy confirming the identity of the blonde woman.

The next search was on Facebook, as every man and their dog had an account. 'Jennifer Thornleigh' produced a selection of names on his screen. Scrolling down the names, he was able to isolate three Jennifer Thornleighs, but only one located in Bristol. Clicking on the link revealed her picture, confirming the fact she'd shortened her name to Jenna, and a short synopsis. This was so fucking easy, there was no doubt in his mind that if she befriended him she would be like most people on Facebook, who never tired of displaying their lives for all and sundry to look at. A picture of a meal they'd cooked; a night out with friends; selfies; family gatherings; what holidays they planned to take, and when. An open invitation for any would-be burglars or stalkers. It beggared belief how stupid people could be and made him innately smug that he resisted the lure of social media.

After trawling Facebook, Twitter and Instagram, he knew everything about Jenna Thornleigh, including the fact that she frequented a local gym three times a week before starting work; a good place to commence his surveillance. What struck him about the woman was the fact that her surname was the same as his mother's maiden name, but he dismissed it as a sheer coincidence.

Getting up early was a bit of an imposition for Daniel, who was a night owl, but exceptions had to be made sometimes. He was on a mission. The thought provoked a shiver of anticipation at initiating a new hunt. Pulling on dark trousers and a thick grey sweater, he searched his wardrobe for a pair of rubber-soled trainers he had recently purchased; a lightweight design that cushioned his feet and would soften his footfall. Throwing on a black parka, he grabbed his car keys, set the alarm and left the house, closing the door quietly behind him. It was getting on for 5am as he pressed the fob on his keyring and got into the Range Rover. Most houses in the immediate vicinity were shrouded in darkness, their occupants yet to rise for the next day's toil, as he headed towards Bristol city centre.

Parking at that time in the morning would prove no problem but he was mindful of not being too conspicuous; it would be easy for someone to spot him in the deserted streets.

The gym Jenna Thornleigh frequented was easy to locate, being part of a prominent hotel in Broad Street, a side street opposite Christmas Steps. From the top of the street, a prime position provided a view of the entrance to the gym. Daniel could easily observe the comings and goings. He had no idea what time she would arrive but, guessing she started work at 9 o'clock, he estimated it could be any time between six and eight. It was now

5.50am and, knowing he could have a long wait ahead of him, Daniel passed the time making mental notes of suitable locations and planning how an abduction could take place, depending on what transpired during his surveillance. At 6am, Jenna Thornleigh appeared, jogging up the street at a brisk pace and so immersed in her early morning routine that she didn't notice the man who moved forward in her line of vision, taking a moment to light up a cigarette in order to get a better glimpse of her. Even if she had taken the time to take in her surroundings, he was confident she wouldn't recognise him as he'd covered most of his head and face with a black beanie.

As he glanced through the cigarette smoke, Daniel noticed that without a screed of make-up she looked younger than he had initially thought, and even more desirable, clad in tight pink Lycra leggings, black running shoes and a pink hoodie. Her blonde hair was gathered into a ponytail, which swung seductively against her slender white neck as she disappeared through the flood-lit glass doors into the gym.

Glancing at his watch, Daniel was satisfied the bitch would be at least an hour inside and he strode past the building, heading back towards the centre. Locating a passageway tucked beside an office block, where he had a good vantage point over the city centre, Daniel patiently waited for her return.

At 7am, a lone woman jogged up to the end of Broad Street, crossed over at the pelican lights and made her way across the centre. As he moved from his hiding place she turned suddenly and looked straight in his direction. Fearing he'd been spotted, Daniel darted back, cursing himself for being so impatient. As he watched from the darkness, whatever had spooked the woman seemed to have passed and after a moment's hesitation she continued her journey past the terraced shopfronts towards Christmas Steps and back home.

Daniel spent several mornings diligently observing Jenna

Chapter 6

Acquisition of No. 26 Christmas Steps
18 months earlier

Jenna sat at the kitchen table, deep in thought. It had been a fraught four months of untold stress, due to incompetent builders. Before departing for a two-week holiday in Italy, she and Alannah had gone over the schedule with the contractor, believing that they could fulfil the brief and keep their promises that the building would be habitable on their return from holiday. The moment they touched down at Bristol Airport and were through Passport Control, Alannah rang Dave, the site foreman, to inform him they were back in the country and would arrive at Christmas Steps within the hour. The conversation didn't go well. Dave informed her that works had been held up as they were waiting for a gas boiler to be delivered.

The phone call caused tempers to flare between Jenna and Alannah and consequently conversions became heated on the way back from the airport and into Bristol. It wasn't until the taxi dropped them off at the top of Christmas Steps that their worst fears were realised. Looking down the narrow, cobbled street, they could see their team of builders sitting on the pavement, smoking, and drinking tea. After the curt conversation with Dave and arguments with Jenna, the sight incensed Alannah.

"Get off your fat, lazy backsides and help us with these cases!" she yelled from the top of the steps.

One of the builders, who was mid-way through swallowing a mouthful of scalding tea, choked when he saw them and spat the remnants down his tee-shirt. Stubbing out half-smoked cigarettes on the pavement, the rest of the crew rushed up to help with the suitcases.

Alannah followed behind them, now in full throttle. "If that fucking house is not finished I'm gonna string you bastards up by your balls."

Jenna noticed that several of the men had gone a deep shade of red and, knowing there was going to be a confrontation, scarpered down Christmas Steps. Inside the building, Dave was talking to a gas engineer, unaware that his team of builders had done a disappearing act. Looking round at the general mayhem in the building, it was clear to Jenna and Alannah that hardly any work had been done, if any, since their departure on holiday.

"What the fuck has been happening here?" Not waiting for a response from Dave, Alannah answered herself. "Not a fucking lot by the looks of it, you lazy bastards."

"Don't you talk to me like that." Dave indignantly squared up to her, revealing a hairy chest and belcher chain as his shirt strained over his considerable girth.

Alannah's temper exploded and to stop herself from physically attacking Dave she picked up the nearest thing to hand – a plaster-encrusted chair – and threw it at the wall.

Jenna, who was momentarily rendered speechless, found her voice and launched into condemnation of the works. Under the barrage of complaint, Dave finally buckled, admitting that during their absence his team had been pulled off the job to attend another site. Believing he could get the project back on track before they returned, Dave had foolhardily accepted the other job. In light of this admission, Jenna and Alannah verbally terminated the contract, ordering Dave and his team off site and telling him his company would be footing the bill for alternative accommodation as they were now technically homeless.

Fortunately, friends rallied round, providing accommodation whilst another contracting company was sought, coming highly recommended and able to pick up the pieces and finish the renovation works. The property had originally been bought as a joint business venture, part-commercial with residential accommodation above, between Jenna and Alannah. Now, some nine months later, fully ensconced in the property and starting the new business, Jenna sensed something still wasn't quite right. The minute they moved in, she had detected a presence, starting with a glimpse of an old lady dressed in a long skirt and leg-of-mutton blouse, a cameo broach on the neckline. Her grey hair was pinned up in a bun on the top of her head. She was sitting on a chair in the kitchen and seemed to be preoccupied with working on a piece of tapestry. Jenna, used to seeing spirits, turned to face the apparition and in doing so the old lady vanished. There was nothing threatening about her presence and Jenna accepted that as the property was built in the early 1800s there was bound to be history attached to it, and with history came the unexplained.

Strange things were also occurring in her bedroom, which was located on the top floor of the building. One night, shortly after swapping bedrooms with Alannah, who had complained that she felt ill at ease in the room, Jenna was woken by a thump on her bed. Opening her eyes and turning on the bedside light, she saw nothing. Convinced it was something she had conjured up in her imagination, Jenna turned the light off and fell back into a deep sleep. The next morning, her faux fur throw was on the other side of the room, its pile flattened in parts, as though someone had deliberately thrown it on the floor and stamped on it. This puzzled Jenna as she didn't recall taking the throw off the bed. She had needed its warmth, it being a particularly chilly night.

A week later, as Jenna sat on a wicker chair in her bedroom, putting on make-up, she felt something move past her, creating a draft in its wake. As she looked up from the mirror, from the corner of her eye she spotted what looked like a small child. Turning her head slightly to get a better look, she saw a pair of twin girls, whose ages she estimated to be in the region of four or five, playing with rag dolls and completely oblivious to her presence. The sighting of these children became a common occurrence to Jenna, who affectionately named them Polly and Molly. There was nothing malevolent about these spirits; on the contrary, they seemed happy to roam about the building, playing their little games with each other. As she became attuned to their presence, there was the odd occasion when Jenna would be the butt of one of their pranks but on the whole they caused no harm or upset and were content to roam between both worlds.

Alannah, who been a childhood friend, since their first meeting in primary school, was aware of her friend's unusual talent. Being afraid of anything supernatural, however, she chose to ignore this side of Jenna's life and remained blissfully unaware of what was happening under her own roof. Knowing Alannah would freak out big time if she knew the building was haunted, Jenna kept the sightings to herself. Lately, however, she had begun to get a sense of unpleasant stirrings within the building, and she knew as this continued that there was no way she could keep her suspicions under wraps.

One day, Jenna was climbing the narrow stairwell to the first floor when something gripped her and pinned her against the wall. The surrounding air turned desperately cold as she fought against the unknown force but efforts to release herself from the entity proved futile. The force was so great that Jenna found herself surrendering to its influence as it transferred its agony, permeating her very being and triggering the onset of a panic attack so violent she began to shake uncontrollably. Just when she thought she was going to black out, the entity left as quickly as it had taken possession, leaving her slumped against the stairwell and gasping for breath. Momentarily, she was unable to move, then gradually her breathing returned to normal, leaving Jenna exhausted, confused and out of control. The entity was nothing like the spirts she'd seen since moving into the property, who seemed content to roam peacefully between two worlds, revisiting familiar places.

After the confrontation on the stairwell, she knew that it was no longer possible to keep her experiences from Alannah. Things were escalating at a frightening rate and there was no alternative but to tell her friend, and seek help before something terrible happened.

Going back downstairs, a second encounter with the malevolent spirit occurred as Jenna entered the kitchen, where she was engulfed by a force so great that it knocked her to the floor. This time, the soul was bombarding Jenna with gruesome visions of a woman being savagely beaten, her attacker possessed by a fury the like of which she'd never seen before. Unable to break the spirit's hold, Jenna was forced to watch, horrified, as the man put his hands round the woman's throat and squeezed tightly until her screams were silenced. The woman's unconscious body was thrown to the ground, where the man defiled and did all manner of barbaric things to her. Jenna watched him wrapping the woman's body in a rug and carrying her away. Then the all-encompassing force left her and Jenna was transported back to her own body, where she lay in a heap on the kitchen floor.

The unearthly vision unhinged Jenna, making her feel it was also some kind of warning. Unable to get the gruesome images out of her mind, Jenna realised that she had been unable to see the man's face yet an image was projected into her mind. In that brief moment she glimpsed the man's eyes, which was enough to stop her heart from beating as she'd seen those eyes in this lifetime, and recently. The realisation the rapist could be someone she knew or came into contact with was too much for Jenna to comprehend. Disoriented, the horrific truth began to dawn on her, that the evil in the vision she'd been privy to took place right where she was sitting, on the flagstone floor of the kitchen.

Her own view from the kitchen window remained the same as it had been then. Flashbacks bombarding her mind provided snatches of the distinct drystone wall surrounding the garden at the back of the property, which was dominated by an aged oak tree. She knew without doubt that she was living in a place where horrendous violence had occurred.

Jenna crawled up against the kitchen units and used their solid platform to lever herself off the floor. Her mind was in turmoil, thinking back to when she and Alannah had purchased the property. Nothing came up during the conveyancing process; no complaints or disputes from adjoining neighbours were lodged, and certainly no inkling of a past murder, although the fact the building had been empty for at least eight years did raise a red flag. A succession of traders had occupied the property, starting up new businesses, but after a short time each had folded. It appeared that nothing worked at No. 26 Christmas Steps; a fact she and Alannah were aware of before purchasing the property, but which didn't deter them. After getting the property for a bargain price they had great plans for the Grade II listed building.

After the visionary warning, Jenna started to imagine all sorts of things, convincing herself that someone was watching the property. Being alone in the house didn't help her paranoia. It was the same sensation she remembered feeling when she left the gym that morning, which made her look over her shoulder to see if she was being followed as she jogged the short distance home. At 7am it was still dark and Bristol city centre was starting to get busy as she crossed by the traffic lights. Increasing her pace, Jenna had jogged past the brightly illuminated rank of shops and offices but could see nothing to justify her suspicions.

Meanwhile, on the other side of the city centre, a dark shape hidden in the recess of a building stirred and moved out of its hiding place to observe her as she ran along the pavement in the direction of Christmas Steps. As she disappeared around the corner, the shadowy shape moved and a man emerged from the hiding place, following her until she reached her destination.

Once safely inside the confines of home, Jenna had briefly glanced between the illuminated displays covering the office window, which advertised the latest vacancies the recruitment agency had on offer. It was still dark outside and apart from a solitary woman dressed in a nurse's uniform, on her way to work in the Bristol Royal Infirmary, Jenna saw no one else. Turning, she walked through the office, opening the door and going into the residential part of the property on the ground floor.

Switching on the lights as she passed into the lounge then into the kitchen to prepare breakfast, Jenna's mind was occupied with the day ahead and the busy schedule of jobs in her diary. Outside, at the bottom of Christmas Steps, the dark shape shifted and left its vantage point.

When Jenna returned home that evening, the house was deathly silent, the only sound the occasional shudder of the fridge-freezer. The recruitment agency was closed and, glancing in Alannah's diary, she noticed a late client appointment, which meant that she was alone in a building where things were off-kilter. The presence of the old lady and the twin girls was acceptable in her strange world but the violent vision had manifested a sense of danger she'd never experienced before. Searching for an answer to the madness, Jenna's thoughts gravitated to the strange incident at Hotel Papiar, and the man who'd accosted her. Luckily for her, Peter had been in the wine bar at the time and come to her rescue.

Jenna's sense of unease escalated as she started to assimilate the unexplained things that were happening. Common sense should have put the incident at Hotel Papiar down to an overly amorous admirer who probably had too much to drink but the more she thought about the man, the more she was convinced there was a familiarity about him. The thought of him brought on a sudden darkness, which took possession of her mind. When the darkness cleared, the same vision depicting the rapist filled her mind. As with the previous vision, his face was distorted, but as the image magnified she saw the same pair of hazel-flecked eyes. Jenna screamed out, clutching her head and trying to shake the image, then suddenly it shot out of focus and disappeared. How was it possible that the eyes belonged to the same person she'd encountered in the Hotel Papiar? The vision she'd seen depicted another time, well before recent renovations to Christmas Steps.

When Jenna first saw the man in the vision, she remembered orange-and-brown patterned dishes on the draining board as he beat the woman's head off a stone sink, her blood spattering and pooling on the crockery. The furniture and style of the kitchen in the vision suggested the 1980s. Jenna emerged from her thoughts knowing it was impossible for the person she'd encountered in the wine bar, being a similar age to herself, to be the same man in the vision, which clearly recounted something which had taken place over three decades ago.

Revisiting the horrendous vision made Jenna double over and retch the contents of her stomach onto the floor. Reaching over for some kitchen roll from the granite work surface, she got down on her knees and cleaned the putrid mess off the floor. She threw the soiled kitchen towel in the bin, ran the tap in the kitchen sink, rinsed her hands and splashed cold water over her flushed face.

The thought process was relentless. Re-jigging mental calculations swirling through her mind, Jenna estimated that if a murder had occurred at Christmas Steps in the 1980s, around thirty years ago, the man who'd accosted her was far too young, yet the returning flashback convinced her otherwise. Whoever attacked the girl had to be in his late fifties by now. The tortured spirit of the murdered girl who came to her purposely focused on the rapist's eyes; the last thing she saw before he strangled the lifeblood out of her. When piecing the snatches of the grisly vision together, there was no doubt in Jenna's mind it was some sort of warning. Everything seemed to lead to the brief encounter with the stranger at the wine bar, making her wonder why the troubled soul had chosen her.

The list of questions bombarding her brain was endless, leaving Jenna feeling that there was something vital she was missing. Jenna felt totally helpless, at a loss as to how she could explain to a long-standing friend that the property they'd bought was not only haunted but could also be the site of a historic murder.

Once Alannah heard the far-fetched sequence of events, Jenna had no doubt her immediate reaction would be to put the property up for sale; a prospect that, after all the heartache they had been through with the renovations, Jenna could not face.

Checking her watch, Jenna saw that Alannah wouldn't be home for at least another hour. According to their business diary, she and Abbey were pitching the new business to potential clients. Realising she would have to deal with her inner turmoil, paranoia set in and threatened to overwhelm her. Not wanting to be alone a minute longer, Jenna retrieved her mobile from the coffee table in the lounge and sent a text to Alannah, inviting her and Abbey to join her in the Three Sugar Loaves pub after their meeting. There was no way she could tell Alannah what was going on but she took comfort at being out of the house for a couple of hours.

Before walking down to the pub, Jenna took the opportunity to trawl the internet on the laptop in the office, starting her search in the mid 1980s. Putting 'Christmas Steps' into the browser bought up a succession of unsuccessful businesses closing as new occupants stepped in and took over the leases. The discovery some traders who weathered different fads and trends still remained in Christmas Steps instilled her with a renewed confidence that their fledgling recruitment business would flourish, given time. Totally immersed in the task, it wasn't until Jenna glanced at the clock on the bottom of the screen that she noticed an hour had passed and realised Alannah and Abbey would be waiting in the Three Sugar Loaves. Closing down the laptop, Jenna gathered her purse off the desk and bolted out of the door, down the cobbled street and into the pub. When she walked in, her friends were sitting at a table in the bottom bar, with a prime view looking onto Christmas Street, chatting animatedly over a couple of drinks. Seeing Jenna approach, Abbey immediately got up to greet her, planting two chaste kisses either side of her face then retreating to the bar to get her a drink.

"Where have you been? I was just about to come up to the house to look for you," Alannah said in an irritated tone as she watched Abbey walk to the bar, out of earshot.

"Sorry, got caught up on the internet."

Alannah was not happy with Jenna's half-cocked explanation. Knowing Jenna of old, she had actually sensed something was wrong. The more she thought about Jenna's behaviour over the last couple of weeks, the more she was convinced there was something her friend was hiding from her. Launching the new business had taken most of her time but she was determined to have a serious talk with her friend, to find out what was going on. Realising this was not the time or place, however, seeing Abbey coming back from the bar, Alannah decided to postpone that talk until they got home.

Several rounds of drinks later, all thoughts of Jenna's strange behaviour were forgotten. It was going on midnight when they put Abbey in a taxi before heading home. Feeling tipsy from over-indulgence, Alannah declined Jenna's offer to make coffee, opting to go bed as she had a busy day ahead of her. Staggering up the stairs to her bedroom, she left Jenna in the lounge, once more intent on her laptop.

The effects of the drink-fuelled evening were evident as Jenna attempted to restart her online search. Realising it was getting late and the words on the screen were swarming back at her, she closed it down and went to bed, hoping sleep would come quickly.

The moment her head hit the pillow and her eyes closed, Jenna fell into a deep sleep; so deep, she was blissfully unaware of the presence in her room, hovering inches from her bed. Despite the alcohol, for the first time in two weeks she was blessed with undisturbed and untroubled sleep.

The next morning, slightly hungover, Jenna awoke with renewed optimism, resolving to meet the disturbing challenges head on. Getting ready for work, she mulled over the events of the past two days, making a mental promise to talk to Alannah that evening, hoping together they would be able to make sense of the extraordinary sequence of events.

Whilst Alannah and Abbey spearheaded the new business, Jenna had elected to keep her existing job, with the intention of coming into Stepz 2 Recruitment at a later stage, when it could sustain another salary. For the time being, she was content to take a back seat. She enjoyed her role as office manager for a firm of architects. She and Alannah had agreed at the beginning of the joint venture that, having no prior recruitment experience, Jenna would be a silent partner until such time the new business grew and was able to sustain three salaries. Meanwhile, it was down to Alannah and Abbey to take the business forward. The arrangement was proving successful and early indicators showed that business was steadily increasing.

Since inception of the business, Jenna often found that she and Alannah were like ships in the night. That evening was no exception, as the office housing Stepz 2 Recruitment at the front of the property was deserted when she arrived home. A note left on the kitchen table told her that Alannah and Abbey were on a return visit to a new client, who was looking to recruit a team of sales people for their call centre. Not wanting their conversion to be put on hold again, Jenna had worked herself into a frantic state. Momentarily, as she studied the note left on the kitchen table, excitement at the prospect of bringing another new client on board distracted her from her anxiety. She was confident that Alannah and Abbey would seal the deal, making a total of four new clients in two days and bringing the possibility of Jenna leaving her job sooner rather than later.

Jenna set up her laptop, determined to find out what she could about the property she and Alannah had bought. There were two avenues open for the search: residential and commercial. She thought she would target the 1980s first but before she had a chance to type in any keywords, Alannah bounded through the front door. Excited at signing up another new client with six potential sales jobs, she quickly filled Jenna in on the news, flew upstairs to her bedroom, discarded her pinstriped suit for jeans and tee-shirt, refreshed her make-up, then whisked Jenna away to Hotel Papiar for celebratory drinks.

On the short distance to the wine bar, Alannah filled Jenna in on the meeting and how they'd played a blinder, taking business from three high street agencies. Abbey was waiting for them when they arrived at the wine bar, with a chilled bottle of Prosecco and three glasses ready to toast bringing on board another new client. The evening was a succession of drinks, good food and laughter. Once again, Jenna's promise to tell Alannah about the spiritual encounters fell by the wayside.

It was early Saturday morning and with her guilty secret still intact, Jenna had managed to convince herself it was prudent to do some more digging before dragging Alannah into something she couldn't fully explain. Opening her laptop, she began another search, trawling through electoral registers and beginning to build a picture of the people who inhabited No. 26 Christmas Steps. At the turn of the century, she discovered it was not unusual for extended family members to live together, packed tightly under the same roof. Going through the details of past occupants, nothing matched what she was looking for. Moving forward into the 1980s, the last residential occupants at No. 26 were a family called Adams: a man called Donald, his wife Marjorie, and their two children, Thomas and Jane. After 1987, there was no trace of the family on the electoral registers. Jenna tried another search but failed to find anything of interest. Just as she was going to call it a day, she typed in 'Adams Christmas Steps 1980s' and a rogue news item caught her interest;

25 September 1986

Jane Adams, 24, late of Christmas Steps, died today after spending 11 months in a coma. To date, no one has been arrested for her murder. Police are appealing for any information from the public as to the whereabouts of her brother Thomas (Tommy) Adams.

Searching through earlier news reports, Jenna discovered Jane's mutilated body had been found in a leafy suburb of Street in Somerset. The article informed her Jane Adams was left for dead after being brutally raped and attacked at her home. No. 26 Christmas Steps. In an attempt to hide the evidence, and presumably believing Jane to be dead, it seemed her attacker had transported her to Somerset and callously dumped her in a refuge bin. She was discovered, clinging to life, by garbage men.

Jenna recoiled in shock as she looked at the grainy black-and-white picture of the young woman accompanying the news article, knocking the laptop which was resting on the side of the sofa in the process. Fortunately, Jenna managed to catch the Mac before it fell to the floor. Composing herself after the near accident, she looked at the photo again, confirming her eyes were not deceiving her. Although the image was poor quality, there was no denying the woman was the same person she'd seen in her vision. An overwhelming feeling of fear threatened Jenna's ability to think logically as she went through the motions of saving the news article into her favourites, to show Alannah what she'd found.

Now Jenna had confirmation that a murder had been committed in their new home, there was no way she could ignore the troubled spirit's warning. The past was now invading her world.

Chapter 7

Hydlebury Farm's Secret
Cornwall

Killing his adoptive parents had been easy for Daniel. It had been on the cards ever since discovering their lies about his adoption. The opportunity arose when they were planning a holiday in France. Having just turned nineteen, Daniel persuaded Stanley and Heather that he was responsible enough to be left at home, under the watchful eye of Edith, the dutiful housekeeper who'd been with the family ever since he was a toddler. Being somewhat a genius when it came to stripping and rebuilding cars, Daniel had sabotaged his parents' Range Rover.

The accident happened when they were travelling between Limogen and Champniers, on their way to Cognac. The car spun uncontrollably over the central reservation, into oncoming traffic, colliding with four other cars before rolling and crashing on the other side. Daniel's mother and father were pronounced dead at the scene, together with three other people, one of whom was a three-year-old child. Police never suspected the mangled mess of metal and body parts was anything other than a tragic accident, attributing it to an over-tired driver who, on the long journey through France, had fallen asleep at the wheel. When Daniel was told the news of his parents' death he played the part of the grief-stricken son, his performance worthy of an Oscar-winner, totally convincing the two police officers who were tasked to deliver the devastating news.

Daniel inherited his parents' fortune on reaching the age of twenty-eight. A house in Stoke Bishop; the construction business, worth in excess of £5 million; holiday homes in Italy and France, not to mention the stocks and bonds Heather and Stanley had amassed during their lifetime. Until he came of age, he was allocated a monthly allowance, which enabled him to pay Edith off and sever all ties with acquaintances and friends who'd been a part of his life as he grew up. The only blood relative remaining on his mother's side was Peggy, the woman he thought was his aunt but who was in fact his great-aunt, who he had met a couple of times on trips to Somerset, and had no desire to meet again. That minor problem was soon resolved. Peggy died several weeks after her sister's accident. It came as no surprise as she had been very ill. It was reported back to him via people who knew Peggy that after on hearing about Heather's death she'd given up her struggle with cancer and died in her sleep. With no surviving family members, Daniel was free to indulge his darkest passions without redress.

In the wake of Peggy's death, Daniel found himself the sole beneficiary of her Will, which included a property in Cornwall, adding to his considerable fortune. It took some time to sort out his parents' affairs, in particular the construction business, as his father's business partner didn't take kindly to the young upstart coming in and throwing his weight around. It was evident from the get-go that Robert Finlay wasn't going to tolerate Daniel's meddling, leaving him no alternative but to sell his share of the business to the highest bidder. For Robert, it was a relief. Ever since first meeting Stanley's son, he had never taken to the boy. There was something about Daniel that made his skin crawl; something unnatural, which he couldn't quite put his finger on.

On receiving his inheritance, Daniel lived like a playboy, indulging in luxuries that were previously out of his reach. Once he'd sold on his part of the business, he took a trip to his parents' villa in Italy, then spent several months touring around, taking in the delights of the Amalfi coast before returning to Bristol.

After narrowly escaping the multi-vehicle collision and temporarily housing his prisoner in the basement of his house, he started going through some old paperwork, coming across a copy of Aunt Peggy's Will. It wasn't until he read it, together with supporting documentation, that he remembered Hydlebury Farm. He'd never made any attempt to see the property before but seeing another opportunity to add to his vast fortune, he decided to take a trip to Cornwall with a view to putting the estate on the market.

The journey from Bristol to Cornwall took him two hours. Coming off the motorway, he took the A30 and followed signs for Launceston, then headed for the small hamlet of Lawhitton. The satnav took him to traffic lights by a bridge, where he took a right turn down a narrow lane. Getting out of the car, Daniel stood for a while, looking at the ramshackle building before him. According to the information supplied by his great-aunt's solicitor after Peggy's death, Hydlebury Farm had been abandoned for fifteen years, the building untouched since the demise of its previous tenants; a brother and sister who had died within two years of each other. After the tenants' deaths, his aunt had been too sick to deal with the property and it was left unoccupied. As Daniel took in the sight of the old farmhouse, which appeared to have collapsed in on itself, he suspected that with the passage of time the structure had become seriously dilapidated. A list of repairs mentally stacked up as he assessed the damage. A roof that sagged in the middle. Delabole slates precariously hanging by a thread at eaves-level, threatening to topple downwards. Most of the windows had long since lost their glass, allowing gale force winds to rip through the farmhouse, unchallenged. Where he stood, wet grass grew long and unkempt, abundant weeds soaking his shoes. At one time, this patch of land may have passed as a garden of sorts.

There was no need to use the keys in his pocket as the front door hung off its hinges, allowing easy access. Making his way around the farmhouse, Daniel accessed the kitchen, dining room, front room, pantry and bathroom, as well as three double bedrooms upstairs. In one of the bedrooms, a man's jacket hung on a hook on the back of a door, a cane walking stick propped against one of the walls. The room was dominated by a dark wooden chest of drawers, on top of which a collection of false teeth sat in pride of place amidst a film of dust; a stark reminder of the room's previous occupant.

Once he'd explored the house, Daniel went back outside and surveyed the two acres of land, discovering two abandoned barns, the first of which had a broken-down tractor parked outside its double doors. As with the farmhouse, the barn was easy to access, its doors rotted and hanging open, making Daniel briefly wonder why squatters hadn't seized the opportunity to take possession of the desolate building. Inside, the barn was stacked full of rusty farming implements. As it was not worthy of closer inspection, Daniel turned on his heel and trudged across the soggy grass to the neighbouring barn, which at first glance appeared to be in better condition. As he entered, a sizeable hole in the roof above the hayloft caught his attention, letting in rainwater, which lay in stagnant puddles on the barn floor.

Although he'd never been to the property before, let alone known of its existence, Daniel was drawn to the south-west corner of the barn, where a large expanse of rainwater covered the dirt floor. As he stood looking down at the floor, his senses told him there was something beneath the water, prompting an urge for further investigation. Taking off his jacket, Daniel rolled up his shirt sleeves. He crouched down, immersing his hands in the dirty water, and felt something solid scrape the tip of his right index finger. Manoeuvring the object up and out of the shallow puddle, he realised it was a ring-pull, which appeared to be attached to a trapdoor. He tugged the metal ring upwards several times and managed to dislodge the trapdoor, upending a slurry of stagnant water, which saturated his trousers and shoes. Cursing as he looked down at his ruined clothes, he threw back the trapdoor, letting it fall with a resounding thud. Standing over the gaping black void, an evil stench of death permeated Daniel's nostrils, invoking memories and cementing the existence of past lives. The vision he'd seen during regression in the therapist's surgery stirred in his brain, and the fact that he'd left the man with no means of tracing his whereabouts. Daniel knew, before descending the wooden staircase, that he had found the cellar that would ultimately lead him on the path into his former life. He stood for some time, considering the next stage of his metamorphosis from present into the past.

As he teetered on the brink of his former existence, memories from his current life presented themselves. On the recent holiday to Italy, whilst in Positano, he had met a woman meandering down a side street, looking in gift shops. Sensing she was a tourist like himself, he watched her for some time before making his move. He discovered the statuesque brunette was American, called Paige, and was on her own in Positano. They immediately hit it off and spent the best part of two days holed up in the rented apartment overlooking the Amalfi coast, gorging on all forms of bondage and punishment. The debauchery ended badly when Paige, who had a penchant for strangulation, allowed him to put the plastic bag over her head, thinking that at the point of asphyxiation he would release her. As Daniel's grip tightened around her neck, making breathing difficult, she started to struggle, indicating that he'd gone too far and the game was over. Instead of stopping, however, Daniel increased the pressure until, weak from the struggle, she drew her last breath, satisfying his lust for killing – momentarily, at least.

Paige's body had lain on the bedroom floor for another two days, during which time Daniel travelled to Sorrento, some five miles away, where he purchased a selection of knives including a boning knife; twine; thick black plastic bags, and industrial-strength cleaning solutions from different traders. With his head covered by a baseball cap, its peak pulled down and obscuring most of his face, he paid cash, ensuring nothing could be traced back to him. The last purchase on his list was a large, brightly coloured beach bag.

With all of his goods stored out of sight in the boot of his rental car, he headed back to Positano with only one thought on his mind: disposal of the body.

Daniel parked in the apartment's allocated parking spot and unloaded the contents of the boot carefully, storing the knives, bags and cleaning products inside the beach bag before lifting its heavy weight onto his shoulder and strolling nonchalantly up to the apartment. To anyone observing him, he was just another tourist coming back from the beach; certainly not a killer with a bag full of sinister tools.

Once inside the apartment, Daniel carried the bag into the bathroom and emptied its contents onto the tiled floor then, going back into the bedroom, he dragged Paige's nude, decomposing body by the ankles into the bathroom and threw it into the sunken bath. Stripping off his clothes, Daniel jumped into the bath with the corpse and selected the boning knife then set about cutting. When he'd finished hacking the lifeless body, all that remained of the beautiful brunette were six bloody body parts: two legs, two arms, a head and a torso, all of which he dumped into black plastic bags and tied with twine. It took several journeys to transfer the body parts to the rental car, which was parked outside the apartment, where the contents from the large beach bag were shoved unceremoniously into the boot.

On the last journey to the car, Daniel encountered a neighbour eyeing his colourful bag with curiosity. The bag, containing the head and arms of the brunette, was heavy and bulky, making Daniel struggle as he carried it, sparking the man's interest as he passed by. Aware of the man's eyes on him, Daniel directed the key fob at the car to open the door and heaved the bag onto the back seat, instead of opening the boot to empty its contents. This proved a wise move as the man glanced back to take another look before walking on. It was then that Daniel realised he was still wearing the plastic gloves he'd used when handling the body parts. Not wanting to draw further attention to himself he left them on, praying the man wouldn't notice the oddity.

The moment of scrutiny passed and the man went on his way without incident. Daniel, who hadn't realised he was holding his breath during that anxious moment, let out a huge sigh of relief. With all body parts shoved in the car, he went back to the apartment and set about cleaning it with the industrial-strength solutions he'd bought, then packed all his belongings. By the time he'd finished cleaning and packing up, it was early evening. He got in the car and drove away from the apartment. His end destination was Naples Airport, from where he would fly back to Bristol. He had two days until the flight he had booked, which gave him time to get rid of the body parts, which were starting to smell in the sweltering heat.

The journey took him past Sorrento, in the direction of Castellammare di Stabia, winding along the Statale 145 peninsula road where, under normal circumstances, the drive would have been pretty and picturesque. The beauty unfolding in front of him as he drove was wasted on Daniel, however, his mind having just one purpose: dumping the body parts without being seen.

As it started to get dark, traffic on the roads became lighter. Passing a country club, he doubled back and parked on the periphery of its golf course until darkness set in, then drove around looking for a dump site. Beyond the club's immaculate grounds lay scrubland. Daniel found a spot deep inside the shrubbery.

Once he'd dumped Paige's remains, Daniel headed back to Naples, driving with the windows open to rid the car of the stench of death. Finding a secluded B & B a short distance from Naples Airport, Daniel spent the rest of his stay there before going on to pick up his flight. In that time, he cleaned the rental car inside and out, eliminating the stench of death and all signs of the American beauty called Paige.

He had chosen his victim well; a single woman on holiday on her own, ripe for the picking. During the two days he spent with her, Daniel had discovered she had split up with her partner after a violent argument and back in Arizona had been holed up in a motel until she could move back into her house, which was occupied by tenants. Luckily for Daniel, this meant there would be no immediate search party as the woman had decided on the spur of the moment to take an impromptu holiday to Italy, giving him plenty of opportunity to escape without incident.

After returning home, flashbacks came with alarming regularity, making Daniel regret his decision to supply the therapist with a bogus name and details; the man could have been useful to get a better insight to his former life. Now, however, as fate would have it, the trip to the house in Cornwall had put him on the right path. Standing over the gaping black void, Daniel realised all he had to do to get the answers he craved was walk down that wooden staircase.

He retrieved a torch from the glove department of his car then descended the rickety wooden steps, into the bowels of the old cellar. Once Daniel reached the bottom of the staircase, he shone the torch round the space and took in its abandoned glory. Clearly, nobody had been in the cellar in centuries, which was evident from the huge cobwebs that hung in abundance from the wooden ceiling, and rusting tools left on the dusty wooden cabinetry. Floorboards creaked underfoot as he shuffled along in the limited light his torch afforded him. A scratching noise made him turn suddenly, catching a large rat in the glare of his torch. The creature bared its teeth, indignant at the intrusion. The two of them eyeballed each other for a moment then the rat scampered off into a hole in the floorboards.

Daniel discovered the floorboards were loose and started to pull them up, revealing a burial site. Mounting excitement made him lose all sense of reason as he looked at a shallow grave that had already given up its treasures. A partially exposed finger-bone pointing out of the soil made him want to dig further. Gripping his torch in his left hand he manoeuvred himself into the void beneath the floorboards. Propping his torch up, he started digging and found a small skeleton entwined with the remnants of a cotton fabric. As Daniel handled the skeleton, part of its eroded leg bone came off in his hands. He looked at the tiny bone and a primeval urge made him stop and sniff it. Holding the bone almost lovingly, he willed his mind to relive the victim's moment of death.

Daniel saw himself as the first boy he'd seen whilst undergoing regression therapy. Lying in a grain field, spying on a girl who was playing with something in the dirt, unaware of his presence. As the traces of the past echoed in his brain, Daniel became aware of a wailing noise, beginning as a low frequency sob and becoming louder and louder, bringing with it excruciating pain. Dropping the bone, he fell to his knees, screaming for the pain to go away, his hands frantically clawing his scalp to rip the ungodly noise from inside his head.

Suddenly, the pain and the wailing stopped and he heard a voice. Scrabbling for the torch he climbed out of the void. Back in the cellar in the torch light, he saw an apparition in the far corner of the cellar, its sudden appearance making him scream in fright. For the first time in his life, the tables had turned on him. Instead of being the instigator of fear, Daniel knew and felt it himself. As the apparition transformed into a solid form, a voice was vibrating inside his head, making him stagger back against the cellar wall.

"You will suffer for what you have done."

No explanations were needed. Daniel instantly knew that the thing hovering before him, which resembled a small child, was one of his past victims.

"Who are you?" he screamed.

The apparition offered no response. Daniel was powerless to move as the childlike apparition glided towards him and engulfed his body. In the instance of contact, all the pain and suffering he and his past selves had inflicted over the centuries bore down on him, making the pounding in his heart flutter. Then everything went black.

When Daniel came to, he was lying on the timber floor, his torch a short distance away, emitting a faint strip of light in the pitch darkness of the cellar. As he attempted to move, a sharp racking pain rocked his body. He remembered clutching his heart before he had blacked out and, fearing the pain was the onslaught of a heart attack, Daniel began to panic, realising he was in the middle of the countryside where no one would hear him and his mobile was out of reach, in the car.

The fear of impending death brought superhuman resolve, making him realise that if he didn't do something quickly he could die alone, left to decay amongst the bodies of his long-deceased victims. Stretching his hand out towards the thin strip of light, his fingers inched through the dirt of the floor and grabbed the torch. Once it was in his hands, he gradually pulled himself up into a sitting position. Flashing the beam around the cellar, there was no sign of the terrifying apparition which had taken possession of his body. All traces of it had vanished, apart from the bone, which lay under the floorboards, inches away from his foot. Rolling away, he stumbled onto his feet, clutching the torch to his chest. The pain stabbing at his chest started to ease, making movement more fluid. Using the wall as support, Daniel inched his way round the cellar until he located the wooden staircase and started to gravitate towards the light in the barn overhead. Reaching the top of the staircase, he scrambled out and slammed the trapdoor back into place. The light was fading fast as he stumbled out of the barn and got back to his car. In no fit state to drive, and with no desire to go back into the farmhouse, Daniel pulled down the back seats in the Range Rover, covered himself with a blanket, locked the doors, and fell into a deep, troubled sleep.

When he awoke, it was early and still dark. Taking a moment to collect his thoughts, he pushed aside the blanket and scrambled across the back seats. Opening a side door, damp air clung to his clothes as he emerged from the stationary Range Rover and stretched his cramped body. The car was parked outside the farmhouse, which loomed like a monstrous demon in the darkness. From where Daniel was standing, the barn was completely camouflaged by the darkness. A shiver went down his spine as he recalled the horrendous sequence of events he'd experienced. His enlightenment about his ability to reincarnate throughout the centuries had come with an arrogant belief that he was immune to other earthbound phenomena. Now he knew he was wrong; the apparition's deadly possession of his body shattered that deluded belief. Handling the bone retrieved from the shallow grave had been the pivotal moment, when he discovered the deceased had been a young girl. Past memories of who she was or when the murder took place evaded him, stirring up anger and frustration. Next time, Daniel vowed, if and when the apparition came, he would be prepared for it and, having found the underground cellar, nothing was going to stop him. Least of all a spirit of a dead girl.

He had plans for the grimy hiding place and there was a lot of work to be done before they could come to fruition. With his resolve firmly in place, Daniel decided to check in somewhere locally whilst he worked on the barn to get it fit for purpose.

He slipped back into his car. As Daniel manoeuvred onto the lane the Range Rover's powerful beams lit up the surrounding darkness, illuminating the farmhouse in all its ruination. Just as he was about to head away he spotted lights in the distance; presumably from another cottage nestling further up the lane, which he had missed when he arrived the day before. A nearby neighbour could prove problematic. He would have to be extra vigilant with his comings and goings. The last thing he needed was some busybody sniffing around.

Glancing at the clock on the dashboard, it read 6.15am: too early to shop for the items needed for the barn project and too early to book into a hotel. Driving four miles back into Launceston, Daniel passed Tesco, where he doubled back, knowing he would find a café inside and toilet facilities where he could freshen up.

After several coffees and an early breakfast, he went shopping for essentials. At 3pm, he found a hotel and checked in as Jason Holden, handing over credit card details matching the false identity. Luckily, he was still in the disguise he had created for himself whilst stalking Peter Shaney, who would remain imprisoned in his Bristol home until alterations to the barn were complete.

Coming down to Cornwall to clear his head whilst he worked out what to do with the bodybuilder had proved more lucrative than Daniel had imagined. Not only was he in possession of a farmhouse that, once renovated, would increase his growing fortune, but he had a place where he could indulge his darkest fantasies without disturbance. The barn was somewhere Daniel could bring the bodybuilder and Jenna Thornleigh, where their screams would not be heard beneath the heavy oak floorboards.

Two days should give him enough time to construct the basic alterations to the cellar and get back to Bristol. In the meantime, Shaney had had a reprieve as on the way to Devon there had been a multi-vehicle collision, forcing Daniel to take the next available exit off the motorway and head back to Bristol. His original plan was to kill the bodybuilder and dump his body on Dartmoor. For the time being he would remain anaesthetised and locked up in the basement of his house. The drug he'd injected into his neck was still swirling round his system. Coupled with the water laced with GHB, which Daniel had managed to feed down his throat, this would keep his prisoner unconscious until his return.

Arriving back at Hydlebury, Daniel unloaded his purchases, ferrying the building materials into the barn and setting up camp in the scullery; the only dry room in the farmhouse.

Over the next two days, Daniel worked tirelessly, around the clock. The first thing he did was block up the hole in the floorboards, sealing up the burial site. He then remodelled the cellar into a fortress, constructing two timber-clad cages complete with heavy-duty padlocks. The existing wooden cabinetry was restored, with minor repairs to the drawers, which now housed an impressive array of tools. Pride of place was a large solid wood workbench, bought as a flat-pack and reassembled in the confines of the cellar. On the top of the work bench, Daniel fitted four steel rings; two at the top and two at the bottom, through which were attached plastic zip-lock ties. In an effort to remain off the radar, and not wanting to run the risk of alerting the authorities to someone occupying the property, Daniel purchased two generators, supplying light and power to the cellar and scullery. In case of the generators failing, he also bought a variety of camping lights, matches and candles.

The only problem he faced was that there was no water supply to the barn but Daniel overcame that by sourcing a water butt and filling it using a bore-hole pump he managed to rig up to the one of the generators. Once the water butt was full, he hauled it onto a trolley and wheeled it into the barn, placing it beside the trapdoor.

Digging a hole, he fed plastic piping through, fitting the end with a plastic nozzle and attaching it to the water butt's tap. On the other end of the plastic piping filtering down into the cellar, Daniel attached another nozzle and tap that could be turned on and off on demand. He hooked this to a steel ring, which he fitted to the cellar wall.

Once he'd secured the pipe, Daniel walked back up the wooden staircase and turned on the water butt's tap, then descended into the cellar to test his handiwork. The crude contraption worked a treat, water gushing out of it the moment the tap was released and stopping immediately it was turned off. All he had to do was remember to close the tap off at the water butt end when it was not in use.

Everything was he set. He had light, power, water and a fully-fortified prison nobody could escape from. A place where he was free to come and go without disturbance.

Chapter 8

Bluebell Cottage
Cornwall

Since the death of her husband five years earlier, Ethel had lived alone on the outskirts of the small village of Lawhitton, tending a smallholding which housed chickens, ducks, and a small but impressive cottage garden. Life was a struggle, and isolated, but despite her daughter Sally's insistence she should leave her beloved cottage and go to live with her in Exeter, Ethel stubbornly preferred to keep her independence and live with her memories. Now in her late seventies, she knew it was only a matter of time before her body would dictate when her independence was no longer an option but until that time she was determined to soldier on.

Although daily routines were monotonous, Ethel took pride in her smallholding, which supplied more than enough produce to keep her fed. Apart from Sally visiting every fortnight as her busy schedule and family life dictated, Ethel was alone. She was wary of strangers and had made it a policy to not get involved with any, apart from the brother and sister who had lived at Hydlebury Farm down the lane.

A couple of days ago, however, she had become aware of activity at the derelict old farmhouse. It was the noise of a vehicle heading towards the farm that alerted Ethel, who was working in her cottage garden at the time. As the noise got nearer, she walked to the line of firs sheltering her land and peered through a gap in the trees, catching a glimpse of a man driving a blue Range Rover, which was passing through the farm's gates and looked to be loaded down with supplies. The man's presence stirred an interest in Ethel, making her wonder what he was up to. The farmhouse, which had stood empty for more years than she could remember, was not fit for habitation. An hour or so later, the car left Hydlebury and headed back in the direction of Launceston.

The following morning, when Ethel heard the Range Rover return, her nosiness got the better of her. She walked down the lane and cut over a field at the back, where she could get a better look at what was going on. She could see that a man was outside the farmhouse with his back to her, in the process of unloading lengths of timber and an oak door that had been secured to the vehicle's roof rack. There was something about the man's demeanour that gave Ethel the creeps, warning her to stay hidden behind the surrounding hedges.

Once the items from the roof rack were offloaded the man started on the contents inside the Range Rover, which consisted of more building materials. Although she hadn't seen his face clearly, from his build and the way he moved she estimated the man to be in his early thirties. As she watched his activities, Ethel recalled a conversation she'd had with Macey, a neighbour from Rezare. Macey, who liked to gossip, had informed Ethel that a reliable source had told her the owner of Hydlebury Farm had died up in Somerset and the property had been passed down to a relative. Deducing that the stranger unloading the Range Rover must be the relative, she wondered why he had taken so long to visit his inheritance. Ethel began to feel awkward about spying on him. Losing interest in his activities, she crept past the hedge line and made her way back to her cottage unseen, leaving the new owner to go about his business.

The thought of a stranger in the small hamlet whose occupants had been whittled down to just her and the other near neighbour, Mr Anstey, was disconcerting but once Ethel became embroiled into her daily routines all ruminations about the stranger were quickly forgotten.

Unaware that he'd been watched, Daniel finished his construction work in the cellar, securing the trapdoor with a padlock. Once he had repaired the barn door, he fitted another padlock. One of his last tasks before leaving the farm was to replace the rotting front door of the farmhouse. After planing the oak door to fit then hanging it and fitting a new lock, he boarded up the downstairs windows to deter any would-be vandals or vagrants. Daniel was encouraged by the progress he'd made, his heart thumping wildly with excitement as images of the blond bodybuilder flashed in his mind. It was just a matter of transporting him from Bristol to the cellar, where everything was ready for the bloody task ahead. Daniel planned to stay overnight in Bristol then, after giving the bodybuilder another sedative, he would bring him down to Cornwall.

On arriving back in Bristol the first thing Daniel did was check the basement where Peter Shaney had been imprisoned. As he unlocked the oak door and switched on the light, Daniel heard muffled noises coming from behind one of the inner doors. He walked down the oak staircase to the lower level, which was occupied by a games room consisting of a fully stocked bar, pool table and cinema section, and a bedroom with en suite for his conquests who weren't worthy of seeing the upper levels of the grand house.

As he padded across the oak flooring into the bedroom, towards the noise, Daniel could hear his captive behind the locked en suite door, pleading for help. The noise level was minimal but he knew it would quickly escalate to full-throttle screams. As he unlocked the door and braced himself for the ungodly racket, he was confident the noise would be contained within the house, given the fact he'd spent an absolute fortune soundproofing the basement area of the property.

Inside was the prisoner, who had been chained to a steel radiator as an extra safety measure. The moment Daniel entered the cavernous bathroom, Peter Shaney lunged at him like an enraged bull but the slack on the chains pulled him up short before he could lay hands on his target.

"You fucking bastard, why are you doing this to me? What have I done to you?" he screeched from a standing point three feet from the door, lashing out with his arms, trying to reach his abductor.

Daniel stood calmly observing his pray. He let the obscenities flow over him without responding until Peter, hoarse from screaming, slumped on the floor, conceding defeat. From where he was standing, Daniel could see that his captive had eaten the food, and drunk the water he'd left, evidenced by empty packets and bottles scattered around the marbled floor. He also noticed that he'd made use of the toilet and the roll-top bath, leaving dirty tidal marks and sodden towels, then ransacked the built-in cabinets in an effort to find anything to free himself. The mess infuriated Daniel, who'd grown tired of the man's ranting. Now it was time for the reveal. Taking off the dark tortoiseshell glasses he stood for a moment, allowing the truth to sink in. The moment Peter looked into Daniel's eyes, he knew instantly who his abductor was.

"It's you from the Hotel Papiar, isn't it? What's this all about?" Then the penny dropped. "Look, man, she's a friend, you would have done the same in my shoes. Nothing personal, just looking after my own. Be reasonable and just let me go. You've had your fun and I'm duly chastised. Let me go."

The begging brought a response Peter hadn't expected. Without uttering a word, Daniel produced a gun from his jacket packet and fired, releasing its potentially lethal ammunition into Peter's arm.

"You fucking lunatic, you've shot me!" Peter screamed, looking down at his torn shirt and observing what looked like a small dart sticking out of his arm. "What have you done?"

These were the last words Peter slurred before passing out on the marbled floor.

Daniel had planned to spend the night in Bristol but decided to move Peter's unconscious body under the cover of darkness, loading it onto the upright trolley, which had been designed to move fridge-freezers, he'd brought with him from Cornwall. Before strapping Peter to its steel struts he dressed him with his suit jacket then pulled him with some effort back up the oak staircase. He wheeled the trolley through an interconnecting corridor to the adjoining three-car garage where, alongside a silver Porsche and the Range Rover he'd just driven up from Cornwall was parked the white transit van, looking out of place beside the premium vehicles. Stopping momentarily to catch his breath, Daniel propped the trolley by the van and produced a set of keys from his jacket pocket. Unlocking the back door, he undid the straps securing the body to the trolley and hauled it inside. Peter murmured as his head connected violently with the side of the van, then slid back into oblivion. After securing Peter's hands and feet with duct tape, Daniel loaded the trolley beside him, along with other provisions, then slammed the door shut and locked it. Going back into the house, he closed all doors, turned off lights, and set the intruder alarm before setting off on the two-hour journey back to Cornwall.

Back at Bluebell Cottage, Ethel's thoughts again strayed to the stranger she'd seen at Hydlebury Farm, wondering what he was going to do with the property. There seemed to be a popular trend for people upcountry investing in country residences as holiday homes and if that was the new owner's plans for Hydlebury Farm then there was nothing she could do about it. After she'd heard him leave she had snuck out to take another look at his handiwork, which displayed signs of barricading rather than renovation. As she viewed the makeshift repairs, the sinking feeling in the pit of her stomach returned, warning her something wasn't quite right.

The way the man had gone about barricading the property with industrial-sized bolts seemed to be a bit excessive given its isolated location, bringing uncharitable thoughts that the stranger was up to no good.

Chapter 9

Hydlebury Farm Cellar
Cornwall

When Peter regained consciousness, the first thing that assaulted his senses was an overwhelming stench of mould and damp. As his vision cleared, a muted light revealed a wooden structure, which had been fashioned into two compartments built up against a timber wall. The structure looked fairly new and robustly constructed, with strutted doors secured by two padlocks. Looking through the bars of his cell, Peter nervously took in his surroundings, wondering where the freak was and what he was going to do to him. Compared to the last place; a designer bathroom inside a house he'd never seen, this dump was hell, instilling him with a renewed sense of fear that shook him to the core. As he frantically sought through his memory banks, nothing jumped out to ease his apprehension. In the house there were no windows in the bathroom and no way of knowing whether it was night or day or where he had been held prisoner. Looking at the date and time on his wristwatch Peter realised it had been five days since his abduction and some two hours since he'd been removed from the house. During that time, Peter could have been taken anywhere in the country.

He remembered going to help the creep from the gym in the multi-storey car park, when he was trying to get into his van, followed by a stab to his neck, falling, then everything had gone black. When he came to in the house, he found himself chained to a radiator and had searched through everything within reach to help him escape. In the end, he was reduced to eating the food and water left by the abductor and making use of the bathroom facilities. The last thing he remembered was his abductor returning to the house, revealing his identity, then a dart being fired into his arm. Looking up a set of stairs leading up to a floor-boarded ceiling and trapdoor, he knew he must be below ground-level. As his eyes rested on a wooden bench with metal restraints in the centre of the room, and the array of tools on the wooden cabinetry, Peter knew this was serious payback.

Peter had been in and out of consciousness and transported from one place to another, like the commodities he skilfully manoeuvred in his job as a stockbroker. As soon as the thought entered his head, his hopes raised a little that someone from Stock Beechley would alert the police when he failed to show up for work. Unauthorised absence was unheard of in his line of work, bearing in mind the amounts of money they handled. High-profile clients demanded nothing less than perfection and constant attention when it came to their portfolios; some of them would be screaming from the rafters when he wasn't at their beck and call. It was Monday evening when he'd been abducted and he was still in his work suit. It was now Saturday morning. His peers would be in a flap.

His wooden prison contained a steel bucket, which Peter assumed was toilet facilities. The other luxuries his captor afforded him were two packs of bottled water and a box containing chocolate, prepacked sausage rolls and pasties. In an effort to stave off a raging thirst from the drugs swirling around in his body, Peter ripped off the plastic encasing the bottled water and gulped half a bottle in one go. Thirst quenched, he realised it was his captor's intention to keep him alive; at least for the time being. As his eyes scanned the supplies, he estimated there was enough for three to four days tops, if he eked it out. It suggested his abductor planned to be away for a while.

The cell was eight paces by eight; just wide enough for Peter to stand and stretch out with both arms and touch the wooden bars either end. They were at least four inches thick and screwed solidly in place. The padlock on the outside securing the strutted door was of a chunky metal construction and, although he could reach through the bars to touch and tug at it, there was no way to release it. Casting his eye around the adjoining cell, he could see it mirrored his in design and also contained a steel bucket and bottled water. The preparation of the other cell led him to believe that some other poor bastard would go through the same trauma. The question was: who?

Another day passed in solitary confinement, with Peter on tenterhooks, wondering how long it would be before the freak returned to finish what he started. Beneath the strong stench of damp and the stale odour emanating from his own body, there was another pungent aroma, which as yet he could not define. Whatever it was, he knew it wasn't going to be good. With limited water and food, time was running out. He'd already drunk half of the bottled water in an effort to flush out the effects of the drugs but he still felt out of sorts.

His original estimate of four days was shot out of the water as he faced the stark reality of his hellish predicament. Dehydration and starvation would be nipping at his heels if help didn't arrive soon. Normally up-beat and optimistic, for the first time in his life Peter felt totally despondent and with all hopes fading, he slumped back on his haunches and cried. When the tears dried, helplessness gave way to simmering anger, building until he found himself screaming aloud.

"Let me out of here, you fucking bastard. Help, someone please help me!"

Peter screamed for his life until he no longer had a voice then he fell in a crumpled heap on the floor.

The desperation of his situation started to play tricks with his mind. His life in its entirety flashed before his eyes. All those months in the gym, honing his body to muscled perfection, only to be imprisoned like a butterfly in a jar and, like the butterfly, which fluttered around madly looking for a means of escape, he still had his strength but no way out. Then it hit him; perhaps all that weight-lifting could be an advantage. Looking at the wooden prison with fresh eyes and having established earlier that there was no give in either side of the walls, the only other option was the bolted door, which was embedded on hinges. As he studied the structure he wondered whether, if he could weaken the hinges enough to release one side of the door, there might a chance of getting out of the cell. Escaping the cellar was another matter but he would deal with one thing at a time. Going to a place in his mind where he zoned in on a strict discipline; a practice he used regularly in the gym to achieve results, taking off his suit jacket Peter lay down on the cell floor, stretched his legs out, and started pounding in cycles of twenty continuous thumps, then rested and continued the routine. At first there was no give but as his powerful legs pounded, between thumps he thought he heard a cracking sound. Scrambling to his feet, Peter inspected the hinges and saw a hairline crack in the wood surrounding them, giving him a glimmer of hope. Inching his fingers between one of the hinges, he started to pick at one of the three screws which secured the hinge, trying to ease it out of its steel casing, but although he managed to pull it out there wasn't enough leverage for Peter to unscrew it. Frustrated, he grabbed the door frame and began to shake it with an almighty force, which made the door rattle beneath his hands. It was then that he noticed the screws in the hinge nearest the floor had loosened much further than those at the top.

Dropping to his knees, Peter rubbed his eyes free of the sweat trickling down his face before starting the delicate operation of wriggling the screws out of their casing. Bit by bit, the first screw slowly moved upwards, enough for him to get a grip on it. Then, with it firmly between his fingers, he started to turn it until it flew out of its steel casing and fell to the floor. Peter could hardly believe his luck as he stared down at the screw by his knees. With a sense of victory and renewed hope, he took up his position on the floor and continued pounding furiously at the door, hoping the vibrations would loosen the other screws enough for him to pull them out. With the gruelling repetition, his legs began to weaken and he knew if he kept it up there would be a likelihood of serious injury. Wheezing from exertion, he stopped and propped himself against the wall, massaging the burning pain in his calf muscles, trying to breathe new life into his throbbing legs. Taking another look at his watch, he realised it was well over two hours since he'd begun thrashing against the door but as his life depended on getting out of the underground prison, he wasn't ready to give up.

Weighing up the task ahead of him, Peter rested a while to get his strength back before starting again. With hopes of escape swirling in his brain and on the brink of exhaustion, his body started to shut down and Peter slid into a trance-like condition. Suspended between consciousness and reality, his pain momentarily disappeared as he floated outside his body, looking down at himself slumped against the cell wall.

Peter remembered thinking that if this was what it felt like when you left this world he would embrace the release from his worldly shackles. A shimmering whiteness began to engulf him, taking control of his thoughts and movements until they were no longer his. Powerless to resist the overwhelming force, Peter found himself in another dimension, where he felt no fear; just a terrible sadness at the loss of a life that wasn't his own. In this dimension, he was transported to another time, where he was forced to witness a pubescent boy rape and strangle a young girl. As she took her last breath, the girl's face at the moment of death was clearly etched in his brain, making him scream out in horror and bringing him back to reality.

"Why did this happen? Why couldn't I help her? What sort of monster would kill a little girl? Why, why, why? And why me? Answer me, PLEASE answer me!" Peter's bellows bounced off an unhearing God.

After that, everything went black. The next thing Peter remembered was convulsing on the floor of his wooden cell. As the tremors subsided, he could smell the stench of death in the aftermath of the gruesome vision. Recognising that it was the same hideous odour he had detected earlier brought the realisation that this was also the girl's last resting place. Bearing witness to the young girl's death tipped Peter over the edge and in a fit of pure rage he lashed out violently against the cell door. The wood cracked and something dropped onto the floor, rolling beside him. As he reached over to see what it was, he discovered his almighty rage had given him the strength to kick out the top hinge. Stumbling to his feet, he gripped the door and started to push it outwards. It moved forward without resistance until he had created a space large enough to allow him to squeeze through. Grabbing his jacket, he put it on and manoeuvred his body onto the other side. By this time, the light, which he had correctly deduced was powered by a generator, had started to fade, meaning that very shortly he would be plunged into darkness.

With no time to lose, Peter ran up the wooden staircase and flung himself against the trapdoor, trying to dislodge it, but it was locked on the other side and all his efforts to shoulder it open were futile. Deflated that he'd come so far only to be thwarted by another hurdle made him want to give up. Suddenly, the image of the dead girl's face flashed before his eyes, forcing Peter to face the stark reality that if he didn't get out of the underground prison before the freak returned, he would suffer the same fate.

Stumbling down the stairwell, he began searching the rack of tools, looking for something to smash through the trapdoor. He spied a lethal-looking axe lying on the cabinetry just below the racks. Picking it up, he charged up the stairs and started to hack at the wooden frame above his head. The moment he pulled his arm back and took a swing at the trapdoor, he knew he was on a hiding to nowhere. The confined space at the top of the stairwell allowed no room to get the leverage he needed to do any significant damage. In a fit of temper, he threw the axe, which rebounded off one of the walls, coming to rest with a loud thump at the far end of the cellar.

Climbing back down the stairwell, his mind was set on finding something to gouge out the framework surrounding the trapdoor; something solid with a long handle that would allow him to strike up. Then, when he was halfway down the stairwell, he heard a noise. Stopping in his tracks, he listened. In the distance, he picked out the sound of a car engine, meaning one thing: the abductor was back. Scrambling down the remaining stairs, Peter sprang into action. Searching through the array of tools for something to arm himself with, he spotted a nail gun. He grabbed it and scrambled back into his cell, pulling the gaping door to and leaning against a small niche between the wall and two cells, which was big enough to conceal the right side of his body and the nail gun.

***

Daniel had been on a mission, knowing there was limited time to snatch Jenna and return to Cornwall before the great hulking oaf in the cellar died. He formulated a plan of where and when the abduction would take place. Leaving nothing to chance, he decided to use the dart gun that had sedated Peter Shaney, as opposed to grabbing her and risking a struggle where she could easily slip from his grasp and without doubt outrun him.

Jenna's early morning route took her past a rank of brightly illuminated shops then under an archway between an office building and a hairdressers. The passageway on the other side of the archway was obscured from view of the road and the only risk was other pedestrians passing through but there were very few at that time in the morning. It was the perfect place for the abduction. The time had come to put his plan into action.

The moment Jenna ran past the parked van and around the corner she sensed something was wrong. Entering the dark passageway, a clicking noise echoed in the deserted space. Something whizzed past her, scraping her neck like a charging hornet, prompting her to stop and bring her hand up. As she touched the contours of her neck, Jenna discovered that whatever had hit her had taken a chunk out of her flesh, leaving a wet, sticky substance in its wake. She instinctively knew it was blood. Whatever had hit her was no freak blow and she started to run through what remained of the passageway to get away from whatever lurked in the dark, confined space. Behind her, something emerged from the darkness. She heard a second click then a missile pierced her leg, ripping through her Lycra jogging pants and digging deep into her thigh. In mid-step, she was disabled. She fell to the ground like a wounded animal. The next thing she was aware of was a pair of rough, powerful hands grabbing at her. Unable to move or cry out for help, Jenna felt her body being lifted and carried away. After that, everything went black.

With Jenna slung across his shoulders, Daniel started to walk through the passageway, when a noise made him freeze in his tracks. Sidling up against the wall, he heard the owner of a nearby newsagents' humming to herself as she opened up shop, blissfully unaware that a short distance away an abduction was taking place. He listened whilst the woman opened the door to the shop and let herself inside.

Satisfied the shopkeeper was out of sight, Peter adjusted Jenna's weight on his shoulder and moved quickly through the passageway and out the other side. Keeping a visual for passing traffic, Daniel ran to his van, which was double-parked outside a rank of shops. He placed Jenna inside the back of the van just as a car's headlights illuminated him with their full beam. Trying desperately not to panic, he quickly shut the door and turned away from the light. Walking round to the driver's side, he got in behind the wheel as the car cruised past without incident and stopped at the traffic lights ahead. Beads of sweat ran down Daniel's face from his exertion, and nerves kicked in. He'd been fortunate as, if the passing car had been seconds earlier, the driver would have seen him putting Jenna's unconscious body in the back of his van and the situation would have been very different. Daniel waited for the traffic lights ahead to turn green and let the car drive off before turning the key in the ignition and beginning the journey back to Cornwall.

It was light when Daniel arrived at Lawhitton. Parking the van outside the farmhouse, he unbolted the door and went inside to drop off a holdall. Everything was as he had left it: damp, derelict and undisturbed by human presence, which suited his plans entirely. Discarding his overcoat, he wheeled out the trolley he had used to transport Peter Shaney from the basement of his home in Bristol and pushed it outside to the van. Daniel listened. There were no sounds of movement coming from inside the vehicle and, satisfied the woman was still sedated, he opened the back door. Light poured into the van's dark interior, washing over Jenna's unconscious body. He briefly studied her unmoving form before lifting her onto the trolley for transportation to the barn. There was no doubting the woman's beauty.

The vibration from the trolley crossing the bumpy ground stirred Jenna from her unconscious state. Opening her eyes, she saw a sea of fields and in the distance a large, dilapidated barn. She saw she was strapped onto a steel trolley, which was being pushed by the maniac who had attacked her. Jenna knew it would be futile to struggle as it would only alert him to her consciousness and achieve nothing. As the barn loomed closer she frantically searched for a way to escape before they reached their destination, coming to the conclusion that the only option was to feign unconsciousness until he freed her of the restraints.

As he pushed the trolley into the barn, Jenna took in her surroundings, noticing the generator and large water butt feeding a pipe into the floor. As the trolley came to a standstill near a trapdoor in the ground, she was tilted to an upright position and quickly closed her eyes as he came from behind the trolley to face her. She smelt his stale breath as he moved towards her then felt a sharp prod to her shoulder as he checked whether she was still unconscious. It took all her willpower to bite back her fear and remain still as his hand caressed her face then lingered on her shoulder. Fortunately, the moment passed, as his attentions turned to a generator, which was making a whining noise. Sensing movement away from her, Jenna's eyes flicked open. The man had his back to her, walking over to the generator to refill it with fuel from the metal canisters stored beside the water butt. The operation took no more than ten minutes, during which time Jenna, with limited visual scope, studied her surroundings, committing them to memory. She watched as he crouched down and pulled up the trapdoor, letting it fall open with a thud, then stood up and turned around. The movement was quick. Jenna closed her eyes, praying he hadn't noticed she was awake. Luckily, in the split second as he turned around, Daniel had been too preoccupied rubbing dirt from his hands. In the brief moment, the image of her abductor's face burned into the back of Jenna's closed eyes. Initially, there was nothing she recognised about the man but something in her memory began to stir, making Jenna feel her abductor was someone she knew.

Each advancing step pounding on the dirt floor brought him closer towards her. There was no time to lose. If she was going to make a bid for freedom, she had to do it now, before he bundled her through the trapdoor to whatever lay beneath. Seconds later, his rough hands were on her and the nylon restraints strapping her to the trolley were released. Before she could collect her thoughts, she was hoisted like a sack of coal over his shoulder. Stopping momentarily to apportion the weight, Daniel started to walk the short distance to the trapdoor.

Do something; anything. Don't let the bastard take you down there! The screaming in her brain propelled Jenna into action.

As Daniel took the first step on the wooden staircase, his shoulder lurched sideways, making him stagger against the wall and drop his load, which fell down the remaining stairs to the bottom. Jenna rolled to a stop, stunned but unhurt. In the vital seconds whilst she struggled to get to her feet, her attacker was upon her. Grabbing her violently by the shoulders, Daniel straddled her. Venting the full might of his anger on the helpless woman beneath him, he started pounding her head against the wooden floor.

"Pleeeeaase, pleeeeeeeeaase don't, let me go, let me go, you bastard!" Jenna screamed but nothing stopped the demon on top of her.

Before she passed out, Jenna looked into his face and saw evil personified. She also recognised him at last: he was the same man she'd seen in the vision at Christmas Steps and who had accosted her in the Hotel Papiar. After that the pounding stopped, everything went black, and once again she slipped into unconsciousness.

Up against the wall in his cell, Peter witnessed the woman fall down the staircase and land on the cellar floor. In the split second it took the abductor to scramble down the stairs after her, Peter leapt into action. Wrenching open the cell door, he slipped behind the abductor, who was too preoccupied hammering the life out of the woman on the floor to notice him disappearing beneath the stairwell, waiting for the moment to strike.

Drawing breath from his straddled position over Jenna's silent, prone body, Daniel eventually looked over at the wooden cells. Something strange registered and it took a moment to realise what it was. The cell housing the other prisoner was empty.

Just as he was about to get up, a sharp pain reverberated through the back of his head. The blow from the butt of the nail gun was delivered with such force that it knocked him off the woman and rendered him unconscious on the floor. Once the abductor rolled off the woman, Peter instantly recognised her.

"Jenna, Jenna, are you alright?"

She could hear a man's voice calling in the distance. As she started to regain consciousness, the fog in her brain began to clear. Opening her eyes, she saw him kneeling over her and instantly recognised the owner of the voice.

"Oh my God, Jenna, are you alright?" Peter helped her to a sitting position.

At first, Jenna was too disorientated to reply. Trying to take in her surroundings, she saw her attacker splayed out on the floor, face-down, a couple of feet away. There were two cells, a wooden bench and a lethal selection of tools waiting for use, leaving her in no doubt that the unconscious freak had torture on his agenda.

Once Peter established Jenna was coherent, he started rifling through Daniel's jacket pockets, quickly finding keys belonging to the padlocks securing the wooden cells. Opening the cell next to the one he'd been imprisoned in, he dragged Daniel's unconscious body into it, bolted and locked the padlock. Once he was satisfied their abductor was safely behind bars, out of harm's way, his attention turned to Jenna, who was struggling to get to her feet. Peter noticed a patch of blood seeping through her blonde hair. On closer inspection, he saw a gaping hole where her head had been bashed against the floor.

"We need to get you to a hospital, that wound needs attention."

There was no protest from Jenna, who was struggling to cope with the horrendous pounding in her head.

"Do you think you can manage those stairs?" Peter pointed towards the wooden staircase leading up into the barn.

"Yes, I'll be alright."

Peter was too preoccupied helping Jenna up the staircase to notice that their abductor had regained consciousness and had his hands through the cell bars, unlocking the padlock. Daniel, who by nature was paranoid, always had back-up contingencies, which paid off handsomely. This time, the contingency was a set of spare keys secreted through a small hole in the lining of his trouser pocket, secured in place on a large safety pin. All he had to do was pick the safety pin back through the hole in his pocket, release the steel pin, and the keys fell into his hand.

Once the padlock was released, Daniel flung open the cell door and grabbed a pickaxe from the floor at the side of the cells. Just as Peter was manoeuvring Jenna onto the third step, Daniel leaped behind him and plunged the pickaxe deep between his shoulder blades. The bodybuilder screamed and fell into a heap at the bottom of the stairs, leaving Jenna exposed and paralysed with fear. She offered no resistance as Daniel stepped over Peter and dragged her back down to the open cell, flinging her inside.

Once the padlock was bolted, Daniel turned his attentions back to the bodybuilder. Peter was bleeding profusely from the wound in his back. He posed no threat. The pickaxe made a sickening squelch as Daniel pulled it out of the muscled back, bringing with it a wad of skin and a fountain of blood, tearing a gaping hole in his jacket in the process.

Daniel momentarily stopped to admire the sharpness of the blade that had ripped into the bodybuilder's back like a knife into soft butter. Turning it over in his hands, he placed it with the other tools on the cabinetry then dragged the unconscious man to the wooden bench. The effort made him breathless as he hoisted him onto it, face-down, tying his hands and feet with zip-ties. Selecting a pair of sharp scissors from the cabinetry drawer, Daniel cut through Peter's trousers. He started from the legs, moving up to the seat of his pants and through his suit jacket and shirt, peeling them aside and exposing the man's body. The sight of the bodybuilder's perfectly toned buttocks excited Daniel, who felt his erection straining against his trousers. Old memories started to resurface where, in another lifetime as a soldier, he had raped and defiled powerless young recruits under his charge. Unzipping his pants, he got on top of the bench and plunged his hard, pulsating penis deep inside the bodybuilder's back passage. Peter, who was drifting in and out of consciousness and losing an alarming amount of blood, offered no resistance to the man who pumped away on top of him until he was fully satisfied.

Jenna, now fully coherent, the dizziness and pounding in her head having subsided, watched in helpless horror through the cell bars, screaming for him to stop. Nothing stopped Daniel, though, who continued sodomising Peter until he came to a shuddering climax. After it was over, he calmly climbed off his victim and zipped up his pants then, double-checking the restraints on the bench were still secure, he walked over to the cells at the far end of the cellar. The woman inside saw him coming and cowered back against the wall as he peered inside, inspecting his prey.

"You are next, bitch, and I have something very special in mind for you." Daniel lewdly grabbed his crotch to emphasise the point. Just as he was about to turn on his heel, the intention leaving her to stew alone, something happened to make him stop dead in his tracks. Instead of the spirited screaming and begging, the woman had suddenly gone very quiet, then she opened her mouth to speak.

"Do you remember me?" The voice coming from his prisoner was childlike.

The temperature had plummeted, making him shiver. Jenna stood rigidly, staring at him with dull, milky-white eyes, her face resembling a death mask; no longer recognisable as the beautiful woman that drove him to distraction. A crackling force emanated from her then something akin to the struggling carcass of a mutant butterfly emerged from her body and came to rest beside her. As the shape before him metamorphosed and started to take on a human form, Daniel found he was powerless to move or look away.

Once the transformation was complete, the manifestation became an embodiment of a young girl; the same young girl he'd seen earlier when he'd discovered the shallow graves, triggering more violent memories. Flashbacks bombarded Daniel's mind, transporting him to another time, and a horrendous crime. He saw himself back in the cellar, watching as a young boy dug a grave then stuffed a small, battered body into the shallow hole in the void under the floorboards. As he looked down into the grave, the face of a young girl stared back at him, leaving him in no doubt that the apparition controlling him and the girl were the same being. His mind reverted to a time centuries ago when, as a boy of fifteen, the killing spree started. A struggle of wills prevailed as he fought against the voice and the image of the young girl in his head, returned from death to confront him. Spasms of fear shook his body as he lashed out at the apparition's controlling force. Inside the cell, Jenna stood motionless. Beside her, the force began to gain momentum, its shimmering form gliding over to the bars of the cell and disappearing straight through them, coming to rest inches away from Daniel.

Daniel stared in horror as the force doubled in size and merged with his body. In that moment, he felt a pain so extreme that he fell to his knees, screaming for his life. After what seemed an eternity, when he thought his life was over, the excruciating pain stopped then the apparition left him as suddenly as it had entered his body.

Daniel staggered to his feet, not quite believing what had just taken place. Screams from past victims just before death always lingered, echoing in his mind then followed by blissful silence. He reasoned with himself that this was a passing echo; nothing to worry about. Nothing could touch him, he was invincible.

Possessing no conscience, Daniel felt no residue of regret for the murders he had committed, going on to find other victims to satisfy his demonic lusts. There had been no comeback for the heinous crimes he'd committed but this was different. Something was attaching this entity to an earthbound cord, which had powers beyond his comprehension. It had tried to take possession of him earlier and failed but now through his prisoner it had succeeded in possessing him. As he looked at Jenna standing still in her cell, a thought entered his head. He knew she was the conduit for the apparition and to stop it from manifesting itself again he had to kill her. Hands shaking, Daniel reached into his trouser pocket for the padlock key but just as he was about to unlock the cell the voice was back in his head and he dropped the key.

"You will remember what you did." The childlike voice returned and Daniel's eyes were drawn back to Jenna.

Past lives flashed through his mind, transporting him back through time, seeing himself again as a young boy born to a farming family. The unearthly apparition possessing Jenna transformed itself into a healthy, living child, sitting at a scrubbed wooden table, playing with rag dolls. Suddenly, like a TV screen in a power cut, the flashback stopped, plunging Daniel into a black, monochrome screen. It flickered, producing an image of a field and a girl playing nearby, unaware of his presence.

Daniel instantly knew this was the site of her death; a death he had caused, and at that point he started to lose his grip on all reality. Sliding back through time, he saw himself standing on gallows before a screaming crowd. The executor's pockmarked face loomed before him just before a black hood was placed on his head. The crowd's baying for his blood reached a crescendo then his body fell from a great height and the thick rope round his neck strangled him to death.

Daniel started to hyperventilate, gasping for breath, desperately trying to rid himself of the grisly death vision. As parts of his memory resurfaced, the vision of a young girl's face flashed before his eyes. Piece by piece, he recalled her death with startling clarity. He was not enlightened to the young girl's identity; just the fact he was being held accountable for her death and the rogue soul persecuting him was seeking retribution for the atrocity he'd committed in this past life. His mind was once again locked in battle with the powerful force, refusing to regurgitate the past murder. A struggle ensued. Daniel's earthly dominance stood its ground and broke free of the deathly apparition, which had no place on this earth. Her time was gone, allowing him to win the battle. Like being sucked out of a deep black hole, he was hurtled back to the present with such force he was propelled across the room, crashing against the far side of the cellar. Dazed, Daniel scrambled to his feet, searching for the apparition that held him in its spell; preparing to continue the fight. But the entity had vanished. The only presence he detected was Jenna, who stood quietly watching him from behind the bars of her wooden cell. As he approached, Daniel could see that although her eyes had reverted from milky-white back to opaque blue, there was something lurking behind them that repelled him. Fearing another onslaught from the unknown force, he picked up the keys, turned on his heel and scrambled back up the wooden staircase, closing and bolting the trapdoor behind him.

When Jenna came out of the trance she found her abductor had fled the scene, leaving her imprisoned, with Peter strapped like a butchered animal against the wooden bench. Regaining her senses, she started calling him.

"Peter... Peter... Peter, can you hear me?"

From the confines of her cell, Jenna tried to assess his condition. Blood poured from the axe wound in his back at an alarming rate, seeping down onto the floor. She knew he would bleed to death if they didn't get out of their prison soon. Screaming failed to conjure any human help that may be anywhere in the vicinity, leaving her hoarse and barely able to speak. Compounding the dire situation was the intervention of the supernatural phenomenon taking possession of her body. The possession left her bewildered, wondering why when placed in such a desperately impossible situation she felt so strongly intertwined with the troubled entity.

As if something was directing her mind, her thoughts immediately recalled the recent events that had occurred at Christmas Steps, pushing her analytical brain into overdrive. Instead of being used as a vessel to convey messages from the dead, it seemed there was something more sinister at stake; something she couldn't quite grasp. The entity haunting Christmas Steps was a young woman in her early twenties, who had been murdered by her brother. The presence attaching itself to her in the confines of the underground prison was a young girl, also murdered by a family member. It made no sense to Jenna why she'd been used as a conduit to channel such horrendous images onto her abductor. She dug deep into her spiritual psyche, trying to reconnect with the entity, desperately seeking answers and a way out before Peter bled to death and the madman returned to finish off what he started. Jenna's sixth sense told her their abductor was a serial killer with an unknown agenda and there had to be more at stake than a stupid squabble at a wine bar.

Thinking back to the moment she met him at the Hotel Papiar, she'd half-known then what he was but she had failed to fully recognise him, as a past soul with unfinished business; business which ultimately signalled the end of her life. To fight against something so evil that spanned centuries, reborn time and time again, its sole mission to murder, was hell incarnate.

Trying to find an answer, Jenna briefly toyed with the grotesque idea that his victims had been selected because of a connection to his past lives. The thought made her shudder yet part of her believed this to be a real possibility. To test the theory further, she attempted to cross over to the other side, seeking a connection between the entities at Christmas Steps and those in the cellar. Nothing came and once again her psychic abilities failed her. With no means of escape and no answers from the other side, Jenna was forced to face the inevitable: she and Peter were the next victims on the killer's unknown agenda. In that desperate moment, she knew she would suffer the same fate as the girl buried underneath the cellar floorboards. With no answer forthcoming, and all hope fading, she fell to her knees and prayed that when the time came to face death it would be swift.

Praying focused her mind, making Jenna take in her surroundings with different eyes. She noticed hairline cracks in the middle struts of the cell, creating a ray of hope. Looking more closely, she realised there was a weakness in the structure between the two cells. Following the path of the cracks, her eyes settled on the slatted door of the adjoining cell. She saw two long screws on the floor. Not quite believing her eyes, she blinked to bring the objects back into focus. She realised that in his haste to flee the cellar her abductor had failed to notice the neighbouring cell door was missing vital screws from its hinges and that was how Peter had managed to escape from the cell. All she had to do was to push through the struts to get into the other cell. Jenna started to tug furiously at the wooden structure, which began to wobble under her hands but wouldn't give. Realising that if just one of the wooden struts loosened there might be a possibility of squeezing sideways into the other cell regenerated her thoughts of escape. Grabbing the struts, she tugged with such force that the muscles in her shoulders burned from the strain, making her buckle under the pain. Despite unrelenting efforts, nothing gave way.

Demoralised at the lack of progress, she slumped on the floor. As she lay reflecting on the impossible situation, a smouldering rage started to build into an explosive crescendo where, without warning, she found herself kicking violently against the cell walls. Suddenly, one of the weakened struts cracked, sending her feet crashing into the next cell and in the process tearing a length of wood from the structure, leaving shattered shards in its wake. Shocked by the ferocity of her actions, it took her a moment to realise her leg was stuck between the two cells. Easing it out of the opening, Jenna scrambled to her feet. She flung the damaged strut aside and inspected the opening but the space was still too small. With no alternative route of escape, she found herself breathing in as she attempted to make her body small enough to get through the opening.

Manoeuvring one leg sideways into the other cell, Jenna squeezed through the gap but her shoulders became wedged between the bars. Jenna dropped into a crouch-like position, using the weight of her lower body to dislodge her shoulders. She discovered the opening was slightly wider lower down. Twisting her body backwards and forwards, like teasing a cork from champagne bottle, the wooden struts started to give way and she tumbled through to the other side.

***

Sound travels in the quietness of the countryside and, unbeknown to Jenna, her screams had attracted the attentions of a nearby neighbour.

Knowing the strange noise wasn't caused by foxes, who habitually conducted their amorous shenanigans in the early hours of the morning and not at mid-day, piqued Ethel's curiosity. She'd heard the pitiful wailing several times and failed to recognise the sound but that day it had been particularly loud and continued for some time, enabling Ethel to pinpoint its source as being in the vicinity of Hydlebury Farm. Assuming the new owner was at the property, as she'd heard a vehicle coming and going, Ethel's initial reaction was to steer clear of the farmhouse as she wasn't keen to interact with him. Sounds of sawing and drilling had made her modify her original thinking, from that of a barricading job to the start of refurbishment works on the dilapidated building. Curiosity, however, got the better of Ethel, who decided to snoop around under the cover of dusk, when lights started to go on, helping to confirm which part of the property was occupied. Her plan was to get up close to the farmhouse and look in the window, into the scullery; the only window that hadn't been barricaded with plywood, to see what was going on. If spotted, she would resort to Plan B and simply introduce herself to the new owner.

Over the years in which the farmhouse had been left derelict, Ethel had taken the opportunity to explore Hydlebury Farm and its surrounding land with her pet terrier, Scamp. Utilising that knowledge, and armed with a torch, Ethel climbed through an opening in the hedge, which led into a field at the back of the farmhouse. She picked her way through the brambles surrounding the hedge and made her way over to the farmhouse, skirting round a white transit van and noticing a light coming from the scullery window. She sidled up against the outside wall to get a look inside. Ethel saw a sleeping bag alongside various boxes and tools, which were strewn on the flagstone floor. In the midst of the debris, a man was kneeling down on his haunches, wailing into his hands like a baby.

Disturbed by the sight, Ethel quickly darted away from the window. Knowing something wasn't right, she moved swiftly away from the farmhouse and headed for a light she'd seen in the distance. Increasing her pace to a slow run, the light led her to one of the two large barns nestled beside the river. There was no noise coming from inside.

A padlock lay on the floor by the barn door, leaving it unlocked. Slipping the latch, she quietly stepped inside, leaving the door slightly ajar. In the dimly-lit barn, Ethel discovered a working generator and a large water butt with a pipe leading down the side of a trapdoor, which was bolted on the outside. Turning off her torch and placing it in her jacket pocket, Ethel walked over to inspect the trapdoor.

Chapter 10

Eve Shalinski
Bridewell Police Station, Bristol

It was Eve's fifty-fourth birthday and she was meeting Brenda at the Glass Boat; a restaurant located on a floating harbour, with spectacular views of the city and harbourside. Living in Winterbourne, she could not remember the last time she had come into Bristol, let alone eaten out. Indulgences such as these were a rare occurrence during her marriage to Mark; a lying, controlling cheat who she had divorced a year ago.

Since then, Eve had struggled to pick up the pieces of her fractured life. During the course of the first five years of marriage she had been treated like a princess, making her genuinely love her husband. Then bit by bit the remaining fifteen years of marriage started to sour to the point where Mark had successfully brainwashed her into thinking she was worthless, controlling her every movement, and isolating her from family and friends, and outside influences which might give her any hope or ideas of independence. The only person Eve had befriended outside her marriage was a work colleague called Brenda who, over the years of working for the same company, she'd grown close to and whom she eventually confided in. Once Eve had summoned up enough courage to confess what was going on in her fractious marriage, the flood gates opened, enabling her to reveal the cruel beatings and mind-controlling games which were a way of life.

Confiding in Brenda had been a major breakthrough and changed Eve's life. With the newly found confidence and Brenda's help, she had found the strength to stand up to the sadistic bully she had married, and leave him.

Arriving early, she was greeted by the Maître d' of the Glass Boat and was seated by a window, from where she could enjoy the dockside view, watching passers-by and the comings and goings of surrounding bars and restaurants. As Eve took in her surroundings, thoughts of her disastrous marriage evaporated and her mood lightened. It was a gloriously sunny June afternoon, bringing people out in droves. Sitting on a nearby bench, she observed a young courting couple snuggled closely together, watching the harbourside activity. The man said something to his girlfriend, prompting a smile. It made Eve feel envious of their intimacy.

Then, at the far end of the cobbled walkway which ran the length of the harbourside, a man caught her attention. Something familiar in the gait of his swagger as he approached made her turn in her seat to get a better view. She estimated him to be in his early thirties, with the lean physique of a person who regularly worked out and took care of himself. As he got closer, she saw he was classically handsome, with shoulder-length mousy thick dark hair and chiselled features; a look reminiscent of a long-forgotten matinée idol. Eve was so caught up with the man that it took her a moment to register he had stopped in front of the restaurant. Embarrassed she had been caught watching him, Eve fiddled with the menu in an effort to avert her eyes.

Behind dark aviator glasses, the man was able to take in his surroundings at leisure. On approaching the harbourside he had noticed an attractive older woman watching him from the Glass Boat. As he came level with the floating restaurant, he took off his glasses and looked straight at the woman, wondering whether she was someone he knew.

Glancing at the contents of the menu, from the corner of her eye

Eve saw the man take off his glasses. Something stirred uneasily inside Eve as she felt his presence linger outside the window. Compelled to look up, she found herself staring into hypnotic, hazel-flecked eyes.

The moment their eyes met, Eve was in no doubt she knew the person standing before her but the man showed no signs of recognition. Whatever made him stop had passed. Placing his glasses back on, he turned and strolled off, leaving Eve in a turmoil and not quite believing what she'd seen. Instinctively, she knew it was him, but common sense told her it was impossible. The person she'd seen was young enough to be her son, not the lover she'd known all those years ago.

***

With the onset of modern technology, policing had come a long way since 1985. Cold cases were now being solved some fifteen, twenty or twenty-five years later. It was a challenge DS Sylvia Piconya embraced and looked forward to, having been recently seconded to Avon & Somerset Police from Basingstoke. It had not been the promotion she had hoped for but as her brother Joe lived in Bristol it came with an added bonus.

DS Piconya had been handed several cold cases, one of which was that of Jane Adams. As she picked up the file, for some unknown reason her mind wandered back to an incident at the front desk a couple of days before. She remembered the middle-aged woman coming into the station, insisting she'd seen a missing suspect wanted for the murder of his sister in the mid-eighties. Sylvia had been loitering by the front desk, talking to one of the PCs about another case, when the commotion caught her attention. The sergeant on the front desk, clearly overworked and disinterested, went through the motion of taking down details, assuring her the sighting would be passed on to the appropriate persons. In reality, with the wave of new cutbacks and staff shortages, it would be added to a long list of outstanding cases waiting to be investigated.

Something the woman said to the sergeant struck a chord in Sylvia's brain, however, prompting her to take a closer look at the file. As her eyes rolled over the handwritten notes made over three decades earlier, the name Tommy Adams screamed out at her. It was the same name the woman had kept mentioning. Coincidences were pretty rare in her book, convincing her that the incident at the front desk and the cold case were connected in some way. She was still poring over the report, contemplating getting the woman's details from the desk sergeant, when a call came in from the owner of an art gallery in Christmas Steps.

Davina McCreedie had been in the back office doing her accounts when the bell on the gallery door rang, announcing the arrival of a customer. Davina went through to the gallery. Alarm bells started to ring when she recognised him as the man she'd seen loitering around Christmas Steps several days earlier. As he browsed through the artwork, Davina became aware that the man, who was taking sly glances towards her, and outside into the street for signs of passers-by, was not interested in art. She found herself intimidated by his presence. He had showed no signs of leaving and in a panic she'd gone into the back office to call the police, convinced a volatile situation was developing. When the desk sergeant took the call, the details were relayed to DS Piconya, who with another colleague was immediately dispatched to investigate. As Christmas Steps was a stone's throw away from the police station and the call had been dealt with so swiftly, the man in question was still in the gallery when they arrived on the scene.

Daniel heard the doorbell chime as two police officers entered the gallery. From the corner of his eye he noticed the owner appear from a back room and saw her talking to the officers, one of whom approached him. It took every bit of self-control not to turn round and rip the head off the interfering bitch, who he realised had called the police. As the police officer addressed him, Daniel calmly turned away from the piece of driftwood he'd been inspecting to face her. Smile firmly plastered on his face, giving the illusion he had no cares in the world, he responded courteously, studying her carefully as she questioned him about his activities around Christmas Steps. As the questioning progressed, Daniel frantically wondered how they'd got him in their sights. Looking at it from the gallery owner's perspective, he realised then that his own actions had given him away. He was only there because the vantage point from the gallery's big glass windows gave him a perfect view of the recruitment agency and with his obvious interest in activities outside the gallery, he must have looked suspicious. He cursed his carelessness.

The other police officer, an acne-faced youngster, joined them, standing silently by his partner and sizing him up. Daniel's fury grew as the questions became more intrusive and then it started to dawn on him they had no idea what he was up to. The story he concocted was that he was a tourist from Birmingham, named Jason Holden, with a keen interest in medieval history, which Christmas Steps had in spades. For an uncomfortable moment, Daniel got the impression the police woman had seen through his lies. Compounding his fears, she reached into her jacket pocket and retrieved a small notepad, into which she wrote down his name and bogus contact details. Just as she was about to question him further, the radio on Acne's shoulder crackled into life, distracting the woman's train of thought. PC Esklick walked to the back of the gallery for privacy. Moments later, he beckoned to his partner.

The incoming call turned out to be a stroke of luck for Daniel, as the police officers were summoned to attend another scene and, for the time being, the spotlight was off him. He smiled slyly to himself at his good fortune, knowing the false name and address would lead them to dead ends. The incident had taught him a valuable lesson as he was escorted out of the gallery, back down Christmas Steps, and sent on his way. As much as it irked him, he knew he couldn't go back to the gallery and deal with the interfering bitch. But now she was firmly on his radar. One day, he would walk back into her life when she least expected it and make her pay the price for her interference.

After leaving the gallery, DS Piconya and PC Esklick responded to a fight between two women, in front of a row of shops in Broadmead Shopping Centre, a short walking distance away from Christmas Steps. When they arrived at the scene, the fight was in full throttle, onlookers forming a circle around them. Some had taken out their mobile phones and were filming the incident. When the police officers were spotted, mobile phones were discretely hidden and onlookers moved aside, allowing them to pull the warring women apart.

It never ceased to amaze Piconya how callous the general public were; no one had the sense to try and stop the fight. Sadly, she knew the dark side of human nature; the fighting women viewed as a bit of sport, which would no doubt be posted on social media later. Keeping the screeching women at arm's length, DS Piconya and PC Esklick established that the fight had started over a scrawny-looking man who was furtively kicking his heels on the corner of the street, a safe distance away. Faced with the prospect of being brought into custody, the women reluctantly settled their differences, were given a warning, and told to head to their respective homes.

Before leaving, both women looked expectantly at the man; the subject of their fight, hoping the pathetic specimen of manhood would make a choice. The lines were clearly drawn and decisions had to be made but after a moment's hesitation he thought better of it and turned on his heel. Skulking away into the distance, he left both women bitterly disappointed, looking like a couple of fools.

Back at the station, PC Steve Esklick began typing up reports of the Broadmead Shopping Centre and Christmas Steps incidents, leaving DS Piconya to focus on the cold case left on her desk. Picking up the file, she studied its cover.

Jane Adams, 1985.

Sitting in front of her laptop she skim-read the handwritten notes, mentally highlighting salient points that caught her eye; an exercise she found invaluable when dealing with large caseloads. At the top of her list was Tommy Adams, the main suspect and the victim's brother, who had mysteriously disappeared. Trawling through the notes she learned that the father, Donald Adams, died not long after his son's disappearance, his strange injuries indicating that foul play had taken place, with Tommy once again the likely suspect. With no other leads, the search had focused on Tommy's girlfriend. Following extensive news campaigns seeking the public's help, and with police tracing her name through the banking system, Eve Shalinski had presented herself at Bridewell Police Station.

It transpired that Eve had left Tommy and was in hiding, fearful of the repercussions for deserting him. As DS Piconya read her former colleague's notes, it became evident that Eve Shalinski, who was away from the property at the time of the murder, had no idea what had taken place. She did, however, give the police a list of Tommy's regular haunts to check, but these had failed to reveal anything useful and the search for his whereabouts continued.

The file also held some old photographs, taken at the home of the suspect, depicting Tommy with Eve, in happier times. Holding one of the old photographs in her hands, DS Piconya was immediately struck by the resemblance to the man they had questioned at Steps Gallery. The eyes were the same but whilst the murder suspect's handsome, chiselled face bore signs of scarring around the chin area, the man they'd seen and questioned was without facial blemishes. Also, the person in the photo looked the same age then as the man from the gallery was now – and the photo was taken decades ago. Nevertheless, she couldn't shake the feeling that they were the same person.

Needing clarification, Piconya got up from her desk and went through the open doorway, shouting over the open-plan squad room to PC Esklick. "Steve, can you come here for a moment?"

Esklick, who'd been typing up statements at one of the hot-desks allocated for more mundane duties, looked up from his computer. Scraping his chair across the hardwood floor, he got up and lumbered over to her office.

"Have a look at this."

Esklick took the proffered photograph and studied it for a moment. "Bloody hell, isn't that the bloke we interviewed at the Steps Gallery? But this picture looks like it was taken in the 80s. Just look at those clothes and that hairstyle." He ran a hand over his buzz-cut as he handed the photograph back to Piconya.

Intrigued by the discovery, Esklick hovered over her shoulder, looking down at the photograph on the desk whilst Piconya went through the possibilities in her mind. She remembered the woman who had come to the station a couple of days earlier. Instructing Esklick to retrieve the woman's details from the desk sergeant, Piconya sieved through the old case file until she found what she was looking for.

Esklick returned shortly after, with an incident report containing the woman's contact details. Inspecting the old handwritten notes and the name typed on the incident report, Piconya found they matched. The resemblance of the man in the gallery to the man in the photograph of the missing suspect; the proximity of Christmas Steps, where the murder took place; Eve Shalinski, Tommy Adams' old girlfriend, coming into the station. These were far too many coincidences to be ignored. Piconya shivered in her seat. The cold case was getting weirder by the minute. From the details the desk sergeant had taken, it seemed Eve Shalinski was convinced she'd seen Tommy Adams. Piconya believed the man at the gallery in Christmas Steps matched Eve Shalinski's description, right down to the hazel-flecked eyes.

After her divorce, Eve had reverted back to her maiden name of Shalinski and so it had been that name she had given when reporting the sighting of Tommy, or the man she imagined was him. Reflecting on her actions, Eve regretted going to the police but, after having dinner with Brenda on the Glass Boat and knowing Bridewell Police Station was in the vicinity, she had acted on impulse. Before she knew it, Eve had found herself outside, looking up at the imposing two-storey building. All it took was one step through those revolving doors and there was no going back. Something spurred her on and without realising it she was in the foyer, speaking to the desk sergeant, telling him about the encounter with the man on the harbourside, who she believed was a suspect wanted for a murder committed over thirty years ago. Despite the fact that he looked too young to be Tommy, the startling similarity to the man she once knew continued to plague her.

Eve's imagination ran wild. Why had the man chosen that moment in time to stop? He could have easily walked past the restaurant but he'd stopped and looked directly at her, removing his sunglasses to get a clearer look. When he took off the dark aviators and she stared into those hazel-flecked eyes, her world turned upside down. Years rolled back in her mind, to a time when she had known Tommy Adams. The bizarre encounter made her fret and worry. Two days later, her fears were realised when she received a call on her mobile from DS Piconya.

Despite Eve's protests that she'd made a mistake and the man she'd seen couldn't be Tommy Adams, a meeting was set up at Bridewell Police Station the following evening.

Eve found herself walking over the threshold into the police station once again. After a nervous wait by the front desk, she was ushered into a small, windowless room containing a large desk and three chairs. She was directed to a single chair at the other side of the desk. Recording equipment and a wad of notepads and pens sat on the side, in anticipation of the pending interview. As Eve took a moment to study her surroundings, a door opened and a young, attractive blonde woman in her mid-thirties entered the room, accompanied by an even younger PC, whose face bore acne scars. Fearful of being reprimanded for wasting police time, Eve was surprised to discover they were exceptionally interested in her sighting. The woman, who introduced herself as DS Piconya, showed Eve a selection of old photographs from the file in front of her, from which she quickly chose a picture of her and Tommy. While she had aged in the intervening years, it seemed that the man on the harbourside was the same person looking back at her from the photo; it was as though he was actually Tommy and that throughout the intervening years, apart from his hairstyle, his appearance had remained exactly the same.

"Have you found him?" Eve whispered as she gently fingered the photograph.

"There has been another sighting of the same man but at this stage we cannot confirm his identity," PC Esklick said.

"Thank you for coming into the station. We will keep you informed if there any further developments," DS Piconya assured her, bringing the interview to an end. Handing over one of her business cards, DS Piconya told Eve to call if she had anything else to add to the investigation and escorted her through to the revolving door which led onto the street.

As there was time to kill before the next bus to Winterbourne, Eve decided to get a coffee; to sit and mull over the strange interview with the police. One consolation was that somebody else had seen the same person, and had also thought the resemblance to Tommy too strong to be coincidental. Recounting the events on the harbourside and looking at the old photograph of herself with Tommy had cemented in her mind the fact that the man couldn't possibly be the lover she'd once known. Nevertheless, conjuring up the man's image again, there was no doubt in her mind that whoever he was there was something very off-kilter about him. The moment she looked into his strange hazel-flecked eyes, Eve saw something that chilled her to the very core. In the confines of the small interview room, paranoia getting the better of her, she regretted having blurted out that same thought to the two police officers. Eve had been adamant the person she'd seen was Tommy but she knew now that wasn't possible. Finishing her coffee, she got up to catch her bus, wondering whether she should have left things alone instead of stirring up a past she preferred to forget.

After the interview with Eve, DS Piconya and PC Esklick went back to Steps Gallery to interview Davina McCreedie. They discovered McCreedie's first sighting of the man known by the bogus name of Jason Holden had occurred when she was walking her West Highland terrier. She told them she usually walked Scarlet early in the morning, before starting work, and that it was about 6am when she spotted the man, sticking out like a sore thumb in the deserted city centre. At first, she assumed he was waiting for someone as he was too engrossed looking at his watch to notice her walk by on the other side of the shops. As she walked back up Colston Avenue, she had seen the Range Rover, which had been parked in the same spot the previous morning, amongst other vehicles displaying a resident's permit. As parking was an issue in central Bristol, and she hadn't been able to park nearby, she took umbrage to strangers using the precious parking spots. She was able to give not only a description but also a partial number plate of the vehicle. As PC Esklick wrote the information down in his notebook, Piconya was beginning to form the opinion that the woman was a tad neurotic. McCreedie went on to explain that after she had taken her dog home she had popped out to get some milk from the Spar shop and noticed the same man peering in through Stepz 2 Recruitment's shop window. Walking back up Colston Avenue, she had also observed him getting into the Range Rover, confirming the fact that the partial plate number she'd given belonged to his vehicle.

The cold case of Jane Adams was beginning to take on a life of its own, with the common denominator being Thomas Adams. Two recent sightings of the person matching his description were discredited due to the man's apparent age but still, having seen the man with her own eyes, Piconya was thrown by the startling similarity to Tommy Adams. Another disturbing fact which came to light when questioning Davina McCreedie was that he was loitering around No. 26 Christmas Steps, which, thirty years ago, was the site of the murder. On the whiteboard beside her desk, Piconya picked up a black marker pen and started to summarise her findings. At the top of the board she wrote 'Jane Adams 1985'. In the middle, drawing a large circle, she penned the words 'Hazel Flecked Eyes – scarring to the chin – Tommy Adams'. From the circle several arrows shot out, each with a comment.

- *Jane Adams murdered - residence No. 26 Christmas Steps*
- *Tommy Adams – main suspect*

- *Ex-girlfriend Eva Shalinski – sights man resembling Tommy Adams*
- *Complaint from Davina McCreedie at Steps Gallery – man in gallery acting strangely*
- *Questioning man called Jason Holden - startling resemblance to Tommy Adams – giving bogus contact details*
- *McCreedie sights Holden loitering outside No. 26 Christmas Steps and getting into Range Rover – partial number plate OVR*

DS Piconya looked back at the whiteboard. Everything was a jumble in her mind but staring back at her handiwork she could see a pattern developing that made no logical sense. Who was Jason Holden and what, if anything, had he to do with a murder that had been committed in 1985? As he had already given them bogus contact details, he was well and truly on Piconya's radar as a person of interest.

Chapter 11

Peter Shaney - Missing
Bristol

Peter had been missing for three days and his flatmate was becoming concerned, especially when he failed to turn up for the match on Wednesday night. In the event that they missed each other in the crowds, they would always meet up at the Dog and Duck, but there was no sign of Peter. Clive had tried Peter's mobile numerous times but it kept going to voicemail. Several messages on the answerphone at home from Peter's employers, enquiring as to his whereabouts, set alarm bells ringing. Peter never missed work, no matter how hungover he was, or how hectic his social life became.

Toying with the thought of calling the police, Clive remembered Peter complaining about the extortionate amount he had paid for a season ticket for the multi-storey car park in Park Row. He decided to check it out first, to see if he could find Peter's car. It was 7.50pm when he got into Bristol and drove into the full car park. He remembered seeing a billboard advertising Rhianna's concert at the Colston Hall, which would have brought out fans in their droves, taking every car parking spot in town. The first available space was on the third floor. As he manoeuvred his Audi into the concrete bay, Clive decided to start his search at the bottom and work his way up to the top. Taking the stone staircase down to Level 1, he walked the concrete bays, inspecting each car, looking for Peter's black Mercedes Roadster.

As Levels 1 and 2 proved fruitless, Clive redoubled his efforts in Level 3 but found it much the same; a sea of cars but none of them Peter's, with his distinctive personalised number plate. Clive began to think that he had set himself an impossible task. At Level 6, however, he spotted a black Roadster at the far end, near the lifts. Clive began to run towards it. A horn blasted from an outraged motorist, who was trying to back up and manoeuvre into a tight parking spot. The person in the Mini drove straight into the space, in the process almost knocking Clive over. Normally, he would have given the careless driver a piece of his mind but as he was intent on getting to the other side of the car park, he dismissed the man with a passing two-fingered salute. Reaching the Roadster, he tried all the doors but found them locked. Peering inside the vehicle, he spotted Peter's briefcase. Peter would never go anywhere without this prized possession, which contained everything bar the kitchen sink. Reaching into his jacket for his mobile phone, Clive once again started to dial Peter's number. As the distinct ring tone blasted out he could hear it coming from inside the car, confirming his suspicions that something was seriously wrong as Peter and his phone were almost surgically attached. Heading down to Level 3, Clive jumped in his car and drove to Bridewell Police Station to file a missing person report.

As DS Stacey Weller interviewed Clive Richards, she knew there was a valid case for concern. Peter Shaney had been missing for three days. According to Richards, there had been calls from his workplace and his car was parked in Level 6 at the Park Row multi-storey car park. The flatmate had also taken pictures of the Roadster, clearly showing the briefcase on the passenger seat. He forwarded the images to DS Weller's email address, along with a current picture of Peter Shaney. After accessing the photographs and hearing the account of the man's disappearance, DS Weller deduced that whatever had happened to Peter Shaney must have occurred in or around the car park. Crime scene investigators were dispatched and made short work gaining access to the car. Retrieving the briefcase, they found the mobile belonging to the missing man. There were no signs of a struggle; everything seemed in order. It seemed the vehicle had been locked and abandoned. Dusting the car, the CSI team had been able to lift several fingerprints, which were being processed. The surrounding area was searched and the Roadster removed to a police warehouse for further testing.

The following morning, DS Weller called Stock Beechley, Peter's employers, and quickly established that Peter was last seen on Monday evening. This gave them a date to work with when requesting CCTV footage from the car park management.

Clive Richards had mentioned Peter having an altercation with another man a couple of weeks earlier. According to the flatmate, Shaney went to the rescue of a woman being hassled by a man, which resulted in a scuffle and the man being ejected from the bar. When pressed further on the incident, Richards couldn't remember the name of the establishment and with a healthy supply of bars in Bristol city centre, checking out the lead would be like searching for a needle in a haystack. DS Weller could only hope that Richards' memory would eventually stump up the information. Experience told her that although the incident at the bar may have at first appeared insignificant, in some instances aggrieved parties would take umbrage at being so publicly humiliated. Richards had been able to provide an insight into his flatmate's daily routine, supplying the name and address of a gym Peter frequented; another lead to check out.

Later that day, the Park Row car park CCTV footage was available for viewing. Armed with takeout coffees, George Whitehead – a conscripted police constable from Traffic Division

– and DS Weller started the painstaking task of sifting through endless footage, searching for the black Mercedes Roadster.

At Stock Beechley, they said Shaney was in the habit of working late so Weller and Whitehead used an initial timescale of between 6pm and 8pm. First checking the footage of Monday morning, they pinpointed the time Shaney had parked the car, watching as he exited the vehicle, briefcase in hand. Scrolling forward to a time line starting at 6pm, they focused on views of the bays by the lifts on Level 6. Being early evening, the car park was a hive of activity, with people heading home. By 6.40pm, as the multi-storey started to empty and a battered white van came into view, parking in the bay next to the Roadster. The occupant of the van sat in the vehicle for some time, heightening their suspicions. DS Weller stopped the footage and they leaned nearer, to get a better view. Moving the footage slowly forward onto the next frame, it showed the driver's side door opening and someone getting out of the van. The occupant appeared to be male and wearing a black hoodie, which obscured his face as he closed the door, walked to the back of the van and opened it. Weller and Whitehead watched as the man rummaged inside, pulling out a trunk – which looked bulky rather than heavy, judging by the ease with which he lifted it. After the hooded man slammed the door, they waited for his next move, expecting him to pick up the trunk and head out of the car park. But he just leaned on the side of the van and looked at his watch, appearing to wait for someone.

During the course of moving the trunk, the man's head had remained hidden, frustrating Weller and Whitehead, as the only time they got a glimpse of his face was when he turned sharply, as if reacting to a noise in the distance. Seconds later, the footage showed lift doors opening and both officers recognised Peter Shaney as he stepped out, alone, onto Level 6.

They inched closer to the screen, watching Shaney as he walked the short distance from the lift over the concrete floor to the bay where his Roadster was parked. The white van's occupant had his back to Peter as he approached and appeared to be struggling to open the back door of his van. Peter casually glanced over as he passed, pressing a key fob in his hand and opening the Roadster. He was just about to get in the car when the man by the van turned and spoke to him. There was a slight hesitation, during which time Shaney appeared to recognise the man. Throwing his briefcase in the car, he slammed the car door and followed him back over to the van, where a conversation took place between the men, who appeared to be inspecting the back door of the van. Shaney turned his back on the other man and started to pull the handle, then suddenly he collapsed to the floor. Everything happened so fast that the officers had to rewind the footage to establish what had taken place.

As they painstakingly rewound and froze each frame, Weller and Whitehead zoomed in and saw the man lunge towards Peter's neck. It appeared he had stabbed Peter with something and, given Shaney's quick collapse, it could reasonably be presumed that it was some kind of needle or dart, primed with anaesthetic or worse. Weller and Whitehead saw a box in the rear of the van, which the man moved before hauling Shaney inside, together with the trunk. Stooping down to pick up Shaney's keys, which had fallen out of his hands as he collapsed, the man swiped the fob, locking the Roadster then putting the keys in his pocket. He turned to close the van doors but something distracted him. Following his line of vision, they saw the lift doors opening and a young woman step out. Fearing she would get caught up in the affray, they watched helplessly as the abductor slammed the van doors shut. The woman walked the short distance to a bay on the other side of the car park, where a light blue Fiat 500 was parked. She appeared oblivious to what was happening, intent only on her mobile phone. The man allowed her to pass without incident, presumably satisfied she was too preoccupied to notice what he'd been doing. Weller breathed a sigh of relief as the moment passed. Little did the young woman realise how close she'd come to danger. The abductor waited for her to drive out of the car park then he reopened the back doors and lifted something out of a small cardboard box. Straddling Peter's body, he appeared to be tying Peter's hands then, climbing back out of the van, he yanked Peter's legs out. At that point, DS Weller slowed down the footage and saw a zip-tie in the man's left hand. They watched as he secured Peter's feet then heaved his body deeper inside the van and relocked the door. Walking round the side of the van, the man got into the driver's seat and started the engine, backed out of the bay, and drove round and eventually out of the car park. All this had taken place in a matter of fifteen minutes, during which time Weller and Whitehead were unable to get a full view of the abductor's face.

The footage showed a number plate and the make of the van. Traffic Division were immediately alerted to the situation and quickly charted the vehicle's progress out of the city, heading onto the M5 motorway towards Somerset. Just past Somerset, they lost sight of the white van when a serious accident involving several lorries and multiple cars stopped all traffic in both directions, until emergency services arrived to attend the devastation. The battered white van narrowly escaped the accident and turned off at the nearest junction, heading back towards Bristol and away from the mangled tragedy.

Back at the station, DS Weller gathered her six-person team together and, with the assistance of PC Whitehead, updated them on recent developments. Now it was established they were dealing with an abduction, the investigation was on high alert to find Peter Shaney.

Weller started barking orders. "Sturgers, I want you and Jones to trawl city-centre pubs to find out whether there have been any recent incidents. We know Shaney ejected a man from a bar after he assaulted a friend of his." DS Weller repeated the scant information Clive Richards had given them, knowing it would be a big ask for her team to unearth anything of use.

"Davies and Pembleton, I want you to look over the CCTV footage. Here are the timelines. Get in contact with the DVLA and find the owner of the white van. I also want you to locate the young woman who owns the light blue Fiat 500. See whether the girl noticed anything unusual in the car park, or had a glimpse of the abductor's face as she walked by. CCTV footage shows her briefly looking up from her phone as she walked past the concrete bays. It may have been an automatic reaction to steer herself in the right direction towards her car and in that brief moment she may have noticed something." The two officers nodded their understanding of the task ahead and took the list of the timelines and registration numbers.

"Michaels, you and Tarrant can question Shaney's neighbours. It is evident that this bastard had his victim in his sights before making his move. Find out whether any of them noticed any strangers in the vicinity." Both officers left the briefing room, armed with Peter Shaney's home address and contact details for Clive Richards. "Whitehead, you're with me, we are going to check out Shaney's gym."

Fitkicks was situated in Welsh Back, near the harbourside in Bristol city centre; a convenient location for Shaney who, according to his flatmate, spent a lot of his time working out. On arrival, they were ushered into the manager's office, where they met Dianne Crossby, a no-nonsense brunette who obviously worked out, making Weller aware of her own expanding waistline, briefly regretting she hadn't taken the time to address the ongoing problem. Proffering their IDs, DS Weller explained the nature of their business, showing a recent picture extracted from Clive Richards' mobile phone. Dianne Crossby immediately recognised Peter Shaney as one of her regulars, telling them he came into the gym sometimes in the evenings but mostly early mornings, before work. Dianne operated a split shift pattern with her deputy, Tina Uttridge, and Dianne tended to take the early shifts. When questioned further about Shaney's routine, another name cropped up. Recounting an incident when she was on the front desk one morning as Shaney was leaving, the manager told Weller and Whitehead that he jokingly remarked about his 'shadow', who appeared out of the male changing area just as Peter left through the revolving doors. The 'shadow' Shaney referred to was a new member called Jason Holden, who'd taken to frequenting the gym at the same time.

Sensing they were onto something and knowing Fitkicks would operate a surveillance system, DS Weller requested access to the footage. Dianne Crossby returned minutes later with another body-beautiful, called Tom Curtis; their surveillance and IT expert. Curtis' fingers flew over the keyboard, entering passwords to open the security system. The screen immediately filled with views of the indoor swimming pool, front desk, and weight-lifting section, as well as the treadmills and shots in and outside the revolving doors. It was an impressive system, allowing management to keep an eye on their patrons should anything untoward happen. Dianne instructed Tom to retrieve footage from just over a week ago, directing him to the gym area where the treadmills were located. Scrolling through, the timeline showed 06.23am, Peter Shaney running on one of the five treadmills. Three of the other treadmills were occupied by women, none of whom were of interest to the officers. As Tom was about to fast-forward the footage, a man appeared on the edge of the screen, heading for the empty piece of equipment to the right of Shaney. The man, who was smaller in build, with mousey hair and wearing dark glasses, nodded briefly to Peter Shaney as he got on the treadmill. On the machine, he occasionally took the opportunity to sneak sideways glances at his neighbour. The officers could immediately see why Shaney referred to the man as a shadow; there was something indefinably creepy about his behaviour.

They watched the complete section of footage, showing Peter finishing his routine, getting off the treadmill, completing cooling-down stretches, then entering the changing room to shower. Waiting several minutes, the man got off his treadmill and turned his body to face the surveillance cameras, providing a clear image of his face.

"Freeze-frame that. Can you print that image off for us?" DS Weller pointed to the screen. Tom nodded in response and seconds later presented her with a colour copy of the man in the footage.

"I spoke to that man when he came in to register. If you give me a moment, I will get you his details." Dianne Crossby left the room, returning five minutes later with a print-out of Jason Holden's membership details with address and telephone numbers. DS Weller and Whitehead thanked Dianne and Tom for their help then left the gym.

Back at Bridewell Police Station, enquiries into Jason Holden, the name on the gym membership, drew a blank. Weller suspected that the details given to Fitkicks were all bogus, which, although frustrating, added to her suspicions that the man had something to do with Shaney's disappearance. Otherwise, why go to so much trouble to conceal his identity? The picture retrieved from the gym footage also failed to match up to facial recognition on the HOLMES database. Pondering on the photograph, Whitehead spotted something. To confirm his train of thought, he started sifting through his handwritten notes from several days before. Once he found what he was looking for, he showed DS Weller his notes.

"I think the man in the CCTV footage at Park Row is the same person from the gym."

DS Weller studied the photograph Whitehead selected from the copies she had on her desk, tapping it at the man's wrist as he referred to his notes. Following the line of his finger, Weller caught a glimpse of what looked like a thick silver bangle, just below the sleeve of the man's sweatshirt. Whitehead proffered his notepad, showing his handwritten notes and timelines. Looking at the notebook on the desk, Weller spotted the word 'bangle', circled with a brief description against it as the piece of jewellery had caught his attention. Checking the photograph of the Fitkicks surveillance, Whitehead loaded up the footage of the multi-storey car park. The frame showed the man hauling Shaney's unconscious body into the back of the white van and, for the briefest of moments, the sleeve of his black hoodie rose to reveal his left wrist, upon which was a silver bracelet. Freezing the frame and blowing up the shot of the bracelet with its distinct engraving, Weller could see Whitehead's suspicions had been correct. It was the same piece of jewellery.

"Well spotted, George, let's get this photo on the whiteboard for the team briefing."

As Weller and Whitehead were standing in front of the whiteboard, mulling over what they had so far, PCs Ed Michaels and Karl Tarrant walked into the briefing room. After a brisk greeting, Michaels and Tarrant disclosed their findings at Peter Shaney's address. It transpired that a neighbour had noticed a dark blue car parked along the street, a short distance away from her flat. The neighbour's observations were due largely to the fact that off-street parking was minimal in the area, leaving residents racing to get precious parking spots outside their homes. The woman, who lived in the flat just below Peter Shaney and Clive Richards, hadn't seen the owner of the vehicle and it had been parked there after she returned from shopping but Maria Clarke told them about the man who she came across as she opened the front door earlier on in the evening; apparently lost and looking for another address. Maria said she had thought that the man, who was studying the names on the top flat's doorbell, was acting strangely. As their house number was clearly visible on the side of the building, as was the case with all the other properties in the street, she wondered why he'd taken the time to stroll down the pathway leading to the property when a quick glance would have clearly informed him he had the wrong address. Maria had escorted the man back up the pathway, pointed him in the right direction of number 12, then got in her car. Before she drove off, she glanced in her mirror and saw the man disappear up the street. The description she gave of the man matched the man in the photograph taken from the gym, which was now pinned in the centre of the whiteboard.

Shortly after the discovery was written up on the board, PCs Davies and Pembleton ambled into the briefing room, finding their colleagues talking animatedly about the photograph. Having located the owner of the Fiat 500, a Judith Canning, they told Weller that the woman was initially of little help as she could barely remember the time of day, let alone recall what she was doing over a week ago in a multi-storey car park. Judith Canning's life revolved round a large circle of friends; an annoying fact that was cemented by constant calls and texts received on her mobile whilst Davies and Pemberton tried to question her in the confines of her small bedsit. The girl did, however, remember one thing that struck a chord, which she mentioned after viewing a series of particularly annoying texts from Liam, her boyfriend. It appeared the texts from him also prompted an earlier memory, when she had left Liam's flat after a blazing row. The argument had been so intense that Judith Canning recalled the time and date, which Davies wrote down in his notebook and which tied in with the time of Peter's abduction. On her journey back to her car, Judith had received a barrage of texts from her boyfriend, begging her to come back to the flat. Davies was trying to stifle a yawn while Judith mentioned getting into the lift, taking her to Level 6 of the multi-storey, and texting a response to Liam. She then recalled looking up from her mobile as she walked to her car, briefly spotting a pair of trainers in her peripheral vision. It came as a surprise to Davies and Pemberton when Judith was able to describe the trainers in graphic detail. Then she explained they were a coveted item in a collection of designer sportswear which was on her wish list but which she could not afford. On hearing this information, six pairs of eyes reverted to the photograph pinned in the centre of the whiteboard, where 'Jason Holden' was wearing the same designer trainers Judith Canning had described.

The latest discovery established without a shadow of doubt that the man in the multi-storey and the man in the gym, who had been seen snooping around Shaney's place of residence, were one and the same person. It was now known that their suspect was using another vehicle apart from the battered white van with fake number plates. It was also established that the man, whoever he was, had expensive taste in jewellery and footwear, which meant he earned a substantial salary or had access to money.

***

In another part of Bridewell Police Station, DS Piconya was pondering her cold case and the man who bore a startling resemblance to Tommy Adams. The deeper she delved into the case, the weirder it became. Piconya came to several possible conclusions; Adams had died, moved out of the country, or was living rough. To support the last theory, it appeared that there had been several possible sightings of Tommy Adams living on the streets in Bristol over the years. It was a hard life and often changed the appearance of those who endured it, who could become unrecognisable to family and friends. Adams could be in plain sight under their very noses, the ravages of time rendering the man unidentifiable. Mental health was also an issue to consider, as no person came out of the experience unscathed; especially after a long exposure to vagrancy. With the scant information available, Piconya's gut instinct told her that Tommy Adams, now in his mid-fifties, would likely be dead or mentally unstable. Either way, there was no merit in investigating that angle unless something happened to steer her in that direction.

Switching tack, Piconya started to look more closely into the life of the murdered sister. The file made for gruesome reading when it came to the catalogue of injuries Jane Adams had sustained during the attack leading to her death. It was remarkable that the young woman had lingered in a coma for so long. Turning the page in the report, Piconya continued to read but stopped mid-sentence, not quite believing what she was looking at. Piconya re-read the words on the page, trying to digest them. The report stated that although Jane Adams never regained consciousness, she'd sustained a pregnancy, producing a baby boy who was delivered by caesarean section just a month before his mother passed away.

"My God, this explains a lot," Piconya said aloud, thinking of the ramifications of a child born a product of rape.

The discovery put the cold case on another level now that there was something tangible to grip onto. Tracing a child's progress lost over thirty years ago may not be easy. It occurred to Piconya that there might be some mileage in tracking down the original detectives, who could have some insight as to what happened to the boy.

***

DCI Gerald Spencer had taken early retirement from the force and was content with his life now. During his career with Avon & Somerset Constabulary, he'd been a party to too many terrible things, which spilled over into his personal life, ultimately wrecking his marriage. Sally had left him years ago and he now lived alone, preferring to come and go when and how he pleased, without the constraints of a nagging wife. Secretly, a part of him still missed her but pride pushed away fond thoughts of the woman who, at one time, he had worshipped to distraction. After the divorce, Sally had gone on to meet someone else, and remarried, living another life with a man who gave her the children she craved. Nowadays, Gerald spent the majority of his time on his garden, which he kept manicured to within an inch of its life. He had also developed an award-winning market garden, supplying not only his needs but those of most of the village, who eagerly bought the excess produce for next-to-nothing after orders had been fulfilled with several local shops. The market garden gained notoriety as a thriving business; one in which Gerald took great pride, giving him not only a lucrative income but another lease of life outside the murky arena of crime.

It didn't take Piconya long to track DCI Spencer down. With PC Esklick in tow, she rang the doorbell and waited on the doorstep for some time before the next door neighbour intervened.

"If you're looking for Gerald, love, you'll have to go round the back. He's usually in his garden." The middle-aged woman, leaning on the adjoining fence, indicated to a back gate.

Piconya thanked her and set off with PC Esklick, up the meandering path that ran along the side of the house to the back gate. On the other side of the gate, the gardens were vast and immaculate, spanning at least an acre of land. A spectacular array of flowers in full bloom in the nearby flowerbeds were a feast for Piconya's eyes as she and Esklick ventured further in, where the gardens were laid to lawn. They could see an athletic-looking man with wild silver hair, garbed out in wellies, old combat trousers and a tee-shirt sporting an emblem of a local football team. He was picking runner beans from what appeared to be a bumper crop. Beside him was a large greenhouse, housing all manner of vegetables and standing proudly in the afternoon sunshine, giving a garden centre a run for its money. Completely immersed in the task at hand, Gerald Spencer was unaware he had company. Piconya called out to him as they approached but he returned no response. It wasn't until they were almost on top of the man that she noticed a dangling white wire leading to his ears and realised he was listening to music from an iPhone tucked inside his shirt pocket.

As their shadows crossed his path, Gerald Spencer turned abruptly, coming face-to-face with the two intruders. Startled by their presence, his manner was gruff as he ripped out his ear buds to find out what they wanted. Piconya and Esklick proffered IDs for inspection. Realising they were Force, Spencer's manner softened, ushering them to some nearby benches, where they could sit and take in the sunshine.

"What can I do for you, Officers?" Gerald Spencer sat on a bench opposite and spread out his long legs in front of him.

"I'm after some information about a cold case relating to Jane Adams," DS Piconya replied. At the mention of the name, Spencer's face clouded over.

As they talked, Spencer's long-forgotten memories started to emerge, some of which had escaped the written reports. Away from the responsibilities of an active DCI, Spencer felt more disposed to talk freely about the bizarre incidents surrounding the Jane Adams case. The years fell away, transporting him back to the 1980s, triggering a recollection of the events leading to PCs Davies and Smithers discovering Donald Adams' dead body in the house at Christmas Steps.

Sensing something out of the ordinary was about to be revealed,

Piconya leaned forward slightly, to capture every word from Spencer's mouth. Following her lead, PC Esklick stopped writing in his notebook and looked up at the man, waiting expectantly for the next part of the story. Spencer appeared to question himself before resuming. He recounted the incident told by PC Davies, as to what had taken place inside the house. Piconya and Esklick listened as Spencer told them that, after finding Adams' body in an upstairs bedroom, PC Smithers had been left upstairs whilst Davies went down to call for back-up and get some fresh air; the stench of death making him nauseous. As he finished the call to Bridewell Police Station, Davies heard screams coming from the house and ran back inside, up the stairwell to the top floor. On the landing, he found Smithers suspended halfway up against a wall, apparently held by the throat by an unseen force. Horrified at the sight, it took Davies a couple of seconds to make sense of what he was seeing. As Davies jumped up to reach his colleague, who was choking and struggling against the invisible force, his own body was scooped up and flung against the far wall, then he tumbled down the stairwell to the first floor. Stunned from the attack, he struggled to his feet and ran back up the stairwell, where he saw Smithers falling to the floor like a rock being dropped from a great height. Quickly scanning the top floor landing for signs of what had attacked them, Davies saw nothing. Smithers was on all fours, gasping for breath. Davies grabbed his colleague and bundled him down the narrow staircase, out of the property and onto the narrow, cobbled street.

Spencer, who'd been the lead figure on the rapid response team and one of the first responders at the scene, discovered the two distressed officers outside No. 26 Christmas Steps. Whilst the rest of the team went inside the building, he stayed with Davies and Smithers, trying to establish what had happened to the officers. Smithers was unable to speak coherently and it was Davies who gave his version of the events that had unravelled inside the house.

Spencer had looked up at the property and in doing so witnessed something defying the laws of nature. The thing he saw with his own two eyes in the upstairs window was unlike anything he had come across before. After hearing what Davies had told him, he was convinced it was the supernatural phenomenon which had attacked his officers.

The strange tale flabbergasted Piconya and Esklick, neither of whom had come across anything quite like this before. Spencer admitted that, had he not seen the apparition in the upstairs window himself, it would have been easy to dismiss the fantastical account Davies had spun. However, as his officers on the rapid response team reported nothing extraordinary at the scene, it transpired that Spencer had kept his mouth shut about the sighting; a decision he bitterly regretted.

Davies and Smithers went on to became the butt of many a joke dished out by fellow officers, who preferred to sweep the supernatural occurrence under the carpet rather than open their minds to the unknown. Spencer painted a sad tale as, one by one, they turned their backs on their two colleagues, labelling them pranksters. As a result, Davies, to save face, convinced himself the incident had been a figment of his imagination, despite the fact he'd sustained broken ribs; an injury consistent with being flung against a wall, ricocheting off it, and tumbling down the first-floor stairwell, all of which was documented in his report. Five years after the incident at Christmas Steps, Davies was caught up in a violent domestic and died from knife wounds; the result of defending the battered wife. Spencer told Piconya and Esklick that Smithers never recovered from the incident at Christmas Steps, which had turned his mind, forcing him to leave the force.

Spencer kept in contact with Smithers for a while, calling him several times to see how he was doing and sending Christmas cards, but as the years passed, contact diminished. He had retained his address but the last time he called Smithers, the landline number registered as invalid.

Taking the piece of paper on which Spencer had written Smithers' address, DS Piconya looked at it briefly before putting it into her pocket. The village of Lamerton in Devon was a place unfamiliar to her and would undoubtedly involve a lengthy journey. She briefly wondered whether Smithers still lived at the same address, making a mental note to get Esklick to check before they made the journey to Devon.

Before leaving Spencer filled them in on the family dynamics, the fact that, beside Tommy Adams being suspected of his sister's murder, Donald Adam had died also in mysterious circumstances. Hearing the peculiar circumstances of his death made Piconya shiver and wonder whether the man had fallen foul of the same entity Smithers and Spencer had encountered. It also came to light that Jane's mother had died of a brain haemorrhage at the age of thirty-four, when Jane and Tommy were children. Piconya glanced at Esklick, both thinking the same: how many more tragedies would strike this family?

Spencer went on to tell them that Jane's mother, Marjorie, had two surviving sisters, Heather and Peggy, and it was Heather who adopted Jane's son.

Chapter 12

Ken Smithers
Lamerton, Devon

Ken Smithers led a simple life in his small cottage in Lamerton, a village bordering the market town of Tavistock in Devon. With the pension from the force and proceeds from his artwork, he was making a decent living. To outsiders, knowing nothing of the incident that destroyed his career, he lived a quiet, solitary life. Lately, however, flashbacks had begun to surface and he'd been experiencing memory lapses. At first, he put them down to a coping mechanism and would have been content with his self-diagnosis had it not been for the latest incident, where he found he'd completed a draft of a painting he couldn't remember doing. When his senses returned, Smithers was horrified at the artwork he'd unwittingly created and was tempted to destroy it. Its destruction, however, was saved by a friend who called by one afternoon and, noticing the painting resting on the easel in the conservatory, went over to look at it. Trevor Buriton, a gallery owner, drooled over the draft and, realising its potential, persuaded Smithers to let him sell it in its present state. At first, Smithers was against the idea but, beaten down by Buriton's persistence, he reluctantly agreed. Within a matter of weeks, the exhibited painting attracted much attention and, despite the exorbitant price, was sold. Spurred on by the sale, Buriton convinced Smithers to paint a series of oils entitled *The Phantom*.

When Smithers layered black and grey oils, forming the phantom, a part of him relived past experiences over and over again, creating a lifelike horror on the canvas. As the coffers were getting low, it was only the prospect of earning some serious money that spurred him on and the hope that the medium of painting could be a way to exorcise the demon which had been haunting him all these years. Smithers completed four oils in a commissioned series of eight and was about to make a start on the fifth when it all became too much for him. Discarding his paintbrush, he walked away from the easel and made a call to the gallery owner to tell him he was unable to finish the commission. Trevor Buriton, although disappointed by the decision, and the money he would lose, understood and arranged to collect the four completed paintings to exhibit in his gallery.

Buriton mounted them in pride of place on the front wall. Standing back to assess the work, his professional eyes roamed the paintings. Canvas One showed a swirling mass of translucent blackness, floating up a narrow oak stairwell, shadows of darkness charting its progress. In the second canvas, the phantom's form became more solid, attaching itself to the stairwell, captured in a gliding motion. Canvas Three showed the black shape gradually metamorphosing into a human form. Buriton stared so intently at the oil painting that for the briefest of moments he felt himself irresistibly drawn into its blackness. Snapping out of the spellbound trance, his eyes shot to the next stage of metamorphosis. Canvas Four was more breath-taking than the other three, depicting a human-like figure emerging from a cloak of black and grey mist. The naked figure inside the mist was fully formed, its skin glistening like gold as one arm broke free, like a chrysalis shedding its skin, heading towards something unseen at the top of the stairwell. The paintings left Buriton wanting more, which meant going back to Smithers to persuade him to finish the series.

The four canvases sat in Buriton's gallery for months, attracting much attention from people who viewed them. Like him, it left them wanting to see more of the artist's work but without the rest of the series there had been no potential buyers. One afternoon, an American walked into the gallery, instantly gravitating towards the Smithers collection. After engaging him in a sales pitch, Buriton found out the American was in Tavistock on business and, having previously viewed the Smithers series on the internet, he wanted to see them in the flesh. The exquisite precision and subject matter of the artwork enthralled him and despite the hefty price tags he indicated his interest in buying the paintings. Buriton let slip that the artist originally planned a series of eight oils and that the rest of the commission had been put on hold. On hearing this, George Wallis wanted the whole series, for which he was prepared to pay an extortionate amount of money if, when completed, they lived up to his expectations. A large deposit was paid to secure the four paintings and a deal was struck between the two men for the remaining pictures. Wallis told Buriton he would be back in England in six months' time, by which time it was agreed the artist would finish the collection. Once Wallis returned, subject to being satisfied by what he saw, money would change hands and the *Phantom* series would be packaged and shipped off to the States.

Buriton visited his artist friend. He was initially met with resistance from Smithers but after hearing the large amount of money involved in the proposed transaction, the former policeman started to waver. Smithers knew the money would set him up for several years but mentally it might either destroy him. Several days later, after much soul-searching, he rang Buriton to tell him he was prepared to paint the remainder of the series. The gallery owner was over the moon and promised to leave him alone until the work was finished. In return, Smithers agreed to keep him apprised with emailed snapshots of his progress. After concluding the agreement, Smithers steeled himself for the task ahead, knowing the final oil would bring a baring of his soul and a fear for his sanity.

Since the paranormal experience all those years ago, he'd been plagued with nightmares about Christmas Steps, believing it to have a connection with the case of Jane Adams. He knew it wasn't just a figment of his imagination. Brian Davies had also witnessed the terrifying event first-hand. Smithers remembered waking up in a hospital bed with no memory of what happened to him. When he was eventually discharged, strange things started to surface from his shocked memory. He replayed them in his mind over and over again, trying to make sense of them. His last recollection was standing on the second-floor landing, looking down the stairwell and seeing a shadow appear from nowhere. As he moved forward to get a better look, the shadow disappeared and, thinking it was a trick of the light, he walked to the edge of the landing to descend the stairwell. Just as he was about to put his foot on the first tread, an all-consuming force had taken hold of him and a living hell came crashing into his life.

The experience left Smithers unable to carry out his work to a satisfactory degree. Coupled with continual snide and insensitive remarks from colleagues, he ended up leaving the police force in pursuit of another life; one where he would find peace and tranquillity. Thinking back, he knew he'd made the wrong decision, as nothing could erase the moment his life became a living hell. Now, he was being forced to expose his demon in the only way he knew possible and, once revealed, it would enable everyone to share his agonies through the medium of art.

As Smithers resumed painting, time was irrelevant and Canvas Five was finished in next to no time. Over the next four weeks, he prepped three other canvases, laying down the familiar background with different degrees of shades and shadows, each process bringing the 'phantom' closer to the top of the stairwell and nearer to human form. The last canvas would depict a scene at the top of the stairwell. Dividing his talents between the three canvases, it wasn't long before he was ready to reveal the entity.

Before putting paint to canvas, he considered the construction of the eighth image, knowing it was going to be an ordeal. The revelation of the phantom would be a pivotal moment, when the stuff of nightmares came to fruition. He would never forget the almighty force which had lifted him off the floor and thrown Davies down a flight of stairs.

Working on Canvas Eight was every bit as traumatic as he imagined. Painting the phantom's image triggered a blinding pain in his head, temporarily disabling him. As the pain subsided, his vision cleared, enabling him to survey his surroundings. For the briefest of moments, he was transported back to Christmas Steps, where all his nightmares began. Images he was seeing defied the laws of physics, his fear conjuring life-like hallucinations.

"Don't feed your fears. It doesn't exist. Get back to the here and now, don't let it reclaim you," the screaming voice of logic resounded in his brain.

Battling against the malevolent apparition, Smithers blinked his eyes furiously in an attempt to dispel the unwanted image and was immediately back in his conservatory, with a lingering sensation of something evil happening as he put the finishing touches to the face of the phantom. As his senses returned, he found he was standing in his conservatory but the eighth canvas was face-up on the floor, at the far side of the room. There was nobody else in the house and no explanation as to why the canvas had come off its easel, landing where it did, unless he'd thrown it in a fit of rage.

Stumbling into a chair, Smithers put his head in his hands and let out a pained howl. Then another noise came, which made him stop and look up. Disoriented, Smithers thought that besides seeing things he was also hearing things. The banging started again and he realised it was coming from the front door, and that whoever it was outside wasn't going to go away. Another round of persistent knocking propelled him out of the chair to answer the door.

DS Sylvia Piconya and PC Steve Esklick stood on the doorstep of the semi-detached cottage, pondering their next move. Despite assurances from the neighbour that Ken Smithers was at home, there was no sign of him opening his door and as they had travelled nearly three hours to get to their destination Piconya was not about to give up her quest to interview the man. Suddenly, she heard a rattling of a key, then the front door opened.

"Yes, can I help you?" The cottage's occupant stood on the doorstep, dishevelled as though he'd been in some sort of a fight and in a state of high anxiety, clearly annoyed at the intrusion, which immediately raised red flags for the naturally suspicious Piconya.

Piconya proffered her ID and she and Esklick were ushered into the lounge. From her seat on the sofa, DS Piconya could see through to the conservatory beyond, giving a view of the back garden. As her cursory inspection of the conservatory concluded, her eyes landed on an upturned canvas in the far corner of the room, traces of fresh paint smeared on the hardwood floor in its wake. She concluded that this was the probable source of Smithers' anxiety. Her eyes reverted to Smithers, who sat in an armchair, facing them.

"Mr Smithers, I believe you may be of assistance in our investigation."

As DS Piconya briefly outlined details of their cold case, Smithers turned a deathly shade of white, clutched his chest and started to hyperventilate. Fearing a heart attack, Piconya was about to rush to his aid when he reached into his shirt pocket and produced an inhaler. Realising he was having some sort of asthma attack, Esklick was already on his feet, watching anxiously as the man took several long puffs from the inhaler. Shortly afterwards, the medication started to take effect and the man's breathing began to stabilise. Esklick went in search of the kitchen to make some tea whilst Piconya remained with Smithers, assuring him it wasn't their intention to open old wounds. As her gentle tone echoed outside the mental floodgates, Smithers' mind began to crack.

Esklick appeared, carrying a tray containing three mugs of steaming tea and a canister of sugar. Seeing the man in a high state of distress, he laid the tray down on a side table and sat quietly next to Piconya, listening in silence as Smithers' pent-up anguish spewed out, unabated. It all came out in a heated rush; the discovery of Donald Adams' body, the attack by the supernatural force, and the voices in his head driving him to the point of insanity. They heard how colleagues brushed the matter under the carpet, unable to understand or believe the incredible sequence of events. After Smithers finished, Piconya got up from the sofa and walked into the conservatory to get some air and to digest what she'd heard. As she passed the upturned canvas, she stopped to look at it. There was no explaining why she'd picked it up, apart from a natural curiosity to find out what had triggered the upheaval in the conservatory. As Piconya placed it back on the easel, a smudged likeness stared back at her, the grotesque image in the centre of the painting bearing an uncanny resemblance to the prime suspect in their cold case. Reaching into her jacket to retrieve her mobile phone, Piconya took several pictures of the painting and walked back into the lounge, where Smithers and Esklick sat in silence, awaiting her return.

The subject of the painting's freakish similarity to Tommy Adams had Piconya's undivided attention and, sensing he was at last being taken seriously, Ken Smithers' whole demeanour changed. From a wreck of a man, who could barely string a sentence together, the retired police constable gained confidence.

The permanently harrowed expression etched on his face disappeared; a significant sign that the inner trauma he had carried for so many years was dissipating. Piconya wanted to know how and why the apparition had not only destroyed a man's career but continued haunting him to the present day. As she attempted to make sense of things, a disturbing thought entered her mind; meeting this man had been predestined. Keeping her suspicions in check, Piconya continued probing Smithers, who told her the image was created during a memory lapse and how a local gallery owner had persuaded him to put it up for sale. At that point, Smithers was only too willing to get the thing he'd subconsciously created out of his home. DS Piconya learned that the painting, which was being sold for a small fortune, was one of a series of eight.

Rising from his chair, Smithers beckoned them to follow him along a narrow hallway, which led to the back of the cottage. At the end of the hallway, he opened a door into another room, where the majority of his artwork and supplies were stored. Pointing to three finished canvases propped up against the wall, Smithers told them that four of the series had already been taken to the gallery, then left Piconya and Esklick looking over the paintings whilst he booted up a laptop on a nearby bench. The screen flickered into life, displaying a gallery website and catalogue of paintings entitled *The Phantom*. Each painting, although dark in nature, was brilliantly depicted, compelling the viewer to see the next stage of metamorphosis and leaving Piconya spellbound, having seen the final reveal with her own eyes. Although the painting in the conservatory had been slightly smudged, there was no doubting the striking resemblance. The image of phantom not only resembled the brother wanted for his sister's murder but also the man known as Jason Holden. Piconya's mind was whirling with possibilities that didn't seem credible. The only possible explanation was that Jason Holden, the product of rape, was also Tommy Adams' son. The child who Spencer had told them was adopted by Marjorie's sister, Heather.

Before leaving Lamerton, Piconya and Esklick witnessed an astounding transformation in Smithers, making him almost serene, like a person discovering religion for the first time. Something he said as a parting comment made Piconya think there was substance in the theory he presented, of a wandering spirit latching onto an earthbound presence to further its mission. Smithers was convinced that although the entity had been unable to possess him fully, due to the intervention of PC Davies, it had found a way back to this earth through another medium, meaning there could have been another incident where a rebirth of its paranormal form had taken place. Regurgitating the horrifying sequence of events in Christmas Steps, Smithers' artwork had enabled him to unlock the vaults of his mind. Now the phantom was exposed on canvas for all to see, the place in his mind where it had been hidden all those years was empty, giving peace to a troubled man. From a sad, frightened individual barely possessing strength to pick up the pieces of his shattered life, he was now able to talk about the possession in a detached manner. He also divulged something he'd not told another living soul, for fear of ridicule; that during the episode of possession, the entity had given him a snapshot of a young girl's essence, trapped in its domain. The passing of this information made Piconya shiver, wondering what else they would discover in the course of their investigations.

Before leaving the force, Smithers discovered from a colleague called Aubrey that he and Sam Dixson, part of the backup team attending the scene at Christmas Steps, also saw something they never reported. Once inside the property, they'd been sent to locate the deceased's body, leaving the rest of the team cataloguing and photographing the scene downstairs. Climbing two sets of stairs to the top floor, and following the smell of death and decay, they discovered Donald Adams lying on the floor, fully dressed, beside his bed in the first bedroom. At the far end of the landing was a second, empty, bedroom.

Aubrey told Smithers that after the dead body had been removed they were the last of the team to leave. Having seen Adams' terror-ridden face, his emotions were heightened. Death came in all guises but he'd never seen anything quite like the expression etched on the old man's face, the image of which played on his mind. Although shaken by the experience, Aubrey kept his feelings hidden from Dixson. After they secured the property, they lingered outside to light up a cigarette. Aubrey noticed something in the top window, looking out onto the street, and nudged Dixson, who also looked up. A dark silhouette emerged from the shadows, appearing to be frantically clawing at the glass. So fierce were its actions to escape the confines of the building that they could hear thumping and see the glass panes shaking in their wooden frames. Suddenly, an anguished howl emanated from the house, the sound amplifying in the narrow street below, then the silhouette disappeared into thin air, leaving Aubrey and Dixson baffled.

Little did they realise that earlier on in the investigation the entity had also revealed itself to DCI Spencer. Going back into the property, Aubrey and Dixson conducted another search, focusing their attention in the top bedroom where they'd seen the howling silhouette, but they found nothing. The glass in the window frames was intact, with no visible signs of damage. The only thing Aubrey detected was a peculiar odour, which smelt like sulphur. As a consequence of seeing something that couldn't be explained, just like DCI Spencer the two officers failed to mention the incident in their report, giving no support to Smithers' story.

On the journey back to Bristol, the satnav directed them through the village of Milton Abbot, down country roads towards

Launceston. On a steep, windy stretch of road going towards Greystone Bridge, Piconya noticed a farmhouse through the treeline, in front of which was parked a white vehicle. Even from that distance, she could tell the building was ancient and in need of attention. She wondered briefly who lived there. As they stopped at traffic lights, just before going over a narrow stone bridge, curiosity made her look again, but the view was obscured by trees.

In the driver's seat, Esklick was unnaturally quiet, which suited Piconya, who mulled over Smithers' theory of an earthbound spirit with the ability to possess its victims. Despite other sightings by Spencer, Aubrey and Dixson, the only tangible evidence the supernatural entity existed was in a set of paintings, which it could be argued were the product of a very disturbed mind. But that still didn't account for the image in the oil painting bearing a startling resemblance to Tommy Adams, wanted for a murder over thirty years ago and ultimately leading back to Jane Adams and Christmas Steps. From the old case file, Piconya accessed photographs and read detailed reports as to how the unconscious victim had been discharged from a wheelie bin into a garbage truck. After she was discovered to be still alive, Jane Adams was rushed to Frenchay, where she remained in a coma and, after giving birth to a baby boy, died having never seen her son. A picture of the newly-born infant still remained in the file but the father of the boy was never found.

Although DNA profiling first started out in the 1980s, it was not until 1986 that it had been made widely available. Police dealing the crime at the time had collected fingerprints and semen stains from the scene but failed to carry out the testing required to prove the theory that Jane had been raped by her brother. Now technology had moved on, Piconya was going to make it a priority to get the testing done. The child was later adopted, which would have been a minefield to investigate had Spencer not divulged the fact that Jane's Aunt Heather had adopted the baby.

Rain started to shower the windscreen as they approached Bristol, turning into a torrential downpour and making driving difficult in the heavy traffic. Electing to seek shelter, Piconya and Esklick turned off at Gordano Services. Parking the car near the service complex, they made a dash inside. As they waited for the rain to subside, Esklick ordered coffees whilst Piconya found a seat away from other travellers, who were descending on the service pit-stop in their hordes, with the same aim of escaping the rain. After queuing for ten minutes, PC Esklick returned, armed with two coffees and a selection of sugary pastries. By this time, the service complex was bursting at the seams, with so many people milling about it was hard to conduct any sort of conversation.

Screaming kids ran around, unchecked by their parents, who turned a blind eye to their behaviour. Piconya found herself counting her blessings that although in her early teens she'd been filled with romantic ideas of finding the man of her dreams and having kids, in reality no one had measured up to her long list of requirements. Eyeballing a young girl stamping her feet and smacking her mother's arm to get attention; the mother in the middle of a heated argument with her husband, Piconya was grateful that love had passed her by. At least when the day ended, she could shut her door to the world and answer to no one.

As Piconya and Esklick finished their coffees, the precocious brat had given up battering her mother and was now screaming at the top of her voice at her father, who ignored his child, hell-bent on finishing the argument he had started with his wife. It was now turning ugly. People nearby were commenting and staring at the family causing the disturbance in the midst of the restaurant. Piconya was about to intervene when a young man in his early twenties, a shiny manager's badge pinned to his jacket, approached the table. A few words were exchanged and the husband stood up. For a moment, all eyes were on the man as he stood facing the manager, fists clenched ready to throw a punch. DS Piconya and PC Esklick got to their feet but the fraught husband, who obviously had second thoughts about starting a fight, spat a load of obscenities into the manager's face and stormed off.

Seeing her husband barge through the heaving restaurant, the wife gathered up her petulant child and followed him, much to the relief of onlookers. As they'd finished their coffees and were on their feet, Piconya and Esklick followed them out and into the car park, where they saw the wife strapping her child into the back seat of a red Peugeot. At that point, they were too far away to hear what was being said between the couple, but their body language had changed dramatically, suggesting a truce of sorts. Putting her arms around her husband, the woman gave him a cuddle. He responded by kissing her on the cheek. It appeared the disagreement had passed and all was well with the argumentative couple as they got into their car and drove off.

Piconya once again counted her silent blessings, to be spared the trauma of relationships, although her isolated lifestyle had earned her the nickname of Iron Knickers between a few misogynist officers who had tried and failed to get a date.

The rain had reduced to a drizzle as they got into their car to continue the journey back into Bristol. As Esklick manoeuvred into the service petrol station to fill up, Piconya reverted to her mental tick-list. First was DNA-testing of the old semen samples, then checking into Heather Thornleigh nee Adams' family. As Esklick entered the service station to pay for the petrol, Piconya's mobile rang. The call was from Bridewell Police Station.

Chapter 13

Hydlebury Farm

Ethel was on her knees with one ear close to the trapdoor, listening for sounds of life. She heard a banging noise, as though something was thudding up against wood.

"Is anyone down there?" she shouted nervously, then listened. Almost immediately, there was an answer.

"Help me, please help me."

Ethel was so taken aback by the piercing scream that she fell back on her knees in fright. It took a moment to collect herself before she was able to answer. "Who are you and what the blazes is going on?" she shouted back, finding her voice.

"He's kidnapped us! Please, we need to get out of here before he comes back!"

To Ethel's horror, she realised that there was more than one person in the cellar and the man she'd seen in the farmhouse with his head in his hands must be a kidnapper. She'd narrowly escaped detection when he came out of the farmhouse and got into his van.

Looking round the dimly lit barn, she frantically starting searching for keys to unlock the padlock but found nothing apart from an array of abandoned farm implements. Searching through a pile of debris stacked up in the corner, she spotted a rusty old crowbar, which she tried to use to lever off the steel plate the padlock was attached to. The thickness of the crowbar made it difficult to get leverage and after numerous attempts Ethel threw the tool aside in frustration. A fraught dialogue began between Ethel and the woman below ground, who'd been listening to her unsuccessful attempts to release it.

"I'm going to get help. Just hold on a little while longer, I can't move the padlock by myself."

"Please hurry, he might come back any moment," Jenna urged, dreading what the deranged maniac would do to her.

Just as Ethel got to her feet, she thought she heard something. She realised it was a car engine in the distance, which, judging by its loud humming, was getting closer by the second. There was a lane that ran between Hydlebury Farm and her cottage, which merged onto a road and a set of traffic lights either side of the Greystone Bridge, filtering traffic from Cornwall over the River Tamar into Devon. Ethel knew that if she didn't hear the vehicle going over the bridge there was only one way it could go. Her fears were realised when she heard a vehicle turn into the lane, heading in their direction. She knew the road was rarely used, apart from by locals who were prepared to manoeuvre the treacherous little lane at ridiculous speeds. As the hum became louder, it seemed apparent the driver of the vehicle was not a local. The kidnapper was returning.

Knowing it was imperative to get out of the barn before he got back, she dropped to her knees and shouted down to the woman. "It sounds like he's back. I will have to go now and get help. I will be back, just hold on." Ethel didn't wait for a response. She got to her feet and ran out of the barn.

A short distance away, as Ethel closed the barn door, a vehicle come to a halt outside the farmhouse. The sound of a door slamming could be heard in the still of the night, then a beam of light cut through the darkness into the field leading towards the barn.

Knowing she had no time to lose, Ethel fumbled in her jacket pocket, located her torch and slid away into the darkness of the field, heading towards her cottage to get help.

He'd only been gone about fifteen minutes, enough time to fill up the van and get some cigarettes, but the moment he entered the barn, Daniel knew someone had been in there. Sniffing the air like a dog trying to get a scent, he detected a faint smell of lilacs then noticed a crowbar abandoned on the floor beside the trapdoor. Bending down to inspect the padlock, he discovered gouges where someone must have tried unsuccessfully to release it. An almighty rage consumed him as the realisation hit him that an intruder had entered the barn and found his hiding place. Lashing out at the portable generator, he upended it with a swift blow from his foot. The sturdy metal object, designed to operate in all terrains, landed on its side, showing no signs of damage. Daniel's foot, however, had taken a battering. Hobbling around in agony, he cursed all and sundry before sinking down onto the floor. Nursing his foot and struggling to get his temper under control, Daniel began to figure out his next move. The main priority was to find the intruder before he or she had a chance to get help. Judging by the smell of lilacs still clinging to the air, the person was female. It seemed reasonable to assume that, being in the middle of the countryside, the woman would be local. Daniel assumed Jenna's continual screaming had alerted the woman to his hideout and cursed himself for not gagging the bitch when he locked her in the cell.

Daniel remembered seeing lights and a thicket of fir trees further down the narrow lane when he drove up to Hydlebury Farm, indicating they were concealing another residence. This train of thought brought forth a number of questions. If there was another property nestled behind the firs, did the woman live there, and did she have family or live with someone? Mulling over the possibilities, he reached the conclusion that the woman had stumbled on his activities alone and, judging by the unsuccessful gouging around the steel latch, she didn't have the strength to release the trapdoor. As he reached for the iPhone tucked inside his jacket, another thought struck him. Looking at its screen, it indicated no signal, which meant that if the woman possessed a mobile she too would be experiencing the same problem, leaving the only option to find a landline to call for help. Assuming the woman was still out there in the darkness and on route to her home, he raised himself from the floor gingerly, putting his foot to the ground. Although painful, it had full movement, which meant nothing was broken. Disregarding the shooting pain from his ankle, he hobbled out of the barn with one aim on his mind: to find the intruder before she could get help.

Ethel was hiding behind the hedgerow separating the fields when she saw the man hobbling out of the barn, shining his high-powered torch into the darkness. As the brilliant beam moved in her direction, she ducked further down. Paralysed by fear, she waited for the inevitable moment of discovery, cringing as the light swept over her hiding place, forcing her further into the undergrowth. The light lingered momentarily, falling onto the contours of her dark coat, then moved further up the field. As the moment passed she let out a strangled sob of relief then peered out from her hiding place. A sinking feeling in the pit of her stomach told her there was no way she could get to her home before him, as she watched the man's retreating back in the darkness, heading towards her cottage. Ethel started to panic, realising that apart from heading into the open countryside – which was fraught with hidden dangers – there was no other option left but to head for the road, with hopes of flagging down a passing motorist.

Decision made, she set off, knowing the chances of any one passing over Greystone Bridge at that time of night were slim.

Ethel estimated it would take at least fifteen minutes to manoeuvre the unpaved roadway to the next cluster of houses in Lawhitton Village to raise the alarm but, as that was some distance away and off the beaten track her best bet was to stay on the road that would lead her back into Launceston. The only glimmer of hope at the end of a very dark tunnel was that, the further she headed towards the town, the better the possibility of picking up a signal on the mobile phone she'd taken with her when leaving the cottage.

Ethel's fears were further compounded when she reached the deserted stone bridge. There was no street lighting, the only illumination in the pitch darkness being two sets of traffic lights situated each end of the bridge. The beam from her torch gave out just enough light to enable safe passage up the unpaved roadway. Then, halfway through the arduous journey, trying to manoeuvre between roadway and hedgerows, she heard a vehicle approaching. Ethel stood at the side of the road and flung her arms about as it rounded the bend. The beam from the headlights was so bright that she was blinded temporarily but she heard and felt it come to an abrupt halt a couple of feet away. As she shielded her eyes against the light a door opened and then she was grabbed roughly and flung up against the side of a van. Ethel struggled, violently clawing at the hands squeezing her throat. Looking into the face of her attacker, lit up from the van's interior lights, she recognised the man she'd seen at the farmhouse. The force on her windpipe made it impossible for her to scream for help as he manoeuvred her around, opened the rear van doors, and threw her inside.

Ethel could feel the vehicle do a U-turn in the road and calculated it would only be a matter of minutes before they reached the farmhouse, where she would be at her attacker's mercy. At that point, she could only surmise that having found her cottage in darkness, apart from the porch light she left on when leaving the cottage, her attacker realised she hadn't reached home and would therefore be heading towards the road. Turning on the torch, which she had pocketed when the van stopped, Ethel shone it around her moving prison and found that it was empty except for a small toolbox. Sliding towards it, she opened the lid and shone the torch inside, disappointed to discover an assortment of nuts and bolts; nothing substantial to defend herself against the monster driving the van. As the hopelessness of her situation hit home, Ethel's body shook with fear and she reached automatically into her pockets for warmth.

Knowing there was no mobile phone signal in these parts, she didn't bother to take the device out of her pocket to check again. As her fingers lingered over the useless device, however, she felt a hole in the old duffel coat pocket. She remembered the Swiss Army knife she'd inherited from her father, which had slipped through the pocket lining whilst she'd been foraging for elderflower to make cordial. Ethel had been meaning to retrieve the knife and mend the pocket but hadn't got round to doing either. Blessing her tardiness, she plunged her hand through the tear and felt along the hemline, where the knife was lodged between seams. She eased it back up out of the lining into her hand. The van swerved left, confirming the fact that the vehicle was entering the farmyard and within seconds they would be at their destination. With no time to think, Ethel adopted a crouching position, ready to spring into action. Grabbing the toolbox, she flicked open the pen knife to reveal its blade and prepared for the fight of her life.

She felt the vehicle judder to a halt, then the engine stopped. Seconds later, the driver's door opened and the kidnapper walked round to the back of the van. As soon as the back door opened, Ethel, who had been clutching the toolbox like a shield, threw it at the man with all her strength. The metal box careered forward, spilling its contents and clipping him on the side of the head, making him stagger backwards. Seizing the moment, Ethel leapt out of the van on all fours, like a feral cat. Daniel was completely overpowered as she landed on top of him, knocking him to the ground. Momentarily winded from the fall, he was at the mercy of a woman whose fist was posed to strike him in the face. He rolled violently to the side, where he was able to deflect the intended blow and instead grabbed the back of her head, slamming it viciously on the ground.

Ethel was rendered unconscious by the blow and lay motionless. Hauling the unconscious woman up under her arms, Daniel threw her slight frame across his shoulders and, guided by the light from the van's headlights, walked the short distance across the fields to the barn. Ethel came to as Daniel entered the barn. The moment she opened her eyes, she realised where she was, what was happening, and that the Swiss Army knife was still wrapped in her clenched hand. Its blade dug deep into her palm; a painful reminder of its presence and a miracle it wasn't lost in the struggle.

Knowing she had to act quickly before she became another prisoner beneath the trapdoor, Ethel opened her hand carefully, manoeuvring the tip of the knife through bloodied fingertips until she got a grip on the handle. Standing adjacent to the trapdoor, her attacker began to unload the body from his shoulders.

Suddenly, he felt her move, but before he could react Ethel had flung her arm back and plunged the knife into the side of his neck. Daniel howled and dropped her, falling to his knees and gripping his bleeding neck. Ethel, who still had the knife in her hand, scrambled out of reach and was on her feet within seconds, running for the barn door. Behind her, she heard him cursing and screaming like a wild animal as she flew into the blackness of the night.

Jenna heard the scuffle and assumed the worst; that he'd found the woman who was their only glimmer of help. From the confines of her underground cell she listened to his cursing obscenities and realised that the woman had escaped as he ranted about what he would do when he caught up with her. There was an almighty crash topside as Daniel hauled himself upright and stumbled against the upturned generator in his search to find something to stem the bleeding from the wound in his neck. Opening his coat, he fumbled under his jumper, tore off a section of his tee-shirt and held it against the wound. Grabbing the crowbar that had been discarded by the trapdoor, he set off for his van to get a torch and begin the search for the woman.

The moment Daniel stepped outside the barn, he was momentarily transported into another world, where it was broad daylight. He saw himself as a young boy playing in fields; these same fields surrounding this farmhouse he had inherited from his great-aunt. The vision invoked in-depth memories of a narrow lane with high hedgerows snaking their way through the countryside. At a fork, the lane split two ways, one leading back onto a main road and the other heading to the village of Rezare. Back the other way was the Greystone Bridge and a road leading to Launceston, where the woman he was chasing had made her earlier escape attempt. He saw three fields surrounded by hedgerows before the land yielded to woodland. The vision faded, leaving Daniel standing beside his van with no knowledge of how he'd got there. All he remembered was standing outside the barn, staring into pitch blackness, in the vain hope of a sign of the woman who'd stabbed him in the neck.

Since his arrival at Hydlebury, memories of his past lives had been flooding back with alarming regularity. On this occasion, the memories served him well, reigniting a suppressed knowledge of the surrounding farmland. Knowing the woman wouldn't make the same mistake twice, and head for the road, the fields would be the first place to start his search.

Opening the passenger-side door of the van, Daniel rummaged about in the glove compartment and retrieved the torch. The high-powered beam cut through the darkness, illuminating a great swathe of ground as he headed into the fields. He covered the first, quickly coming to a turnstile. On the other side was a second field, just as vast as the first. Shining the light across the land, he could see nothing, and hear nothing, to indicate anyone was nearby. As he went deeper in, he found the opening he'd seen in his vision, leading into a third field. As Daniel did a 360-degree turn he saw a faint light in the distance, heading towards a wooded area. Increasing his pace to a run, he charged through ankle-height grass towards the source of light. His breathing became erratic as he contemplated an unthinkable scenario: if the interfering bitch was to make it to the wooded area. It was imperative to catch her before she entered the forest as, once inside, the trees would provide shelter and the odds would be stacked in her favour.

Ethel could see a powerful beam in the distance as she struggled to reach the shelter of the woods, their damp, peaty aroma filling her nostrils as she got closer. Just as salvation was in sight, her foot struck an old tree branch and she stumbled into the undergrowth, dropping her torch in the process. Unhurt but shaken, Ethel scrambled to her feet and made the final dash across the field. With total darkness hampering her progress, she careered into a thicket of brambles, which trapped her inside its thorny nest. Panicking, Ethel pulled away the thorny branches, which tore at her duffel coat and injured her hands as she broke free. Moments later, she was running full-pelt through open fields towards the woods, her progress chartered by her pursuer's powerful torch beam.

"I've got you now, bitch!" were the last words Ethel heard before a steel crowbar knocked her legs from under her, rendering her immobile and in horrendous pain on the sodden ground.

As she looked up, her attacker loomed over her, shining the torch in her face, the crowbar raised high above his shoulders, poised for the next onslaught. Ethel rolled to the side as the crowbar made its descent, missing her head by inches and sinking into the soft, mossy ground beside her. She heard the man cussing as he struggled to dislodge it from the sodden earth and she seized the opportunity to grab the pen knife from her pocket. Luckily, as she'd had the presence of mind to slip the knife back into the pocket without the tear. Flicking open the bloodied blade and knowing she wouldn't get far on her injured legs, she prepared to defend herself.

Giving up on the crowbar, Daniel rounded on Ethel, who managed to roll a short distance away; nearer to the woods but not far enough to effect an escape. As she tried to crawl away, two rough hands tugged at her shoulder blades and turned her over. Ethel thrashed out, bucking against him as he straddled her body and placed his huge, strong hands around her neck. The only means of defending herself was in her right hand, which was pinned under his body. As he squeezed her neck, she felt the lifeblood starting to drain away from her body. She didn't want to die like this.

An almighty rage consumed her. With one push from her powerful hips, she was able to rock his body to one side, in the process releasing her right arm.

Once again, Daniel was caught off-guard by the woman, who struck his face with deadly force before he was able to regain his dominance. The advancing blade aimed wildly at its target and missed his cheek by millimetres, passing through the fleshy end of his nose. Ethel heard the sickening sound of tearing flesh as she pulled the knife back. Howling screams pierced the darkness of the surrounding fields as he fell off her and rolled into a foetal position, hands across his face to stem the bleeding.

"Fucking hell, fuck, fuck, fuuuuuuuuuuuuuuuuuuuuk!" In his haste to capture the woman, he'd forgotten about the knife.

The light from the torch, which had been dropped during the altercation, shone up from the ground nearby, illuminating the aftermath of the struggle. Darkness gathered around them like a black cloak as Daniel rolled around in pain. Ethel lunged for the torch and crawled to the perimeter of the wooded area, where she stumbled across a load of broken branches. Using one of the branches, Ethel managed to manoeuvre herself upright, relieved to find that, although painful, her legs were not broken. Working through the pain, Ethel inched deeper into the woods with the aid of her wooden crutch. Feeling her way in the darkness and failing torchlight, her fingers located a hollow at the foot of a tree. Further investigation revealed it was big enough for her slight frame. Scratting around the base of the tree, Ethel found enough broken branches to wedge into the opening. Wriggling inside, she barricaded the opening to the outside world and turned off the torch, to conserve the last of the failing batteries and conceal her whereabouts, then sat still and silent, hoping she'd done enough to stay hidden and avoid capture.

Meanwhile, in the dark field below the wood, Daniel was in serious trouble. With blood from his wounded nose running like a small river into his open mouth, he knew he had to do something. Faced with two options: to go after the bitch who had injured him or staunch the bleeding before he drowned in a pool of his own blood, he chose the latter. Staggering across open fields in the pitch blackness, using the distant farmhouse lights as a homing beacon, he knew his biggest hurdle would be the turnstile he had crossed earlier; now a formidable fortress in the blackness of the countryside. It took several attempts to scale its battlements, before he landed feet-first on the other side, in a heap of soggy mud that seeped over the top of his trainers. By the time

Daniel reached the farmhouse, he was delirious with rage and bleeding like fury. A low hum from the generator supplying power and light greeted him as Daniel flung open the door and rummaged around the supplies he'd bought in Launceston. In one of the plastic bags, he located a roll of gaffer tape. Emptying the contents of a small holdall, he picked up one of his clean shirts. With the aid of a Stanley knife, he tore it into strips. Pressing the cotton against his bleeding nose, Daniel ran the gaffer tape over the wound until the whole of his nose and part of his face was covered, making him look like a walking zombie. Taking a bottle from his stash of water, he washed the remaining blood from his face and neck then changed into a clean shirt, discarding the blood-splattered tee-shirt in a black plastic sack containing remnants of building rubble.

Without a torch to guide his way, Daniel knew it was hopeless to pursue the woman in the pitch blackness; his only comforting thought was that she faced the same predicament, as the torch batteries were failing. Looking at his watch, he saw it was 11.15pm, and with hours to wait before daylight came, time was on his side. But the first priority was to find a hospital and get his injuries attended to.

Daniel remembered having seen signs for Launceston Hospital but he decided against going there as it was too close for comfort. Questions would be asked and at that time of night it would be assumed he was living in or within the catchment area of Launceston. Being a small community hospital, he doubted whether they had facilities to treat his injuries anyway. Setting the satnav, he started the journey to Plymouth.

Daniel reached Derriford Hospital just before midnight. The journey into Plymouth had been long and painful but light on traffic. With blood oozing from the gaffer tape on his face and his neck sporting an open wound crusted with dried blood, he looked desperate as he entered the Accident & Emergency unit. Medical staff took one look at him and ushered him into a cubicle, ahead of the queue in the waiting area. Shortly, a doctor with a stethoscope hanging round his neck, who introduced himself as Sadiq Patel, removed his temporary dressings and inspected the wounds on Daniel's nose and neck, prompting a barrage of questions. By this time, Daniel was delirious with pain and incapable of thinking straight, let alone coming up with plausible answers to intrusive questions. Patel instructed a harassed nurse, who'd been called away from another patient, to collect a wad of medication. Returning to the cubicle, under the instructions of the doctor she administered an injection with quick precision, its contents shooting into Daniel's arm and easing his agony. As luck would have it, Daniel was informed, a cosmetic surgeon with a speciality in facial reconstruction was on call that evening. The man was quickly commandeered to attend Daniel's wounds. He was transferred into a mini operating room, where he was inspected under high velocity magnifying mirrors, injected with more substances to numb his nasal area, and then stitched up. As the cosmetic surgeon worked on his face, Daniel closed his eyes, willing the ordeal to be over.

It was getting on for three in the morning when Daniel eventually left the hospital. He had told medical staff his injuries were caused by falling on a Stanley knife, whilst carrying out renovations to a house he had recently purchased. Embellishing the story further, he told them he was carrying the knife when he tripped over a box of floor tiles. In an effort to cushion the fall, he inadvertently held up the hand containing the knife. In the process, it sliced his neck, then ripped into his nose before he hit the floor. Giving them a bogus name and address in Plymouth, he was not convinced they believed his story. Either way, he didn't care; his main goal was to get back to Launceston and finish off what he started. In his head, he had it all planned; at first light he would find the interfering woman and bring her back to the barn, where he would kill her and the blond bodybuilder, then bury them under the floorboards of the cellar.

In reality, when Daniel reached Hydlebury totally exhausted by his ordeal at the hospital, he'd fallen asleep and missed first light, which meant the woman hiding in the woods under the cover of darkness had a head start and a real possibility of reaching help.

The thought enraged him and he woke in a panic and sprang out of his sleeping bag, the blood rushing to his head and making him feel faint. Slumping back down again, he waited for the moment to pass, then tentatively rose to his feet. This time, his legs supported his weight. Stumbling around like a newly delivered foal, he found the painkillers the hospital gave him, threw a couple of capsules down his throat, washed them down with a gulp of bottled water and prepared for the search.

***

In the dark confines of her hiding place, Ethel's thoughts had run amok. Who was this monster? Why was he doing this? And how was she going to get out of the woods alive? Knowing she'd done enough damage to the man to warrant medical attention, she silently prayed his injuries would slow him down and buy her time until it was light enough to find help. In the meantime, frightened witless, injured and alone, her thoughts reverted to a time when Hydlebury Farm was tenanted by a brother and sister. She remembered the sister, Gracie, with fondness but had not known the brother well. Gracie was very independent and, after her brother died, had preferred her own company. To Ethel's knowledge, no one other than she visited Hydlebury and this had been just once a week, when she dropped off shopping for her elderly neighbour, whose health was rapidly declining and who was becoming housebound. Ethel's concerns about Gracie were realised when, during a weekly visit to the farmhouse, she found her unconscious at the bottom of the stairwell, having taken a tumble down a flight of stairs. After a frantic call to the emergency services, Gracie was rushed to hospital, where she was diagnosed as having had a stroke. She died three days later, having never regained consciousness. Ethel remembered quite clearly the day she found her neighbour's unconscious body. The terrified expression on the old woman's face had left a profound effect on her and instigated many a nightmare for years afterwards.

Since then, Hydlebury Farm had remained uninhabited, still in the possession of the Thornleigh family. In the eighteenth century, it was rumoured, a young boy living at Hydlebury was found guilty of murdering two children and had been hanged for his crimes. Local gossip passed down through the years embellished a tale about the farmer's daughter, who went missing around the time of the two murders. Stories of curses became commonplace when talking about Hydlebury, and the popular belief was that the boy, the young girl's cousin, was responsible for her disappearance. There had also been talk about another boy called Thomas, born some hundred years later who lived at the farm. The second Thomas had died in a farming accident. After his death it was discovered he'd been responsible for several unsolved murders, one failed attack leaving a victim alive to tell her tale.

Ethel recalled one afternoon whilst she sat in the kitchen having tea with Gracie how the subject had reared its ugly head. At the time, Gracie had laughed, dismissing local gossip as complete fabrication, but her eyes told another story. A fleeting thought now crossed Ethel's mind, making her wonder whether something happened in the farmhouse to trigger Gracie's demise.

After Gracie died, Ethel had continued to walk her dog over the land surrounding Hydlebury, and down along the bank by the

River Tamar. One afternoon, she had decided to take a different route, which took her past the second barn. It was a sunny afternoon in mid-May and Scamp, the beloved terrier she'd had back then, ran ahead, having spotted a rabbit who had ventured out of its warren to enjoy the summer sun.

Whilst Ethel rested by the side of the barn, catching her breath, there was not a soul in sight, apart from Scamp chasing the rabbit, who clearly had the upper hand. Suddenly, her reverie was broken when she sensed something behind her. Turning, she had seen a small girl run back into the barn. Stepping over the rotten carcass of the barn door, which, dilapidated with the passage of time, lay rotting on the ground, Ethel followed the girl inside, calling out, but there was no sign of her. Puzzled, Ethel once again scanned the barn, assuring herself she wasn't imagining things. As there was only one way in and out of the building, and she was standing by the doorway, she knew no one had got past her.

A noise had startled her. She turned to find Scamp behind her, brushing up against her legs. Sensing something wasn't quite right, Ethel was relieved to have his company, but as she bent down to pet him he started to growl and bare his teeth. Alarmed, she pulled away. Scamp, normally a mild-tempered dog, turned into a snarling wolf, taking a running dive into the barn at something unseen. Ethel followed him inside but despite commands to heel he continued to scratch frantically at the dirt floor, trying to dig something up.

Forgetting the search for the girl, Ethel had walked over to the spot where Scamp was digging. Finding nothing but a pile of dirt and a shallow hole, she had chastised the dog and dragged him by his collar out of the barn. Ethel realised why thoughts of her dear departed dog all those years ago had entered her head. If she had allowed him to dig a little further, he would surely have unearthed the trapdoor. Whatever had spooked Scamp must have lain below; possibly another prisoner in the cellar.

As darkness gave way to light, Ethel moved the barricade of branches from the entrance to the small hollow. Checking the coast was clear, she wriggled out from her hiding place on all fours but as she attempted to stand a stabbing pain shot up her left leg, making her stumble against the tree for support. The pain subsided after a while, allowing her to bend down and check her leg. Ethel saw the source of her pain. A huge black and yellow bruise had developed where the crowbar had found its target but despite the gripping pain nothing appeared to be broken. Putting her right foot down, she gingerly moved her left leg but the pain was excruciating, making her scream and fall back against the tree once more. Momentarily winded, Ethel began to take in her situation, realising her scream echoing through the empty fields could have given away her hiding place. A mixture of fear and determination snapped her back to reality and with superhuman effort she raised herself upright. Putting all her weight on her right leg, she began to hobble painfully through the wooded area. On the precarious journey through the trees, she sourced another a broken branch, which she utilised as a support, easing the pressure bearing down on her left leg. Progress was slow and it was fully light by the time she made it to the river bank. Looking around to get her bearings, she realised she was well off-course. Instead of reaching the small village of Rezare, she was heading for the grounds of Clarissa House; a grand five-star hotel set in acres of unspoilt countryside.

With the hotel in sight, she heard someone in the distance scrabbling through the adjoining fields. Frantically, she searched for somewhere to hide, knowing instinctively that any moment, when her attacker rounded the hedgerow, he would see her. As far as the eye could see, there were swathes of meadowland separated by hedges, leading onto manicured lawns where the hotel perched on a hill, overlooking the expansive valley and river. Ethel was a sitting duck; she couldn't run and there was nowhere to hide. Just below her, the river was at its widest and deepest point.

Without thinking, she abandoned the broken branch and rolled down the steep incline into the water. She hit the river with a splash, just as she heard a man's voice somewhere behind her, uttering obscenities. Within seconds, he would be standing on the river bank, near to the spot where she'd gone in. Filling her lungs with a big gulp of air, Ethel dived into the water, hoping the murky depths would conceal her presence and praying she could hold her breath long enough to reach the other side.

Daniel scanned the surrounding countryside. There was no sign of the bitch but he was certain he'd heard something before he rounded the hedgerow. In frustration, he kicked the branch by his feet into the river then hurtled towards the hotel.

On the other side of the bank, Ethel had just come up for air in time to see her attacker running off. Scrambling back up the bank, she crawled through the tree line, behind which lay another field. Shielded by the trees, she lay on the soft grass, counting her blessings and trying to get her bearings. With the river between them, Ethel felt a glimmer of hope. She had to get as far away as possible but with nothing between her apart from meadowland, Clarissa House and the road in the other direction, there was only one clear choice: to get to the road before he backtracked.

It was still early when Daniel reached Clarissa House. Watching from a safe distance, he observed a porter transporting luggage into a guest's car. There were no visible signs to indicate the bitch had made it to the hotel and raised the alarm, meaning that once again he'd miscalculated her actions. Fury gripped him when he realised the only other direction she could take was to go back to the road. Pivoting on his heels, Daniel ran back the way he had come, to catch the interfering bitch before she reached the road.

Back at Clarissa House, Georgina was busy clearing a guest's room but stopped briefly to admire the view from the window. It was a view she never tired of; not like her job, which at first she enjoyed but which was now becoming a chore, with the unsociable hours. In the distance, something caught her eye, making her curious enough to open the window and get a better look. She saw a man running through the fields towards the river, where she could just make out another figure standing on the bank before disappearing into the water. Jenny, another chambermaid, had just entered the room and was about to replenish the toiletries in the en suite when Georgina called her over.

"What do you think is going on there, Jen?" Georgina asked as they watched the retreating figure in the distance.

"Don't know, perhaps it's a country runner."

Digesting the plausible explanation, Georgina still thought it strange to encounter a runner this far off the beaten track, as the hotel was virtually in the middle of nowhere, and private property. Also, where was the other person who had been on the river bank?

"Come on, Georgie, Kathy will be here any minute to inspect the room." Jenny's irritable tone made Georgina turn from the window and, contemplating the impending visit from the housekeeper, who did not tolerate shoddiness, returned to the task at hand. All thoughts of the runners vanished as she plumped up the pillows on the bed, just as Kathy entered the room. Had Kathy been more approachable, Georgina would have been inclined to mention the strange sight she had witnessed from the window. Instead, the incident was soon forgotten as Georgina became embroiled in the busy work schedule.

With an injured leg and sopping wet clothes slowing her down, Ethel started to have serious doubts as to whether she could reach help before the man caught up with her again. Following the course of the river, she could see her cottage in the distance, and the barn at Hydlebury, where the woman was imprisoned. Despite pains shooting up her left leg, desperation spurred her on towards a place where a phone and car would be at her disposal. The journey would, however, involve crossing the river and going back over the land at Hydlebury. It also struck her that it was highly likely the monster pursuing her would inevitably come to the same conclusion.

Finding a shallow point in the winding river, Ethel once again stepped into its murky waters, this time wading across. On the other side, she hauled her body up and over the bank and rolled into the adjoining field. Her teeth were chattering from the effects of cold water again saturating her clothes, not to mention the fear she felt as she struggled to pull herself into a standing position. Scanning the surrounding farmland, there was no sign of the man as she hobbled towards Hydlebury, with the intention of retracing her steps, skirting past the farmhouse through the fields to the hole in the hedge where her property lay, back along the lane.

Daniel, meanwhile, was making his way back to Hydlebury, frantically searching for the woman who had not only succeeded in escaping him twice but was also responsible for the injuries to his face and neck. In his numerous incarnations, no one had inflicted so much damage and lived to tell the tale. This bitch would be no exception. His nose, although stitched and repaired at the hospital, hurt like hell. Breathing through his mouth was excruciatingly difficult, meaning he had to stop frequently to gain his breath before continuing. The summer sun was beginning to rise in the sky as he slumped down on the damp grass, reflecting on the dire situation. He was not in control. The fact a woman had outsmarted him was unbearable, making his temper boil over. In sheer frustration, he screamed out loud.

"I am going to get you, bitch, and when I do you are going to suffer and pay for what you've done to me." Daniel's fury-ridden voice echoed over the deserted fields.

As Ethel climbed through the hole in the hedge, she heard the screaming in the distance. The words were unclear but there was little doubt in her mind that they emanated from the deranged male. As she stepped onto the lane, her injured leg underwent a crippling spasm and she stumbled against a hedge, which cushioned her fall as she fell to the ground. Determined not to give up, Ethel started to crawl and roll the remainder of the way up the narrow lane, until she reached the side of her property. She swung open the latch of the gate. She could hear Poppy going berserk inside her cottage as the gate creaked open, announcing her progress up the pathway to the side door, which, out of habit, was always kept unlocked.

Chapter 14

Jenna Thornleigh, missing

Alannah was sitting in the kitchen, contemplating the busy day ahead. Looking at her diary on the table beside her breakfast bowl, she studied her comments against the two o'clock appointment – Maxwell Carnegie (Solicitor) wanted a supervisor for his typing pool and a legal secretary with experience in family matters. The staffing requirement itself was not an issue; the problem was Maxwell Carnegie himself. Disgruntled staff coming into the agency, seeking alternative employment, told her the man was an absolute nightmare to work for and an utter bully. It had come as no surprise to Alannah when she received a call from the head of the law firm, inviting her to meet with him to discuss his staffing issues. Being a new agency on the block, Alannah had figured it was only a matter of time before Carnegie landed on their doorstep. During their telephone conversation, in which he barked his long list of requirements, she was tempted to turn away the new business, but curiosity got the better of her. She wanted to meet the man for herself, to ascertain whether what she'd been told held any truth. When pitching for the new business, she planned to take Abbey, reorganising other appointments to accommodate the Carnegie & Co visit.

By 8.45 am, she was suited and booted, ready for the day ahead. She picked up her diary from the kitchen table and went through to the front office to prepare to open the doors to the public. It was then that she realised she hadn't heard Jenna return from her early morning gym session. Walking back upstairs, Alannah went in search of Jenna, discovering her bedroom empty and showing no sign of her return from the gym. This was strange; she could normally set her watch by her friend's routine. The minute Jenna returned to the house, she would fling off her Lycra exercise gear and trainers, run downstairs to the bathroom on the first floor, take a quick shower, dress, then apply make-up for work. Followed by a hurried breakfast, when she and Alannah would share a brief conversation, before Jenna headed off.

Going back downstairs, Alannah rang Jenna's mobile but it went straight to voicemail. Abbey arrived in the office but there was still no sign of their friend. By 9.50am, despite several calls to her mobile, there was no response from Jenna. The business phone rang. Thinking it was a client or candidate, Abbey answered then passed the call over to Alannah. It was Alan Turnbull, senior partner at the firm of architects Jenna worked for, enquiring as to her whereabouts. Alan was concerned as Jenna hadn't turned up for work. It was totally out of character for her not to phone and let him know if there were any problems.

Having met Alan on several occasions, Alannah had become friendly with him and confided that Jenna had failed to return from the gym, admitting she was starting to get worried. She promised to call Alan the minute Jenna turned up. Then Alannah called Trim Trail and spoke to Glenda Rowen, who confirmed Jenna had visited the gym that morning, leaving at her usual time of around 6.50am. Thanking Glenda, Alannah ended the call with a feeling of dread, wondering what possibly could have happened in the short distance it took to cross the centre, along the rank of shops and offices to Christmas Steps. Leaving the gym clad only in Lycra sportswear and trainers, there was no logical place Jenna would go other than home.

The phone calls with Alan and Glenda fuelled Alannah's panic, making her reflect on Jenna's movements over the past few weeks. There was nothing out of the ordinary, apart from the incident at Hotel Papiar. Alannah had felt something else was preoccupying Jenna recently, though, and recalled her saying there was something she needed to talk to her about but, being embroiled with the new business, they had never got round to that discussion. Alannah knew something was seriously wrong. With a scheduled appointment due to arrive in ten minutes, which Abbey was going to deal with, Alannah left the office and walked through to the residential part of the property, to call the police on the landline. She was put through to PC Michaels in the incident room, who took down details of Jenna's disappearance, including the incident at Hotel Papiar. What he'd just heard was a significant lead connected to their current case, which prompted Michaels to inform Alannah someone would arrive shortly at Christmas Steps to take a statement.

***

"Boss, I've just taken a call reporting a missing woman from Christmas Steps," PC Michaels tripped over his words in an effort to get the information out in a rush. "Alannah Corby of Stepz 2 Recruitment reported Jenna Thornleigh, her friend and business partner, missing when she failed to return from an early morning gym session. She also mentioned that the missing woman was assaulted by a man a couple of weeks ago in a local wine bar."

Telling Michaels she would respond to the call, Weller caught up with Whitehead, who had just finished updating the whiteboard on the Shaney case. "That can wait until we get back. Michaels has just taken a call about a missing woman with a possible connection to the Shaney case."

On the way to Christmas Steps, Weller filled Whitehead in on the scant details Michaels had managed to retrieve during the phone conversation with Alannah Corby. Now they had two missing people to deal with, it had to be more than coincidence. Ten minutes later, they were at the recruitment agency where they greeted by Alannah Corby, who was in a total meltdown in the wake of her friend's disappearance.

She took them through the office and into the lounge, where they questioned her about Jenna's last known movements. Going through Jenna's daily routine, Alannah told them about the information she'd received from Glenda Rowen at Trim Trail, adding that the gym manager had been on reception at the time and seen Jenna leaving. A knowing look passed between the two officers after she finished talking then DS Weller spoke.

"When you reported Jenna missing, you also mentioned something about an altercation at the Hotel Papiar."

Alannah reiterated to Weller and Whitehead what Jenna had told her about the assault at Hotel Papiar and how Peter Shaney had come to her aid. They listened as Alannah told them that Jenna had mentioned she felt like she was being followed and that there was something important she had wanted to tell Alannah.

"How well does Jenna know Peter Shaney?"

"He used to go to the same gym and is a friend of Jenna's. I've met him, he seems like a nice guy." Alannah's voice was a little unsteady, realising something wasn't quite right. "Why do you want to know? Has he got anything to do with her disappearance?"

"We are following another a line of enquiry. It is important that you tell us anything you know about Peter," prompted DS Weller. At that point, Alannah said she had nothing else to add.

"OK. Well, let me know if anything else comes to mind. Now, can we take a look around her bedroom? Does she have a laptop?"

"Yes, follow me." Alannah led DS Weller and PC Whitehead up two narrow staircases to the top floor, where she watched from the doorway as they searched Jenna's bedroom for clues, quickly discovering the laptop tucked away on a shelf in a built-in wardrobe. Weller rested it on top of a small bureau and turned it on. A screen-saver depicting a sandy beach over which the sun was setting flickered into glorious technicolour.

"I don't suppose you know her password?" Weller asked.

"Yes, as a matter of fact I do," Alannah rattled it off.

Weller had immediate access to Jenna's files, where she found two directories called 'Family Tree' and 'Diary'. Opening the diary and skim-reading it, she discovered a startling account of events happening in Christmas Steps, and a mine of information that needed in-depth investigation. "We will need to take this away for further investigation."

Closing down the laptop, it was clear Weller was onto something she wasn't about to divulge to Alannah.

"Yes of course, take what you need if it will help to locate Jenna."

As she showed them to the door Alannah remembered something that Jenna had told her about the assault at Hotel Papiar, which she had failed to mention earlier. "I think the man who assaulted Jenna threatened her and Peter after he was thrown out of the wine bar."

"Can you remember what Jenna said?" Weller prompted.

"No, not exactly but I think he said he would get even with them. Oh my God, you don't believe he's taken Jenna?" Standing on the step leading down to the office, Alannah appeared to waver. Weller turned swiftly and held her by the shoulders to steady her.

"Alannah, I know it's difficult but we can't jump to conclusions and I assure you we will be looking at everything." A moment passed while Weller assessed Alannah, wondering whether she was going to be alright, then let her go.

Alannah gathered herself together as she stepped down into the office and walked over to the front door to let them out. Pausing in the doorway, Weller handed Alannah a card before leaving with Whitehead, promising to call the minute they had any news.

Back at the station, the first thing Weller did was boot up the laptop and access Jenna's diary.

No. 26 Christmas Steps

When we viewed the property, I sensed a presence but made no mention of this to Alannah. I knew it would freak her out and as we were hell-bent on buying No. 26, I kept quiet. It was some time before we could move into the property, which was a total renovation project. Right from the start, there were problems with incompetent builders, who not only failed to complete the project on time but ultimately left us homeless. It had been agreed with the contractors we engaged to undertake the renovation works that the property would be ready to move in when we returned from holiday and on that proviso we vacated our rented flat.

I'll never forget the moment we returned from two weeks in Italy to find that hardly any, if any, work had been done in our absence. I could barely contain my anger when we entered the property and in all the years of knowing Alannah, I'd never known her to lose her temper like that. As I looked around at the shambolic building site, Alannah picked up a plaster-encrusted kitchen chair and threw it at the wall in anger. A screaming match developed between Dave (the foreman) and Alannah. He admitted taking on another job whilst we were away on holiday. Unable to take any more of his pathetic excuses for the lack of progress on our build, Dave and his crew were sacked, ordered off site, and presented bills for alternative accommodation until the building was habitable. It was another eight weeks before the renovations were completed and the building was signed off by building control. If I'd known then that this was only the start of things to come, I would have slapped the property back on the market and sold it.

When we moved in, Alannah chose one of the top bedrooms but after a couple of nights she started to complain about strange things happening there. I swapped rooms, fearing the presence I'd detected when we viewed the property was making itself known. It was nothing that I couldn't cope with but for Alannah it would be difficult. At that point, I felt confident I could contain the presence and in time help it to pass to the other side.

As we settled into our new home, I discovered the presence of two young girls in the top bedroom I was now occupying, in addition to a woman in her mid-fifties who materialised in the kitchen one evening, taking me by complete surprise. It soon became evident very early on in our occupancy that the property was a portal for numerous visiting spirits. Then one evening, when I was alone in the property, something happened to change everything.

As I was halfway up the stairwell to my bedroom, something pinned me down on the steps. I could see nothing but experienced a pain so great that when I eventually broke free of the powerful force it left me reeling. I fled downstairs into the kitchen, away from the force, to get a glass of water and to make sense of what had just happened. Never in the years in which I had come to terms with my extraordinary gift have I experienced something so horrendous. My hands were trembling as I filled a glass with water over the kitchen sink.

Without turning, I instinctively knew the presence was back and before I could turn to face it I was attacked from behind. The glass fell from my hands into the sink as I was lifted off my feet and thrown to the floor, and engulfed by the presence. I was transported in time and subjected to gruesome visions of a young woman being brutally raped. Trapped inside the horrendous vision, I screamed to the rapist to leave her alone but the man continued his foul mission. I watched the scene unfolding, helpless on the periphery as the young woman put up a valiant fight, clawing and biting her attacker. The man, who was bigger and stronger, easily overpowered his victim, pinning her against the kitchen units, where she lost her battle. I watched in revulsion as her head was pounded into a pulp against a stone sink, rendering her unconscious. After the rape, the man fell off his victim and howled with grief like a demented animal when he saw what he'd done. After a while, his senses returned and he wrapped the body of the young woman in a mat.

As the vision began to fade, I came to, lying on the kitchen floor, trembling with fear in the aftermath of what I'd just witnessed, instinctively knowing the crime was committed in the very spot where I lay. I initially thought the entity was male, due to the ferocity of its presence, but as my thoughts cleared it began to dawn on me that the troubled soul was female and whoever she'd been in a previous life had come back through the vortex of time to get vengeance on her rapist, or to convey a warning. Either way, I know I am somehow connected to her past life and I am convinced that the property we bought harbours a grisly secret. This new enlightenment has filled me with a sense of foreboding for the future occupancy of No. 26, which is something I can no longer keep from Alannah.

A week has passed with no further incidents. I have built myself up into a frenzy at the thought of telling Alannah the truth about the property into which we've poured our life savings. Thinking it best to tell her away from No. 26, as I knew what her reaction would be, I organised an early evening meeting in the Hotel Papiar, where it would be quiet and we wouldn't be disturbed. As I arrived at the wine bar, I received a call on my mobile from Alannah, telling me she'd been caught up in a business meeting and she'd try to catch up later. That evening, I never got round to telling her, as I met up with another group of friends and although I ended up staying at the Hotel Papiar, Alannah never showed and something else happened *to take my thoughts off the decision I faced.*

I saw the black aura clinging to him like a cape the moment he entered the wine bar. Although he tried to be inconspicuous, it was evident he was studying me from behind the cocktail menu he was holding. I watched him from the corner of my eye as he gave up studying the menu and approached our group. With his hypnotic presence, he ingratiated himself to my friends and managed to single me out, persuading me to leave the group under the guise of helping to fetch another round of drinks. He followed behind me as I manoeuvred through the crowds. As I got to the far right side of the bar, where the crowds were less dense, he took me by surprise. I felt the hardness in his pants as he pushed his body up against me. In the struggle to get away, I managed to manoeuvre myself forward and face him head on. He was inches away from my face, forcing me to stare directly into his strange, hazel-flecked eyes. In that instant, the vision I'd seen in the kitchen came flooding back to me, allowing me to glimpse the soul of a murderer. That's when I realised that the man in front of me, although it seemed impossible, was the embodiment of the rapist who attacked and killed the young woman on the floor of my kitchen. The crowds surrounding us at the bar were getting thicker as I struggled to get away from him. Mistaking my fear-ridden panic for impatience and wanting to get to the bar, a man pushed me out of his way, back towards the very person I was trying to escape from.

The music in the wine bar was so loud and noisy that my heated words of warning to the man to keep away from me were drowned in the heady party atmosphere. I was desperate and in a tight spot. This sadistic bully was clearly enjoying every minute of my distress as he pursued me amongst the thronging crowds. Searching for my friends, I discovered they'd disappeared to the other side of the bar and were out of sight. It was then that I noticed a powerfully built man with blond hair towering above the crowds, heading in my direction, pushing people aside until he reached me. As he got closer I realised it was Peter. The crowds started to shrink away from us as Peter grabbed the back of the man's jacket and hustled him towards the door. Knowing there was going to be a confrontation, people nearby edged away, allowing easy passage through the crowded bar. Following, I watched as Peter threw him onto the street. The man turned to face Peter and momentarily their eyes met, like two gun-slingers at the OK Corral, waiting for the first one to draw. I thought then that the defiant man standing on the pavement outside the wine bar was going to retaliate but, sizing up the muscle-bound body builder before him, he obviously had second thoughts. Before he left he took a long, lingering look of pure hatred, which chilled me to the bone; as though he was dissecting what could have been if he had his way. His parting words frightened the shit out of me – "You are going to suffer for what you've done to me." Then he turned on his heel and vanished into the night.

Peter and I looked at each other in astonishment then went back into the wine bar to join my friends. The evening was a total disaster as I couldn't get the man and the heated words he spat at us out of my mind. The whole affair freaked me out and when Peter offered to walk me home, I readily accepted, not wanting to walk the short distance alone. I thanked him once again for his help and we said our goodbyes on the doorstep. Once inside No. 26 I walked through the office space and up the side staircase, passing Alannah's closed bedroom door. Noticing her light was off, I carried on to the top floor, to my bedroom. Just as I was about to close the curtains, I looked down onto the street and for the briefest of moments I thought I saw something move from the shadows of the buildings at the bottom, where the cobbled pathway curves round to meet Christmas Street. I looked again but saw nothing but darkness, where the street lighting failed to reach into the dark recesses, then a group of drunken revellers stumbled into view, evidently on their way to one of the clubs on lower Park Row. I watched them pass and in their wake silence reigned. Nothing stirred from the shadows. Alone in my room, my thoughts started to escalate. As I write this diary I know my thought process is totally irrational but I am even more convinced that what I'd seen in that horrendous vision had now presented itself in the flesh.

As Weller finished reading the diary extract, she had mixed feelings. She could deal with a sexual assault but the presence of a ghostly apparition was another thing. Perhaps the other file, called 'Family Tree', would give up some more information. After emailing it to Mark Casey, head of the tech department, for in-depth analysis, she sat at her desk for some time, pondering the two cases. It was evident they were linked but for the life of her she couldn't think why some random man at a wine bar would abduct two people just because of a drunken spat. The more Weller thought about the bizarre situation, the more she was convinced the two missing people were connected in some way. If that was the case, why had he taken Peter? It was clear Jenna had been the man's focus. It could be that Peter's intervention had resulted in him inadvertently becoming collateral damage. Perhaps this man, whoever he was, had such an ego that rejection was not an option. Getting up from her desk, she went to the briefing room to go over her jumbled thoughts, update the whiteboard, and inform her team about the latest development.

The following morning, Weller and Whitehead returned to Stepz 2 Recruitment, to speak to Alannah Corby a second time as the contents in the diary began to take on another significance. The vivid account Jenna Thornleigh wrote about the man who'd assaulted her in the Hotel Papiar made Weller's flesh crawl. A devil incarnate with strange hazel-flecked eyes and chiselled features, there was no doubt in Weller's mind that he was a person of interest. Even more astounding was Jenna's claim that No. 26 Christmas Steps was haunted by a presence who'd been murdered in the property in the early 1980s.

When some of the contents of Jenna's diary came to light, it was obvious Alannah was distressed. As her behaviour was bordering on hysterical, Weller stopped short of telling her about the theory that No. 26 Christmas Steps was the site of a murder, opting to concentrate of any scrap of information Alannah could provide about the missing woman.

Her main concern now was that it was six days since Peter Shaney's abduction and with Jenna's disappearance the situation was escalating. The only blessing was that Alannah had been quick off the mark to report it, which gave her hope they might find Jenna before the madman did whatever he was planning to her. The first forty-eight hours would be crucial. Everything, no matter how insignificant, had to be looked at.

***

After Weller and Whitehead's departure, Abbey and Alannah cancelled the remaining appointments and closed the office. Hours later, they were still dissecting Jenna's uncharacteristic disappearance, trying to make sense of the situation. Alannah's world was turned upside-down: one minute, she was going about her daily routine then, in the blink of an eye, everything changed. As time marched on with no sign of Jenna, and DS Weller's tight-lipped attitude, it was evident there was more to her disappearance than the police were prepared to divulge. All Alannah and Abbey could do was wait, and hope that she would be found safe and well, but a strong sense of foreboding prevailed, making Alannah believe things were going to end badly.

Thinking back to when they bought the property, Alannah

realised that even then things were somewhat out of kilter. The strange occurrences in the top bedroom, which she swapped with Jenna, began giving her cause for concern. When they moved in, Jenna had graciously given her first choice of the three bedrooms, and she'd chosen the top bedroom because of its quaintness, beamed ceilings and shuttered windows with a great view onto the cobbled street below. The moment she moved her possessions into the room, however, strange things started to happen. From the get-go, Alannah had a sense of being watched, her paranoia increasing at night when, alone with her thoughts, her overactive imagination took flight.

One night, she had been woken by a rocking sensation, then she felt someone jumping on her bed. Screaming in the darkness of her room, she reached out and turned on the bedside light, ready to face the intruder, but she could see nothing on her bed, or anywhere in the room. Throwing back the duvet, she got up and checked underneath the bed, then opened the wardrobe doors and peered inside, to satisfy herself that she was alone. Unnerved by the incident and unable to get back to sleep, Alannah had picked up the book she'd been reading and turned onto her side, facing the door. Selecting the page with the turned-down corner, she continued reading in an effort to steer her mind from the strange thoughts that were popping into her mind. After finishing a chapter, her eyes were heavy with sleep, but as she reached to turn the bedside light off she felt something move beside her. Turning quickly, she could see an indentation in the duvet, close to her feet. To her horror, it spread and started to move across the bed. Alannah sprung up like a scalded cat, watching the indentation as it sunk into the soft down of the duvet. Paralysed with fear, she was unable to move as she tracked its progress over to where she was standing. As the last indentation vanished from the bed beside her, for the briefest of moments a rush of air whipped round her legs, snapping Alannah out of the fear-ridden trance.

Like a woman possessed, she jumped on the bed, thrashing at the bedclothes and beating away the invisible intruder. During the moment of madness, she felt nothing and could see nothing. The unhinged terror was gradually replaced with denial and, to retain her sanity, Alannah almost convinced herself that what she'd seen was all in her imagination. Totally spent and exhausted, she slumped back on the bed, where she spent the rest of the night guarding her room like a nervous sentry in readiness to ward off another attack from an invisible enemy. Nothing further happened but Alannah knew there was no way she was going to spend another night in that bedroom.

The next morning, she had related the experience to Jenna, who immediately offered to swap rooms. Alannah gratefully accepted. After moving into the bedroom downstairs, there were no invisible visitors invading her space, and nothing further happened. Then, a couple of weeks later, Jenna and Alannah were at home watching the TV when a heated debate developed between them, sparked by the latest episode of a programme about benefit fraud. In mid-sentence, Jenna turned her head suddenly, as though she'd seen something. Following her line of vision through the glass-panelled French doors leading into the kitchen, Alannah could see nothing. When questioning Jenna about the sudden distraction, her friend had shrugged off the incident, but the startled expression on her face gave her away. Regaining her composure, Jenna offered to make tea and went into the kitchen to put the kettle on. From where she was sitting, Alannah could see Jenna was mesmerised by an empty chair, which had been pulled away from the table. Whilst the kettle was boiling, she walked over to the chair, which Alannah thought for a moment she was going to push back in line with the other three. Instead, she stood in front of it and reached out, appearing to clutch at something unseen. The smile on her friend's face told Alannah that something was happening but, not wanting to witness any more of Jenna's strange behaviour, she looked away and tried to focus on the TV. A couple of minutes later, she heard the kettle boiling, then the clatter of metal against pottery, signalling tea was being prepared. Shortly afterwards, Jenna returned with two steaming mugs and resumed her position on the sofa opposite her friend, picking up their heated debate where they'd left off.

Knowing Jenna possessed the extraordinary gift of being able to see dead people, Alannah started to get a dreadful feeling that something she didn't understand was happening in their home. This was a side of her friend's life that she refused to acknowledge, and avoided at all costs. As much as Alannah was loath to admit it, she was getting the distinct feeling that the property they had bought in Christmas Steps was haunted, and briefly toyed with the idea of confronting Jenna about it.

Three weeks later, after the incident in the kitchen, Lesley and Rebecca, Alannah's sister and niece came to stay for a couple of days. They were given the top two bedrooms and Jenna camped downstairs in the lounge. The following morning, Lesley came bounding into the kitchen, flushed and excited.

"What a night I have had, I think you may have some visitors upstairs," she exclaimed.

Alannah, who was biting into a hot buttered crumpet, looked at Jenna, who was sitting next to her at the table. Becky was still in bed, allowing her mother free rein to speak.

Despite the look of warning on Jenna's face, Lesley continued to tell them about the two little girls she'd seen playing in the bedroom. From her graphic description, they learnt the children were about four or five years old, wearing pinafore dresses and laced boots. According to Lesley, they were totally oblivious to her presence as they played with a china-faced doll with huge glass eyes, and she watched them for some time before falling asleep. She saw them again in the early hours of the morning, telling Jenna and Alannah she had been disturbed by a movement on the bed. Describing the moment, she turned on the bedside light, discovering the smaller of the two children jumping on the bed whilst the other played with a doll on the floor. As the penny dropped, Alannah turned a ghastly shade of white, knowing she'd been through the same experience but had not seen the two young girls. She struggled to keep her emotions at bay whilst Lesley continued telling them how she called out to the girl, who stopped jumping on the bed and looked straight at her. For the briefest of moments, in which Lesley tried to communicate with the child, the girl held her stare before turning to her sister, then the two of them giggled mischievously and disappeared into thin air. Without realising it, Lesley cemented Alannah's fears that No. 26 was haunted. Getting up from the table, Alannah left her breakfast uneaten, making excuses that her first appointment in the agency was due any moment. It had been evident to Jenna that it was not the real reason for her friend's hasty retreat.

Lesley and Becky stayed longer than scheduled. Jenna put Lesley in the picture about Alannah's fears and the extraordinary goings-on in the top bedroom were never discussed in front of her again.

Considering the unnatural occurrences at Christmas Steps, and unaware of Peter's abduction, Alannah began to wonder whether they were connected with Jenna's disappearance. DS Weller had alluded to Jenna's diary containing references to paranormal activity. Her initial reaction was of horror; even thinking about it made her skin crawl. But she was desperate and would do anything to help find Jenna. Fingering the card DS Weller had given her, she was tempted to ring her and run it by her but decided it was too far-fetched to consider. Having spent the evening alone with her fears, however, by morning she relented.

Getting through to Bridewell Police Station, she was informed that DS Weller had tried to call her but as her mobile number was engaged she was on her way over to see her. Just as the call ended, the doorbell rang. DS Weller and PC Whitehead were standing on the doorstep.

"Hello Alannah, can we come in?" Weller's easy smile gave nothing away as they walked through to the lounge.

"Have you found her? Is there any news?" Alannah asked anxiously.

"Take a seat, we need to discuss something with you." The serious tone of the woman's voice made Alannah stop pacing and slump down on a sofa, facing the police officers.

DS Weller wanted to know if she remembered anything else about the incident in Hotel Papiar.

"No, I'm sorry, as I told you before I was not there. Why don't you talk to Peter – he would be the one who could fill you in on this." Alannah was getting irritated at being asked the same questions.

The mention of Peter's name paved the way as DS Weller dropped the bombshell that he was also missing and they suspected both incidents were connected. Alannah was totally floored by the news. A flood of emotions threatened to overwhelm her as she desperately tried to make sense of the latest development.

"I know that we have already briefly touched on Jenna's diary and I don't know quite how to put this, but is Jenna a psychic?" Weller asked.

"What makes you say that?"

"Things she's written suggest that Jenna believes she possesses a supernatural gift," Weller replied.

Something about the softly-spoken police officer prompted Alannah to open up and confide in her about the unexplained occurrences happening at No. 26. As she spoke, she noticed Whitehead look up from the notepad he was scribbling in and look round the room, as if willing a supernatural occurrence to happen in front of him, for verification. It was obvious to Alannah that the young PC was doubtful of her claims, whilst DS Weller was treating the matter more seriously. Unburdening her innermost thoughts and first-hand experiences in the top bedroom left Alannah exhausted and only served to make her more fearful for Jenna's safety.

"Surely you can't believe this has anything to do with Jenna's disappearance?"

"At this stage, we cannot discount anything, but we think that the incident at the Hotel Papiar has something to do with their disappearance."

The comment from Weller left Alannah in no doubt the situation was serious and confirmed her earlier suspicions about the man who accosted Jenna in the wine bar.

"Will you be alright?" Weller asked as they prepared to go back to the station. Her parting words only served to panic Alannah further.

Alannah smiled a weak response but inside she was screaming, *No I'm not alright, my friend is missing, probably kidnapped by a fucking lunatic, the place I'm living in is haunted, no I'm not fucking alright.*

Before the two officers reached the bottom of the Christmas Steps, Alannah was on her mobile to Abbey, accepting her offer to stop over for a few days until Jenna was found. No way was she going to stay another night on her own in No. 26.

Chapter 15

Jenna Thornleigh's Family Tree
Bridewell Police Station

Further exploration through the contents of Jenna Thornleigh's laptop served up more surprises. Mark Casey opened the file entitled 'Family Tree', which began with a basic graph of the Thornleigh ancestors, dating back to the 1700s, with accompanying notes.

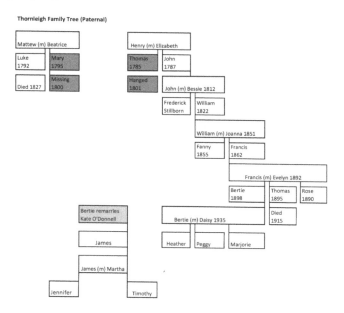

Thornleigh Family - notes

1700s - 1790s Hydlebury Farm, Lawhitton, Cornwall.

Ancestral home of Matthew Thornleigh, his wife Beatrice, and his two children, Luke and Mary. Having hit hard times, Matthew's brother Henry, together with his wife Elizabeth and their two sons, Thomas and John, moved in, increasing the household to a total of eight.

Mary Thornleigh, born 28.11.1795

Mary Thornleigh, daughter of Matthew and Beatrice of Hydlebury Farm, Lawhitton, Cornwall, disappeared at the age of five. Last seen playing in a field within the curtilage of the farm. Evidence of a scuffle in the field was recorded, together with a discarded doll left by the wayside. After Mary's disappearance, nearby neighbours and friends who had travelled from Launceston launched an extensive search of the surrounding countryside, including outhouses, but found nothing. Matthew and Beatrice were questioned, as was Luke, their son. Attentions then turned to Henry, Matthew's brother, but during the time Mary went missing he along with his son John had travelled into Launceston some four miles away with their horse and cart, spending most of the day collecting supplies for the farm, which left Thomas unaccounted for and who quickly became a person of interest. Officials conducting the investigation found nothing to link him to Mary's disappearance and according to Elizabeth, his mother, he spent most of the day ploughing the fields.

Thomas Thornleigh, born 04.04.1785

Son of Henry and Elizabeth, aged 15 was found guilty of murdering two children: Catherine Kernow (aged 7) and John Peese (aged 4). Hanged in Bodmin Gaol 18.11.1801. At that time, it was the popular belief within the local community that Thomas was also responsible for the disappearance of Mary Thornleigh. Nothing in old newspapers or police reports suggested Thomas admitted responsibility for her disappearance. A detailed transcript after his death was written in the Execution Book at Bodmin Gaol and reads:

Fifteen-year-old Thomas Thornleigh was a farm labourer at Hydlebury Farm, Lawhitton near Lansan. Thomas was an attractive young man with pitch black hair and hazel-flecked eyes but with no social skills he was not accepted by local lads and girls who reported him to be mean and moody and gave him a wide berth. One local girl called Emma Wykeford, the same age as Thomas Thornleigh, reported that after persuading her to go for a walk round the ruins of Lansan Castle he tried to molest her. Thomas Thornleigh protested that Emma Wykeford was promiscuous and led him on. After hearing his plausible explanation as the girl was well-endowed and appeared to forward for her years he was let off with a caution. Shortly after, still seething from Emma's rebuke, he came across Catherine Kernow (aged 7) who was on her way to a local baker to pick up bread for the family tea. He followed her though a series of narrow lanes. Away from prying eyes, Thomas Thornleigh was able to drag her into a nearby field where in a fit of rage he raped and strangled her. After killing Catherine Kernow he left her body in the field, naked and exposed to the elements, then walked away. On the walk to the outskirts of town where he had tethered his horse and cart he discovered his trousers were muddy and grass-stained and made a detour by the banks of the River Tamar. Taking off his trousers he rubbed and washed them in the river, wringing them tightly to get the water out, then put them back on. As it was a warm day, by the time he got home his trousers were almost dry. That evening, he sat with the rest of his family devouring the meal that had been put in front of him without a second thought for the poor dead girl he'd left in the field.

Several months later John Peese (aged 4) was playing on the narrow pathway outside St Mary Magdalene Church in Lansan with another boy called Peter Perkins. John accidentally kicked a ball into Peter's stomach and a fight erupted between the two boys. In retaliation Peter kicked John viciously on the shin then ran away. John howled in pain and hobbled off in the direction of home, shouting at his friend and swearing he would tell his parents. Thomas Thornleigh, who had been taking a short cut through the grave yard which led through to the town centre, witnessed the boys' spat. Watching the two boys he waited until Peter was out of sight then swooped down on John Peese, dragging him back through the grave yard to the other side of the church, where a lane led to a cluster of cottages then through to open countryside. With murderous intentions on his mind when he set off on the horse and cart from Hydlebury Farm to collect the weekly supplies he came armed with a piece of rope in his pocket and a neckerchief he'd stolen from his father's bedroom. He used the rope to tie the boy's hands behind his back and the neckerchief to gag him. As they neared the cluster of cottages he forced the sobbing boy to climb over a wooden turnstile, which led into the surrounding farmland. They walked for some time until they came across a derelict barn, where Thomas Thornleigh killed John Peese.

Once he was done with the young boy, Thomas Thornleigh went down by the river and cleaned the blood off his hands and clothing then walked back into the centre of Lansan to collect supplies from the hardware and grocery store. The Thornleigh family's order was always made up of the same supplies, stacked in readiness for his visit, which was paid for at the end of each month when his father or uncle Matthew made the journey into Lansan to pay the account. Nodding a brief greeting to the store owner, he grabbed the string-like bag and loaded it onto his shoulders then without a backwards glance set off to collect the horse and cart.

It took three hours of interrogation before Thomas Thornleigh confessed to killing Catherine Kernow and John Peese and, after putting on a show of tears and regret, developed another personality. The personality was described by interrogators as evil, distorting the boy's facial features to resemble a snarling, beast-like creature. As they questioned the prisoner he spoke in a strange, guttural tone expressing great delight at how he tortured and killed his victims. The boy, who had been secured to a sturdy wooden chair by rope restraints, terrified the two hardened interrogators, Hayden Littlemoor and Arthur Trecarrel, who jumped back out of reach, fearful he would break free and rip them to shreds. The prisoner launched into a tirade of undecipherable abuse, spitting and screaming at them as the chair shook violently under his weight. Thomas Thornleigh possessed super-human strength, enabling him to shuffle the chair close enough to Littlemoor and Trecarrel, who had taken refuge against the cell door. He moved with lightning speed and before they knew it the prisoner was upon them, trapping the two men as they struggled to open the door before the beast-like creature lunged at them. As the grotesque thing in the chair advanced Littlemoor screamed and dropped the keys to the door. In the seconds it took him to retrieve them and open the door Trecarrel was right behind him attempting to close it after them but it was too late. Littlemoor, who was on the other side of the door, heard a blood-curdling scream as he boy sunk his teeth into Trecarrel's hand. Leaping forward to his defence, Littlemoor pushed the boy away with such force that the chair containing the prisoner skidded across the floor and a huge chunk of skin and bone came away from Trecarrel's hand in the separation. The screaming alerted another guard, who ran through the warren of underground tunnels. Finding the interrogator on the floor screaming in agony, with half his hand missing, he pulled him to *his feet and led him away to get help. Behind them, Littlemoor slammed and locked the door but before following his colleagues he took one last look through the bars into the cell. The sight before him made him gasp as he watched the monster in the chair devour the remnants of Trecarrel's hand, licking his lips after the feast like a snarling beast. After consuming the human flesh, the beast-like creature's head spun round to look at Littlemoor, who fled through the underground tunnels into the fresh air.*

Hayden Littlemoor told his account to the prison governor, John Doidge, whilst a doctor attended to Arthur Trecarrel's maimed hand. Littlemoor reported that, despite being privy to all manner of evil during his years as a law enforcer, never had he seen anything like the beast-like transformation which came about as they interrogated the fifteen-year-old boy. Littlemoor's fear was so great that he admitted vomiting on the stone floor before they were forced up against the cell door. He also told the governor how the prisoner's extraordinary strength helped him to loosen the rope binding him to the chair. John Doidge was inclined to dismiss the farfetched report from the interrogator but seeing Trecarrel's badly mutilated hand before he was dispatched to the infirmary, he wanted to see the prisoner for himself, to verify Littlemoor's account. In the company of two armed guards, the prison governor marched back through the warren of tunnels down to the cells. As they approached the cell, there was no sound coming from within. He looked through the bars. Inside, the boy, who had freed himself from the rope restraints, rushed the door like a crazed animal. John Doidge fell back in alarm, overwhelmed by the putrid stench of death coming from the boy's mouth as he attempted to bite him through the confines of the bars. Had he not witnessed the insane creature the other side of the cell door for himself, and heard the chilling account given by the interrogator of the two children's deaths, Doidge would have been at a loss to believe a fifteen-year-old boy could be responsible for such evil.

The coroner's report concluded that in excess of thirty knife wounds found on John Peese's tiny body were testament to a deranged, sadistic killer, who deserved to be hanged by the neck until he was dead. With the confession, and the mutilation of the interrogator's hand, there was no shadow of doubt that Thomas Thornleigh was an insane monster, guilty of brutally murdering John Peese and Catherine Kernow. After the vicious attack on Trecarrel, Thomas Thornleigh was chained to the wall of his cell, restricting movements from his bed to a metal bucket to relieve himself. Guards were extra vigilant, always checking to ascertain the prisoner's whereabouts before entering the cell. On one occasion, the boy tried to bite a guard who ventured too close as he tried to get an empty food tray. After that incident, wooden poles were used to retrieve the empty trays. Over the course of two months the boy, who sat in blood-stained clothes, stinking of death itself, became strangely quiet and withdrawn, indicating that whatever madness possessed him had now passed. During his incarceration, there were several visiting requests, one of which came from his mother, but having considered the severity of Thornleigh's crimes against children, the governor denied the request to see her son. Another request to visit the prisoner came from a pitiful woman suffering from Tuberculosis, who was convinced a murderer's touch could heal her. As there was no hope for the woman the governor granted her last wish. As the prisoner had given them no trouble lately, the woman was let in the cell and left alone with the boy. The guard heard the screaming from the other side of the door and unlocked the cell door to find her grotesquely shaped body lying on the floor, dead at the feet of the prisoner. Rage overwhelmed him as he looked at woman's body. The guard turned on the prisoner, who took the beating without retaliation until the man was pulled away by two other guards.

Father Dominic was called upon to take Thomas Thornleigh's last confession. Despite being warned the boy was evil incarnate the priest, being a god-fearing man, was determined to give the prisoner his last rites before he was despatched into eternity to meet to his maker. Having observed the prisoner and established the boy was in a stable condition Father Dominic entered the cell alone. Half an hour passed without incident then prison guards heard urgent shouting and banging on the cell door. Benjamin Beale, the guard who opened the door, found Father Dominic trembling and clearly distressed but in his haste to get the priest out of the cell he broke the cardinal rule and turned his back on the prisoner. As Beale was within easy reach, Thomas Thornleigh grabbed him by the throat and started to strangle him. Beale was a small, wiry man and no match for the boy who, possessing extraordinary strength, started to choke the man with his hands as Father Dominic cried out for help. Two guards came hurtling down the stone passageway towards the cell and found Beale as the last vestiges of air were squeezed from his body. Defiant words spewed from the fifteen-year-old's mouth as the dead guard was dragged from his grasp, out of the cell, and Thornleigh was flung against the wall. They watched as he got to his feet, laughing and unhurt.

"You can hang me but I will never die," the door closed on the piercing screams.

Thornleigh's words invoked fear amongst the guards, filtering down to prisoners believing the beast in the end cell had strange powers which could travel through walls and kill them. Amongst the prisoners there was great unrest inside Bodmin Gaol to be rid of the inhuman creature before he could strike again. It was little under three months since the boy's incarceration and the death toll was mounting. A woman suffering with Tuberculosis, Benjamin Beale, Arthur Trecarrel's massacred hand and the traumatised priest earned Thomas Thornleigh the nickname "The Demon". Interrogators Hayden Littlemoor, Arthur Trecarrel and the prison governor had little doubt the priest had encountered "The Demon" but further questioning proved futile, the man being too traumatised to utter a word of what transpired between Thornleigh and himself.

Thomas Thornleigh, born 24.02.1895
Son of Francis and Evelyn, sister Rose, brother Bertie. Killed in a farming accident when a plough he was operating hit a rock. It rebounded, catching Thomas' arm as he tried to get it upright. He bled to death where he fell in the field before help could get to him. Thomas was 20 years of age. After his death a young girl came forward to make a complaint that she was beaten by him. This sparked rumours in the community of Lansan and another woman made it known that Thomas had sexually assaulted her and beat her within a heartbeat of her life. When questioned by officials as to why she never came forward when he was alive Flora Down said that it was better to keep it quiet as Thomas threatened he would seek her out and kill her if she told anyone. She broke down and cried saying that no one would believe her anyway as the assault took place five years before he died.

Mark Casey was taken aback by the account, his eyes going back to the ancestral chart on the next page. The names of Thomas and Mary Thornleigh were highlighted in red, which he assumed was the link that sparked the missing woman's interest. Underneath the chart, confirming his theory, were the Thornleigh Family notes and bullet-pointed names, which Jenna Thornleigh had flagged up following an extensive search. After reading the improvised extract from the Execution Book and unearthing the family's dark secret, Casey's radar started to tune into something, making him want to read more. Adding to the intrigue was the fact there had been two boys called Thomas born into the same family, albeit some one hundred years apart, who both appeared to be sexual predators. Casey made a mental note to himself to do some more digging into the second Thomas, to see if he could unearth anything during that time period to link him to anything else. His inner radar was telling him that having had a young woman come forward after his death, with complaints of sexual assaults and beatings, there could possibly be more unreported incidents, or worse. Two hours passed before he glanced at the clock on the laptop, putting him in a spin. Realising the lateness of the hour and with the prospect of DS Weller breathing down his neck for his report, Casey was mindful of getting results for the ambitious detective sergeant, who didn't take kindly to be kept waiting. The thought of the dark-haired beauty, with colour rising in her face as she chastised him like a young boy, was appealing and still fresh in his mind from his last run-in with her.

Snapping out of his reverie, he reverted back to the abduction of Peter Shaney and Jenna Thornleigh and what, if anything, this Family Tree extract, could reveal to help their current investigation.

Despite Jenna's obvious fixation with Thomas, her long-deceased ancestor, Casey could not find any connection between the Thornleigh family and the current abductions, and wondered whether DS Weller and her team were having more success with the diary.

In search of a sugar fix before resuming the search, Casey got up from his desk and walked out of the office. At the end of the corridor a vending machine bulging with all manner of sweet treats and fizzy drinks beckoned him. Retrieving a battered leather wallet from his jacket, he fished round for loose change and fed the machine, selecting two chocolate bars and a regular coke. Hands full with treats, he retraced his steps and collided with DS Weller just as he was about to enter his office.

"Casey, have you got anything for me yet?" Weller said a little abruptly, annoyed they had almost banged into each other.

"Not enough to give you an informed opinion," he replied, ripping open a chocolate bar with his teeth.

"Well get on with it, we have two missing people and I need results pronto."

Weller walked away, leaving Casey drooling in her wake but knowing there was no chance in hell she'd date someone like him. Recent rumours coming to his attention of her being gay dropped the possibility to zero. His initial reaction to the station gossip was one of disappointment but Casey refused to be drawn into the unfounded speculation, probably started by some egotistical twat having had the brush-off from the feisty brunette.

Sitting back at his desk, Casey scrolled through Jenna's bullet-pointed synopsis of her maternal family tree.

Maternal side of the Family

• **_Albert Matthews born 1890_** - _fought in the Battle of Jutland. Died at the age of 26 on 31ˢᵗ May 1916 when battle cruiser Queen Mary was struck five times and went down within sixty seconds. Albert went to his grave in the North Sea leaving behind a wife Margaret and a daughter Annie aged two._

• **_Lucinda Matthews born 1827_** – _sailed on the first iron ship SS Great Britain. Built by Isambard Kingdom Brunel to carry 700 passengers and launched in Bristol's floating harbour by Prince Albert on 23ʳᵈ July 1843. Its maiden journey starting from Liverpool to New York on 26ᵗʰ July 1845. The ship was later used to carry emigrants and gold seekers to Australia._

Lucinda, aged 18, was discovered to have run away with her wealthy lover, a George Tremain who was fifteen years her senior. The last sighting of the love-struck pair was buying two tickets for the maiden journey from Liverpool to New York. On

26th July 1845 Lucinda and George set out on the journey to New York, leaving their respective families behind. George's parents Frederick and Agnes did all they could to track down their sole heir and beneficiary of their vast fortune made in transportation but the trail went cold. Despite posting several advertisements in prominent American papers and employing the services of private detectives in England and America, nothing further was heard from George or Lucinda.

For some unknown reason, the account of Lucinda Matthews intrigued Casey. Back in 1845, policing was basic and tracking people in another continent was nigh on impossible, making it easy for people to disappear without trace. He wondered what became of the woman, hoping she had a full and happy life with her lover. Writing on an A4 pad, Casey noted the lover's name: *George Tremain – wealthy, check descendants, trace the money – find Lucinda.* The other tragedy which struck the family was when Albert Matthews died in May 1916, serving his country in the Battle of Jutland. He was a relatively young man, dying at the age of twenty-six. A pattern was forming within the family history, bringing Casey to the conclusion that these descendants rarely survived to an old age.

Apart from the mention of Lucinda and Albert Matthews, the family tree focused solely on the paternal side, a family of farmers. In Jenna's notes, Casey found that Mathew and Henry, descendants of Joseph and Catherine and their respective families, lived together at a farmhouse called Hydlebury in a small hamlet in Cornwall called Lawhitton. Henry married Elizabeth and had two sons, one of whom was Thomas Thornleigh, hanged for the murder of two small children. Casey found extracts from the *Royal Cornish Gazette* reporting the confession of Thomas Thornleigh to murdering John Peese aged four and Catherine Kernow aged seven, corroborating some facts from the Execution Book at Bodmin Gaol. Thomas Thornleigh's hanging was a ghoulish occasion, with people travelling for miles to witness the spectacle, his death covered by the ancient newspaper with great relish. His last moments described him as a demon staring out at the baying crowds, with bewitching hazel-coloured eyes searching for the next victim to come under his spell. The crowds whipped themselves into such a frenzy that several women fainted and fell to the floor before the executioner had the chance to cover Thornleigh's head with the black hood. As his face disappeared beneath the hood a lull descended. In the deadly silence that followed the trapdoor could be heard clearly as it creaked open in the gallows' floor. Seconds later, Thornleigh fell eight feet, suspended by coiled rope until he choked to death. The crowds cheered the moment his hooded head disappeared through the trapdoor into eternity and damnation. After his body was cut down, the paper reported a bartering process for ownership of the rope that had strangled Thomas Thornleigh, believing it to contain healing powers. Casey felt sick to his stomach as he envisaged people like hungry buzzards, fighting over the remnants of the executor's rope, trying to get the best deal for the gruesome trophy.

Casey discovered that Mary Thornleigh, aged five at the time of Thomas' incarceration, had also mysteriously disappeared, heightening his suspicions. In newspapers it was speculated Thomas Thornleigh was responsible for her disappearance but with no body, and the absence of a confession from her cousin, the mystery remained to this day.

At the end of the research into her family tree the missing woman rambled on about reincarnation and parallel lives. Casey was stunned at what he read next. It appeared Jenna was under the delusion that she was leading a parallel life to Mary Thornleigh, her long-deceased ancestor, based on the fact that this blood relative was born 28/11/1795. The twenty-eighth day and the same month as her own birth, albeit a different century. What startled Casey the most was her theory that Thomas Thornleigh possessed the ability of reincarnation, being reborn to continue his killing rampage right through to the 1980s when he struck again. Casey referred back to the graph and Jenna's notes. In addition to Thomas born in 1785, the other ancestor called Thomas, born in 1895, again caught his eye. Having read about Jenna's theory of reincarnation, he started thinking there might be some credence to the possibility of another reincarnation into the same family. He started to make some notes on his A4 writing pad and decided to do some digging on the second Thomas, to see what else he could find. Jenna also alluded to a warning from a troubled spirit haunting No. 26 Christmas Steps, the property she had recently purchased with her business partner, but without access to the diary offering up more information he was at odds as to what Jenna Thornleigh was referring to. Making reference to reincarnation and the 1980s killing in his notes, Casey wondered whether to bring this to Weller's attention or disregard it, to avoid risking appearing stupid, but if he could find anything on the second Thomas this may prove the theory going through his mind and corroborate Jenna's thoughts.

Chapter 16

The Link
Bridewell Police Station

DS Weller and Whitehead got lucky when one of the PCs tasked to cover Shaney's neighbourhood came across Josh Reardon; a neighbour who, having been burgled twice at previous addresses, had installed a state-of-the-art CCTV surveillance system to deter any would-be thieves. The system, which was linked to his wrist watch and accessed by an app, revealed footage within a mile's radius of his property, logging data direct to a cloud format. This nugget of information was gleaned after PCs Tarrant and Michaels briefed the team on a neighbour called Maria Clarke, the attractive redhead who lived in the same building as Peter Shaney and who had encountered a strange man on the doorstep of their building. Once Tarrant and Michaels finished their briefing, PC Declan Connor, also tasked with door-to-door enquiries in the area, stepped up to address the team, passing on information about Reardon's surveillance system and his high-tech watch, suggesting the surveillance data may contain images of the doorstep stranger. Agreeing with his train of thought, DS Weller instructed Connor to make arrangements to bring Reardon into the station.

Josh Reardon was a beanpole of a man, wearing baggy jeans which kept slipping down to reveal the waistband of his designer underwear. A woollen beanie pulled over his head, emblazoned with the words 'The Man', partially obscured his small, beady eyes. Hip-hop gangster spiel did no favours for the white boy in his late twenties, who was an obnoxious runt with the personality of a worm. As they interviewed him, it was clear to Weller that Whitehead was exasperated by the boy's evasive attitude. When questioned about the evening Maria Clarke had encountered the man at her door, the only information Reardon offered was that he was out 'taking care of business' and saw nothing. Weller kept her temper in check long enough to get Reardon to part from the expensive-looking wrist watch, making a mental note that once it was handed over to the techies to extract the data to keep a close eye on Reardon. Parted from his precious property, Reardon complained bitterly, refusing to move until the watch was returned to him; it was enough to make Weller convinced it had been acquired through ill-gotten gains.

"Look bro, I have to have ma watch back pronto," Reardon leered across the interview desk, his attempt at malice completely lost on them.

Realising he was getting nowhere, Reardon started bleating on about two previous burglaries, how much gear was stolen, and his suspicions about being targeted through Facebook. He followed this up by saying he foolishly gave an edited view of his gangster lifestyle on Facebook, admitting reluctantly how he 'put it out there'. A bad mistake, thought Weller, who'd recently been involved in a case where constant bragging on social media sparked a trail of stalking, ultimately leading to a disastrous situation for the victim.

"It shouldn't take too long," promised Weller as she terminated the interview, bringing an unexpected wave of gratitude from Reardon, which made her attitude soften towards the stroppy young man. He was deposited at the front desk, where the sergeant instructed him to take a seat in the foyer whilst waiting for the return of his prized watch.

It didn't take long for the techies to come up trumps with the feast of data. Living two doors away from Maria Clarke, a date and approximate time when the neighbour encountered the man at her front door narrowed their search perimeters. The surveillance data enabled them to watch as the glamorous redhead opened the front door and spoke to a man on her doorstep. After a brief conversation, they watched as she walked up the pathway from her house to the gate and directed the man to a location further up the road, before getting into her car.

Once she'd driven away, the footage showed the same man doubling back and reappearing outside the building. They watched as he loitered outside for a few minutes, looking up at the top flat. Then he walked away and disappeared at the top of the street.

Fast-forwarding the data, there was no sign of the man until some two hours later they noticed someone driving up and down the narrow side street looking for a parking spot. Slowing the footage they watched as the car manoeuvred into a tight spot just up from Shaney's flat. Watching the occupant disembark they realised it was the same man they'd seen earlier.

Maria Clarke had also arrived back armed with heavy shopping bags she was dragging from the boot of her car. The man noticed the woman obviously remembering her from their first encounter and hurried off down the street out of sight. He reappeared as she was entering the building and watched as another man entered a property a couple of houses down the street. Reaching into his pocket he produced a set of keys. Pointing them in the direction of a dark blue Range Rover parked several yards away, the vehicle's locking mechanism released and he got inside.

The time stamp on the data surveillance read 8.46pm as the driver manoeuvred out of the tight parking spot and made his way up the narrow street. At the end of the street the driver stopped and indicated to take a left turning.

Under the glare of a lamppost, the vehicle's number plate was clearly visible before the car disappeared from view and with it their suspect.

The transference of data took less than an hour then the watch was returned to its owner, who by this time was pacing the front foyer like an expectant father. "'Bout time man, I was 'bout to complain," Reardon snatched the wrist watch from the sergeant, who'd just taken possession of it from the tech department and who watched him swagger through revolving doors onto the street outside.

With the technical information now in her possession, Weller made enquiries with the DVLA for details of the registered owner of the Range Rover. The information revealed the owner of the vehicle was Daniel Overton of Cranleigh, Beaton Moore Road, Stoke Bishop, Bristol. Further investigations into Overton revealed that his parents, Stanley and Heather, had died in a car crash whilst they were on holiday in France, after which he inherited a construction business and the family fortune. Shortly after his parents died, an ageing aunt passed away, also leaving him a small fortune. Overton proved to be a bit of an enigma; never spending too much to draw attention to himself, living well under the radar for someone so wealthy. Overton had no criminal record, nothing that would raise a red flag in his life until now, as a suspect wanted for the abduction of Peter Shaney, last known sighting in a white van heading towards Devon.

After narrowly escaping a multi-vehicle pile-up on the M5 just after Cullompton, the van Daniel Overton was driving had evaded the tracking cameras and Weller had her team searching through anything in the suspect's background that linked him to Devon or Cornwall. By mid-day, the team hadn't got any further with their enquiries, apart from the fact that shortly after receiving his inheritance, Overton sold his father's share of the construction company for an exorbitant amount of money, the proceeds of which had allowed him to upgrade to a grand six-bedroom residence in Stoke Bishop.

The incident room was a hive of activity as Whitehead stepped outside to have a crafty fag. On the way back, he took a detour to look in on his mate Steve Esklick, with the intention of hooking up with him for a drink later on in the week. There was no sign of Esklick as he walked into the squad room, at the end of which was an office he shared with DS Piconya, whose speciality was cold cases. On the way through, he saw the desk sergeant chatting to PC Staverous. Looking through the glass-partitioned office, he noticed it was empty and stopped to ask them if they knew the whereabouts of Esklick. The desk sergeant immediately shook his head, only having come on duty in the last ten minutes, but Staverous told him DS Piconya and Esklick had taken a trip to Devon, to interview someone in connection with a cold case they were working on.

"Ask Benson, he'll know more, he'll be back on duty in about an hour," Staverous offered, looking at his watch.

"Thanks, mate, I'm in the middle of an investigation, I'll just pop into his office and leave him a note." Whitehead made straight for Esklick's desk, in the corner of the small office. After finding a yellow post-it pad he wrote, 'Fancy a drink later? Give me a bell. Whitey' and left it on by his friend's keyboard. Just as Whitehead was about to leave the office, he caught sight of the whiteboard, on which were several pictures with arrows leading to written comments underneath. Curiosity made him move closer. What he saw stopped him in his tracks.

"Fucking hell, it's the same bloke." Standing for a moment, with the footage from Josh Reardon's app fresh in his mind, Whitehead took in the sight before turning on his heel and heading back the same way he had come.

Busting into the busy incident room with the finesse of a baby rhino, he announced to DS Weller, "Boss, you're gonna want to see this."

Weller followed Whitehead until they reached the east wing of the station. As she followed Whitehead's retreating back into a small office, she wondered what had him all stirred up. Then she saw it.

"What the hell is this?" Standing in front of the whiteboard, Weller started to take in its significance.

It was glaringly obvious Whitehead had stumbled across a link to their case. Weller digested the comments surrounding two photographs in the centre of the whiteboard, one of which appeared to have been taken during a family gathering; maybe some sort of celebration – the man stood with a can of beer in his hand, smiling for the camera. Weller assumed it had been taken in the 1980s, evidenced by the mullet hairstyle and style of clothes. The other photograph was a print-out from a mobile phone, of a man in an art gallery, catching him unawares as he studied a piece of artwork. The whiteboard was headed 'Jane Adams, 1985'. The old photograph was circled, with the words 'Hazel Flecked Eyes – scarring to the chin – Tommy Adams'. Another arrow shot from the picture taken on the mobile phone with the person named as Jason Holden. As Weller compared both photographs, the resemblance was startling. Apart from some scarring to Tommy Adams' chin, and decades separating the two men, they could pass as twins. Below Adams' photograph were more arrows:

- *Jane Adams murdered - residence No. 26 Christmas Steps*
- *Tommy Adams – main suspect*
- *Ex-girlfriend Eva Shalinski – sights man resembling Tommy Adams*

Below Jason Holden's photograph the arrows read:

- *Complaint from Davina McCreedie at Steps Gallery – man in gallery acting strangely*
- *Questioning man called Jason Holden - startling resemblance to Tommy Adams – giving bogus contact details*
- *McCreedie sights Holden loitering outside No. 26 Christmas Steps and getting into Range Rover – partial number plate OVR*

To all intents and purposes, it appeared Jason Holden had an agenda focused in and around Christmas Steps, which Davina McCreedie had been quick to point out and wise to bring to their attention. Weller experienced a mounting sense of excitement as she assimilated the similarities with their case. The partial number plate and make of vehicle matched the Range Rover they had tracked from Josh Reardon's surveillance footage, leading them to Daniel Overton; a prime suspect wanted for the abduction of Peter Shaney.

Weller eyed the photograph of Tommy Adams again; the brother wanted for murdering his sister. Apart from the astonishing similarity between the two men, it appeared DS Piconya had found a link connecting them, but Weller was at a loss to ascertain what that was. Before her was the face of a murder suspect going back thirty years, and a young man photographed in an art gallery, who looked to be the same person who was caught on Josh Reardon's surveillance footage. According to Piconya's whiteboard, the man was known as Jason Holden. Weller could also identify him as the same person stalking Peter Shaney at Fitkicks Gym in Welsh Back. Not only was he one and the same person but a dead ringer for the murder suspect Tommy Adams, who had to have undergone a complete face-lift to make him years younger or Holden, aka

Overton, was Adams' offspring. Studying the photograph taken in the gallery with more intensity, Weller discounted the face-lift option as medical science hadn't progressed to the point of eradicating the ageing process completely. Tell-tale signs of age were always present and those differences were evident as Holden reached out to examine a piece of sculpture in the gallery, showing youthful hands with perfectly manicured nails as the sleeve of his jacket rose up to expose a silver bracelet. There was also the recent abduction of Jenna Thornleigh, who was also linked with Peter Shaney. Turning away from the whiteboard, she started to issue orders.

"Well spotted, Whitehead. Take that whiteboard off the wall, I want it in the incident room. Get DS Piconya on her mobile and patch her through to me."

"DS Piconya and PC Esklick are on a field trip in Devon but Benson is due on duty shortly and knows more about it," Whitehead replied.

"When Benson comes in, bring him to me." Weller shot through the door, leaving Whitehead prising the whiteboard out of its fixings whilst he waited for Benson to arrive.

As she entered the incident room, Weller spied PC Michaels.

"Michaels, we've just got another hit on that woman who has gone missing from Christmas Steps, and Shaney. Whitehead will be along shortly with a whiteboard from DS Piconya's office."

Michaels, used to his boss's rapid-fire statements, nodded his head and fell in tow with the rest of the team, awaiting her instructions.

Chapter 17

DS Sylvia Piconya - Sharing of Information
Bridewell Police Station

"Piconya," she said, answering her mobile as Steve Esklick came out of the petrol station shop carrying a bag of what looked suspiciously like chocolate and crisps. Another lapse in his so-called diet, she thought, before giving the caller her full attention.

"Sylvia, it's Stacey Weller. Where are you?"

"Filling up at Gordano Services, why?"

Esklick got into the car and started the engine. He glanced over at his boss as he manoeuvred the car back onto the motorway towards Bristol, a shocked expression on her face as she listened to Weller informing her of the bizarre turn of events overlapping with her cold case. Able to hear just one side of the conversation, Esklick was intrigued.

"Bloody hell, if what you are telling me is correct we could be looking for the same man. We are leaving Gordano services now. Allowing for traffic, we should be with you in about thirty minutes," Piconya said.

Back at Bridewell Police Station, Weller ended the call and turned to address her team, who were gathering in the incident room just as Whitehead entered, carrying the whiteboard.

"Put it over there," she instructed. Whitehead walked to the front and propped Piconya's board against theirs.

"Have you located Benson yet?" Weller asked.

Whitehead shook his head, explaining he'd been called out to attend a burglary on the outskirts of Clifton Village.

Looking at her watch, Weller replied, "Don't worry about Benson. DS Piconya will be with us in about twenty minutes, then we'll know more of what's going on with her cold case."

A lull descended over the room as Whitehead moved away, allowing the team to take in the contents of the whiteboard, then all eyes reverted to Weller and questions started flying.

"Okay, okay, settle down. As you can see, we have some new developments. At this stage, we are waiting for DS Piconya to arrive and share information that could very well assist our investigation. Michaels, grab a marker pen and draw up two tables of information. One headed 'Abduction', the other 'Cold Case Jane Adams 1985'. We'll start with the abduction then list the information DS Piconya has on her whiteboard."

ABDUCTION

Peter Shaney
Missing 6 days – abducted from Park Row multi-storey car park

Josh Reardon (neighbour) – footage from mobile phone showing man and Range Rover OVR – owner Daniel Overton

Fitkicks (gym) - CCTV footage revealing Shaney's stalker – identified as Jason Holden also known as Daniel Overton

Overton – inherits parent's fortune and ageing aunt's estate

Jenna Thornleigh
Disappeared after leaving Trim Trail Gym

Hotel Papiar – man assaulted Jenna in wine bar - thrown out by Peter Shaney

File called Family Tree found on Jenna's laptop – waiting report back from Mark Casey

Diary Extracts found on Jenna Thornleigh's laptop – reveals paranormal activity at 26 Christmas Steps

COLD CASE JANE ADAMS 1985
Jane Adams murdered - residence No. 26 Christmas Steps

Tommy Adams – main suspect

Ex- girlfriend Eva Shalinski – sights man resembling Tommy Adams

Jason Holden
Complaint from Davina McCreedie at Steps Gallery – man in gallery acting strangely

Questioning man called Jason Holden - startling resemblance to Tommy Adams – giving bogus contact details

McCreedie sights Holden loitering outside No. 26 Christmas Steps and getting into Range Rover – partial number plate OVR

Looking at the facts coming together side by side, it was evident to Weller they were dealing with something far stranger than she had ever seen before. Glancing at her watch again it informed her Piconya was due to arrive shortly.

When DS Piconya and PC Esklick entered the incident room, all eyes turned to face them. Weller ushered Piconya and Esklick into a side room, along with Whitehead, where they combined the facts of each case and learned about the background Piconya had gathered on the Adams family that wasn't on the whiteboard, before emerging into the incident room to discuss the collective information and possible ways forward for the joint investigation. As it appeared that Daniel Overton was the prime suspect in the abduction of two people with links to the cold case, he immediately became their main focus.

The team watched Piconya walk over to the whiteboard, pick up a marker pen and add further information from their visit to Devon. The addition of the Adams' family dynamic revealed the staggering fact that Jane Adams, the young woman murdered in 1985, had also resided at the same property as Jenna Thornleigh. The enormity of this sequence of events happening brought a silence to the room as everyone in turn tossed around the strange possibility but, although a pattern was forming, they still had no idea where Overton was.

Weller started to split the available manpower into teams of two, designating each team to a particular task. The main focus was Daniel Overton's last movements, when he was sighted heading towards Devon in a white van. Michaels and Tarrant were tasked with contacting Devon & Cornwall Police, putting an alert out on the van and Daniel Overton, whilst the other team sifted through Overton's personal life, hoping to find someone who would know him well enough to provide them with any clues to his whereabouts.

Whilst DS Piconya and Esklick went back to their office to write up reports on their Devon field trip, Weller studied the whiteboard intently, knowing that somewhere amongst the information in their possession was the key to Overton's location. As her eyes lingered on the name of Peggy Thornleigh, Overton's aunt, something in her memory stirred. She remembered one of her PCs saying something about the aunt's estate as the item was added to the board. As she fished around in her memory, it came to her. Piconya had mentioned that Peggy Thornleigh was Heather Overton's sister and had lived in Somerset, which was near to where the multi-vehicle collision took place; the last place the white van Overton had been driving was seen. Picking up a marker pen, she put asterisks against it on the whiteboard.

ABDUCTION

Peter Shaney
Missing 6 days – abducted from Park Row multi-storey car park

Josh Reardon (neighbour) – footage from mobile phone showing man and Range Rover OVR – owner Daniel Overton

Fitkicks (gym) - CCTV footage revealing Shaney's stalker – identified as Jason Holden also known as Daniel Overton

Overton – inherits parents' fortune and ageing aunt's estate**

<u>Jenna Thornleigh</u>
Disappeared after leaving Trim Trail Gym

Hotel Papiar – man assaulted Jenna in wine bar - thrown out by Peter Shaney

File called Family Tree found on Jenna's laptop – waiting report back from Mark Casey

Diary Extracts found on Jenna Thornleigh's laptop – reveals paranormal activity at 26 Christmas Steps

COLD CASE JANE ADAMS 1985

Jane Adams murdered – residence No. 26 Christmas Steps

Tommy Adams – main suspect

Ex-girlfriend Eva Shalinski – sights man resembling Tommy Adams

Retired DCI Spencer – reveals birth of baby boy adoptive parents Heather (nee Thornleigh) and Stanley Overton

Heather Overton – Marjorie Adams' sister, also Jane's mother

Donald Adams (Jane's father) – died in suspicious circumstances at Christmas Steps

Retired PC Smithers – confirms supernatural occurrence at Christmas Steps

Jason Holden

Complaint from Davina McCreedie at Steps Gallery – man in gallery acting strangely

Questioning man called Jason Holden - startling resemblance to Tommy Adams – giving bogus contact details

McCreedie sights Holden loitering outside No. 26 Christmas Steps and getting into Range Rover – partial number plate OVR

Weller walked purposefully across the busy incident room to Michaels and Tarrant, who were sifting through footage of the multi-vehicle pile-up on the M5 near Cullompton, just before the white van containing Overton had disappeared. Tarrant was on the phone to Traffic, giving them a full description of the vehicle, its number plates, last known whereabouts, and its possible location, requesting a wider search of Devon and Cornwall, ending the call as Weller joined them.

"Pass what you are doing onto Kangers and Phillips, I want you to dig into Peggy Thornleigh's estate. Find out who dealt with the Will and let me know what you find."

As Weller strutted off, the two PCs immediately immersed themselves into the new task. Michaels gave Kangers and Phillips an update on the search for the van and handed everything over to them. Picking up the phone, Tarrant called the court's office in Somerset, asking if a will had been filed for Peggy Thornleigh and coming up trumps with the name of the solicitor who'd dealt with the estate.

It took forty-five minutes for Christopher Trelawney, senior partner of Trelawney, Phelps & Beaton, to call back. He was reluctant to discuss the nature of Peggy Thornleigh's estate over the telephone, inviting the detectives to make an appointment at his offices, with appropriate authority to discuss the matter directly with him.

"Pompous arse," Tarrant muttered under his breath as he put the phone down and went to inform Weller of his conversation.

DS Piconya was standing next to Weller when Tarrant came bounding over, complaining about the stonewalling solicitor. As Trelawney, Phelps & Beaton's offices were located just off the centre, not far from the station, Piconya volunteered to take Esklick and call in to interview Trelawney without the obligatory appointment. Tarrant sniggered to himself as he walked away, wishing he could be a fly on the wall when DS Piconya arrived at the solicitor's offices uninvited. She was not a woman to be messed with.

Trelawney made Piconya and Esklick wait twenty minutes and was every bit as pompous as Tarrant had described. Piconya was in no mood to suck up to the middle-aged prima donna, who was obstructing police enquiries, and made no bones about the fact as she flashed her ID. Chastised and embarrassed by the senior police officer, Trelawney led them into his office, where Piconya spotted a file on his desk entitled 'Thornleigh Estate'. Sitting at the other side of the desk, she watched as Trelawney picked up the pink file and flicked through its contents. Piconya and Esklick learned that Daniel Overton had inherited the whole of his aunt's estate. As Trelawney listed the contents, he mentioned a farmhouse called Hydlebury, located in Cornwall. Piconya knew then that they had their connection. This could be the place their suspect was heading when they lost sight of him on the M5.

At her request for a copy of the Will, Trelawney pressed the intercom on his desk and barked at his secretary, who entered his office and took the file away.

Ten minutes later, armed with a photocopy of the Will, Piconya and Esklick left the offices of Trelawney, Phelps & Beaton and headed back to Bridewell Police Station.

Chapter 18

Ethel
Bluebell Cottage

Ethel was on the phone to the emergency services when she saw him through a side window, running up the path to her cottage. Panic-stricken, she threw the phone back in its cradle and fled through the house, looking for somewhere to hide. Poppy had also heard someone running on the gravelled drive and jumped at the front door, to confront the intruder. Calling Poppy to her side, Ethel ran through the kitchen, expecting the Westie to follow her. She was about to turn back for her dog when the front door opened and Poppy started growling. Expecting the inevitable confrontation, Ethel heard a yelp, following by swearing, then the door slammed shut. Judging from the screeching and cursing coming from the man inside her cottage, Poppy had succeeded in taking a chunk out of him, but was now outside, flinging herself against the door, trying to get back inside to finish the job.

"I know you're in here, bitch, I'm going to find you, and when I do you're going to suffer." His angry voice boomed through the cottage as she ran down the narrow passageway, through to the lounge.

Opening French doors, Ethel slipped outside into the back garden, closing the doors behind her. As she ran for cover behind a large laurel bush, she could hear him in the lounge, screaming obscenities. From the cover of the laurel, she saw him at the

French doors, looking into the garden. She froze as he looked straight towards her. Expecting him to open the doors and come after her, Ethel prepared to run for her life but, instead of charging out into the garden, he moved from the window and through the lounge, searching the rest of the cottage. Relief flooded over her when she realised he'd not seen her but it would only be a matter of time before he worked out she was not in the cottage and came looking for her outside. After all she had been through, it looked like the monster would ultimately get his way. Tears cascaded down her face as the reality of the insurmountable odds came crashing down on her. Then something soft brushed up against her and she realised Poppy had come in through the bank of hedges to find her. Hugging the dog briefly, glad for her company, an idea came to her.

"Poppy, go and fetch Mr Anstey. Get help, Poppy, get Mr Anstey!"

The dog looked at her quizzically, holding its head to one side as though digesting her owner's words, then bolted out of the hedge back the way she had come. Just as Poppy ran into the garden, the French doors opened and the intruder stepped outside, heading towards Ethel. Paralysed with fear, waiting for discovery. She could see his legs through the thick foliage. All he had to do was lean forward into the hedge and he would see her. But then he saw Poppy.

"Bloody hell, what was that?" Daniel turned quickly to see a white blur vanishing up the side lane leading into the countryside.

"Fuck, fuck, fuck! The bitch has gone, and taken the mutt with her," he ranted, stamping his feet so close to Ethel he almost stepped on her fingers.

Ethel held her breath, not daring to move a muscle as she waited for his next move. She felt him hesitate then he started running in the opposite direction to Poppy, back towards Hydlebury Farm. Ethel was beside herself with relief. At that stage, she could only assume was that he was going back to the farm to get his vehicle.

Once the coast was clear, she struggled out of the hedge and limped after Poppy. It took ten minutes of walking, then running; dragging her injured leg behind her, to get to Trimbledon Farm. Just as the farmhouse came into view she heard Poppy barking and a man's voice.

"Come here, girl, what's going on? What's this on your fur?"

Poppy continued a barking frenzy as Mr Anstey kneeled down to examine her coat. The dog allowed him to get closer and he realised the red stain on her white fur was blood.

"Is it Ethel, girl? What's wrong, Poppy, do you want me to come with you?" Poppy jumped up against him, almost toppling him off his knees in an effort to get his attention.

"All right, Poppy, it's all right, I am coming." Mr Anstey stood up and was about to turn back to his cottage for his keys when he saw Ethel limping up the lane in his direction.

"Thank God you are here, I need your help," Ethel spluttered breathlessly as she reached him. Tears streaming down her cheeks, she bent over, clutching her knees and struggling to catch her breath.

"What the hell is going on and what's this blood doing on Poppy's coat?" Ethel felt strong arms around her as Anstey led her towards the cottage, with Poppy in close pursuit.

Anstey bundled Ethel into his messy kitchen. Moving a stack of newspapers from a nearby stool, he sat her down and fetched a glass of water while she regained her breath. Passing the glass to her, Anstey noticed the deep cut, and blood on her hands and her injured leg.

After taking several gulps, Ethel recovered enough to start talking. When the account of her ordeal came out in a heated rush, her startled neighbour couldn't believe what he was hearing. His immediate response was to call the police, then he disappeared briefly, returning with the shotgun that he used for shooting pheasant.

"Don't worry, I'm not going to use it, it's just for protection in case that madman decides to come and find you," Anstey said, seeing the alarm registering on Ethel's face.

"I just hope the police get here before it's too late," Ethel replied, her thoughts on the woman incarcerated below the trapdoor in the barn.

"They told us to stay put and do nothing until they get here. Meanwhile, I'm not taking any chances." The old farmer waved the shotgun menacingly at the door, indicating he wouldn't hesitate to use it. Ethel was grateful and with Poppy at her side they hunkered down in the farmhouse kitchen and awaited the arrival of the police.

***

Knowing time was against him, Daniel ran towards Hydlebury Farm. The first thing he was going to do was get his bags out of the cottage and load up the van, then go to the barn and dispose of the woman and the bodybuilder; if he wasn't dead already. In Daniel's mind, he was already taking on the identity of Jason Holden who, with the help of a forged passport, was going to disappear. As soon as he finished his business at the farm, he was going to dump the van at an industrial estate, where he'd seen a used car dealership. He would buy a car for cash, transfer his belongings from the van, then head back towards Bristol, where he would get a flight to Rome, hire a car and head towards Tuscany and a remote villa he had purchased some time ago under his assumed name. With cash he'd squirrelled away in the Holden bank account from his inheritance and investments, he could live very comfortably.

All his possessions inside the van, Daniel headed towards the barn. A fury built inside him, propelling him into a state where he thought he would physically pull the woman apart with his bare hands. As he got closer, the first thing he heard was her cries for help, her voice cracking and failing from prolonged screaming. Soon, that screaming would be no more and he would be out of there.

From below the trapdoor, Jenna could hear the barn door slamming. She stopped screaming, wondering whether it was the woman returning with help. She listened but the footsteps coming from above ground were far too heavy and dense, indicating that it was one person, of a sizeable weight. She could draw only one conclusion; the kidnapper was back. It had been some time since the woman left and in her heart Jenna hoped she had managed to escape but with the evil presence topside, her mind wrestled with the dreadful possibility that she had never made it.

Looking over at Peter, it was evident that without help he would die shortly. After escaping from the cell, the first thing she did was try to get a response from him then, releasing the hand ties, she took his ripped jacket off and wrapped it round the axe wound in his back. It was now saturated with blood and he'd long since lost consciousness. There was nothing more she could do for him but hope and pray he wouldn't die.

As she heard the monster above pound towards the trapdoor, screaming obscenities to himself, that tiny sliver of hope evaporated. Reality sank in. Rescue was not an option; Jenna was in no doubt of the fate that awaited her once that trapdoor opened.

The only way out was up the wooden staircase. Jenna knew that even with the element of surprise on her side – he wouldn't be expecting her to be free of the cell – he would have the upper hand. That left her one option; to somehow overpower him as he came down the staircase, but with her strength failing and nothing to arm herself with, any hope of this seemed remote.

Jenna sank into complete despair. A white mist appeared before her eyes and she felt herself drifting out of her body into another dimension, where she saw the spirit of the young girl again full of life and vitality before being killed and incarcerated in the grave below the floorboards of the cellar.

As she tuned in to the spirit world, Jenna realised her purpose and why she'd been chosen. Everything came together in that moment in time, allowing the spirit to use her as a way into the living world. Jenna saw the killer as a young boy, strangling and raping the girl in the field then hiding her in the cellar. She saw the horrifying incident in every minute detail as the boy raped the tiny, lifeless body before burying it in the hole he'd dug then covered it with soil. The little girl's body had lain in the shallow grave, undiscovered until now.

The connection with a living being allowed the dead girl release from the place of death. Jenna was powerless to stop centuries of pent-up aggression possessing her mind and body. The loss of a life so young, in such horrendous circumstances, brought overwhelming grief, making Jenna struggle for breath amidst the spirit's great fury. The last thing Jenna's conscious memory recorded was the trapdoor in the floor above her opening, and the monster descending the stairs into the cellar.

As he walked down the wooden stairwell, Daniel was unaware that his prisoner was no longer of this world. Mary Thornleigh had returned to the earthly plain and was finally able to confront her killer.

As Daniel put his foot on the last step, he saw Jenna standing stock-still by the side of the cell. Somehow, the woman had freed herself, but that didn't bother him. She was no match for him and he relished a struggle, which would only serve to heighten his appetite for murder.

As he approached, Jenna was in a trance-like condition, which he mistook for sheer fear. A few paces away from her, Daniel suddenly hit something solid. Momentarily confused, his arms floundered around in mid-air, searching for the obstruction, as there was no logical reason why he couldn't move forward or backward. An unseen force surrounded him, holding him in its epicentre. Jenna showed no signs of moving, standing like a statue just inches away from him. As he looked into her face, it no longer resembled the beautiful young woman he had abducted; he saw the face of a child, striking a fear so great in his heart that it almost stopped beating. He knew the day of reckoning was upon him. His last thought was that the girl was going to make him pay dearly for her murder, and there was nothing he could be to prevent it. The tables were turned and his life was now in her hands.

Mary Thornleigh's soul radiated through Jenna's eyes, hypnotising him and pulling him towards her host's body. Struggle wasn't an option. The vice-like grip holding Daniel was like a straitjacket, controlling every part of his body apart from his facial muscles, which were distorted in fear as he plummeted back in time to stand accountable for his crime. Hurtling through a long, dark tunnel, he came out into another dimension, where he stood face-to-face with the embodiment of his long-deceased cousin. This time, however, she was not a defenceless little girl.

***

The 999 call came in at 6.58am. Although the caller was hysterical, Janet Freestone, the operator handling the call, was a seasoned pro and was able to decipher the woman's location in between gut-wrenching sobs, before a scream ended the call. Fifteen minutes later, another call came in, from a farmer in the same vicinity. At 7.20am, Devon & Cornwall Police were galvanised into action. Responding to an earlier alert, which concerned a suspected abduction, an urgent call was made to Bridewell Police Station in Bristol. It was patched through to the incident room and answered by PC Michaels.

"Guv, you need to take this," Michaels shouted across to Weller, who was deep in conversation with Whitehead and the early morning shift. Conversations stopped and all eyes were on her as she took the call. She listened then barked orders to the caller on the other end, and placed another call just as Piconya and Esklick entered the incident room.

"We've found something," said Piconya, holding the copy of the Will in her hand as Weller finished the second call. "Overton owns a property in Cornwall, called Hydlebury Farm."

Weller stared at the section Piconya had asked the solicitor to highlight. Last night, Piconya had gone back to the station to find Weller but she'd gone out chasing down another lead. A call to her mobile went straight to voicemail then a second call with no response told Piconya that she was in an area of no signal, or the battery on her mobile had died. It was close to midnight when Piconya decided to get some shut-eye and catch up in the morning.

"Jesus, we've got him. Devon & Cornwall have just called to say they had a 999 call from a woman living in the vicinity of Hydlebury Farm, reporting a kidnap. The operator heard screaming and the call finished before she could give any details. Then another call was received shortly after, from a farmer called Anstey, who said he had his neighbour at his farm and there was a woman held captive, possibly with another person, in a barn at Hydlebury Farm.

"Local plod are getting together an armed response team. I've just spoken to Chief Constable Crump, who has already sanctioned a helicopter, which is on its way to collect us. Devon & Cornwall will be sending local intelligence via smartphone during our journey. Piconya, I want you and Esklick with me. Whitehead, you are coming with us, too. Michaels, organise Kevlar vests. We want to hit the ground running when we get there."

The sound of rotor blades could be heard above the early morning traffic as the helicopter appeared on the horizon. The team of four were waiting on the large expanse of roof designed to take the weight of a landing helicopter. Weller saw the pilot in the cockpit, signalling to the landing crew as he prepared to manoeuvre the craft on the target zone. When the helicopter landed, its doors were flung open and the team headed by Weller ran under the rotating blades and climbed into the aircraft, aided by co-pilot Terry Hargraves. Once securely fastened into their seats, the helicopter took off, soaring high in the sky over Bristol city centre and attracting curious stares from people stuck in the rush hour traffic.

It took little over five minutes to clear the city. Just as they were heading towards Somerset, Weller received a call from DCI Stansbridge in Cornwall. The DCI informed Weller that an armed response unit would be meeting them at Clarissa House, where a helicopter landing pad and squad cars were awaiting their arrival. The suspect had been located two miles away from Clarissa and police were already at Bluebell Cottage, a property bordering Hydlebury Farm.

Motorways and swathes of land flashed by and before long Captain Swayne informed them ETA was eighteen minutes. As they neared their destination, Weller could see Clarissa House, set in acres of rolling countryside. Another call from DCI Stansbridge told her that three squad cars were waiting nearby to transport them to Hydlebury Farm, which he informed Weller was seven minutes away. As the helicopter prepared to land, she hoped they would be in time to save Jenna Thornleigh and Peter Shaney.

When the team disembarked, DCI Stansbridge greeted Weller and Piconya, informing them that Ethel Wetherington, the woman who'd made the first 999 call, had been interviewed at a neighbour's farm. Because of Bluebell Cottage's close proximity to Hydlebury Farm, she was advised to stay with Fred Anstey, the neighbour, whilst the raid was underway. Ethel had confirmed the presence of a female and a possible second prisoner in a barn located in one of the fields belonging to the farm.

A squad car with two armed officers had been dispatched ahead to Bluebell Cottage, with strict instructions to observe and wait for the arrival of the rest of the team. The armed officers reported back to DCI Stansbridge as they crept through fields, heading towards the farm. The front door was ajar and they were able were able to slip inside and establish that there was nobody inside the farmhouse. Moving on, they spotted a van parked in front of the property, keys in its ignition. Heading for the barn, they moved swiftly round the side of the building, where they observed the open door and waited for instructions and the arrival of the rest of the team. Five minutes passed without incident. Nobody entered or exited the barn and the officers assumed that both kidnapper and victims were inside the barn.

As the convoy of squad cars turned into the narrow lane leading to Hydlebury Farm, DCI Stansbridge, who was travelling in the lead squad car with Weller, received a call from one of the armed officers, informing him they could hear shouting and that the situation inside appeared to be escalating. The DCI told them they were entering the grounds of the farmhouse, and to hold their position until the rest of the team were in place. Ditching the squad cars at the entrance to the lane, the team continued on foot through the farmhouse gates. The armed response unit, who had their instructions before arrival at the farmhouse and knew the lay of the land, immediately made for the barn, skirting round the side and giving cover to the advancing officers. Within minutes, they joined the two other armed officers at the barn door and, having ascertained the building was empty, slipped quietly inside, guns raised, ready for confrontation.

Weller and Piconya followed DCI Stansbridge into the barn and watched as the armed response team silently moved forward, towards the generator, which Ethel Wetherington had described, locating the open trapdoor. Suddenly, they heard a blood-curdling yell and the voice of a man screaming filtered up through the open trapdoor.

"Keep away from me, you can't be Mary, the bitch is death. Don't touch me, keep away, keep away. You can't hurt me, you're dead. No. Nooooooooooooooooo. Nooooooooooooooooo!" Daniel groaned as though he'd been struck with something then everything went quiet.

Sergeant Pickler, head of the armed response team, dropped to the ground, slid along to the trapdoor and peered down into the cellar. It was a few seconds before he rolled back to safety and reported his findings, which filtered along to the rest of the waiting team. From his brief sighting of the area in the cellar, the officer had spotted two people; a man and a woman. The man, who had his back to the officer, was facing the woman. Apart from the earlier screaming, nothing seemed to be happening between the two people, who appeared to be transfixed, in a trance-like state. Sergeant Pickler had also spotted a wooden bench, on top of which lay a half-naked male, who was bleeding and motionless.

DCI Stansbridge had medics on standby at Bluebell Cottage, ready to intervene at his request. After a brief regroup, the armed response team was pulled back and DS Weller, who had experience in hostage negotiation, crawled closer to the trapdoor, flanked by Sergeant Pickler, in an effort to start up a dialogue with the kidnapper.

"Daniel, this is DS Weller of Avon & Somerset Constabulary. I am here to help you. Will you allow us to give medical attention to the injured man with you?"

Seconds passed, during which there was complete silence below and above ground.

"Daniel, can you please speak to me so we can sort this situation out?" Weller tried again but no response was forthcoming.

Sergeant Pickler inched carefully forward and looked inside. To his surprise, the two people remained unresponsive and hadn't moved from their earlier position. Leaving Weller behind him,

Pickler signalled silently to his second-in-command, who crawled slowly to his side and peered down into the cellar. Moving away, the two men and Weller had a hushed conversation and another regroup took place. After hearing about the strange standstill, DCI Stansbridge proposed tactics to enter the cellar. Decision made, Pickler was followed by Hollingshead, with the rest of the team close on their heels. They crawled over to the trapdoor. Weller, who'd been pulled back, watched the proceedings from a safe distance. Pickler looked inside then immediately signalled the team before slipping silently through the trapdoor. Within a matter of seconds, the whole team had disappeared into the cellar. Topside, Weller braced herself for the inevitable screaming, the worst scenario being gunshots, but all was strangely silent. Suddenly, Pickler's head appeared through the trapdoor, requesting urgent assistance from the medics.

Pickler climbed back down, barking orders to Hollingshead, then he climbed topside to update DCI Stansbridge on the situation below. Weller and Piconya moved closer, to hear the armed response officer's initial report, but what they were hearing made no sense. Until they were able to assess the scene for themselves they were having difficulty comprehending the situation. Stansbridge immediately put a call through to the waiting medics at Bluebell Cottage, galvanising them into action. Once the armed response team had successfully secured the scene below ground, Stansbridge, Weller and Piconya climbed in single-file down the wooden staircase, after Sergeant Pickler.

The crime scene was as Pickler described; an injured man lying unresponsive on a wooden bench, covered with a blood-soaked jacket, with Jenna Thornleigh and Daniel Overton in a complete stand-off, inches away from each other, apparently locked in a comatose state. Attempts at dialogue with the man and woman proved fruitless. Two armed response officers trained their guns on them whilst the medics removed Peter Shaney, who remained unconscious.

One medic stayed behind to assess the situation, whilst the rest of the crew prepared to transport Peter Shaney into a waiting ambulance, destined for Derriford. It wasn't until they'd got the injured man out of the cellar that they realised he had taken a turn for the worse. As the medics worked to save his life, they knew their patient wouldn't survive the forty-minute drive, prompting an urgent call to Cornwall Air Ambulance, who were on site within minutes. Shaney was secured in the helicopter and on his way to the hospital, where a theatre had been prepped and staff awaited his arrival.

After the helicopter lifted off, the medical team waited topside for further instructions as the situation unravelled underground. Weller and Piconya, under observation of two armed response officers, ventured closer to Jenna Thornleigh and Daniel Overton, who remained unresponsive, eyes locked and standing motionless in front of each other. With Overton in their sights, Weller inched ahead of Piconya. It had been some fifteen minutes since entering the cellar and despite Weller's attempts to facilitate a dialogue between them, neither Jenna nor Overton had moved or uttered one word in response.

As Weller got closer, she asked a question. "Who's Mary, Daniel?"

Suddenly, the spell gripping the two people was broken and all hell broke loose.

Chapter 19

Mark Casey - Discovery
Bridewell Police Station

The A4 writing pad started to fill up with Casey's thoughts

Thomas born in 1785 – see Jenna's notes

Thomas born in 1895 – following a theory of reincarnation and the continuing male bloodline

1915 (information coming to light after second Thomas' death)
• Young girl reported to officials of being beaten by Thomas – no name recorded
• Flora Down reported being beaten and sexually assaulted by Thomas – a sure sign his sadist behaviour was escalating

Thinking about Flora Down's statement, indicating that the attack happened five years before Thomas' death, Casey started to focus his search in 1910, looking for anything that connected back to the Thornleigh family. Trawling the internet, he discovered a murder of a notorious prostitute who used to ply her trade in and around Lansan, a name used by the locals for the small town of Launceston in Cornwall. Maggie Wood was found by a fellow prostitute one morning when she called round to her home and found the door wide open. Going inside the terraced property, she had found Maggie naked on the floor by her bed, her throat cut and bite marks on her thighs, as though she had been savaged by a dog. At the time, there was a big hue and cry over the murder but the case remained unsolved.

Two months later, a scullery maid called Sarah Llewellyn, from one of the local manor houses, was attending a Suffragette rally when she was plucked unseen from the back of a crowd. The spellbound audience were intently listening to the speaker, who whipped them into a frenzy about the injustices women suffered at the hands of men. After Sarah's disappearance, a woman called Maisy Clothier came forward and told officials that she and Sarah had exchanged greetings then become embroiled in the rally. When the speech was over, Maisy looked for Sarah but she had gone. This puzzled her as she felt certain the girl would have stayed to talk afterwards and couldn't understand why she had left so abruptly. There were no other sightings of the scullery maid, who seemed to have vanished into thin air. Months turned into years and no information was forthcoming as to her whereabouts. With no body, the case was left open.

In 1911, a Lansan woman walking home after a long shift in a nearby ale house mysteriously disappeared. The proprietor of the ale house, James Geake, told officials that she had left the same time as usual, just after midnight. After he let her out of the back door, the proprietor stood for a while taking in the night air, supping from a pewter tankard. He spotted someone lurking by the trees on the far side of the ale house just after Nellie had left. He called out to the person who, on hearing his voice, disappeared into the trees. Thinking he may be one of his patrons who'd gone to relieve himself, James Geake stood for a while, waiting to see if he emerged from the trees, but the man vanished and, finishing his ale, James Geake never gave it another thought. Going back inside, he locked up for the night. After questioning James Geake, officials realised the man in the trees might have had something to do with Nellie's disappearance. Her body was never discovered.

A pattern was beginning to form and it began to seem likely that they had a serial killer in their midst. Two beaten women, one of whom was sexually assaulted, another found with her throat cut, and two missing women. Thomas Thornleigh had been identified by the first two women. The deaths of the prostitute, and the disappearances of the scullery maid and Nellie from the ale house were left unsolved. With Thomas Thornleigh dead in his grave, that line of investigation hit a stone wall.

Whoever the killer was, he was either burying the bodies or taking them somewhere they couldn't be found. Either way, years had passed and the chance of resolving these murders would be zero. Under his notes, Casey started to draw up his own version of the Thornleigh family tree, starting with Thomas born in 1895 and charting his progress until his death in 1910, adding the discoveries he found during his research.

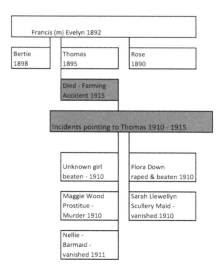

Looking back through the first graph of the Family Tree, the last three descendants – Heather, Peggy and Marjorie – Casey could see where Jenna figured in the ancestral chart. Bertie had three girls and it became clear that Bertie was a bit of a lady's man, as there was a report of domestic disturbance, when his wife caught him with another woman. There was one other woman in particular, a god-fearing Catholic girl, who on first glance it would appear that butter wouldn't melt in her mouth but there were no holds barred when it came to other women's husbands and she'd got her hooks into Bertie. It came to light that Bertie's affair began before and continued long after his marriage to Daisy, much like all the others, with the thrill of the chase. The woman's name was Kate O'Donnell. The affair turned into a lasting relationship, with Bertie leaving his wife and three children, and setting up home with his mistress. Once the scandal died down, Bertie gave up his philandering ways, starting a family with Kate.

Casey found there were startling similarities between the two boys called Thomas – their taste for rape, and the fact they were both family members living at Hydlebury Farm, albeit a century apart. The farm, he thought, would be a good place to start, if it still existed. Getting up from his computer, he decided it was time to have a chat with DS Weller and tell her about his bizarre findings.

The squad room was alive and buzzing as Casey walked in. Weller and Whitehead were not to be seen as he approached PC Michaels, who was talking excitedly to PC Tarrant and gesticulating with his hands.

"Where's DS Weller? I think I may have something for her."

"Haven't you heard? there's been a break in the case."

Chapter 20

The Reveal
Hydlebury Farm

Daniel staggered away from Jenna, leaning up against the cellar wall for support whilst she watched, rooted to the spot, taking in his every movement in transfixed horror. The man's demonic expression chilled the very bones of the onlookers, who kept their distance, assessing his next move.

"Put your hands in the air and don't move!" Sergeant Pickler barked as the armed response team trained their guns on Daniel, fearing resistance.

The man made no attempt to escape or retaliate. His mind was in another world, talking wildly to himself or an unseen presence, much of his speech indecipherable. As Jenna was moved away from him and ushered behind a protective column of police officers, she became aware of her surroundings.

"Don't go near him, he's possessed!" she screamed.

DCI Stansbridge ordered Weller and Piconya to keep the woman back as the armed response team advanced on the man, in an effort to apprehend and cuff him. Suddenly, the area surrounding Overton started to heat up, turning the temperature within a two-foot radius of him scalding hot and making the team retreat a safe distance away from the invisible source of heat. Before the armed response team could regroup and consider their next move, a flame sparked from Overton. Everyone in the watched in horror as a fire appeared to burn in his chest area then spread to his stomach. So intense were the heat and flames that no one could get close enough to help him, leaving the armed response team on the periphery, completely helpless. A paramedic witnessing the impending carnage charged up the wooden staircase to the rest of his team, to get help. People were shouting and running about above ground, whilst below ground time seemed to stand still. Moments later, two paramedics scrambled down the wooden staircase, clutching fire blankets and an extinguisher taken from the ambulance, but as they reached the bottom step they found it was already too late to save Overton. The fire burned so ferociously that it consumed most of him, silencing his pitiful screams and leaving in its wake a charred body, which disintegrated to ashes in front of them.

As the flames petered out, the two paramedics were able to get close enough to inspect the remains of the body. The fire had wiped out all signs of human life, leaving in its wake just a portion of clothing, which was virtually untouched. Amongst the ashes, a booted foot and a hole in the floorboards where Overton had stood were the only evidence; a gruesome souvenir of a fire which had killed the man whilst the rest of the area remained intact. Those witnessing Overton's blood-curdling demise were horrified and baffled in equal measure. There was no apparent spark, flame, or reason why a human body could catch fire when there was no obvious source of ignition nearby, and then burn so fiercely without igniting anything around it.

The man had gone to his grave screaming, in horrendous agony; a sight which Piconya kept re-playing time and again in her mind, ammunition for many nightmares to come. Some members of the armed response team were also visibly shaken. DCI Stansbridge scrambled topside, his mobile phone pressed urgently to his ear.

Piconya quickly ushered Jenna up the wooden staircase into the barn, freeing her from the underground prison. Paramedics rushed to attend her but, apart from the gash on the back of her head which was crusted over with congealing blood, and suffering from shock and dehydration, she appeared to be unharmed. Whilst Jenna's head wound was cleaned and dressed, DCI Stansbridge received a call from Derriford Hospital. Clive Penhally, the surgeon who had operated on Shaney, told the DCI that the bodybuilder had flat-lined and been pronounced clinically dead at 11.43am, for ten minutes, before being successfully resuscitated. The surgeon advised that the next twenty-four hours would be crucial and that if Shaney did recover, brain damage could not be discounted.

Stansbridge received the update just as they were preparing to hand the scene over to Forensics. On hearing parts of the one-sided conversation, Jenna knew from the look on the DCI's face that Peter's life was in a precarious condition.

After they left Hydlebury Farm, Jenna Thornleigh was taken by DS Piconya and DS Weller back to Launceston Police Station, where they were allocated a room to conduct further questioning. All eyes were on Jenna as she walked through the open-plan office, with Piconya and Weller leading the way down a long corridor and into a room at the bottom. The same sergeant who had directed them through the police station appeared five minutes later, carrying a tray with three mugs of tea, a bowl of sugar, and several spoons. Jenna picked up a mug and took a sip of the scalding liquid, which looked like tar with a hint of milk. She grimaced as the tea assaulted her palate but no complaint was forthcoming, her thoughts focused on the harrowing sight she'd witnessed in the cellar, and Peter, who lay in a hospital bed fighting for his life.

During the course of their questioning, DS Weller and Piconya discovered that the trance holding Jenna Thornleigh and Daniel Overton was not of this world. The officers listened, stunned, as

Jenna explained about Mary Thornleigh, whose last resting place was beneath the cellar floorboards, and how the girl had used her as a conduit to this world so that she could hold Daniel Overton accountable for her murder and put a stop to his killing spree. Jenna told them about Christmas Steps being a catalyst, enabling the entity to fulfil her mission. Having read sections of Jenna Thornleigh's diary and interviewed Alannah Corby, DS Weller knew what was coming. Piconya, although she'd been privy to the paranormal experiences Spencer and Smithers had witnessed in No. 26 Christmas Steps back in 1985, was caught completely by surprise by the present-day revelation. Both officers listened in silence as Jenna described the paranormal activity in the Grade II listed property.

Piconya shivered involuntarily, imagining how terrified she would be in that situation. No ordinary person could even begin to understand the emotions this young woman must have endured as she was torn from one dimension into another.

Jenna described having seen the attack on the young woman at No. 26 Christmas Steps and how her research and worries had culminated in the encounter with Daniel Overton at Hotel Papiar. She broke down in tears, thinking that if only she'd gone home after Alannah failed to turn up, perhaps the agonising death of one man, leaving another fighting for his life, may not have happened.

Piconya jumped to Jenna's defence, telling her that she couldn't blame herself for what happened. Jenna took a moment to consider her words before continuing, knowing the police officer was right.

Describing the moment she saw Daniel Overton enter the bar, Jenna told Weller and Piconya about the black aura surrounding him, instantly alerting her to his presence. She recounted how that night, as Peter walked her the short distance from Hotel Papiar to Christmas Steps, she couldn't shake the feeling that they were being watched and was relieved to get back to the safety of her home. After leaving Peter on the doorstep, she went up to her bedroom, booted up her laptop and searched her files, finding the family tree she'd started all those years ago when she was at school. Drawn by an invisible force, she was plunged back to the 1800s and the farming branch of the family tree, where an ancestor called Thomas Thornleigh was hanged for murdering two children and suspected of murdering his cousin, Mary Thornleigh.

Jenna started to shiver uncontrollably, despite the stuffy confines of the interview room. Looking across the desk, she saw Weller and Piconya staring at her in disbelief, hanging on her every word.

Despite having witnessed Overton's horrendous demise, both police officers struggled to understand what Jenna was trying to tell them. She believed Daniel Overton to have lived many lives, each time coming back to this earth and leaving a trail of murders, which was somehow connected to the historic attack at No. 26 Christmas Steps.

Weller and Piconya were silent, considering this strange possibility and knowing about the link to Marjorie Adams (nee Thornleigh), Jane Adams' mother. Jenna started to recount her incarceration; Peter's escape and Overton's attack on him, culminating in the horrific rape. She shivered as she recalled him walking over to the cell afterwards, silently assessing her. Their eyes locked and in that moment she saw the pure evil possessing his soul, leaving her in no doubt what was in store for her.

She recalled speaking to the woman who had tried to break in to the cellar, then her terror when the woman never returned but instead came Daniel Overton. Then she had found herself possessed by Mary Thornleigh's spirit. The energy emanating from the spirit was beyond anything Jenna had ever experienced, holding her in a suspended vacuum as it left her body, targeting the man in front of her. Once it had found its intended host, the spirit bombarded the abductor with images of his past. Jenna was able to see the crimes the man had committed while he howled in agony, trying to get away, but he was trapped in his own living hell. Amidst the trail of misery and devastation, a young girl emerged. Pointing an accusing finger, she projected him through a wall of fire. He relived her killing, the flames licking and scorching his skin as he passed though the fire. On the other side, the young girl watched the murderer trapped in his own personal damnation as his body began to burn from the inside out. When his body disintegrated, the energy force ceased and Jenna had found herself back in the cellar, staring at the charred remains and surrounded by police, with no recollection of how and when they had appeared on the scene.

She vaguely remembered being bundled away up the staircase and through the trapdoor, to the waiting medics, who checked her over and wanted to take her to hospital. Jenna had no care for her own health, insisting on knowing how Peter was, only to be told he had been taken by helicopter to Derriford Hospital, where he was undergoing surgery.

Tears freely flowed down Jenna's cheeks as she finished recounting the terrifying events. Weller suggested they regroup the next morning, as Jenna was mentally and physically exhausted. Accommodation had been pre-booked at a local hotel. As Jenna was in no state to object, she went along with the two officers with no protest. Ensconced in her hotel room, she rang Alannah, who had already been informed by the police that her friend was safe and well. Hearing Jenna's voice at the other end of the phone, Alannah burst into tears of relief. She wanted to know everything but Jenna had no stomach to rake over the grisly affair another time and said she was staying in Launceston for a few days, to help police with their enquiries. Alannah, sensing her trauma, accepted Jenna's reasoning. After the conversation ended, Jenna put the phone back in its cradle on the bedside cabinet, dropped back onto the bed fully clothed, closed her eyes, and fell into a deep sleep.

Piconya and Weller stayed in the hotel bar, drinking coffee, discussing the case and comparing notes. After leaving Launceston Police Station, Piconya had received a call from Forensics, informing her that the sample DNA taken shortly after the baby was born revealed the child in the Jane Adams cold case bore familial DNA, linking the rape to her brother. To date, nothing was known as to Tommy's whereabouts; only that he'd gone on the run and had never been found. Despite questioning neighbours and friends, and urgent news appeals, no further information came to light.

Piconya revealed what had occurred when she and Esklick had had driven down to Devon and tracked down Ken Smithers; how years later, the effects of the traumatic experience at No. 26 Christmas Steps were evidenced in his artwork. Piconya proffered her mobile, showing Weller the photo she'd taken of one of his paintings.

Weller gasped in horror as she looked at the 'phantom', expanding the screen to enlarge the image and not quite believing what she was looking at. "My God, it's a wonder they haven't consigned Smithers to a mental institution. What the hell are we dealing with here?"

Piconya was at a loss to explain.

"I don't know about you but I'm bushed. Let's see what happens tomorrow," Weller suggested.

The two women went to their respective rooms, agreeing to meet for breakfast, each pondering what the following day would reveal.

When they convened at Launceston Police Station the following morning, Piconya started the meeting by telling Jenna about Ken Smithers. She showed Jenna the image Smithers had painted. Jenna reached over to get a better view but the sight on the mobile phone made her sway in her chair. Weller rushed round the side of the desk, grabbing her before she toppled off the chair and staying beside her until she gathered her senses. Piconya continued with Smithers' account of what had happened to him and PC Davies at No. 26 Christmas Steps. Jenna, who said nothing, pictured the whole event unfolding in her home as Piconya conveyed the events that had happened over thirty years ago. In her mind, Jenna knew the spiritual intervention recurring with alarming regularity had been a warning. It was as portal for wandering spirits and it was the same spot she had encountered the entity known as Jane Adams.

Piconya also went on to tell Jenna and Weller about DCI Gerald Spencer, describing the black shadow in the upstairs bedroom overlooking the cobbled street. Jenna knew DCI Spencer had described the malevolent spirit lingering before its demise, and assumed it had already sown its seed elsewhere. Smithers had been the recipient of its evil vibrations but she knew he'd been spared possession, leaving him mentally unbalanced, with two other police officers in denial to its existence.

Although the revelation someone else had experienced paranormal activity in No. 26 Christmas Steps had shocked Jenna, it also gave credence to her story. Jenna furiously tried to put all the pieces of the puzzle together. Piconya suggested they take a break to gather their thoughts and the three women left the confines of the police station for a nearby restaurant. Jenna, who'd skipped breakfast at the hotel, wasn't in the mood for food and picked at her chicken salad, whilst Piconya and Weller devoured their meals. During lunch, conversation reverted to mundane chit-chat but Jenna knew that before the day was over there would be more mental hurdles to cross before Weller and Piconya could comprehend the level of paranormal intervention that had resulted in the death of one man and life-threatening injuries to another. An hour later, they were back at the station, with Jenna ready to expose her innermost fears. Whether they would be accepted remained to be seen.

Back in the interview room Piconya, sensing something monumental was coming, perched on the edge of her seat, leaning forward onto the Formica table between them. Jenna told them the image of the phantom on DS Piconya's smartphone was the entity she saw in her vision; who had raped the woman identified as Jane Adams. The revelation stunned the two police officers. Then, adding more fuel to the fire of disbelief, Jenna put forward the theory she'd been toying with, telling them that before raping his sister Tommy Adams had been possessed by the malevolent entity, allowing it to impregnate Jane Adams. Once the rape was over and the entity had sowed its seed, enabling it to be reborn and continue its evil manifestation, in the persona of Daniel Overton, it had left its host as suddenly as it had taken possession. In Jenna's vision, it was apparent that Tommy Adams had no knowledge of the rape taking place. Afterwards, she witnessed the entity leaving him and the horrified expression on his face when he realised what he'd done. Tommy Adams frantically tried to dispose of his sister's body, not knowing at the time she was still clinging to life. No one would believe what took place on that kitchen floor. They would blame him.

The theory linked Daniel Overton to Piconya's cold case, supplying an answer to the bizarre sequence of events. Jenna returned to Mary Thornleigh and how, over the years, she'd dreamt of her being trapped under the floorboards of the cellar, and her spirit, which had waited to get its revenge, materialising during her captivity at Hydlebury Farm. As soon as she was thrown into that cellar a matter of feet from where Mary had been buried, the troubled spirit had a way to leave the place where she'd been left to rot centuries ago.

During their careers, Weller and Piconya had been a party to a wide range of strange events. This case would have topped the realms of fantasy if it had not been for the fact that they and the rest of the team in the cellar at Hydlebury Farm had witnessed Daniel Overton's fiery demise with their own eyes.

After going over everything that happened, Jenna reverted to the 'if onlys'. If only she and Alannah hadn't bought No. 26 Christmas Steps, none of this would have happened. This led to Peter Shaney, who had unwittingly been caught up in Overton's evil web. Everything culminated with Mary Thornleigh, whose troubled spirit had lain in wait until a window of opportunity allowed her to come back to this world and take revenge on her killer. Little did Jenna realise at that stage how another piece of the bizarre puzzle was going to challenge her to the limits, when Piconya revealed who Jane Adams was. After the trauma she'd been through, both police officers thought it wise to keep this information back, until she had time to come to terms with what happened at Hydlebury Farm. Even then, Piconya wondered whether Jenna would get over the shock of discovering that Jane Adams, the murdered woman, belonged to another branch of her family tree.

Forensics established Daniel Overton's time of death as being 11.43am. The time was recorded by the medic, who happened to look at his watch, knowing that even if he had been able to get close enough to the raging heat his attempts to save the man's life would have been futile. The fire burned upward inside Overton's body, leaving the surrounding area with little more than smoke damage. Suggestions for a logical cause of the fire were gas-producing intestinal bacteria or a build-up of the body's vibrational energy. The fact remained, however, that as human bodies are about sixty percent non-flammable water, no physical or medical mechanism could explain why Overton's body had self-combusted. The man's flammable clothing extracted from the top of the boot, being a mix of cotton and polyester blends, was the only surviving evidence he had existed, and had served to fuel the fire. It was discovered there was also a rare medical condition the coroner considered called Stevens-Johnson syndrome, which could account for a spontaneous combustion; a skin disease which could be triggered by a toxic reaction to medications. But as this was a case without the presence of a body on which to conduct further investigations, and with no former medical history, the coroner found no plausible explanation for the man's death.

Three skeletons were also discovered beneath the floor of the cellar. One belonged to a female child, dating back to the 18th century, alongside two adult females. It was established one of the females was in her twenties and the other slightly older; both killed and mutilated, their shrivelled body parts stored in glass jars found buried with their remains. Identification of the three bodies proved difficult, as all that remained were bones and slivers of skin preserved in formaldehyde. Fragments of twine were found tied around the top of the glass jars and attached to the end of one was remnants of a type of label too disintegrated to be of use. Bone fragments from the two older females suggested they were killed in the 1900s, the gap in time suggesting two different killers.

Reading the forensic report, and having witnessed the macabre scene in the cellar, there was no doubt in Piconya's and Weller's minds that the theory Jenna Thornleigh presented was credible. The remains of the young female dating back to the 18th century could have been Mary Thornleigh's.

After the crime scene had been sealed off and interviews conducted, Weller, Piconya and Jenna were driven back to Bristol. Once they'd dropped Jenna off at Christmas Steps, Weller and Piconya continued on to Bridewell Police Station. The team had been kept abreast of the developments in Cornwall, leaving Weller the unenviable task of reporting the events leading up to Overton's death. During the de-briefing with her team, Weller noticed Casey slip into the room and sit quietly at the back until she had finished speaking and answering the flood of questions that followed.

After the briefing as she was about to pack up her notes and make her way out to her office Casey approached her. "I think I may be able to help ID the two other skeletons found at Hydlebury Farm."

Weller, rendered speechless by his statement, allowed him to continue.

"Something I have found in the Thornleigh family tree suggests that one of Jenna's ancestors may have had something to do with the death of two missing women going back to the 1900s," Casey informed her.

He took her down to his office where he had the graph from Jenna Thornleigh's family tree pinned to a large cork board on the wall by the side of his desk, along with a copy of his handwritten notes. As Weller inspected his research, it quickly became obvious that Casey was referring to another ancestor who, like the first Thomas, had all the hallmarks of a sadist killer. Reviewing the historic evidence of two missing women; a scullery maid called Sarah Llewellyn and the barmaid called Nellie, Weller was coming to the same conclusion. There was a strong possibility they had found the link to their skeletons. Weller's heart missed a beat when she realised what this revelation would mean to Jenna Thornleigh and the implications that would follow. To discover one killer in your family history is devastating but two couldn't bear thinking about. Meanwhile, Forensics had to be updated with Casey's discovery.

First, she rang Piconya. "Hi Sylvia, there's something I think you should see. Can you come up to the Tech Department?" Weller pocketed her mobile and looked at Casey. They were both looking at the cork board, in deep conversation, when Piconya arrived.

"What's this all about?"

"Casey has unearthed some Thornleigh family history – take a look at this graph then Casey will fill you in with the rest," Weller said.

Casey and Weller watched whilst Piconya digested the contents of the main graph pinned to the wall. Like Weller, it didn't take her too long to establish the existence of another Thomas, then Casey showed her the second graph and his discovery notes.

"Bloody hell – this means that we've got two historic serial killers born to the same family. What the fuck is Jenna gonna say about this, and the fact that Jane Adams is also her relative?"

Casey was momentarily taken aback by Piconya who, unlike some of her female colleagues, rarely swore.

"Doesn't bear thinking about," replied Weller, wondering how the hell she was going to break the news as it was obvious from the information and notes Jenna had made on the main graph that she'd not got round to looking into this ancestor in-depth.

"Who's Jane Adams?" Casey asked.

Piconya picked up a marker pen and under Marjorie's name starting filling in the family graph to reveal the woman had two children called Jane and Tommy, explaining that Jane had been murdered in the mid-80s, by Tommy. Casey stood with his hands on his hips, gaping at the cork board. The information before him was explosive. Three murderers in one family tree. The addition of Tommy Adams far surpassed the realms of fantasy.

***

Jenna Thornleigh, meanwhile, was considering the daunting prospect of facing Alannah, and the future of No. 26 Christmas Steps. Knowing her friend's reaction would be to put the place up for sale, Jenna could only hope that she may, after time, come to understand their home and business were worth keeping now that the entity had passed over.

Peter Shaney was transferred from Derriford to Frenchay Hospital in Bristol, where they were better equipped to deal with his condition. He regained consciousness two weeks later. Waiting by his bedside, Jenna was accompanied by DS Piconya, who had stopped by to check on his progress.

As they sat quietly talking, Peter opened his eyes, looked over at Jenna and smiled. "It's so nice to see you again, Jenna."

The sound of his voice and the words spoken chilled Jenna to the bone. She stared in horror at the man lying in the bed, who looked every inch like Peter Shaney but was not the person she had once known. As Piconya looked into his strange, hazel-flecked eyes, she also sensed something was off-kilter.

"Who are you?" Jenna demanded, seeing the black aura surrounding the man in the bed, gathering like a storm cloud.

He smiled then closed his eyes, leaving Jenna lost for words and Piconya hanging for his response. They watched as Peter Shaney's eyes flickered beneath closed lids, expecting them to open again any moment, but instead he slipped back into a deep sleep. After the strange exchange, Piconya and Jenna sat in stunned silence, neither daring to put into words what had happened.

The nursing staff were summoned and after a cursory inspection of the patient they were informed it may be some time before he woke again. They decided to return the next day. Before leaving the hospital, Piconya proffered her card to the ward sister, asking her to call the moment he woke. Up to that point, Weller and Piconya had elected to keep their discovery about Jenna's family tree under wraps, until Peter Shaney was in a more stable condition and she was able to handle another trauma.

The next morning, Peter Shaney woke alone in his room. Getting out of bed, he searched a cupboard for his clothes and found nothing. Sneaking out of the room, he looked to both ends of a long corridor, which was empty bar one porter disappearing through the double doors at the end, transporting a patient in a wheelchair to another part of the hospital. Seizing the moment, Peter darted along the corridor, opening each closed door as he went, discovering a locker room where he found a jacket hanging on a coat hook and a pair of trainers left by one of the nursing staff.

The trainers were too small but he managed to squeeze his feet into them, leaving the laces undone and his heels hanging over the backs of the shoes. Making his way swiftly through the maze of corridors, he found a lift and pressed the button. Within seconds, it arrived and he was inside, plummeting down to ground level. Being early morning, the reception area was deserted, apart from a receptionist chatting to a nurse. The two women took no notice of the man as he walked past, trying not to hobble in the ill-fitting trainers. He reached the double entrance doors without incident and disappeared into the car park outside. As Peter had no money and couldn't get far on foot, he loitered around the car park, wondering what to do next. He noticed a woman get out of her car and walk over to the ticket machine. Instinct told him the woman had not locked her car. She had her back to him as he opened the car door and slipped into the driver's seat, finding the keys in the ignition. The engine burst into life. Putting it into gear, his foot stomped on the accelerator and he sped out of the car park.

The owner of the vehicle turned from the pay machine in time to see her car being driven out of the car park at breakneck speed and ran after it, uttering obscenities at its fast-disappearing shape, cursing herself for being so careless. Luckily, she'd had the sense to pick up her handbag containing her mobile phone when she left the car, enabling her to call the police to report the theft.

Chapter 21

Tommy Adams
Bridewell Police Station

Back at Bridewell Police Station, what had started as a bad day turned into a nightmare for DS Weller. Having received word from Frenchay Hospital that Peter Shaney had absconded, stealing a car, she was on the point of calling Piconya to tell her about the latest development when PC Whitehead barged into her office.

"Guv, there's a man at the front desk demanding to see you. He won't speak with anyone else. Looks like a tramp, has weird eyes, sort of multi-coloured."

Weller shivered involuntarily, conjuring up a scene of close proximity with a smelly vagrant in one of their interview rooms, and was contemplating passing the matter on to one of her counterparts when something Whitehead said jump-started her memory banks.

"What colour did you say his eyes were?"

"Hazel with green flecks," replied Whitehead and a knowing look passing between them as the penny dropped.

"Tell him I'll be with him shortly. Get an interview room ready, with plenty of air fresheners and water. You can sit in on this one." Whitehead left Weller's office to carry out her instructions.

After the door closed, Weller called Piconya, informing her about Peter Shaney's escape. Acting on a gut feeling, she also invited her to be present during the interview with the tramp. Ten minutes later, Piconya appeared and they strolled along the corridor towards Interview Room 3, where they viewed the man through a two-way mirror. The tramp sat facing Whitehead, drinking from a polystyrene cup, his hands shaking as he spilled half the contents down himself. Weller studied him, taking in his jacket, belted with a dressing gown cord, and holes in the soles of his boots, exposing threadbare socks. Most of his face was obscured by a full beard, which looked as though it hadn't been groomed for years. It was only when she looked into his eyes that the idea which had been swirling around in her mind since his arrival at the station hit her head-on. The man sitting in their interview room could be Tommy Adams. Under normal circumstances, the tramp would have escaped their attention, had he not come into the station of his own volition, but with the recent atrocity and Daniel Overton so fresh in her mind, Weller was on high alert.

Inside the interview room, Whitehead was struggling to get a name from the tramp, who stubbornly insisted on speaking to DS Weller before divulging his identity.

"Come on, Sylvia, let's see who this person is and what he wants," Weller said, not wanting to share her thoughts just yet.

"What the hell is Peter Shaney playing at, leaving the hospital, and stealing a car in the process?" Piconya quipped as Weller opened the door.

"Let's deal with this first," Weller said quietly. "I've put out an alert on the stolen car. The hospital have informed us that Shaney still needs medical attention and won't get far in his condition. I've got his flat under surveillance, should he turn up there. Friends and family have also been informed."

The overpowering smell of sweat and stale body odour, mixed with an undercurrent of something sweet and cloying, was untouched by the air fresheners that Whitehead had strategically placed out of sight in the far corners of the room. Piconya gagged slightly as she followed Weller into the room, taking the seat Whitehead had vacated. Weller sat next to her, facing the tramp. Before speaking, she reached over and pressed a button on the recording equipment then leaned back in her seat, taking a long look at the man before her.

"For the benefit of the tape, the time is 3.31pm on Wednesday 31st July. I am DS Weller, beside me is DS Piconya, and standing by the door is PC Whitehead. I gather you want to speak to me," Weller directed her conversation to the man in front of her.

"I said only you," the tramp spat through yellow stained teeth, a sliver of spittle dripping down his beard.

"It is policy for two officers to be present during an interview," Weller replied.

The tramp seemed to think about what she'd said. Weighing up the situation, his eyes fixed on PC Whitehead. "You will need to get rid of him before I say anything."

Knowing they were getting nowhere, Weller reluctantly granted his request. "Again for the benefit of the tape, PC Whitehead is leaving the room."

Weller nodded to him, knowing full well that Whitehead would make his way to the adjoining room to watch the remainder of the interview, ready to intervene should any problems arise.

"For the benefit of the tape, can you state your name, please?"

The man looked at the police officers in front of him, curiosity evident on DS Weller's face. There was a silence in the room whilst they waited for his reply then he mumbled something unheard into his beard.

"Sorry, we didn't hear that, can you speak up?" Weller's impatience showed.

"Tommy Adams," he said, raising his voice.

Despite confirming her earlier suspicions, Weller found herself taking a deep breath to mask the gasp escaping from her lips, her eyes darting sideways to Piconya in the process. Taking a moment to compose herself, she continued in a softer tone. "Tommy, we've been looking for you for a long time. Where have you been?"

Looking at Weller, he considered her words then embarked on a long tale. Weller and Piconya learned that after his attack on Jane, Tommy's first reaction was to flee the country, but with no money and no passport he had no choice but to remain in Bristol. In the following months, he found a hiding spot deep inside the Downs parklands, setting up camp with the meagre possessions he'd taken from his home. Then early one morning he left his hiding place and started walking, until he came to the Clifton suspension bridge over the Avon Gorge, heading towards Ashton Court. Half-way across the bridge, he stopped and looked down at the steep drop. Before he knew what he was doing, he found that he'd climbed onto the top of the railing and was preparing to jump off the bridge when a whooshing noise in the distance startled him. Instead of hurling himself into the steep drop, Tommy fell backwards, onto the safety of the bridge. As he lay crumpled on the sidewalk, a cyclist stopped and helped him up.

Unbeknown to Tommy, in the brief moment he'd been on the parapet contemplating his demise, the cyclist, who was focusing on the view from the bridge, hadn't noticed his attempted suicide as she sped along. It was only when she got closer that she saw someone on the ground, which made her stop and get off her bike. As the man turned to face her, all she saw was a tramp who needed a helping hand; not a person wanted for murder.

Tommy, winded from the fall, offered no resistance as she propped her bike against the railing and helped him to his feet. Seeing he was unsteady, she offered him her arm, picked up her bike, and together they slowly walked to the other side of the bridge. With assurances that he was all right, the good Samaritan got on her bike and continued her journey. As the bike disappeared in the early morning light, Tommy realised with a start how close he'd come to ending it all. It also flagged up his bedraggled appearance. In the wake of all the media attention, it was a miracle the cyclist hadn't recognised him, but it also confirmed that he would be able to move freely throughout Bristol, where most people gave vagrants a wide berth.

Tommy ventured back into the city, finding spots in underpasses to sleep at night and places to beg for money during the day. By this time, he was unrecognisable, his former clean-cut self now sporting a full mane of hair and a long, straggly beard; the ensemble topped off with a peaked baseball cap, hiding his eyes from anyone attempting to get closer. In essence, Tommy Adams became invisible; a currency for passing through the city unchallenged, becoming a regular fixture in certain spots where nobody bothered him.

One favoured spot he frequented was outside a newsagents' in Christmas Street, where he was able to see the coming and goings of the clientele and observe Dorothy Baker, the proprietor. Tommy knew Dorothy, she having served him on many occasions when he lived a stone's throw away in Christmas Steps, and who loved gossiping with her regulars. If anyone knew what was going on, she would, and he figured if he hung around long enough, sooner or later he would hear something about Jane. Whilst sitting on a filthy blanket on the cobbled street begging for money from passers-by, Tommy learned his sister was found alive and in intensive care at Frenchay Hospital. The news stunned him. He was so certain he'd killed Jane that in his haste to get rid of her body he had failed to check for signs of life. If he had, things would have turned out differently. Bit by bit, he gleaned snatches of conversations through the open newsagents' doors. The attempted murder had rocked the small community, where everyone had something to say about the savage attack, enabling him to get a snapshot of what happened after her body was found in the garbage bin. The revelation that his sister was alive chipped away at his conscience, making Tommy toy with the idea of handing himself into police, but the idea of being confined to a cell for the rest of his natural life quickly quashed those thoughts.

Tommy had been begging outside the newsagents for four days running when he noticed Dorothy giving him curious looks from inside the shop. On the fifth day, she came out and walked up to him. Fearing he had been recognised, he was about to snatch up his blanket and scarper, but before he could move Dorothy was upon him, looking him straight in the face. For a brief moment a flicker of recognition flashed across her eyes then to his relief she asked whether he would like some chips. Tommy was relieved that his guise as a tramp had passed muster and overwhelmed at the woman's kindness as she crossed over to the chip shop, a few doors away. He heard her order a large portion, loitering by the open door so she could keep an eye on her shop whilst she waited for the chips to be parcelled in newspaper. Returning with the steaming package, she handed the chips over then went back into her shop. Tommy was grateful to Dorothy on three counts: for the food, as he was ravenous; that she failed to recognise him, and that the incident had focused his mind. He knew he had to get to Frenchay Hospital and find his sister.

He took his time walking the four-mile route through St Werburgh's and St Paul's to Frenchay, sleeping in shop doorways and underpasses and begging on the streets. At one point, he'd got hassled by a prostitute, who accused him of frightening off her punters. To avoid drawing attention to himself, Tommy heeded her words and moved to another spot to beg.

On arrival at Frenchay Hospital, Tommy spent days hidden on the perimeter and nights loitering around the car park, watching the coming and goings, trying to gauge an opportunity of slipping through the automatic glass doors, unnoticed. At 3.20am, with daylight another three hours away, the receptionist manning the front desk disappeared from her post. Seizing the opportunity, Tommy slipped inside and ran the full length of the corridor to another door, hiding behind it as he heard the door to the ladies' toilet open. He could hear the receptionist in the corridor walking its length towards him, making him panic and freeze. Just as the woman was about to pull the handle to open the door, the whoosh of the automatic entrance doors rang in his ears. He was seconds away from discovery when Tommy heard what sounded like a woman stumbling into the reception area, weeping and wailing in pain. The receptionist turned and quickly went to her aid, leaving Tommy on the other side of the door, counting his blessings. With the commotion unfolding, he knew that at any moment the A&E team would be galvanised into action. Assessing the maze of corridors ahead, Tommy wondered which way to go next, heading for a sign in the distance. As he got closer, he could see an arrow pointing to his right, informing him the Intensive Care Ward was on Floor 3. Not chancing the lift, Tommy took the stairwell up but had to dip off at Floor 2, when he heard a door open and footsteps descending the stairwell. As the clatter of feet echoed past him on their way to the lower level, Tommy re-emerged to climb the remaining stairs, knowing it was imperative to keep out of sight. His tramp-like appearance in the early hours of the morning would raise alarm bells.

Tommy found the intensive care wards were key-coded and closely monitored by nursing staff, making entry impossible. Disheartened he'd come this far only to fail at the last hurdle, he was about to leave when he noticed a nurse coming out of a side room. From his hiding place, he saw the door swing open, catching sight of a patient hooked up to a bank of machinery. Interest piqued, once the nurse was out of sight, he snuck out from his hiding place, slipping unnoticed into the room. All was quiet, apart from a low hum from the machinery. The patient in the bed was asleep, her arms exposed above the sheets. A tube was imbedded in her hand, leading to a drip overhead and other wiring hooking her up to the bank of bleeping machinery. As he got closer to the woman, he saw her face bore the scars of an atrocious beating. Standing beside her, it took Tommy several minutes to realise he was looking down at Jane. The realisation struck him like a thunderbolt. It was one thing to learn that his sister had survived the vicious beating he inflicted upon her, but another to see her in the flesh.

A conflicting storm of emotions plagued him as he stood over her, contemplating what he should do next. If she regained consciousness, she would be able to tell the police her story, and he couldn't afford for that to happen. Before he could act, however, he heard footsteps outside then the door opened. A knee-jerk reaction made Tommy throw himself on the floor and scramble under the bed. He struggled to suppress the nervous panting coming from his throat as he watched shapely ankles in a sturdy pair of flat black shoes walk beside the bed. The owner of the shoes stopped then he heard her picking up something from the end of the bed. The nurse studied the chart in her hands then stopped and sniffed the air.

"What the hell is that god almighty smell?"

The words reverberated in Tommy's brain, screaming discovery; his own stench was to be his downfall. Cringing under the bed, he waited for the moment of discovery then another nurse entered the room. He knew he could deal with one woman but now there were two the odds were stacked against him.

"Hi Linda, how's she doing?" the other nurse asked.

"As well as could be expected under the circumstances. The C Section was performed two days ago."

"My God, a lot has happened since I've been on holiday. Did the baby survive?"

He couldn't believe his ears. A baby? What were they talking about?

302

Not daring to breathe, Tommy waited for the conversation to continue.

"It was touch and go for a while but he's a little fighter."

"It's a boy then, where is he now?" The other nurse replied with a smile in her voice.

"Come on, I'll show you." The arrival of her colleague made Linda forget about the putrid smell emanating from beneath the bed as they left the room.

When the coast was clear, Tommy slithered on his stomach from beneath the bed and got to his feet. Looking at his sister, so pale and battered, tore at his heart strings. From earlier thoughts of murderous intent, he began to question himself. What the fucking hell had he done now? As a consequence of his actions, he'd sired a baby boy.

At that point in the interview, Weller was sorely tempted to tell Tommy about Daniel Overton, who'd grown up to became a killer, but decided against it, preferring to hear the rest of Tommy's story now he was on a roll and determined to finish what he had started.

Before leaving the hospital room, Tommy had bent over Jane's bed and whispered into her ear. "Please forgive me, Jane, I'm sorry, I didn't know what I was doing. Please forgive me, I will be back. I will somehow make things right."

There was no response from his sister as she lay at the command of beeping machines monitoring her every movement. Tommy sighed and turned to leave the room then, remembering the nurses talking about the baby, he went in search of the boy.

As the door closed Jane, who'd been in a comatose state since discovery of her body, showed signs of stirring. Below closed lids, her eyes started to roll sideways. A familiar voice pierced her comatose state, enabling his words to reach her. As the words 'I'll be back' echoed in her fragile mind, Jane's pulse began to race, setting off alarms and alerting the medical team. By the time they reached the room, she was in the throes of a heart attack so massive that it obliterated her already weakened state. Despite the best efforts of the medical team working relentlessly on her, Jane gave up the fight for life. Time of death was recorded as 4.18am.

From down the corridor, Tommy heard the loud, piercing beeps as he looked through the window into the incubation ward, wondering which one was his child. In all, there were eight babies and at the bottom of each cot was a chart with the name of mother and baby, the last one denoting the mother as being Jane Adams – baby's name unknown.

Tommy's heart was beating wildly as he described the moment he clapped eyes on the child and the murderous thoughts in his mind. At that point, he didn't care anymore. He'd come to the end of the road, with only one way ahead.

An inner rage grew as he looked at the sleeping infant. Suddenly, as though it detected his presence, the child opened its eyes and stared straight at him. In that moment of contact, he felt violated by the same thing that had possessed him at Christmas Steps, forcing him to rape his sister. Something permeated Tommy's soul, making his knees buckle. Throwing his hands forward to break his fall, he rebounded from the glass window, coming to a painful halt as his shoulder collided against a wall.

To unsuspecting observers looking into that cot, all they would see was a cute baby, but Tommy saw something else, which had possessed his soul and ruined his life. As he struggled to his feet, he contemplated going into the incubation ward and killing it. Raising a clenched fist, he smashed it against the side wall and howled in pain as the impact shuddered up his arm. Clutching his bruised hand, he made his way to the entrance of the incubation unit and was about to wrench open the door when he noticed another keypad entry system and realised that without the right combination he would never get in. As he contemplated his next move, in the distance Tommy could hear people clambering up the corridor towards the room he'd left, then a voice rang out in the mayhem.

"Hurry, she's arresting!" Then the door closed and all he could hear was the muffled shouts of the medical team.

Following the commotion, Tommy came up short, realising the muffled shouts were coming from his sister's room. Fearing he would be discovered, he found an empty room at the far end of the corridor where, with the door slightly ajar, he strained to hear what was going on. It seemed an age before the door to Jane's room opened again. He could make out Linda's voice amidst subdued tones.

"Poor mite, didn't stand a chance."

Tommy couldn't make out the rest of her conversation as they walked back to the Intensive Care Ward but from the general air of the medical team, he knew that Jane was dead.

***

In the early hours of the morning, noise carried easily through deserted corridors, reaching the Intensive Care Ward. Sister Carole Pendergan, who'd just come on duty, thought she heard something and by chance glanced at the monitor connected to the baby unit. As she looked at the monitor, she saw a bearded man thumping a wall outside the unit. Alarmed by the strange sight, she immediately called Security, then all hell broke loose as an alarm went off and a medical team was scrambled to attend the patient in Room 2, who, according to the bank of machinery monitoring her progress, was having a heart attack.

By the time Security reached the baby unit, the man Sister Pendergan had seen on the monitor had disappeared. Despite an extensive search, he was nowhere to be seen, and it was assumed that he somehow reached the main doors having managed to avoid detection. Playing back the security footage showed a man who looked like a tramp standing outside the baby unit, staring at one of the infants at the far end. The tramp, who appeared to be mumbling to himself, stumbled and fell. After getting up, he threw a punch at a side wall, appearing to utter a load of unheard words to himself. To unsuspecting eyes, the footage showed a vagrant who'd wandered in off the street; probably in a drunken stupor, judging by his earlier fall.

This was no interrogation for Weller and Piconya; it had the feeling of a long-awaited confession, from a man who had evaded capture for thirty years. His contemplation about killing the child he'd sired through rape made Weller feel as though she'd been dropped from a great height into a deep black hole. His rank breath wafting over the Formica table added to her queasiness. Under normal circumstances, she would have been exhilarated at the prospect of a murderer handing himself in but she was at odds with herself, convinced there was something else she was missing. The sweet, cloying smell emanating from the tramp invaded her senses, making her flashback to a death she had attended a couple of years ago. She'd been the first through the door of the flat after the battering ram had split it open and found the body of the female occupant lying dead in a bath of putrid water, her body having lain there for months before discovery. Shaking off the morbid thoughts, Weller refocused on the task ahead.

Like Piconya, she pondered Adams' emerging confession. Everything pointed to an episode of complete madness or possession, culminating in the rape of his sister. Weller shivered involuntarily, remembering what they had witnessed in the cellar at Hydlebury Farm, making her lean towards the latter explanation.

Reliving the rape all those years ago, Tommy could feel his

sister's warm blood on his hands and see it splattered all over the Belfast sink, in full technicolour. Over the years, he had tried to suppress these memories but failed, knowing that the day they stopped it would signal his own death. Once again, they appeared in his mind's eye like it was only yesterday.

Continuing with the discovery at the hospital, he told Weller and Piconya how afterwards he found himself staring at a road sign leading into St Werburgh's, having no recollection of how he got there. The last memory he retained was the conversation between the two nurses discussing Jane's death, and seeing the child in the baby unit. The very thought of the monster he'd seen in the cot making him keel over and throw up on the roadside. All he wanted to do was drift into oblivion and forget what he'd seen at Frenchay Hospital. Armed with money made from begging, he went into an off licence and bought a carrier bag full of cheap, gut-rotting scrumpy cider and went on a bender in an attempt to block it all out. Days and nights rolled into alcoholic oblivion then one morning, as he woke with dew-saturated clothes, he found himself straddled across the bottom of Christmas Steps. Nearby was a pool of vomit, which had clearly come from his mouth, leaving a trail down his long, unkempt beard. Shuffling onto all fours, he had attempted to get upright but staggered and fell, rolling to the bottom of the steps and lying there for some time before he attempted to rise again. As he stood swaying on his feet, looking up at Christmas Steps, he wondered how he'd got there. This was the last place he wanted to be, yet he was inexplicably drawn to the area time and time again. Not wanting to cross the path of No. 26 for obvious reasons, Tommy elected to go back on the street leading him into Broadmead Shopping area, to check out the bins of the restaurants, where tasty morsels of leftover food were often thrown out.

As he turned to leave, he glanced at the stone staircase leading up through the centre of Christmas Steps. Something in the misty air stirred. Thinking it was a trick of the early morning light, he looked again. This time, there was no mistaking the solid mass hovering mid-way up the stone staircase. As he watched, it appeared to be moving towards him, gaining momentum. Tommy froze. In the blink of an eye, it was upon him, consuming him, invading his very soul. He screamed and fell, clutching his head, trying to shake free of the malevolent invader and rolling around like a fish out of water, battering himself violently against the cobbled floor.

At the top of Christmas Steps, two nurses who'd just finished their shifts were taking a short cut through to the city centre and saw the commotion at the bottom, rushing to his aid.

Sharinda and Petra could smell the alcohol fumes coming off the man before they got to him. His eyes were rolling about in his head and he was muttering something indecipherable to himself. As they tried to stop him from hurting himself further, he took a swipe at Sharinda, knocking her over. Petra, seeing the situation was escalating, grabbed Sharinda and together they ran to the centre, where they located a phone box and made a 999 call. Once the call had been placed, they went back to wait for the emergency services. When the ambulance arrived four minutes later, Tommy was still thrashing about on the floor. It took the combined strength of the two paramedics to overpower him and a shot in his arm before he finally stopped struggling and they were able to transport him on a stretcher into the ambulance.

On arrival at Bristol Royal Infirmary, Tommy was rushed to A&E, where he was examined by Dr Christopher Abbotsfield. The doctor was asking Tommy all types of questions. "Who is the Prime Minister? How many fingers am I holding up? What day and year is it?"

The encounter with the supernatural force on Christmas Steps, and discovering his sister alive only to die ten minutes later, had pushed Tommy's already fragile mental state closer to the abyss.

All it would take was one more push to lock him away in that dark place forever. Getting no intelligent response, Abbotsfield decided that the man needed to be sectioned for his own good. He couldn't risk allocating him a bed in a main ward as he'd been reported to be violent by the paramedics who'd brought him in. Still under the influence of the drugs shot into his arm, Tommy lay whimpering whilst the doctor made arrangements to have him removed to a secure facility, where he would be assessed and given treatment for his fragile mental condition.

Tommy spent the next four years in Blackberry Hospital; a secure unit specialising in mental health issues, where he was fed, clothed and kept in a drug-induced state of altered reality. Each day rolled into one; the only thing that changed was the staff. In the beginning, there was a conscious effort to find out who Tommy was, and where he came from, but that soon fell by the wayside, in the wake of Tommy's refusal to answer any of their questions. Nearing the end of his fourth year there, he was allowed to go into the gardens to sit in the fresh air and take in the extensive grounds. It was during these weekly jaunts outside that his mind started to regurgitate old memories, taking him back to a time when he was happy and carefree. As these memories stirred, Tommy acquired the will power to dispense of the drugs, which were having less effect on him anyway. Each morning and evening, when the nurses fed him the tablets with a cup of water, he pretended to swallow, skilfully moving the pills under his tongue and taking the water down in one gulp. When the nurses left, he would spit out the tablets and poke them into a gap in the skirting board. Bit by bit, as his fragmented memories returned, he became stronger and more rational.

Not letting on to the medical staff that he had regained control of his own mind, Tommy still acted as though he was heavily sedated, waiting for a chance to escape. One morning, as he sat on a bench in the garden, he noticed a laundry van drive into the grounds to the rear of the unit. Getting up from the bench, he strolled nonchalantly round the grounds, ending up at the rear of the hospital and watching the van as its driver unloaded the contents. Tommy repeated his observations each week, until he established a routine that was going to be his ticket out of the secure unit.

On the day he planned to make his escape, he was delayed by one of the nursing staff, who decided to stop and talk to him. Time was of the essence and he was getting impatient. Suddenly, one of the other residents who'd been sitting in the grounds nearby started to have a fit, diverting her attentions.

With her back turned, he wandered off towards the back of the hospital, darting between trees and bushes before arriving at the spot where he could see the laundry van. His plan worked a treat; the minute the driver was inside the hospital delivering the clean laundry, Tommy dived into the back of the vehicle, having worked out the number of loads it took to finish the delivery. Once inside the van, he squeezed through the empty wheelie pallets, hiding at the back, out of sight.

As the last pallet was loaded onto the hydraulic platform and pushed into the van, Tommy breathed a sigh of relief, then the back doors closed, plunging him into darkness. Tommy felt the vehicle drive out from the hospital and turn onto the main road back into Bristol. From the writing on the van, he knew where he was going and how long it was going to take to get there, but had no idea what would happen at the other end, or how long he would be in the back of the van before it was opened.

As chance would have it, when he got to the other end he didn't have long to wait as another load of laundry was scheduled for delivery. The back doors opened and Tommy blinked as daylight flooded the van. From his crouched position on the floor, between the slots in the pallets he could see the same driver starting to unload the vehicle and with the evacuation of the empty wheelie pallets came the danger of discovery. He started to panic, getting ready to rush the driver to make his escape.

With Tommy primed and ready to spring into action, as the driver reached for the next pallet something diverted his attention. Then Tommy heard someone calling him from the depot building. There was a flurry of excited conversation between the driver and the depot staff, allowing Tommy to slip out unnoticed and duck behind a row of parked vans. He edged his way to the entrance gate. Beyond was a side road. Cars sped by and a man walking his dog gave Tommy a curious look as he hurried down the road. There was a block of shops, at the end of which was a boarded-up retail unit. Slipping round the back of the unit, he discovered a vandalised door, which with a bit of brute force he managed to open, allowing him access to the abandoned shop premises.

Back at the laundry depot, the driver of the van was being questioned and his van searched. The call came from Blackberry Hospital too late. Tommy was already in the wind, leaving the supposedly secure unit with no answers as to his escape route and buying him more time to effect his freedom.

He knew there was no way he could wander the streets in the blue institutional clothes supplied by the hospital. It would only be a matter of time before a local spotted him and reported him to the police. Under the cover of night, Tommy ventured from his hiding place, heading for a residential area where, in a back garden, he spotted washing flapping in the wind. Eyeing up the clothing on the line, he saw a pair of beige chinos and a checked shirt but the house owners were still up, judging by the light in their conservatory. Now it was a waiting game, hoping they would leave the washing out for the evening, otherwise he would have to find another house. Luckily, being a balmy night, the washing was left out and two hours later all lights went out in the household. Slipping in through the back gate, Tommy crossed a lawned area to the washing line and had just taken the trousers and shirt when the back light activated, catching him red-handed. Bundling the clothes under his arm, he fled back out through the garden gate, along the lane at the back of the house, before the householder had the chance to open his window to find out what had activated the lights.

With his change of clothes and a wash in the retail unit's rusty sink, Tommy was able to blend into normality. Mindful of keeping a low profile until his beard and hair had grown back, hiding his face, he spent years wandering aimlessly from place to place, begging in the streets for his fix of booze and food, taking shelter at local drop-in centres when the weather got bad. Nobody bothered him as he kept to himself, preferring not to engage in conversation.

Charities helped him get by, with offerings from their soup kitchens and changes of clothing. Life slipped on and before he knew it, Tommy had been on the streets nigh on thirty years. In his early fifties, he now looked like a man well over seventy. Life on the streets had taken its toll and his health was deteriorating, attributed to drinking and harsh weather his body had endured.

No amount of cheap booze, however, blocked out the memories of that fateful day that led to the death of his sister, which kept resurfacing like a cork bobbing on water, refusing to be submerged. Each time the memories resurfaced they were attached to something else, making him feel as though something was living a parallel life inside him, providing glimpses into its life. Getting pissed on cheap cider failed to blot out these episodes, only serving to enhance the vivid images coming to him whilst intoxicated, plaguing him through to soberness and lingering for days afterwards.

It got so bad that Tommy barely slept, fearing he would be devoured by the image of a boy that had grown into a man, playing cruel tricks with his subconscious mind. By this time, he was convinced his guilty mind was seeing the seed he'd plunged into his sister; the product of the rape.

Tommy started muttering to himself. As it was getting on for eight o'clock in the evening and sensing the man had nothing more to offer, Weller called a halt to the interview. Arrangements were made to lock him up in a cell for the night, with something to eat. Whitehead came into the room to escort Tommy to the cells. Weller and Piconya watched the broken man shuffle off with Whitehead, offering no resistance. It was as though he'd already given up, accepting his fate and the sentence that was going to be served upon him for the death of his sister.

The next morning, the man in front of them was a different person. With a good night's sleep and some food inside him, he seemed more alert, and keen to continue his confession. Once again, Weller pressed the button, activating the recording machine before starting the interview but this time it was Piconya who spoke. "Tommy, can you tell us something about these images you've been seeing?" Piconya had spoken to Weller about this and they thought there was mileage in this line of questioning as she had a theory, albeit somewhat off the wall.

Tommy scrutinised the policewoman who spoke for the first time, wondering whether to trust her. Taking a moment to mull things over he decided that, having confessed to his sister's murder and revealing that he spent four years of his life locked up in a mental institution, they already had him pegged as a nutter so he had nothing to lose by releasing the rest of his demons.

It was harrowing and difficult to explain to people who'd not lived hand-in-glove with evil. He could pinpoint the moment it started as he clapped eyes on his son in the incubation unit at Frenchay Hospital. Then, he was an infant, but as that child grew

Tommy could feel its attachment clawing at him. Traumatic landmark events affecting its life were projected into his mind, enabling Tommy to see all manner of depravities. One night as he slept fitfully in an underpass, covered with a filthy duvet and cardboard, he awoke with a start. Although he was wide awake, the nightmare continued in the darkness of the underpass. At first, he thought he was re-visiting the attack on his sister but as the nightmare continued as he realised it was not him but someone else. He screamed for it to stop, banging his head against the stone wall beside him, then slumped into blackness. The next thing Tommy remembered, it was getting light and he had woken up with an egg-shaped lump on his forehead. He felt disorientated and frightened by the night's events but little did he know that it was just the start of things to come.

Over the passing years, nightmares became a fixture of his life, each one bringing insight into the child's life as the boy grew into a man. Tommy knew there was a high risk of being labelled a madman for divulging his innermost thoughts but talking about it was like an anaesthetic balm to his soul and he would do anything to rid himself of this constant darkness.

"Tell us what this apparition looks like," Piconya encouraged.

As he began to speak, Tommy had a coughing fit. Piconya reached over and passed the box of tissues from the corner of the desk. Reaching into the box, he extracted a wad and spat a stream of phlegm into them. Weller cringed as she watched him, wondering whether he was fit to continue the interview. Neither officer noticed the blood-splattered tissue as Tommy balled it and put it into his jacket pocket. After taking a sip of water, he cleared his throat and continued speaking.

Tommy conjured up the devil that had tormented him throughout the years, describing it without borders. Its build, its hair colour changing in every episode of violence yet retaining the same style, cut just above its collar. Digging deep into his scarred memory banks, he resurrected its face, remembering the fine chiselled features and hazel flecked eyes. As he described its eyes, Piconya and Weller looked at each other in astonishment, waiting for Tommy to finish.

There was a moment when he paused, debating whether to continue. "The last thing I saw was a younger image of myself, engulfed in fire, burning from inside out. After it died, there was blackness and a blessed silence in my head for the first time in years. I was devastated the following day, when its presence came back." Tommy paused, thinking he'd gone too far.

Weller leaned forward and gestured for Tommy to continue, intrigued by what he was going to divulge.

"I don't know how I know this but it didn't die."

Weller and Piconya were dumbfounded by the revelation.

"What makes you think that?" Piconya prompted.

"Because it has someone else."

"What do you mean?" Weller composed herself enough to ask the question.

"My visions have started again. I know it's the same evil but in another form."

Seeing their confused looks, Tommy told them about the latest vision, in which he saw a blond, musclebound man. Weller knew immediately he was describing Peter Shaney. A silent look of understanding passed between the two police officers as Weller terminated the interview, knowing they needed to confer before continuing. Before leaving the room, Weller informed Tommy they were going to take a break and convene later, asking whether he wanted something to eat. He shook his head, requesting only a cup of sweet tea. As Tommy watched the two police officers disappear through the door and shut it behind them, he knew that would never happen. Resting his arms on the Formica table in front of him, he lowered his head and closed his eyes.

Fifteen minutes later, PC Whitehead entered Interview Room

315

3. The first thing he saw was the tramp asleep, his head on the table. Putting the cup of tea on the table beside him, Whitehead nudged his arm to wake him but he was unresponsive. A second nudge failed, then a third only served to dislodge him from the table and he fell to the floor.

Alarmed he'd been over-zealous in his attempts to wake him, Whitehead leaned over to help the man up but as he crouched down to lift him he realised there was something seriously wrong with Tommy Adams. As he turned him over, staring eyes reflected echoes of shock; the man's mouth open as though to say something but never passing his last words on to a living soul. Whitehead leaned forward, pressing his fingers to his neck, desperately looking for a pulse, but there was none to be found none. Rushing out of the room, he summoned help but when the resident doctor arrived it was confirmed that Tommy Adams was dead.

A repeat prescription in his jacket pocket and checking on the doctor who had issued it revealed that Tommy Adams had advanced lung cancer, which had eventually taken his life; a life spent in hell, plagued by a supernatural spirit and reliving the murder of his sister.

Weller could only hope that wherever he was now, he was in a better place. Behind him, he left a trail of unanswered questions. The main one being, where was Peter Shaney?

Weller wondered whether, however far-fetched it appeared, whatever possessed Tommy Adams could be resident in another host, to continue its cycle of murder and mayhem. That would never be established until they found Shaney, and when they did there was only one person who would believe them.

Little did Jenna Thornleigh realise that it was all about to start again. This time, not only had the entity gained knowledge to use against them but it seemed its energies might never be extinguished, as it continued its life seamlessly, jumping from one person into another.

With no option left, Weller had to share the discovery Casey had made, about another relative called Thomas in her family tree, and Jane Adams' identity.

She hoped that this information, along with Tommy Adams' death, would not push Jenna over the edge.

Acknowledgements and artwork images

The artwork is a collaboration with artwork by Zac Morris and design input from Paul Crow.

Zac is a talented young prize-winning tattooist working at Skinzophrenic Tattoo Studio in Hereford. Paul also lives and works in Hereford and is a published artist.

CPSIA information can be obtained
at www.ICGtesting.com
Printed in the USA
LVHW050914050819
626526LV00003B/457